VERY

KINGS

Jane S. Wonda

Very Bad Kings

First semester

KINGSTON UNIVERSITY SERIES – PART 1

Uitgeverij Zomer & Keuning

ISBN 9789020559897
ISBN e-book 9789020559910
ISBN audiobook 9789020559927
NUR 343

© 2025 Uitgeverij Zomer & Keuning
Postbus 13288, 3507 LG Utrecht

© 2021 Jane S. Wonda
Originally published in German as *Very Bad Kings* by Wondaversum,
Germany.

Cover design © Wondaversum
English cover Liesbeth Thomas, t4design
Editor Claudia Matheis

www.zomerenkeuning.nl
www.janeswonda.com

Zomer & Keuning believes it is important to use natural resources in an envi-
ronmentally friendly and responsible manner. The paper that was used for the
edition of this title, is guaranteed to have not resulted in deforestation.

For all those who always see the good and dream of the bad.

Your naked body should only belong to those
who fall in love with your naked soul.
Charlie Chaplin

SOUNDTRACK

The Magic of Kingston
Mae | Berlinist

Very Bad Kings
Sharks Don't Sleep | Berlinist

Sylvian
Tanz für mich | Provinz

So Many Secrets
Kingdom of Burmecia | TPR

The Game Has Only Begun
Blood // Water | grandson

Mable & Harper
La Vie En Rose | Emily Watts

Jaxon and the Kings
We are Gods | Audiomachine

Campus Life
Death Bed | We Rabbitz und co.

Crescent
Your Self Lingers | Echos

Complete Playlist available on Spotify at:
Very Bad Kings Soundtrack by Jane S. Wonda

TRIGGER WARNING

Every sentence in this book could fuck with your brain.
Some of them definitely will.
Proceed with caution.

Very Bad Kings ends on a cliffhanger and may contain triggers, including bullying. Mobbing, attempted rape, mentions of suicide, (sexual) harassment, (sexual) violence, psychological torment, (mentions of) death, alcohol and drug abuse, and knife play.

Please take these content notices seriously.
Your mental health matters.

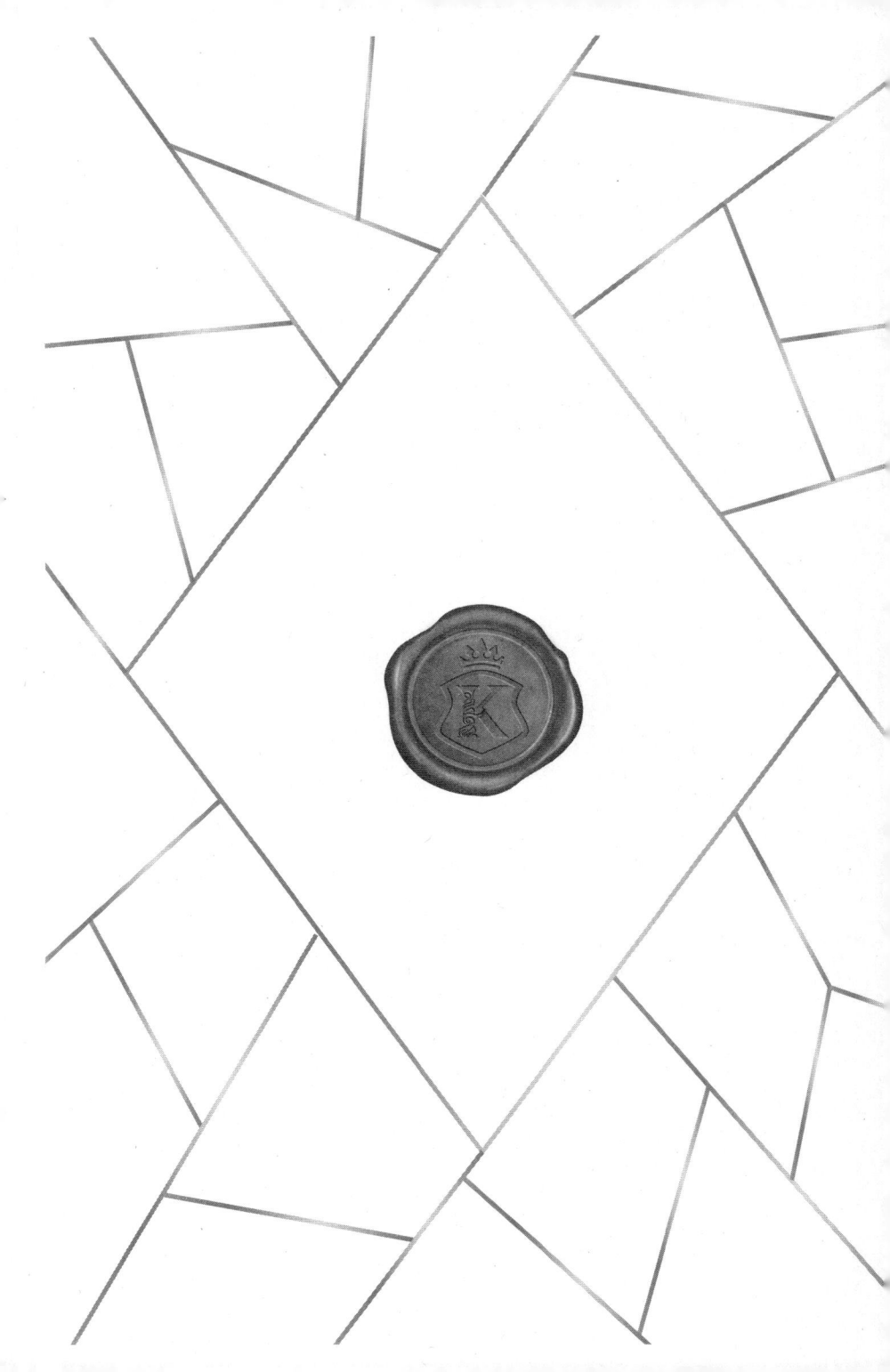

We're going to play a game.
We're cruel bastards,
moving people like pawns
and sacrificing them at our whim.

You're the stakes we play for.

And you, and you, and you.
I put your pretty head on the checkered board
and have you capture the enemy king.
Maybe you're my bishop.
My rook.
My knight in shining armor.
Maybe you're even my queen.
Who can tell?

GAME OVER

They're coming at me like a pack of dogs—or wolves, their eyes trained on the kill. There are five of them, as different from each other as night from day, and yet they all share one thing:

They're full of desire.

They're full of thirst.

For revenge.

For retribution.

For me.

Five pairs of eyes are fixed on me, five dark faces hidden behind the black-and-gold masks of the Kings, the eyes and lips of only three uncovered. Each of their mouths is twisted into a different kind of sadistic smile.

I'm trapped.

They've won.

The chair I'm chained to won't move across the floor.

I need to flee but they're coming closer.

I can already hear their breaths.

They're close enough their seductive scents cloud my senses.

The middle one steps forward, roughly grabbing my hair and yanking my head back as he approaches my lips. His finger strokes across my cheek as if he were running a blade over my skin.

"You lost," Jaxon hisses, his voice reminiscent of a hunter on the prowl. Silent and dangerous and beautiful enough to lure me into his trap time and time again, to lure me to my death. "Why didn't you just run while you still could? Didn't you know a chess match is almost always over once the queen is out of the game? Seems they haven't told you that. And here I thought this was one of the best universities in the country."

Laughter ripples through the room like rain washing over me. I am not alone. Not alone with these five sinister figures, no. The entire lecture hall is full. We have an audience, a faceless collection of students who can't wait to finally see me fall.

I will not fall.

Nothing, no one will make me leave Kingston before I graduate.

This is my only chance to make more of my life than the hell it used to be, and the hell it's once again become as the Kings try to destroy me.

I won't let a single one of those sons of bitches win, though.

"You still don't seem very scared of us," Jaxon whispers, coming close enough that I can't ignore the electric tension he's always ignited in me. For a brief moment, a memory of his hot body on mine surfaces. I remember him thrusting deep into me. The way he held my head between his hands, drinking in every minute movement of my face, watching what Reece and Sylvian did to me and how it turned me on... Then I remember everything he's done to me, and I'm instantly cured.

"Oh, I am incredibly scared of you," I tell him with mock fear, in a voice I can see is driving him crazy even now. Every time I challenge him, he comes closer to losing his cool.

I have long understood that Jaxon wants to defile me all the more when I refuse him. More than defile, even: he wants to destroy me emotionally.

And he very nearly succeeded.

"Too bad Kingston wasn't even able to teach you manners.

You really should know," Jaxon tuts, "better than to lie to me, little Belle."

"Oh, but I studied under the master of deceit, didn't you know?" I just can't help but provoke him.

Here I am, tied to my chair, surrounded by a crowd of gawking students, and facing five sons of bitches yearning to devour my soul, and I can't stop myself from provoking Jaxon Tyrell.

The king among the *Kings*.

The man on the throne of the elite.

My downfall in human form.

Mine, and that of hundreds of other women stupid enough to fall for him.

Jaxon Tyrell.

Maybe I am suicidal after all. Wasn't I always told that no one at Kingston University opposed him if they planned to keep studying here?

Jaxon's cold blue eyes squint. His is the only face I can read in spite of the mask, as easily as if we were meeting in bright sunlight. I know Jaxon Tyrell. I know him all too well.

Everyone else blurs into the faceless mass behind him. Those who don't want to be recognized are disguised, their faces covered with scarves or dark hoods pulled down low.

I wonder if Harper's in the audience.

"You almost won the game, Belle." Jaxon speaks louder now as he steps back. "You impressed me. I'm almost sad to have to say goodbye to you. It was so close"—he holds up his thumb and index finger, only slightly apart—"and so *very* entertaining. I wouldn't have wanted to miss a moment of these last few months."

I grit my teeth as I struggle to bear Jaxon's arrogance. The lights at the back of the lecture hall turn on, illuminating the entire aisle.

The audience, craven idiots that they are, shrink back into the rows of seats and away from the cone of light. Three women stride through the door at the top of the hall.

Three masked women. My heart breaks the moment I realize who has made their appearance.

There they come, my enemies, my rivals. Each of them stabbing me in the back in her very own way.

Their shimmering white ball gowns hug their slim figures. All three of them are beautiful: impeccably so. It's just their personalities that render them uglier than anyone else in the room.

Sylvian and Reece step away from the other Kings, toward the women before leading them back to the center.

They betrayed me.

Each in their own way.

They delivered me to Jaxon Tyrell and now they want to watch my end alongside their lying brides!

"Oh, are you sad Sylvian picked someone else?" Jaxon asks me. Lightning-fast, he bends toward my ear, though he doesn't lower his voice, allowing everyone to hear him. "How could you ever believe he'd choose scum like you?"

His words hit me hard enough I have to fight down tears.

The audience jeers when Jaxon suddenly pushes my chair back. I scream, panicked, I can't catch myself, but he grabs me at the last moment. Reaching around the back, he unbuckles the belt binding me. Then he drops me the rest of the way. Lying twisted on the floor in front of him, I prop myself up on my elbows.

"Run," he whispers, and this time I'm the only one to hear him. His voice has lost all sense of performance or showmanship. He's done playing. The only thing he wants now is retribution.

I glance at Reece, then at Romeo and the other King whose name I don't know. Is it Zayn? All three are staring back at me from behind expressionless, golden masks. They're going to help Jaxon—that much is clear. They'll do anything to make their leader happy.

And he won't be happy until I'm lying broken on the floor, never to rise again.

Until I'm held down by inescapable chains.

Until I'm bleeding.

Until I'm screaming in pain.

"I'll run tonight," I whisper to Jaxon. "But I'll be back in time for the first class of the new semester."

His attractive, sculpted face morphs into a hateful grimace. "You wouldn't dare."

"No one, not even you, will keep me from taking advantage of the best opportunity I can expect in my life. You picked the wrong enemy for your game. You'll have to kill me to keep me from coming back."

The look Jaxon is giving me is too close to a killer's stare. I start backing away across the floor. He'd kill me. I've known that for a good, long while. That means I have to make sure that he can't do so without facing the consequences.

I'll have to be trouble for him on all accounts.

For all of them.

One last time, I look around the crowded, dimly lit hall. I look into Jaxon's face, then into Sylvian's behind his mask, as he demonstratively links hands with his princess. The gesture alone is enough to drive a spike through my heart.

Reece seems as calm as ever. I almost regret having to declare war on him. Once I truly make myself his enemy, he surely won't be as… nice anymore.

"See you next semester!" I call, getting plenty of boos and hisses in return. I look at eight hate-filled pairs of eyes before I run. I flee.

But only so I can return better equipped.

The war hasn't even started, you sons of bitches!

Not a single one of you will ever find their way back into my heart!

JAXON

Hello, beautiful.

Welcome to Kingston.

It's awe-inspiring, isn't it? This university, founded by our ancestors so people like you and me could acquire knowledge no one else could teach us.

But you're wrong. Kingston isn't a place for impoverished scholarship students like you to study business administration, philosophy, politics, or science.

The only thing you're going to learn here is how to survive among people like us.

The elite.

But trust me on this.

Your lessons will be hard ones.

And if you don't do your homework properly, Belle, I'm afraid we'll have to punish you…

1

MABLE

The taxi looks like a space ship between all the luxurious black sedans. It's a spot of yellow that just won't blend in, standing out like a sore thumb in this sea of Bentleys and BMWs. I've never seen this many expensive, extravagant cars in one place before. Not to mention drivers opening doors, pages loading suitcases onto gilded carts, and fashionably dressed young adults saying goodbye to their rich parents in polo shirts and designer suits.

The taxi crawls down the congested street. The line of luxury car upon luxury car just won't end. I fold the directions to my dorm smaller and smaller before trying to smooth it out and then starting again, all the while on the lookout for someone who doesn't look like they shop on Rodeo Drive. Isn't there anyone normal at this university?

"House 17, ma'am?" the driver asks me with a thick Southern accent.

I nod at him. We couldn't be any farther removed from Texas.

"I'll stop up there, then."

I nod again as he flicks on his blinker and waits for three pages to cross the street with ten suitcases. The student next to them, talking on her phone as she walks, looks as if she's never touched a suitcase in her life.

The moment the group has crossed the street, a red sports car speeds past us, engine roaring, only to brake right in front of the taxi and slide into the only free parking spot anywhere in sight.

A student in a close-fitting azure shirt, his hair golden brown, steps out, casting a glancing look our way before turning to a blonde with three suitcases as she jumps up and down to welcome him, screaming like some groupie.

"Dickhead," I mutter, watching the guy's hands, sporting several ostentatious signet rings, slide under the girl's tiny skirt. He reeks of money like a dung heap reeks of manure.

"I can't stop here, ma'am," the driver says with an apologetic smile. He ends up parking at the very end of the row of cars. Half a mile away. "That's twenty-eight dollars fifty, ma'am."

I give him thirty. I can't even really afford that, never mind a proper tip.

When the driver gets out of the car, I enjoy a moment where I feel like I might have help, like the other freshmen. Instead, he unloads my many bags, two totes, and broken suitcase onto the sidewalk, before clapping me on the shoulder and driving away without another word.

There I am, standing on the fringes of elegant society, with more luggage than I can carry, and at least half a mile's walk to my dorm.

It's alright. The euphoria of being accepted to *Kingston University*—by far the most renowned in the country—drowns out the ache of not belonging here.

With two bags over my shoulder, my suitcase's handle in one hand and the two totes in my other, I set off down the sidewalk. Everything else has to stay behind for the moment because I simply can't carry it on my own. I feel eyes on me as soon as I pass the first group of parents and students embracing.

Keeping my head high, I pretend not to notice the derisive

sets of their mouths, the disgusted eyerolls, and the pointed pity on the adults' faces. I stubbornly trudge along, feeling more and more like a condemned woman on the way to the gallows with every step. That's bullshit, of course. I've been accepted at Kingston because I worked hard for it.

Why would I feel bad about that?

Even from afar, I can spot the red sports car with students crowded around it. I focus on a spot in the distance as I keep walking, dragging my suitcase and ignoring the way the tote cuts into my hand.

No one offers me any help. I hadn't really expected it, but the part of me that enjoys a good fairy tale would've loved to be wrong about that. Once I finally reach the red car, I drop my totes and suitcase to treat myself to a break. From here, I have to turn onto a footpath through the park. Just a little farther now.

"Oh, look there. A homeless girl from the city." The high voice comes from the students by the car. Some glance over with wry smiles before turning away again. The blonde who just spoke studies me like I'm an animal in the zoo, a different species that may have wandered here by accident. "Isn't she cute? Maybe we should give her a few bucks for a new tote. That one's going to break any second."

The women standing around the blonde all laugh.

"Leave her alone, Clarisse," one of them tells her even as she revels in the arms of a muscular man. Her lip curls when she sees me looking at her. "This charity case is *not* worth your notice."

With a mirthless smile, I bend down to pick up my things. I've barely taken two steps before the blonde moves away from the group to stand in my way.

"You don't belong here, Cinderella," she hisses, her pretty eyes narrowing to slits. Her personality is hideous, but not even that can take away from her amazing looks. Her doll-like face is free of blemishes, her figure as athletic as it is elegant. She's wearing a modest blouse and a short skirt, and I remember she was the one who greeted the guy who stole our parking spot. "Go, crawl back to where you came from."

Clarisse. The name fits her.

My mouth goes dry as I struggle to respond. A smart response, some glib retort—why can't I think of anything? All these rich people looking at me like they hate me isn't easy. I might've imagined a hundred times what I would do or say in this sort of situation, but the reality feels so much worse.

Since the blank space in my head just won't form words, all I can do is step around the stranger and simply pass her by. I should've expected her to make it a bit harder for me, but her brutality still comes as a surprise. Clarisse deliberately steps into me, pushing me. Laden as I am, I lose my balance and fall.

The contents of my totes scatter across the sidewalk, and laughter surges around me. Blushing hot, I scramble to my feet, picking up my things from the ground, and only notice I cut open my right hand when blood stains my new notebook. Fuck it all. Tears burn in my eyes. I keep my head down as I stumble away with what I could get my hands on quickly, leaving my suitcase behind. I need to get to my room. That's the most important thing right now.

Maybe everyone will have disappeared into their own luxury apartments—unsurprisingly, there are barely any simple dorms at Kingston—by the time I come back.

Luckily, none of them are following me when I step through the door to House 17. The acrid smell of cheap detergent envelopes me as I walk down a corridor that looks like it hasn't been inhabited in years. Nine scholarship holders were admitted to the Tyrell Foundation's program along with me. *Where are they?*

"Hello?" I call out cautiously. There's no response. The building seems abandoned. I find my room, trying the key I only just collected from the main building. It fits, and I enter. But the door wasn't locked, and my room isn't empty.

Sports Car is sitting on one of the two beds, his head thrown back, his legs spread wide, and a delicate woman is on her knees, blowing him.

I freeze, staring at them. It's the only thing I'm able to do for a moment: Stand there. Watch. Watch the girl's lips sliding up and down the guy's dick. I've stayed far enough away from men so far to avoid experiencing what my mother did, but I still know this guy is rather well-endowed. It's not like this is the first time I've walked in on someone having sex. It's not rare to see johns fucking our neighbors on a Saturday night in the trailer park.

This is different, though.

The entire guy is different.

His azure T-shirt is pulled up to reveal an athletic, impeccably chiseled stomach. The signet rings on his fingers seem elegant now, rather than ostentatious, and his hair catches the sunlight in a golden shimmer, making his relaxed expression look down-right angelic.

Since this is my dorm and I do need to put my things down, I clear my throat to draw their attention.

When the guy opens his eyes, it's like the air gets sucked out of the room. His expression captivates me, so intense the skin on my arms breaks out in goosebumps. Then his hand is on the back of the woman's neck, holding her down. She whimpers when he presses her head into his lap, and he keeps his cold eyes fixed on me.

They flash with lust. His lips go slack, his hips twitch, a shiver skates down my back. As he comes, this stranger looks at me like I'm the one getting him off. Like the girl kneeling between his legs isn't even here.

Following his orgasm, he drops back, releasing his hold on the girl, and treating me to a lopsided smile. "Does the hole you crawled out of not have doors?"

"What?"

The girl sits back, casting a shy glance at me as she wipes her mouth, but she stays on her knees in front of him, like the women in the trailer park do when their johns want them to pretend to be submissive.

"I asked if you've ever seen a door before," the Adonis repeats, his fly shamelessly open. "Since you don't seem to know to knock before you enter a room."

Now that he's entirely uncovered, I can see his impressive length. His shaft is glistening, wet, capturing my attention as if I've never seen a dick before.

"And cocks are new to you, too, eh?"

Biting my tongue, I look to the ceiling. "This is my room and I'd like to put my stuff away now."

Neither of them make a sound, and I try to pretend they aren't there while I put the books in my arms on the other bed. As I turn back to the door, I hear his voice.

"Leave."

I vaguely understand he doesn't mean me. But I'm not planning on staying either, so I reach for the door handle.

"I didn't mean you."

Blushing deeply, I turn around while the girl—slim and wearing a skimpy summer dress—slips past me. "I'm aware," I tell him firmly. "But the last thing I'm going to do is take orders from someone like you."

The stranger raises an eyebrow, straightening to his full height and buckling his belt. The rings on his hands flash in the sun. "Is that how it is?" His rough voice makes my stomach tingle as he advances on me.

Even though I'm frantically searching for words to throw at him, my tongue curls up and I can't manage to say a thing. Once again, all I can do is flee.

"You mean you won't suck my dick just because I tell you to?" he asks, his voice even lower.

The question is so impertinent, his behavior so disgusting, I want to hurt him. And I could. I learned early on how to defend myself from men.

When I turn around to look at him again, however, the world grinds to a halt.

He's smiling at me from underneath his long eyelashes, and my heart skips a beat.

Maybe it's just not my day. Maybe I'm dehydrated, or all the super-rich students out there have melted my synapses. In any case, I'm frozen, unable to do anything other than stare at the stranger as if he's glowing. As if he's reflecting his surroundings like clear water. His eyes are as blue as the sea, and his smile is as welcoming as a warm summer morning. Feelings stir in me, a flicker of yearning, the certainty that this man has sprung right from a fairy tale my mother told me when I was a child.

A savior.

A prince.

A promise that will last forever.

His face could've been sculpted by a great artist. Striking cheekbones and jawline frame a straight nose and sensuous lips. He truly does look like an angel. A fallen one.

"No, I won't," I mutter, responding to a question that feels like it was asked a lifetime ago. When he takes another step toward me, pushing past the invisible threshold of polite distance, I move back and hit the door.

Though the guy is definitely an asshole, I'm finding it hard to think a single clear thought. His entire posture is brimming with confidence and masculinity. His movements are determined, his muscles well-defined, and his fashionable clothes bring it all together to complete his perfect appearance.

My mouth goes dry as he reaches for me. I freeze again, filled with the conflicting energy his nearness inspires in me—preparing myself to push him away while at the same time expecting him to grab me—when he reaches past me to open the door.

"Pity. I'm sure in your mouth I could come again right away."

I move aside to let him through. "In your dreams."

"Oh, definitely." His smile pulls into a lopsided grin as he swings the door farther open. Before stepping through, though, he treats me to another look. His expression changes. The look on his beautiful face disparaging now as a dangerous gleam lights his eyes. "What's your name?"

"Mable," I say immediately, before biting my tongue. Why am I even answering this guy instead of ignoring him?

"Amabelle Weaver?"

I gape at him. How does he know my name?

"I'm Jaxon. Jaxon Tyrell."

My breath catches.

"My father is funding your new life of luxury, and I'm going to make it hell. The way you're looking, you won't last a week. Less than that if you don't blow me now and then. Think about it, Belle. Maybe you'd like to take orders from me after all." His mouth twists into a diabolical smile before he yanks the door all the way open and then slams it shut behind him.

I don't dare take another breath before the last sounds of his footsteps in the hall are gone. "Fuck," I mutter, trying to rub the goosebumps from my arms. That was not how I imagined meeting Jaxon Tyrell, son and heir of the Tyrells, whose foundation is funding my scholarship. I didn't even know he was still studying here. Even so, I try not to take his threat too seriously. He's clearly the sort of spoiled asshole who's looked down on everything and everyone all his life.

Once I've pulled myself together—and waited long enough for Jaxon to get lost—I go back outside to get the rest of my stuff.

The dorms are concealed behind the other, more imposing buildings on campus. It's much calmer here, in the shadow of those architecturally impressive structures, than out on the main street. This seems to be one of the buildings that hasn't been fully renovated yet. Hotel-like apartment buildings with glass-enclosed balconies, floor-to-ceiling windows, and white-painted trim loom on either side.

My building is an eyesore between them.

Did they do that on purpose? Is Kingston University making sure we don't forget our place?

As I walk down the gravel path, I notice a student leaning against the building across from me in the shadows. I smell tobacco and I look into the guy's face the same moment he looks into mine.

Everything about him is dark, as if the shadows around him are a part of him. His black leather jacket with sleeves rolled up, his black boots, black chinos, the black tattoos on his forearms, and all that aside from his eyes, his hair, and his stubble.

I nod at him, maybe because I think being accepted at the country's best university means I'm expected to be polite.

He doesn't respond, merely taps the ash off his cigarette and keeps his eyes fixed on me as I pass by.

Okay, I tell myself, almost like a mantra. *The college is full of freaks. The important thing is not to let them keep you from studying.*

Back on the main street, I notice splashes of color scattered across the meadow. I pass by quite a few without paying them any mind, but then I see the black-and-white script of my favorite jumper in the grass. The many scattered spots are my clothes.

"What the fuck!" I look around for whoever's responsible for this idiocy, then lay eyes on the blonde who blocked my way before.

She's leaning against Jaxon on the hood of the red sports car, watching me with an ugly smile on her face and surrounded by her clique. He's wearing sunglasses now and seems to be the only one who isn't interested in what's happening with my stuff.

I roll my eyes at the incredibly childish prank and start gathering my clothes. "Too funny!" I call out to the group once I've collected everything and stuffed it back into my tote. "Looks like you've made it to kindergarten level. Too bad this is college." There. That's a reasonably cool retort. But the next moment, I wish I'd just kept quiet.

The blonde doll breaks away from Jaxon and moves toward me. Her pretty lips are curled up in disgust, her eyes reflecting pure hate. "You're nothing but garbage, just like your cheap second-hand clothes. It's hardly our fault they begged for a proper funeral to spare them from being worn by you again."

Picking up my suitcase, I ignore her.

"Go home, bitch!" she calls after me. "You and your tragic clothes will never belong here!"

Laughter follows me across the lawn. My knuckles turn white from clutching my suitcase handle with all my strength and anger. What do these rich kids have to gain from treating me like this? How can they be so ridiculously cliché? They seem to have stepped out of some documentary miniseries about bullying at elite schools and picked *me* as their favorite victim for some reason.

Just great.

If the next four years are going to play out like a Netflix show, I'm fucked.

Two more steps down the path, my suitcase's handle suddenly tears off. *Argh!* My arrival at college is slowly but steadily turning into pure torture. Dragging my suitcase behind me, I once again meet the gaze of the guy in the shadows. He's still leaning against the wall. He's still smoking. He's still barely moving.

"Thanks so much for your help!" I yell.

He doesn't even twitch.

"Fucker," I mutter, fighting my way to the dorms. I'm not surprised anymore that no one's helping me. I seem to have fallen into a parallel universe of rich people who see me as nothing but the worthless embodiment of the lower class. I heave my suitcase up the steps to the building's entrance, only for my bag to slip from my grasp at the last moment. "Shit!" I'm almost in tears watching the few things I brought to college tumble down the stairs.

"Oh no!" A shrill voice comes from my right, and a woman rushes forward, trying to catch the notes and printouts I prepared for my first week of lectures as they're swept up by the wind and headed for the lawn.

"It's alright, thank you." I take the papers from her and start to turn away, not expecting anyone to be nice to me without a good reason today.

"I'm so sorry about your suitcase." The stranger bends down again to collect the contents of my toiletries bag. "I once dropped a suitcase down an escalator. It was in Paris, in the Metro. They have these enormously long stairs there, and in the end, it broke open and all my souvenirs shattered everywhere. It sounded like such a cheap excuse when I tried to explain it to my friends." She straightens, pushing the filled toiletries bag into my hands. "Hi, I'm Harper."

"Mable," I respond warily, finally looking at her properly.

Her hazel eyes widen when she hears my name, and her full

lips part slightly. Her entire appearance is enchantingly elfin. I'm starting to feel like I wandered into a fashion show where I don't belong at all. How can every single person on this campus be so pretty? Harper's dark blonde locks frame her narrow face perfectly, and I can't imagine her ever doing anything mean. *Don't let her looks deceive you…*

"That's a beautiful name." Her voice is reverent as she repeats, "*Mable.*" When she says it, it sounds a good deal prettier than I'm used to.

"My full name is Amabelle, but—

"Mable is prettier, definitely."

"Thank you." Uncertain of what else to do, I turn away and stuff everything I just collected into my totes.

"I brought your things along."

"Hm?"

Harper points at my backpack on her back and my bag she's holding, one of the ones I'd left behind on the sidewalk earlier when I couldn't carry everything at once.

"You carried them all the way here?" I ask, perplexed.

"I wanted to help." Harper winks at me, brushing a strand of hair from her face. "I know, there aren't many here who would. They're almost all just spoiled rich kids. I'm in my second year, and I've had to watch them bully people like you so often. This time, I'm here to help." She gives me a radiant smile and I don't know what to say.

"That's nice of you…"

"Nice? I'm throwing myself to a pack of hungry wolves for you! It's not just nice! It's reckless!" She laughs a tinkling laugh, shoulders my bag, and opens the door for me. "I'll come inside with you, and once you've put away your most important things, I'll give you a tour of the campus!"

Since I don't want to offend her by telling her I'd rather be alone after all of this, I follow her to my new dorm room without another word.

Harper stops in the middle of the room for a long moment before heaving a sigh. "Well, at least you don't have to share it."

"I don't?" That's a surprise.

"The ground floor has ten rooms. There are five girls on scholarship. After your first term, you'll rush sororities. At least that's how it's always been. Yeah, I think the bedbugs are the only company you're going to have."

My head jerks up, but Harper is laughing again.

"Just kidding. There shouldn't be any bedbugs. But… well." She puts my things down on the bed on the left, then drops onto the other one.

Harper might think the room's small, but it's generously sized for a single person, more space than I've ever dreamed of having. The window faces the park, and a desk and dresser flanks each bed. The whole setup screams luxury as far as I'm concerned.

"Where are you from, Mable?"

"Woodlyn, Philadelphia."

"Oh, that's not too far from here. Are you going to spend many weekends at home?"

"I might…," I evade. In truth, I should go home every weekend to check up on Mom and my sister. On the other hand, I'm glad to have escaped the trailer park, and Mom won't miss me as long as I keep sending her money.

"Do you want me to leave you alone?" Harper asks. She's leaning back on her hands with her legs crossed, bouncing one of them up and down. I'd really like to say yes, but I shake my head.

Maybe she can explain what just happened, and why I've barely been on campus for an hour but already feel like the university's elite have teamed up against me.

"That's great. I wasn't planning to." Harper jumps up, clapping

31

her hands. "Do you want me to help you unpack, or would you rather do that later? I can show you around. I don't have anything to do until six tonight."

"A tour would be great," I admit, smiling as well now. Harper's radiance is catching.

She threads her arm through mine and leads me out of the room. "You've already seen the ugliest building on campus, which is an important part of any proper tour. They've been debating whether to renovate this last dorm building for years, but they end up bickering about whether it shouldn't just be torn down instead." She stops in the middle of the corridor. "The ones who don't want to tear it down think the building should be a protected monument, preserved for its historical significance. See?" She points up at a fine line of ornamental woodwork running along the walls. "They say Jefferson lived here."

"The president?"

"That's the one. They've already torn down the dorms where the other nine presidents of the Kingston era studied. Seems they might want to keep the Jefferson one, though." Leading me out the door, she turns to the right. In contrast to me, in my simple jumper and comfortable leggings, she's fully made up. Her wrists jingle with golden bracelets, her white sneakers are decorated with logos, her jeans fit her slim legs so well they have to be tailored, and her top bears a Fendi logo that's impossible to miss. "This is the physics building. Two lecture halls, a few study rooms, and the physics lab."

Harper has brought us to one of the many architecturally stunning buildings situated on the edge of the round lawn. The campus is enormous, with many nooks and corners, and full of places that look more like the castle in Harry Potter than a modern university. But instead of on a mountain top, it's built in the middle of what feels like an infinite forest, visible in all directions and surrounding Kingston like a defensive wall. It not only renders cell phone reception terrible but also creates an always-mystical atmosphere even on a sunny day like this one. Even though I printed out a map and learned it by heart, I'm very grateful for the tour. "You know, I've been most interested in physics so far. Maybe I should change my major."

We walk through an atrium that connects a hallway of faculty offices to the lecture halls. The benches and lanterns peppered through the manicured lawns are decorated with metal embellishments, making them look like particularly precious pieces of furniture.

"What are you studying?" I ask.

"Law," she says, miming putting a finger down her throat. "My father is the chief justice."

"Wow. Robert Mitchell is your father?"

"Yeah. That degree is, unfortunately, sort of a family tradition." She sighs, beckoning me onward. "What's your major?"

"Business administration. I'll try to take as much philosophy as I can, though."

"Oh, that's exciting. The philosophy of success. That's quite the interesting combination."

"Combining opposing disciplines appeals to me."

"You'd consider money and philosophy opposing disciplines?" Harper looks thoughtful for a moment. "Isn't it just that philosophy is a way to explain the money? Money doesn't really have any intrinsic value at all. It's just paper... Oh, no, that's psychology. Psychology is a really cool subject, too."

I'm about to launch into a long answer but realize just in time that her question was purely rhetorical, and she's already moved on to the next subject in her head.

"The library." Harper stops again, gesturing widely. "No student with her wits about her would study here. That makes it the perfect place to avoid everyone."

"Got it."

"You know, Mable," she starts after a while, once she's shown me around the important parts of campus and taken me through the main building's atrium with all of its awe-inspiring, historied lecture halls. "I'd love to end this tour in the student restaurant, but there's one more thing I need to show you first."

She leads me up some spiraling stone stairs toward a number of crowned lion sculptures and down a long corridor made to look like a grand hall with its high, ornamented ceiling. The walls are hung with pictures, starting with immense paintings, followed by yellowed photographs, and ending in brilliant, sharp ones. All of them depict men. Young, white men posing in front of a wood-paneled wall reminiscent of a hunting lodge. "The Hall of the Wise Men," Harper says derisively, stopping in front of the last picture with me. "Here they are."

I need a moment to recognize the man posing with three others behind an armchair in the last photograph. Jaxon.

"Remember these faces, Mable, and stay away from them. Stay as far away from them as you can."

I'm tempted to ironically add "or else?" but I can imagine the answer. Three of the four men look like predators thirsting for something. The way Jaxon Tyrell stands there, patronizingly resting his hand on the backrest of a chair that might as well be a throne, his near-invisible smile that of a devil hiding behind angelic beauty, shows he's enjoying his role as the ruler of hell to the fullest.

Tyrell's eyes glint like opals poised to break into pointed, cutting shards if he's angered. His sensuous lips like forbidden fruit in paradise. His attractive, symmetrical face suggests kindness and openness, but I know that his bright eyes and dark blond hair only camouflage the darkness inside him. It's as if the photograph speaks to me, as if his spirit's been captured in the picture. I only met him for a few minutes, but his threat and the roughness of his words, along with the memory of him getting blown, are impossible to push from my mind.

I already know I'll take Harper's advice and stay away from him. I don't need a second helping of his arrogance.

Although Jaxon's the central figure of the photograph, someone else sits on the red cushions: A young man who captures my attention for longer even than the cruel angel by his side. Unless I'm very much mistaken, this black-haired man is the one who'd been smoking in the shadows earlier.

The photograph makes him seem a lot less dark. He almost looks pious with all his tattoos covered by his stylish suit. The circles under his eyes are less pronounced than they'd been today. I'll admit, I'm somewhat perplexed by how his actual looks differ from the man in the picture.

"Sylvian Silvano," Harper whispers behind me. "The guy in the chair. Jaxon Tyrell right next to him. And this one is Reece Crescent." She points at the man to the left of the throne-like chair. His hair is somewhat lighter than Jaxon's and his beauty even more perfect. If Jaxon is the fallen angel, then Reece is still flying high. He's the only one in the picture sporting a broad and friendly smile, which makes him stand out from the others. He doesn't really seem to belong. Like he's far too nice to associate with someone who would say things like what Jaxon said to me today.

"Who's the guy at the very back?"

Harper sighs. "Romeo."

"His name is Romeo?" I giggle and quickly clear my throat. Harper seems a bit too serious for jokes right now.

"Don't imagine he's anything like Juliet's Romeo. Romeo Portcharles is a sharp knife, a living weapon. Stay away from the others. Run fast and hard from Romeo."

Her words send a shiver down my spine. Compared to the other men, Romeo seems quite nondescript, nearly fading into the background next to those three beautiful faces. His hair is dark like Sylvian's, but his eyes are dull, almost dead.

"Jaxon, Sylvian, Reece, and Romeo. They rule the campus and have been in control of everyone and everything for three years now. Even the professors do what they say. They make no secret of hating the scholarship students. Jaxon hates his father, and his father established the foundation that pays for those scholarships after all." Harper turns to face me with a serious look. "Mable, I'm so sorry to tell you about it this openly, but hardly anyone here on a scholarship makes it through their first year."

I raise an eyebrow at her, but all I can say is "What?"

"The program is in its fourth year. In that time, fifteen women have started studying here on scholarship. Three of them are still with us. Just... Don't let them bring you down, okay?" Harper looks concerned.

Once again, I don't know how to respond, so I change the subject. "What do students have to do to get into one of these pictures? Be particularly mean?"

Harper's still serious. "Finish each year at the top of their class."

So they're mean *and* smart. "Is there a group like this for women, too?"

"There is not."

"So women don't get their photograph hung in a fancy hallway if they perform the same or better...?"

Harper makes a face. "This is Kingston. Just be glad they let us study here at all."

I raise both eyebrows but say nothing. In everything I read about the university, I haven't come across a bad word about it. Yes, Kingston has a conservative attitude and political activism is pretty much absent from campus. But they maintain a strict female to male ratio and support students of all origins—as long as they have enough money.

"You think I'm making this up, don't you?" Harper asks, turning away from the wall and toward the heavy double doors at the end of the hallway. "I'd love for you to still believe that after the first few weeks. Maybe this year will be different, hm?"

I nervously wriggle my fingers. Harper's warnings aren't particularly uplifting. "What happened, exactly, that so many scholarship students left?"

Harper gives me a bitter smile. "Many things. Listen to me and stay away from the Kings. That'll make things easier."

"The 'Kings'?" I ask, chuckling.

"The Kings," Harper repeats seriously. She lets a few seconds pass, the silence of the empty corridor reinforcing her words, before suddenly beaming at me again. "So, what next? Do you want to go get some coffee? I'll pay!"

JAXON

Five new girls.
Five new toys.
For five rich bastards.

What do we have this year? One with almond-shaped eyes who'll drop to her knees at the snap of my fingers; a skinny redhead who'll surely be the first to give up and drop out; a little bookworm with glasses bigger than my balls; a fuckable blonde we'll definitely keep around for a while; and a good girl from the slums who won't last a day on campus if we set our minds to getting rid of her.

Come on, boys! Place your wagers! I bet I'll be the first to fuck them all. And I don't just mean their little pussies.

I mean their fucking lives.

2

MABLE

Jaxon Tyrell.
Sylvian Silvano.
Reece Crescent.
Romeo Portcharles.

Four names, each committed to memory, especially because Harper didn't tell me much more about them, and I didn't want to seem pushy. But what are "the Kings" all about?

My afternoon ended up being a lot more pleasant than my arrival on campus. Harper made me laugh so often my ribs ached by the end. I stopped thinking about my clothes scattered across the lawn or the sound of people laughing at me. Setting up my room brings up more complicated feelings than I'd expect it to. On the one hand, I'm grateful to be on my own. On the other, having this much space to myself is unfamiliar and uncomfortable.

Even just having a proper room with proper walls is like living in a palace after the trailer I shared with my mother and sister. It makes me feel rich. Like I've escaped poverty. At the same time, I'm full of guilt about leaving my sister, Olive, behind…

Around seven, I put on simple black pants, a matching shirt, and my worn but comfortable sneakers, then add a bit of makeup, a little blush and a touch of mascara. My walnut-colored hair gets tied back in a ponytail. The girl looking back at me in the mirror has fought for many years to earn her place at Kingston. There's strength in my eyes, along with a fear of failure. Courage as well as doubt. Now I'm here, and it'll take more to drive me away than a few mean comments from some awful bitch.

My scholarship provides for me to eat in the student restaurant for free, but everything else will cost me . Since there aren't many jobs available around this remote university, I'm going to have to work on campus. How mean are the other students going to be to me if I'm the one serving them and carrying their beers across the room? And always with the risk that I'll spill on their expensive pants or fine dresses.

My lips curl into a smile as I leave the dorms for the fifteen minute walk to the other end of campus. The owner of the moderately filled bar doesn't ask me any questions about myself. He just pushes a loaded tray into my hands, watches me carry it across the room, and then shows me how to handle the taps.

I'm keeping a lid on my excitement, but I feel like hugging Derby, a man in his midthirties, for giving me the job just like that.

"You'll be working here four nights a week, is that clear?" he says, gesturing to the schedule hanging behind the door in the tiny kitchen. "The other days you'll be on call. If business is slow, you can use that corner there to study." The table he points at is tucked into the niche between the bar and the kitchen door. "But only if it doesn't bother anyone, so don't start reciting nonsense while you memorize things or anything like that."

I nod dutifully.

"You keep your tips, but never even think of asking me for a raise. Apart from that, the job's really simple. You oughta be able to do it no problem if you made it through the admissions process for this place."

That makes me smile, which he misses.

My first shift proves that getting a job waiting tables was the right decision. Derby leaves me alone and I can move between customers and take orders no problem. The harder and more demanding my studies get, the more relaxing I'll find a job that doesn't require me to do much thinking.

I used to work in a bar back in Philadelphia. I liked it there, too. It allowed me to wind down.

Half an hour before the bar closes, a solitary guest appears. For a moment, I'm confused by the feeling I've seen him before, but then I recognize him. He's one of the Kings, and he's taking a seat in the rearmost corner and watching me aggressively.

His appearance raises the hair on the back of my neck. If Harper was telling the truth, and Sylvian Silvano is part of the clique around Jaxon...

"Hey, there's a new guest," Derby calls out to me from where he's sitting with his newspaper in the niche near the kitchen.

"Sorry," I mutter, grabbing my notepad and walking toward Sylvian, my face as impassive as I can make it. I can't stay away from him, even though I'd like to. I don't want to get in any trouble, and Harper hadn't sounded like she was joking about the so-called Kings.

Even approaching him makes me feel like the ground is about to turn to lava under my feet, and my knees get a little wobbly.

Sylvian's eyes on me are dark as the night, and he radiates danger in a way that doesn't quite fit with the guy in fancy clothes getting his picture taken for being a top student.

I focus on his torso to avoid looking him in the eye. It doesn't help. Every inch of him sets off alarm bells in my head.

Sylvian's wearing the same leather jacket as he was earlier, sleeves rolled up to expose his tattoos. His nails are trimmed short, his hands rough, and he's also wearing rings on his fingers. One of them is a signet ring. Is that the same design that's on Jaxon's?

The only thing he's wearing that doesn't make him look like a criminal are his white sneakers. They shift his appearance toward fashionable, a little dark but certainly familiar from current magazine covers.

An expensive gold watch adorns his wrist. Or at least I assume it's expensive. The name *Richard Mille* reflects the weak light, but that doesn't mean anything to me.

"What'll you have?" I ask in my regular, friendly tone, staring at the notepad in my hand.

I wait for him to respond, but he says nothing, forcing me to look up.

He's holding the menu with maybe ten drinks listed and seems to be reading every single word. Looking down at him from above, I can't tell what color his eyes are, but I do notice the dark circles under them. They make him look like he's gone days without any sleep. Though he doesn't look bulky, he's clearly in great shape. The campus has three gyms that are better equipped than quite a few in town, and it seems like Sylvian makes good use of them.

"Sit down," he says without looking up. He's clutching the menu now, his knuckles standing out white. I'm not sure what to think of that demand and wonder if I simply misunderstood because I was distracted by his looks.

"Sit down, Mable."

Hearing my name and the extremely commanding tone he says it in makes me obey.

My face grows hot as I feel the cheap synthetic leather of the bench under my legs. What is Derby going to think I'm doing here? Yet, I seem to be tethered to the table as if by magic.

It's like I can't help but obey, even though that makes no sense. "Look at me."

A cold shiver runs down my neck as Sylvian gives me another order in that rough, dark voice. Without a thought, I raise my eyes from his knuckles to his face.

His eyes seem to grab me like a grappling hook between ships on the open sea. I am caught. My body refuses to react. The ambient sounds of the bar blur. My breath, in contrast, is loud in my ears and my heart is beating so hard he must be able to hear it from where he's sitting. Being so close to him affects me to my core. As if anchored by an invisible chain, I'm forced to remain right where I am, waiting for permission to escape.

"You never should have come here," Sylvian begins, unblinking, forcing his low voice through gritted teeth.

I hear a thrumming in my ears. His words make no sense. Why would he say that? What does he care where I go to school? Why is he interested in me at all?

Once again, I can't get the words out. This time it's like I'm afraid of what I might say. Instead, I focus on maintaining a neutral expression, which isn't easy when I'm looking at Sylvian. The Kings aren't just top students. Each one of them is damn attractive in his own personal way.

Sylvian's long, black lashes frame his eyes, as his curved lips do his mouth.

His eyes are so deep a green that I'm losing myself in them.

Black hair falls over his forehead.

His face is crowned by shadows.

My hands turn sweaty. A voice in my head yells at me to run, while another insists I stay put until he tells me I can go.

"You can still leave. Go back home. It's not too late," Sylvian explains without putting down the menu. He's holding it between us like a wall, a border that will not be breached. A shield. "If you stay, your life will be hell. Harper told you, didn't she? If you're not going to believe me, then trust *her*. This entire university is going to fuck up your life until it's crushed you into the ground and you're trapped, crawling out from behind its walls, something that used to be human but will never be entirely whole again."

The fascination that had me entranced a moment ago is replaced by fear. Who is Sylvian and what does he want from me? Why is he warning me? Why are they *all* warning me? "What kind of game is this?" I whisper.

He leans farther forward, and a whiff of tobacco and vanilla wafts toward me. "Forget your studies. You can have a better life just by finding yourself a good guy. He could save you and he could save your sister. But if you stay at Kingston, you'll destroy both your lives."

His words are like a slap in the face. *Destroy both our lives? Who would want that? Why?*

"How do you know about my sister?" The fog his appearance induced is lifting. "Who are you anyway? What do you want from me?"

Sylvian keeps his eyes fixed on mine. "I want you to leave."

"You're not the first one to say that." I lean back to get some distance. "You seem to really hate us scholarship students, don't you?"

"It's not about *hate*," he explains calmly, sweeping his gaze across the room for a moment. "It's about... things you'll never learn about. And that's just as it should be. Not knowing will protect you. I only have one thing to ask of you." His eyes soften, pleading in a way that confuses me more than anything else. "Please go."

I blink at him a few times. I don't know what else to do. "I fought too hard to be here. You can come up with all kinds of nonsense, but I'll be staying. Even if my clothes in the grass was only the beginning—I don't expect you to make it past kinder-garten-level bullying."

His hands curl into fists. Naked fury is audible in his voice. "Stop pretending I'm warning you about Clarisse."

"Who else?" I ask cynically, crossing my arms in front of my chest. "I won't be cowed. Certainly not by a few mean comments."

"That's not what this is about," he hisses without opening his mouth. His eyes roam the room again. "You're still beautiful. Beauty is all you need to have a good life these days. If you stay, they will take even that from you. You will have nothing. *Nothing.*"

That word echoes through me.

Beautiful.

"Who would want to take everything from me?"

"Someone who thinks you're a problem, someone who wants to get rid of you before you can harm them." Sylvian lowers the menu, once again reading it so intently it's as if it holds some secret message. "For them... for *us*, you're nothing but collateral damage. A gust of wind. Air to breathe in and then out, consume, gone in a moment. Human lives are nothing but numbers to those in power, like dollar signs in their bank accounts. They have no meaning. Just a means to an end. This isn't about college or about a few students. This is about something much greater. You're worth more than what will happen to you if you stay. You must leave Kingston. Right away."

His words feel like an invisible hand closing around my throat.

"If you refuse to believe me, if this conversation isn't making an impression on you, then you're more stupid than I thought."

"Why would I believe you...?" I sound a bit less confident than I would've liked. The urge to obey him is overwhelming. It's as if he's holding the leash to lead me with. But I can't leave Kingston. Never. Not until I've made the most of this opportunity.

Sylvian closes his eyes for a second, as if in torment. "There are people who don't want you here. They would rather *kill you* than let you finish college. This goes deeper than simple bullying. Believe me."

I stare at him. His face is expressionless. Hard and expressionless enough to push my fear into panic. I can't believe him, though. This is a joke. They're fucking with me. The Kings. Their clique. That's what they're doing. He's probably recording my reaction on his phone right now. Anyone who spreads another person's clothes through a field to drive them away can't be that serious.

"Was that all you had to tell me?" I ask flatly, pushing myself back from the table. My palms are sweaty, which he luckily can't see. I'm about to get to my feet when he reaches out for me.

His fingers close on my wrist, sending liquid heat coursing through me. Sylvian pulls me close over the table, bringing my face toward his, and my body obeys as if it's not my own.

He raises his hand and reaches out. Even though I *should* be moving away from him, I can't. As his fingers touch my cheek, it, too, is burning, and an aroused sound that doesn't fit the situation, Sylvian, or what he just said, at all, breaks free from my throat.

"You will be destroyed," he whispers, and though his words sound like a dark promise, his rough voice is full of feeling. "And the only thing I'll be able to do is watch you suffer through it."

He takes me by the throat and pulls me even closer before he completely surprises me by pressing his soft lips to mine.

A sigh escapes me. The kiss is short.

Like a breath.

And yet, my entire body burns like he spent hours touching me everywhere.

He lets go of me just as quickly as he pulled me toward him, and then storms out of the bar without another word.

It takes me a few seconds to gather myself before I slide off the bench and return to the counter. Derby is waiting for me, eyebrows raised.

"What the hell was that? Did Silvano need some personal advice about which one of the ten drinks on the menu to pick?"

"I'm sorry..." I'm not surprised that Derby is familiar with Sylvian's last name.

"It's your first night, so I'll let it slide. But stay away from any guys—or girls—in the future and just do your job. If you want to flirt with anyone, do it outside. While you're not working. Is that clear?"

"I wasn't flirting," I mutter, but Derby already stopped listening. I'm lucky he didn't see Sylvian kiss me. There's no way I could've explained that. I for sure would've been out of a job immediately.

My shift ends, and I walk back to my dorm.

I lock my door behind me.

Even so, I get the sense it won't make any difference.

Maybe nothing will make a difference for me.

Maybe Sylvian spoke nothing but the truth.

3

JAXON

The whores are boring.

Their naked bodies barely hold my interest, and the plaintive looks, so grateful for anything I might toss at them, are more pathetic every time.

Two women switch off, taking turns sitting on my dick, moaning like we're shooting porn, riding me because I don't care enough to put in the effort to fuck them. I don't even know their names, I realize now. They're blonde and stupid, which makes them exactly like a hundred other bitches on this campus.

Soon I'll be through with all of them.

Not a single one of them will ever be able to hold me.

My fingers, adorned with my signet rings, dig into one of their hips, urging her to move over my cock until I finally come and, for a moment, feel more than just hate.

I was born with contempt in my blood, or maybe my father's constant contempt has infected me with his hatred.

He hated my mother.

He certainly hated me.

And I hate anyone who dares stand in the way of my revenge against him.

Anyone who keeps me from paying him back for what he did to *us*.

I know my father is hatching plans to destroy me for good. He knows no honor and would disempower even his own son.

My father wouldn't establish a fucking foundation and then show absolutely no interest in whether his scholarship students stay on to complete their studies at Kingston—or whether we drive them away. No. There's another reason for it that has *nothing* to do with his impulse to be a good Samaritan.

And I think I know what that reason is.

That's why I'll make sure *none* of them, not a single scholarship student, will ever get their shitty degree.

Not even you.

The campus looks at me and thinks I'm about establishing justice. That I'm punishing those impoverished scholars for *daring* to invade Kingston when they haven't paid a dime to be here.

Really, though?

Those poor innocent little scholarship students are nothing more than pawns in my fight against the man who wants to take away everything I have: My father. If it weren't for him, *I wouldn't have a single fuck to give* about those pussies and their bottom-class male counterparts.

Well played, Tyrell.

You're balls deep and the only thing you're thinking about is your fucking father.

Find a better one next time.

The image of the little trailer-park girl flashes in my mind at that thought. *There's something so very innocent about you. It makes me want to wrap my hands around your tender throat and take your breath away. And there's just enough defiance in your eyes to be sure things won't get boring, eh?*

No. You're certainly not boring.

You're special.

Chocolate-colored eyes, a high-set ponytail, and hot enough that even clothes from Walmart can't hide it.

A proper challenge?

Do I even know what that is?

Me, the King?

I make these boring bitches lick my cock clean before I rise from the chair and buckle my belt. Everyone in the room is long used to my habit of unabashedly fucking in crowded rooms and broad daylight. I can't be bothered to find a quiet corner for it. After all, this is *my* throne room, in a manner of speaking, so I'll be a goddamn king in it.

This room on the main building's second floor is accessible only to a select few. *The door* situated at the end of a hall of paintings of our ancestors, at the very heart of campus.

It's wooden, heavy, and large enough to accommodate a giant.

That door remains closed to anyone who isn't sufficiently capable. Sufficiently smart. Sufficiently brave. And all the other shit our rational stick-up-the-ass grandfathers came up with.

Furnished in the same old-fashioned way as everything else in Kingston, the room concealed behind that magical door is stuffed with books. Book after book after book, and all kept from gathering dust on the impossibly tall bookshelves by Pinch, the hunchbacked janitor, and Pinch only. He comes in with his ridiculous rag to wipe them off every single week.

We've updated the premises a little. We got rid of the table long enough to seat twelve that used to stretch down the center of the room, instead arranging five of the chairs in front of the floor-to-ceiling stained-glass windows.

Anyone entering could be forgiven for mistaking the place for an actual throne room. A throne room for five Kings. I move over to settle on the middle chair, throwing one leg over the armrest.

I don't need a throne. I don't need a hall or even a single fucking follower to know that this university is mine, just as it was my ancestors'. I *am* this university.

It was founded by Eduard Kingston three hundred and fifty years ago. My mother is a Kingston, even though she gave up that name. The blue blood of the American elite is flowing in our veins, and our family has ruled this land for centuries.

And my father, of all people, is trying to keep us from continuing with it.

In another time, I wouldn't have to fight for my place at the top at all. I simply would've inherited it. Still, I conquered every obstacle to follow in my ancestors' footsteps, and I'm close to the final milestone, being initiated into the *real* secrets of Kingston University by graduating.

Nobody is going to take that position away from me.

Least of all one of the pathetic scholarship students who never would've been able to so much as set *foot* on this campus without my father's foundation.

The double doors are thrown open and it admits three men into the room.

Zayn and Reece flank Sylvian, looking like they're escorting a criminal rather than accompanying him.

Shadows battle on Sylvian's face. A glance at my watch tells me they're late.

Some heads in the room turn to take in the new arrivals. Some of the *inner circle* are permitted to spend time here. We frequently study together in the chairs or at the smaller, separate tables, which actually *is* truly effective. Other times, we might bring in some girls from campus, allow them to breathe the air of fame for a few hours before banishing them again as whores. A few *peasants* are among the guys now watching Sylvian, Reece, and Zayn. Young students who've earned the privilege to be our servants.

They're as helpful as they are pathetic. They're *nothing* compared to us.

"Did you have to summon me here like some criminal?" Sylvian asks as he stops a few steps away.

I light my post-fuck cigar. Romeo takes a seat next to me, handing me an ashtray as if on cue. Sometimes they make me feel like the godfather.

Like someone who rules tough, but fair.

Except, to families like ours, the Mafia is barely better than dogs, pieces to be used, moved across the board, and rewarded with a bone for a job well done.

Reece and Zayn take their seats and get just as comfortable there as I am.

"You tell me, Sylvian," I say, my voice brittle. "Did I have to? Or would you have come on your own?"

Sylvian clenches his teeth. He's more important to me than anyone else. Not even Romeo gets close, and Romeo is my *shadow*. But if I had to shoot one of them, I wouldn't even hesitate to put the bullet in Romeo's head.

But I'm pissed off now. He went to you to warn you about us. That makes you even more attractive to me. But I won't have my best friend stabbing me in the back because of you. Sylvian has been keeping secrets from me. The term has barely even started and he's already fucked all the Kings' principles with his arrogance.

Where is this going?

Why can't he just be honest and admit that he'll never learn?

He's trying to protect you, but he's the real threat. No girl is safe from him.

Least of all you.

"What did you tell her?" I ask. "I mean, did you actually explain *everything* to her? Really let her in on what's in store for her this term? Or did you have the decency to *not fuck us quite so deep* even while you betrayed us?"

"She's not the one, Jax," Sylvian says with a huff, but not before taking in each of our faces first. He's trying to justify this. *Fuck. Is it possible I'm not the only one who sees that you're special?* "Go easy on her. She'll break otherwise."

"Oooh, she'll 'break,'" I mock, making Zayn laugh. "That never would have occurred to us, of course. Who'd ever want to break those lousy little scholarship students while they're here getting a degree they don't even deserve to look at shoved up their asses with my family's money? Thanks for the advice, Sylvian. We'll be sure to take it to heart. *You fucking bastard!*"

My final words surge into the room, and everyone looks up. The peasants, the inner circle, even Romeo, who usually maintains his dead-eyed stare until something important happens.

"Fuck you, Jax." Sylvian's voice is low as he returns my gaze, unflinching. A wall rises up between us.

What did he do, Belle?

He wants you to leave and is prepared to protect you at all costs? Doesn't he know how interesting he's making you? Far more interesting even than what our brief encounter sparked.

Romeo leans toward me when I lift my hand. "Send everyone out," I whisper. Without hesitation, he rises to flush our fellow students out of the seating area.

I'm curious now, and sort of pissed off. It's better if this conversation is kept between us Kings. For all I know, Sylvian's been watching Amabelle for weeks, and continues to do so, but he hasn't told me anything about her.

I'm very familiar with his tendencies. He's not a stalker. He never lets his victim know he's watching them, nor does he lurk in doorways or tail them down dark streets. He doesn't even let them know he's interested. In fact, he won't do anything any nerd with a crush and no balls wouldn't do. He just watches from afar.

"What's so interesting about her?" I ask casually before taking a deep drag from my cigar and letting the crackling of embers hang in the air for a beat. "Sylvian, you know you make us curious when you act like this."

"There's nothing *interesting* about her," he claims, feigning confidence. He's the only one who dares oppose me. Not even Reece would have the guts for that without Zayn. "We can find someone better. She won't work out. She can't handle your sick games, or mine, or Crescent's. She just won't be any fun. Pathetic, boring, that's all she'll be."

"You didn't mention Romeo."

Sylvian takes a step forward, teeth clenched and eyes narrowed. "If Romeo so much as *touches* her…!"

I throw my head back and laugh. "Fuck, you've really got it bad for our sweet *Amabelle*."

Romeo's out of earshot, but Sylvian's never cared what Romeo thinks of him anyway. Those two have hated each other since their disagreement about… that thing last year. I don't mind keeping them separated, but I certainly understand if Sylvian wants to keep Romeo away from *someone*.

Romeo—my shadow—is a rabid wolf. My right-hand man for any dirty work that needs doing on this campus, and yet, he's a bit too uncivilized for the club's rules.

That's one reason I'd always pick Sylvian in the end.

"What I *feel* doesn't even begin to come into it," Sylvian continues. "I learned from last year. We can't treat every woman who crosses our path like a toy to be broken. Sometimes it's about more than just our fun, Jax. Her mom is just wallowing in that trailer of hers. A potted plant has more initiative. And Mable has a sister. If we destroy her, her baby sister goes down with her. Can you get that into your sick skull? Do you even care?"

Something pangs in my chest. I'd never expect Sylvian to talk this way. To paint me as a monster and himself as a saint. *I'm not a fucking monster, Amabelle. I am a king. I only do what I do to keep my subjects happy.*

"You call her Mable." That little fact certainly didn't escape me. "You have a nickname for her already. That's just perfect."

Usually, you all share a single pet name. Dole. A wonderful bit of British slang that sums up what you are to us: Something between a doll and a charity case, a dole. Why, then, is Sylvian acting like you're already above all the other Doles, hm?

"You will tell me what this shit is about, right now!" I motion around me, reminding him that he's standing in front of us like he's on trial, instead of sitting among us where he belongs. Have I lost him? What do I have to do to win him back?

While the rest of us spent our vacations in the Hamptons, in Europe, and in Russia, he remained here, holed up in one of his regular clubs, stalking a girl whose very existence drives me crazy.

He was shadowing you, Amabelle. But why?

When I get no answer, I straighten in my chair.

Why are you doing this to me, Syl?

This motherfucker knows me better than the right half of my brain knows the left. He knew all it would take is a single look at Amabelle to make me want her. If Sylvian feels the same way, we could already be having so much fun together.

But my best friend has made a secret of who Amabelle is and what she looks like. He's watched her and he didn't tell me.

He hid you from me.

Has he already forgotten that he owes me his eternal loyalty?

I rescued him off the street like a dog. He would be nothing without me.

"Are you actually telling me that you stalked a girl all summer long, only to realize, on the first day of the semester, that you don't want her after all? I'm hardly the one here playing sick little games, you lying bastard. That's *you*. Don't you try to make me out to be the bad guy here, and tell me why you want to protect *her* of all people."

It's true, Belle. Just like I said: If my father weren't in the picture, I'd hardly care about you at all. The other Kings, though... They hate you for baser reasons. Normally, Sylvian would be champing at the bit to destroy you.

But now?

Did you manage to awaken his conscience?

"I wasn't stalking her," he growls, crossing his arms. The energy emanating from him is like a hurricane rushing toward me. Usually, he's solid as a fucking rock. Nothing gets through his shell. He's a victim of his own guilt, his self-flagellation, and his blind hatred. "I'm telling you we shouldn't do it. Accept it or ignore it. But I won't be joining in. I'm out."

He's grown up. That's cute. I don't feel like playing anymore either. I'm tired of all of these games. For me, taking this seriously is the fun part. Maybe it's time to let him in on the details. Maybe I should tell him why I'm doing all this. There *is* a reason. There's a reason for everything, and it goes far beyond the fact that we're bored. But is he ready to learn the truth?

Can I trust him with my biggest secret?

Maybe he already knows.

"What do you mean 'out'?" Reece asks, his tone mocking. "Don't you want to go on to the Kingston master's program after undergrad, Syl?"

"Of course I do," he snarls. "And none of you are going to stop me."

"Is that so?" I ask, rising to saunter over to him. "Think very carefully about what you say next, Silvano. Between the two of us, I'm not the one who spent my summer watching a girl from the corner of some shitty club. How many times have you imagined her buying a hit from you, or some cocaine, and then jerking you off in a dirty bathroom?" I smile. That's exactly what he was thinking. He's obsessed with her. The way he watched her when she left her dorm, lurking in the shadows so he wouldn't miss a thing. Sylvian is not the only one here who knows how to observe. I know what's happening around me, too. "Don't play if you don't want to. You can spend the whole term focusing on your studies if you like. Or you can try to. You won't be able to stand it, though. You *need* it. You *want* her. You're not trying to protect your little trailer-park bitch *from me*, but *from yourself*. I know you, my dear friend. You and I didn't just make this fucking game up. We *lived* it. We can't simply stop playing. We *are* our game. It's our life. Has been for a long time."

I can see in how Sylvian's looking at me, he knows I'm right. Trying to protect Amabelle from us was a feeble attempt to resist his inner demons. But we're the Kings. I'm nothing without him and he would be even less without me. No one stands in our way.

Not even our own fucking conscience.

It's true, Amabelle. Two hearts beat in my chest. I have a lofty goal, and I'll get rid of anyone who stands in my way. But I also have my... friends. Sylvian, Reece, Zayn, and Romeo. And one thing unites us in this game. It binds us and satisfies every one of our darkest desires.

That's why we can't just stop.

Even if—when I defeat my father.

We'll never stop seeking out victims.

It's an addiction. It's sick. And you're going to love it.

"Tell me, Sylvian," I whisper into the silence, circling him like a wolf calling its mate to play. "How many times did you imagine what would happen once she came to Kingston? What were you imagining? Don't lie to me. I know you've already pictured her naked before you. Before *us*. Imagined us *sharing* her. You won't give a shit about her useless mother or her neglected baby sister once Amabelle is kneeling in front of you, sucking your cock, while we watch. Isn't that right?"

The muscles in Sylvian's jaw twitch. Every word I say is true, and the things in his head are probably much, much worse. "That doesn't change the fact that this has to stop."

"What has to stop, Syl?" I ask him ironically. "You keeping fucking secrets from us? Yes, that needs to stop! You're not a stalker. You're not the type to hide in the shadows. You're a fucking King. What is it about that little girl that has you so enthralled you won't even tell us the truth?"

Sylvian stays silent. He does that a lot, and all I can do in those moments is try and figure out what he could be thinking about. It doesn't help me now.

"Right. Listen up, Silvano. Let's make a bet."

He perks up then, and the Kings in their chairs sit up straighter too. Gambling between Kings is serious business. Never to be taken lightly. Bets are binding. They're dangerous. They can be *deadly*.

I extend a hand to Sylvian. "Whoever gets her first decides her fate."

He snorts. "You understand *nothing*, Jax. I won't touch her."

I'm not the only one laughing then. None of the other Kings believe his bullshit either. "Then I bet that you won't be able to stand it. You won't be able to stand not fucking her. Not even that soft, delicate mouth of hers. You'll want it. You'll want it so bad not even this newfound conscience of yours will be able to stop you."

Sylvian's expression doesn't waver.

"And while you're still struggling to talk yourself out of it, she'll already have fucked me. Whatever you tell her and whatever she finds out about me, in the end, she'll pick me. And I'll be the first."

Now his eyes light up. "You're going to lose."

"Will I?"

"I bet she chooses me. Even if I stay away from her all term."
A brittle smile twists his lips. He grabs my hand and squeezes it
tightly. "If I win, she's out. Mable will stay here, go to class, and
your family's foundation will pay for that shit until she gets her
fucking degree."

"Cute," I say in a singsong voice. "What is it about her that
suddenly made you grow a heart?"

"Deal, Tyrell?"

"The bet's on, Silvano."

He immediately drops my hand like it burned him.

Reece inhales deeply and shakes out his legs. "Are you done
measuring your dicks? Want to bet she won't pick either of you?"

"No need," Sylvian grumbles, shoving his hands in his pockets and turning to drop into one of the reading chairs without
another word.

Reece frowns, but I just keep on smoking.

"Let him mope," I tell the others. "He'll be the first to wreck
Amabelle when the time comes. Do you have your lab assignments for this year yet?"

JAXON

Would you like to play a game?

I'm the King. You can be my Queen.

But watch out: There's only one player who can control you.

We'll just have to see who that is .

No matter what, I just put you on the board. Now, your life is mine to win or lose.

Whether you like it or not.

4

MABLE

The other scholarship students are nice. We bonded right away over breakfast in our shared kitchen. It feels good to be able to joke about Clarisse and "the Kings." One thing connects all of us: Our own hard work has brought us here, not our parents' income. In addition to language skills in something like Russian, German, Chinese, or Japanese, a year of work on a social project is mandatory. Since we couldn't simply *buy* that placement like the other students did, we all have exciting stories to share about what we did after high school. The male applicants also need to present proof of one to two years of military service, which I find somewhat outdated, even though it means virtually no freshman is younger than nineteen.

Lien is the only one of us who doesn't join our group. She's come out of her room but hasn't talked to me or to any of the others. I didn't share what I walked in on her doing with Jaxon, even though I haven't stopped wondering why she did it. Or why they picked my room, of all places. Does she know Jaxon? Or did the "King of the University" just have to walk in to make her fall to her knees in front of him? Did he blackmail her? Did he threaten her like he tried to threaten me? Maybe Lien thinks she has to do what he tells her in order to keep her scholarship…

That's the thought that makes me angriest, and I can't banish the image from my mind. Jaxon sitting there smugly, getting blown by Lien as she kneels in front of him.

Jaxon's self-satisfied grin follows me into the shower, which I delayed until after breakfast so the others could go first. I wish I could just shake off the memory, but the heat of the water only makes it worse and worse. Soon enough, I can practically feel his body on me, pressing me against the shower wall with that devilish smirk on his face. Touching me. His lips move to my ear, lascivious and hot, and I succumb to his cruel fantasy.

Fuck. He's not the only one to show up. Sylvian is there, too. Sylvian, so close and menacing, the taste of his mouth on my lips. *What would it be like to have them both here with me in the shower? If they took turns...?*

Without my permission, my fingers slide between my legs, and only the fact that this is a communal shower makes me bite back a moan.

How many girls think of the Kings when they touch themselves? How many imagine more than one of them at once?

I know I must be just one of many. One of thousands drawn to the charm, the looks, and the irresistible style of those assholes. Still, I allow it to happen. I let that delicious tingle race through my body as I imagine them touching and kissing me one after the other.

Damn. How depraved am I, really?

I turn the shower to cold and then dress myself as quickly as I can.

***

We walk over to the main building together, and it feels much safer than risking running into Clarisse alone. Climbing the wide staircase toward the lecture hall as a group even makes the stares from the other students somewhat bearable.

They look at us like we're lepers, or aliens who dared to invade their campus. I try not to think about that, though. I don't care if they like me or not.

I was accepted to Kingston, damn it.

That's all that matters to me.

Nothing could mean more to me than that.

We all slide into the third row together.

As the room gradually fills up, Harper grabs the open seat next to me on the other side.

"Hi, Bella," she chirps at me, putting one of two coffee cups on my desk. "I don't suppose the coffee machine in your dorm is any good, is it?" She treats me to a broad smile, and once again I notice how pretty she is. Her rosy cheeks glow, and her golden jewelry accentuates her lovely face just perfectly. She's wearing a slim gold watch and a loose shirt emblazoned with *Prada* in huge letters. Every single one of her fingers bears a ring, and she repainted her nails since yesterday.

They're now a glaring pink.

"Isn't this the orientation event?" I ask her.

"Of course it is. Who's going to tell you how things really work if I'm not here, though?" Her conspiratorial smile makes me wonder, Why's Harper being so nice to me? Is she suffering from some sort of helper syndrome? Is she trying to prove to herself that she's a good person by befriending poor, destitute scholarship students?

Quickly brushing those thoughts aside, I reach for my coffee and direct a grateful smile at her. Maybe Harper simply likes me, like I like her.

Just because it's what I'm used to at home, doesn't mean everything is the result of self-serving calculation.

"Look, you're in the same year as Ashley Cohen." She nods

at a new student who just appeared in the doorway on the right side of the huge lecture hall. "I heard she's going to alternate between studying one semester and acting the next. Isn't she just amazing?"

Even though I haven't seen an entire movie with her yet, I do recognize Ashley Cohen, one of Hollywood's most popular up-and-coming actors. "Don't her movies bring her enough money? Why is she here?"

"Well." Harper brushes strands of her long mane behind her ear. "You don't study at Kingston to earn money."

"You don't…?"

"You'll get it soon enough." Harper reaches for her coffee, takes a sip, and doesn't seem inclined to divulge any further information.

While I consider telling her about Sylvian's warning, something has me questioning whether I can trust Harper at all. Both of them speak in riddles.

You don't study at Kingston to earn money.

This isn't about college or about a few students. This is about something much greater.

Are they making fun of me? Are Sylvian and Harper *both* playing a nasty joke?

I watch Ashley Cohen thoughtfully as she takes her seat in the front row and opens her MacBook. Even though her profile is familiar from trailers and movie posters, right now, she looks very much like any other student waiting for her first lecture. Why would she be studying here if not to make money?

For me personally, money is absolutely the reason I'm here. My mom spent her entire life in a trailer park, and I had to leave her and my sister behind for this. Money could change everything. It's freedom, security, independence, health, and peace. I would've attended any college as long as I could land a well-paying job after four years, so I can finally free my sister and myself from the misery of sharing a tiny mobile home between three people. I'm deeply grateful that Kingston University, of all places, accepted me and that I was awarded a full scholarship. I wasn't even aware that stars and starlets like Ashley would also be studying here.

The one thing I know is that virtually every president of the United States has attended Kingston, and virtually all the highest-ranking positions in politics and business associations are occupied by Kingston graduates. Is that "what it's all about"? Do you go to Kingston to get into power?

"You should brood a little less." Harper nudges me, almost making me spill my coffee. "Take a look around. Reece has arrived. We're about to start."

Hearing the name Reece makes me sit up and take notice. I haven't forgotten that he's one of the guys in the photo Harper showed me yesterday. Another one of the *Kings*. However, when he walks to the front of the room, arranges the papers he brought, and looks expectantly at the crowd, every bad thing I've heard about him vanishes from my mind.

Reece Crescent is as hot as liquid gold. My fingers tighten on the cup in my hand, and I fight to swallow a few times. Looking at him is like looking into the face of a statue. He's a flawless specimen of humanity.

"He's an attractive devil, isn't he?" Harper whispers.

I'm not the type of woman who reveals every feeling stirring in her, but there's no way I can lie about this. I nod, trying to hide behind my coffee.

"Hello, and welcome to Kingston University." Reece's voice, melodious like music on a gentle summer breeze, sends warmth flooding into my belly. He's dressed simply and elegantly in cream-colored jeans and a red sweater that emphasizes his sculpted physique. His eyes are blue, though not quite as icy as Jaxon's, and his face radiates pure, beautiful masculinity.

It's the kind of face you want to introduce to your parents. That you want to marry. That would inspire you to give up your dreams, become a housewife, be at your husband's beck and call, if that's what it took.

"Alright, Mable," Harper whispers. "You need to stop staring at him like that. Remember what I told you yesterday. Reece is one of the Kings, right? The Kings are top-tier assholes. You need to stay away from them, even if it doesn't seem like it right now because he's being nice."

Mm-hmm, I think, *it doesn't seem like that at all.*

"I hope you're looking forward to college," Reece continues. "And finally being here. I'm in my senior year, and I'll be with you during your orientation week. And anyone taking Linear Algebra in the General Studies program will be taking one of my classes, so get used to my face right away." He smiles and I'm already looking forward to math. "You have four tough years ahead of you. If you qualify, you can continue on to a two- or three-year master's degree program. If you get the opportunity, I'd highly recommend that you take it. More than half of the senators in Washington right now are Kingston alumni, after all. I don't know of a single listed company without a top Kingston graduate in the C-suite or board. That kind of success doesn't come easy, though. This university is one of the most demanding in the world. However, preparation and networking will help you. Trust me when I say that this week will be the last time you get a day off. Take the opportunity to get to know each other now. Familiarize yourselves with everything the university has to offer so you can use your time as efficiently as possible in future."

I soak up every one of Reece's words, allowing the sound of his voice to comfort me. It seems meant to lull me to sleep and spirit me away, and I find it hard to focus on anything. Ten minutes later, I look around and realize I'm not the only one under his spell. A stab of jealousy grounds me once more. Reece could have anyone he wanted in this auditorium, and that probably includes a few of the men. I don't need to waste a minute ogling him like a particularly lush piece of chocolate cake. It's far more important that I pay attention to what he's telling us.

"His mother is a supermodel and heiress to an exclusive fashion label," Harper whispers after a while. "The Crescents are luminaries of the design world. We wear today what they thought of yesterday. Forget about any of the flashy brand names like Dolce or Chanel. The Crescents are richer than all of them put together."

"Why are you telling me this?" I ask with a sad smile, making Harper laugh. "You're just making him even more interesting."

"It's good to know your enemy. Reece is a spoiled rich kid who's never had to work for anything before. He's only leading this lecture to scope out the girls he's going to bang in the first week. Don't let his angelic smile fool you, Mable. He can destroy you if he sets his mind to it. But I'll be here to protect you from him."

I look at her, stunned. What is she talking about? She almost makes it sound worse than Sylvian did!

I don't even get a chance to ask Harper any questions after the lecture because Reece calls her over as soon as he finishes. She rolls her eyes at me before joining him.

I follow the other scholarship students outside.

There, leaning against the wall in the entrance hall, is Jaxon, surrounded by his adoring clique. He fixes his gaze on our group, and I'm suddenly uncomfortable.

"Go ahead," I tell the others as I hang back to wait for Harper. I'm nervous that Reece wanted to talk to her. How well do they know each other? Can I trust her judgment of the *Kings*? Why else would she warn me about them?

"See you in a bit, Mable!" Rachel calls to me, tying back her red hair as she goes. She lets the flow of the crowd carry her away while I remain behind.

Since Jaxon and his clique continue to stare at me, returning to the lecture hall seems like the wiser course of action. The room is large enough that I can avoid hearing Reece and Harper's conversation, provided I stick close to the door.

But my entry doesn't interrupt any conversation. Reece has Harper pressed against the blackboard, one hand casually resting beside her head, and his other arm crowding her in. She's stiff, hands clenched into fists and expression defiant.

I'm rooted to the spot, uncertain of whether what's happening here is something I'm supposed to see. The two seem so intimate... Are they together? Is that why Harper wants me to stay away from the Kings and, by extension, from Reece?

They turn their heads in my direction at the same time. Hot fire scorches my skin as I feel Reece's interested gaze on me. The look he gives me is so intense it makes me want to run out of the building as fast as I can.

Shit. I'm really not used to attractive men checking me out. Is that a good thing? Or are they just as perverted and cheap as the guys from back home?

"Leave me alone, Crescent," Harper hisses, pushing his hands aside. He allows it, because he's distracted... by me? "And leave Mable alone! I'm warning you!"

Reece's picture-perfect lips curl into a crooked smile as he leans against the blackboard, arms crossed, while Harper rushes toward me.

"Come on, let's go," she mumbles and pulls me along with her. "Amabelle?"

It's as if a tornado picked me up and whirled me around. Of course, turning toward Reece is a mistake. I should've listened to Harper and ignored him. That's hard, though. My name just sounds so damn seductive when he says it.

"Amabelle Weaver," he says, pushing himself off the blackboard and taking a few steps toward us. He moves like a god walking Mount Olympus, no trace of so much as a single dark thought in his eyes. "I'm having a party Friday night. You should come."

"Just leave her be, Reece," Harper mutters at my side.

His eyes shine brightly and he stops in front of us to fix me with a broad smile. "Harper hates me. I reminded her that she can't afford to skip any lectures, even to make new friends. That's why you should join us on Friday evening. We don't normally invite freshmen, but I'll make an exception for you, Amabelle."

"Just Mable."

"Do Harper a favor and go with her, Just-Mable. And make sure she doesn't skip another lecture to pine over me."

"I'm not pining over you!"

Reece raises a perfect brow. Now that I know his mother is a model, his flawless looks make sense. He's stunning and radiantly beautiful. "Of course you're not, Harper. Well. Are you coming?" Reece is smiling at me broadly enough to make me swoon.

There's no escaping it, and before I can think twice, I've already agreed.

Something flashes in his eyes. "Wonderful."

"No!" Harper snaps.

"Party commitments are binding at Kingston. See you Friday night."

"She's not coming!"

Reece's expression turns almost pitying as Harper groans loudly, grabs me by the arm, and drags me away.

"See you Friday," Reece calls after us, his deep baritone sending a vibrating buzz right into my stomach.

"I told you to stay away, and you turn around and accept an

invitation to one of their parties," Harper mutters as she stomps down the hall, pulling me along.

"He was nice!" I try to defend myself, glad we're alone now that Jaxon's gang's disappeared. "I don't think he lied just then. He's worried about you. Did you really skip your lecture?"

"But he *is* lying!" she says, throwing up her hands. "It's all just lies! God... It shouldn't be that hard to *not* fall for their stupid looks." She's pushing through the door, still holding onto my arm, and dragging me out into the daylight.

I have just a second to notice the stone staircase shining strangely and feathers scattered on the ground before it happens.

Harper's feet slide out from under her, and she pulls me down with her. I fall hard on the top step, crying out in surprise as Harper slips away on the soapy water.

"You need to get to the edge!" she calls to me as she moves closer to the building's wall, slipping on the stone time and time again.

I try to follow suit, but I take another fall, hitting every limb on the hard stone.

"Mable!" she calls, pointing above me.

I look up in time to have sticky liquid poured over my head.

Laughter erupts around me. With my eyes glued shut, I can't see who's responsible, but when I finally manage to wipe my eyes clean, I see white snowflakes dancing around me.

Snow?

No, that's feathers.

I stare at my hands in disbelief, then at the yolk on my clothes and on the steps. Feathers cover every exposed inch of my skin, making me look like a chicken. Most definitely. I can't help but laugh.

"Are you alright?" Harper asks as she carefully slides over to me.

Hundreds of students stand in front of me, looking up from the bottom of the stairs and laughing. I'm laughing, too, though. I can't help but find the entire thing hilarious. This prank is so stupid, and that stupidity is what makes it somehow good. And I'm on board with that.

Harper's laughing along with me. She starts out cautiously, restrained, but she joins in when I take a handful of feathers and throw them at her. Most of them remain stuck to my fingers, but a few fly toward her.

"Only the first day proper day at Kingston and already your second kindergarten-level prank," I shout, still laughing as we toss feathers at each other.

Harper defends herself, screeching, and a few precious seconds pass where we're just having fun. A carefree moment. Chicken eggs and feathers are ridiculously tiny issues compared to what my life was like before.

Actually, they're no issue at all.

There were nights in the trailer park when I was afraid I'd be shot.

Days when I thought my mother would never wake up again.

I've survived drug raids at my high school and been frisked by the police more than once.

What are a few feathers compared to that?

We slide down the stairs together, unable to stop giggling. I never want to stop laughing like this. I want to treasure this moment. It was a prank. Just a prank that some students thought up for us. All in all, it was a pretty good, mostly harmless prank.

At my high school, "jokes" involved holding a gun to someone's head and threatening to kill them if they didn't hand over their cell phone…

On the bottom step, memories of my past catch up with me. I know I can't pretend it's over. My sister is still living in the trailer park. I can't laugh while she's suffering. Things might be getting better, but they aren't good yet.

"Hey, don't worry about it," Harper says after we make it to the grass where we're safe from slipping. "You're right, it's kindergarten style."

"Yeah," I reply quietly, my mind on other things. "It is."

"Why were you laughing along?" Rachel demands as we reach the scholarship students. They also have plenty of feathers and eggshells on their clothes, which Brittany and Kady are currently picking off each other. "Don't you get that they're making fun of us all?"

I turn and glance at the crowd behind me. Little by little, people are breaking away from the spectators and moving toward the library, where we have our next orientation event. The demonstration is over. Clarisse continues to stand there, giving me a cold, aloof look. Next to her, Jaxon sits on a wall, blatantly disinterested and staring off at nothing. It's strange to see him from a distance. He makes me scared and angry all at once. He makes me want to run away and be caught at the same time... Damn. Harper is right. It's hard not to fall for their charms.

I turn away from Clarisse and shrug. Trying to explain how I see this entire situation, I say to Rachel, "It's just childish. They'll have to come up with a lot more to get to us, won't they?"

"I hope they don't," Rachel grumbles, stripping off her sweater without any further ado. Rachel graduated from high school at sixteen and completed her first undergraduate degree in three years instead of four. She did an internship abroad in Japan before being accepted to Kingston. She's pretty, with red hair, two navel piercings, and some tattoos that show she must have sported a more alternative style in the past. "What's *she* doing here?" Rachel asks, nodding in Harper's direction.

"I have no use for silly pranks either— Harper says defensively.

"Isn't Clarisse your best friend?" Rachel interrupts her. "Every picture on Instagram shows you together. It's kind of weird that you're suddenly sucking up to Mable, isn't it?"

Harper's eyes go wide. "How do you—"

"You accepted my friend request. I saw it when I had a signal for a change. I know you maintain public and private profiles. You were careless enough to open your private one to me. I saw the picture you posted last weekend and deleted last night."

"That's crazy," Harper replies, crossing her arms in front of her chest. "I have no idea why you hate that I like Mable."

"Like her? You hardly know her!"

"But you do?!

"Alright, calm down, girls," Brittany interjects. She's been among the quieter members of the group so far. Someone more shallow would never expect her to get into Kingston. She looks cheap and her makeup and bleached hair make her seem… empty-headed. That's just an illusion, though. The few things she's said have made it clear that she's insanely smart. "None of us enjoyed that very much. I'm impressed by your ability to see the humor in it, Mable."

What else could I do? I want to ask her, but I hold back. I really couldn't care less about having eggshells or feathers tossed at me.

"Agreed," says Harper, giving my shoulder a friendly squeeze. "See you for lunch." With a confident smile, she goes the opposite way.

Awkward silence descends once she's gone.

"Believe me, Mable—I wouldn't make something like that up. Really!" Rachel implores.

I give her a nod. Why should she? I didn't believe that someone like Harper would try to be friends with me without ulterior motives anyway. I'm cautious. Just the same, I don't automatically trust Rachel either. Or anyone else.

I convince the others not to go change in the dorm. It'd take far too long and make us late for the next lecture. They agree to simply own the prank and we respond with heads held high when laughter greets us in the library. Us laughing along seems to take the fun out of it for those idiots, so it subsides quickly.

The rest of the day continues uneventfully—apart from some annoying comments. I'm glad to finally get out of my sticky clothes in the evening.

On my way to Crown's, I get turned around and find myself standing in front of a large hedge. I'm not sure how I lost my bearings so quickly, but without a map and with cell phone reception as bad as it is, I just have to retrace my steps. Rather than getting back onto the proper path, though, I eventually end up outside of a chapel. I remember this from my map and know that I just have to walk past it to get to the other end of the Crown's parking lot.

The tiny church is all lit up. Curiously, I take in the lights behind the stained-glass window. I can't imagine that any students are all that pious, but they certainly work hard to keep up appearances.

However, as I walk past the open door, I see that there's no mass being held.

My heart skips a beat and I retreat into the shadows to watch the scene.

A chair has been placed right in front of the altar, with a woman tied to it. A black cloth hood has been pulled over her head, and something about her posture tells me she's panicking.

She's surrounded by five figures.

All of them wear black masks, decorated in gold, and they circle the victim in their midst menacingly.

I freeze and forget what I have to do for a moment. Then I reach for my cell phone, about to call the police, only to find that I once again don't have any signal.

Five figures?

One of them seems to be Jaxon, actually. That tall frame, the athletic body...

"It's not that hard," I hear someone say inside the church. "All you have to do is be honest. It's quite easy, isn't it? Just open your little mouth and *TELL US THE DAMN TRUTH!*"

The voice echoes, distorted by the speaker's mask—or maybe he's using a device to distort his voice? The victim, whoever she is, doesn't respond.

"Why are you getting involved?" the same voice asks. "Why are you pretending that you suddenly care about what happens on this campus? What will it take to make you tell us the truth? Does he have to fuck you before you'll talk? I liked you better when the only thing that mattered to you was you."

"There's nothing to see here."

I almost shriek when someone speaks behind me. *Fuck.* My heart hammers in my throat.

A person dressed in black moves to stand in front of me. His face is concealed by a black hood and a completely black mask that doesn't even expose his eyes.

"That's the acceptance ritual for the Omega-Phi Society," he explains. "We don't like any disturbances."

"There's a woman tied up in there!" I say, my voice trembling, as I back away from the masked figure. I don't know his voice. "And that didn't sound like any sort of ritual. It sounded like they're threatening to rape her!"

I can't rule out the possibility that he's telling the truth, though. If students play pranks with eggshells like a bad Hollywood movie, why wouldn't they hold weird rituals for their even weirder societies?

"Yes. That was meant figuratively. You better leave before they catch you. Surely you don't want any more enemies on campus than you already have, do you?"

75

I find it impossible to calm my breathing, but I eventually give in. There's no chance Sylvian was talking about this when he tried to warn me, right? Harper couldn't have meant the Kings tie people up and threaten them either, could she?

How many college movies have I seen where much worse things happen before people are accepted into an exclusive fraternity or sorority?

I still don't know if I did the right thing when I reach Crown's. Maybe it was wrong to look away. Or maybe that's the only way to survive this university.

JAXON

I know you crawled out of some dilapidated hole, a dirty and insignificant place, just like all the ones before. You're nothing special, even though you might think you are. Quite the opposite, really. They all live the way you do. It's half a wonder the sun shines for you at all. But hey, don't you worry about it. You've got us now. We'll drag you out of the shadows and into the light. We'll light you up like a sparkling fucking star in the big blue sky. We'll be awestruck by your radiance. We'll turn you into an angel in no time at all.

We'll give you wings and carry you to the loftiest heights.

Unfortunately, we'll also let some of you… simply fall.

Spread your wings wide, little angel.

The fall will be a long one.

5

MABLE

I make an effort to keep my distance from everyone for the rest of the week. Not just "the Kings," but also the other scholarship students in the dorm. And Harper. After everything that's happened so far, I'm more comfortable not trusting anyone at all.

I pick a seat as far toward the back as possible at the orientation events and I get lunch to-go from the student restaurant. Being unfamiliar with the complicated names of their dishes, I just stick with pasta and salad. Away from other students, I eat my meal in the shade of a tree and am glad to be spared any further attacks.

Of course, I can't avoid everyone entirely. On Wednesday evening, I stepped in a puddle as I entered the dorms. Rachel pushed a bucket into my hand, frantically telling me, "They've flooded the entire bathroom!"

It took us three hours to mop it up and the floor is still somewhat damp.

I felt connected to them again for the few hours we had to work together. I enjoyed laughing together with Rachel, Brittany, and Kady, even if the prank was annoying.

I dropped into bed, dead-tired, on Thursday night, but a sharp cry woke me from my doze just a few minutes later. It brought us all running into Lien's room together. Like me, she'd kept to herself during the week.

Something nasty was in her bed. It turned out to be a toad, and she claimed she had no idea how it got there.

I slept badly that night. I kept imagining other college students breaking in to cover me in toads.

All of this only encouraged me to withdraw even more.

Fortunately, the content of the orientation session distracted me from what Sylvian, Jaxon, and Reece said. I can't wait to dive deep into the many subjects at hand, even though I know the basic courses in economics are going to be a challenge. All of my philosophy professors dress casually, some even in track suits, while the faculty in the business administration department dress in tailored business suits. The content follows similarly. Every philosophical topic seems more exciting than the last, while the economics faculty's offerings are limited to how best to use capitalism as a tool. I'm going to need a few terms to get the big picture. But that's what I'm here for.

Around lunch on Friday, after my last philosophy lecture of the week, Harper races up to me like a whirlwind. I've managed to avoid her, but the many messages she sent me had already warned me that she wouldn't stand for that forever.

"Gotcha!" she yells vehemently, pulling me close. "Never avoid me like this again, will you?"

I stand by her side, unimpressed. I don't owe her, or anyone else, anything. My expression seems clear enough, and she heaves a theatrical sigh.

"I'm *not* friends with Clarisse," she insists.

"That's not the point."

"Yes, it is. You don't trust me."

"No, I really don't care who you're friends with. We barely know each other."

"Why are you mad at me then?"

"I'm not mad!" Only now do I realize that I'm going to need to give some explanation. "I just want to focus on my studies, alright?" *And I don't want to get caught up in some sick frat game and end up tied to a chair.*

Harper lifts one of her perfectly plucked eyebrows, waiting a moment to see if I can come up with a better excuse.

"Weren't we going to that party tonight?" I say quickly. "That'll give us time to talk."

Her brows creep even farther up.

"We had all of those lectures, I got a job at Crown's and there was a string of stupid pranks in the dorm…"

Harper sighs heavily. "You don't owe me any excuses, Mable. I'm sure the entire week has been shitty enough for you as it was."

I nod, even though I secretly disagree. But telling her I don't want to trust her seems a bit harsh to me. I'm not the sort of person who enjoys offending people. My week wasn't actually bad. I loved every single second of my lectures.

"We do need to talk though," she insists. "I just have to… Well, *I* owe you some explanation, okay? Will you give me one more chance?"

"I really don't care who you're friends with—"

"Stop that," she interrupts me with a groan. "No one's going to believe that. You're not stupid, and you have every right to distrust me. Coffee?"

I agree, even though I feel guilty about it. I can't afford the coffee on campus. Harper invited me last time, and once again she hands over her credit card to pay for my seven-dollar latte. The cheapest coffee in the store is five dollars. The employees probably pet the coffee beans before grinding them.

Harper carries our cups to an empty table in the middle of the room. The din of multiple lively discussions allows us to talk undisturbed. However, I can't help noticing that everyone is watching me. It's crazy, but for this entire week I've felt like I'm more famous than Ashley Cohen. The constant stares are annoying. That's another reason why I kept to myself.

"They're waiting for something," Harper whispers, low enough that only I can hear her.

"And what's that? Eggs dropping on my head again?"

"For what the Kings are going to do to you."

I snort, stirring my coffee, unimpressed. "And what's that supposed to be? The most they've come up with so far was a toad in Lien's bed and flooding our bathroom."

Harper brushes her hand over her forehead as her eyes roam for a moment. Just like Sylvian, she seems to want to check whether there's anyone nearby she doesn't want around. "The Kings would never—never ever—put a toad in your bed. Or baptize you with chicken feathers. Those were just dumb pranks by... petty people too immature for college."

"They're missing TikTok, aren't they?" The university network blocks certain apps and websites. We don't even have Facebook. Students can chat with each other via Kingston's dedicated portal, but no one would upload a video of themselves dancing there. Of course, you can use your cell phone to get online if you have to, provided you can find a place where the signal isn't barely sufficient for a phone call. Many areas on campus don't have any kind of signal at all.

"This isn't about TikTok." Harper closes both hands around her cup as she stares down into her frothy milk. "I'm not allowed to tell you as much as I'd like to."

"And why's that?"

"Because Big Brother is watching over this campus. Assume we're being watched at all times, and if it seems that I'm helping you too much, they won't leave us alone at all."

"Big Brother?" I ask, perplexed. "You mean as in George Orwell? Big Brother as in surveillance state?"

She nods as if it's the most normal thing in the world *not* to speak freely to each other. "First of all, though, this is about Clarisse and me, anyway, isn't it?"

"As I was saying—" I begin, only to have her interrupt me again.

"I know, I know, you don't care. You're a really bad liar, Mable. And so am I. So... the truth is this: Clarisse is my best friend. Or rather, she used to be. Until recently. It really hasn't been long since the last time I posted something with her and me. After all... I've known her since nursery school, and we've always done everything together. Everything. We even shared the stupid crown at the prom. We... we were like sisters. And that's why I tolerated her starting a thing with Jaxon. And then, over the last year, it changed her. You got to know her as a... proper bitch, but I remember what she's really like. I was clinging to that knowledge until just before the semester started. Then... two weeks ago, she made a big fuss and proved to me I *can't* be her friend anymore. It was about something... something terrible that is far too awful to joke about. I finally told her the truth. I told her what I thought of all the things she was doing and what she had become. And... well... she threatened that if I didn't take back everything I said, she'd reveal my deepest secret. And... I didn't take it back so she followed through."

"Oh," I say sympathetically, "I'm... sorry."

Harper smiles brightly, though her eyes are glassy. "I deserved it, you know? I put up with all her nastiness and never stood up to her. Her betrayal only proves to me what she's really like."

"And that's why you... helped me?" I conclude.

Harper nods. "It is. Clarisse ousted me from our clique. I do have a few acquaintances from boarding school on campus, but there's a reason they never made it past acquaintance level. I thought I'd just go straight to those who would be in greatest need of a friend. The entire term is going to be so fucking hard, Mable. And I'm glad not only that I can help you make it through, but also that I like you. Which makes me feel guilty again because you're not the only one who needs help, but… I think I'm just really selfish because my parents taught me all my life that I should be. I'll do my best to change, though. Alright? Give me a little time. I'll need some to learn."

Once again, my tongue seems tied. What am I supposed to say to that? "Thank you."

"Whatever for?"

"For carrying my backpack and the rest of my bags to my dorm room." I smile suddenly, and then I look around conspiratorially, leaning forward to make sure no one can catch my words. "In a way, we're annoying Clarisse just by talking, aren't we? Friends or not, I'll do anything to get back at that bitch."

Harper's eyes light up. "Whoa, Mable. I might just kiss the hell out of you. You're so cool and so brave and just amazing!"

"Am I?" I ask, astonished. Honesty is something I have trouble with, it seems. Self-confidence certainly is.

"You're totally right! We should do something together just to spite her. We can get back at all of them. I'm not actually allowed to talk to you at all, after all." She blinks in shock, quickly covering her mouth with her hand.

"No one heard you," I mumble.

"I shouldn't have said that," she whispers back.

"Who makes those rules? Jaxon and his super-smart Kings? Weren't you just saying they're more sophisticated?"

Harper cracks an agonized smile. Something about it tells me this is as much as she'll say on the matter.

Even though I refuse to take their ridiculous code seriously, I'm grateful for my coffee and the time I get to spend with Harper. She opens up an entirely new world for me, and it's a world that I'll inevitably *have to* immerse myself in if I want to take something away from college beyond a degree. I need to understand how the people who'll be my colleagues, supervisors, and well-paying customers think. I have no idea how someone can walk around carrying a bag that costs enough to feed a family of four for half a year back home. I don't understand why people are so very concerned about their looks, constantly fixing their hair and putting on makeup or changing their outfit multiple times a day, like some of the freshmen I met during the week do.

There's a lot the students at Kingston take for granted that I don't have the first idea about.

As we leave the café to walk back to my dorm, we run into Sylvian. He's sitting on the broad staircase of the physics building, smoking. His eyes are fixed on me as we walk past, but Harper pretends not to notice him.

She trembles by my side as we pass by.

"What's wrong?" I ask, dismayed when I see the tears running down her cheeks.

"Oh, it's nothing," she mumbles and wipes her face. "Just allergies."

"To Sylvian?" I tease, which makes her laugh, at least for a moment.

"More like an addiction to Sylvian."

"You used to be together?"

"Together?" She laughs again, bitterly this time. "Mable, these guys... they aren't with anyone but themselves."

"What happened?"

"Nothing happened. He knows how I feel about him, and I know how he feels about me. Absolutely nothing has happened." She dries the tears under her eyelashes. Her mascara seems to be waterproof. In any case, it hasn't run yet. "That's the secret Clarisse revealed. I didn't want Sylvian to ever know I have feelings for him, and then… she told him everything. I'm just stupid, that's all. Stupid and an idiot in love."

"Nonsense," I try to reassure her. Suddenly I feel guilty because I haven't told her about Sylvian's speech at Crown's yet. I can *never* tell her that he kissed me. Even without knowing he doesn't care about Harper's feelings, I wouldn't put any store in that kiss anyway. Arrogant guys with the money to buy whatever they want just kiss whoever they want, too, right? And fuck whoever they want. Sylvian probably has a different girl in his bed every day, just like Jaxon does.

I just feel sorry for Harper. Even without knowing the Kings any better yet, I can imagine it's not exactly easy to be in love with one of them.

"Just be grateful if you never have to meet him." She recovers her composure, lifting her head as we continue on our way toward my dorm. "I don't know anyone who hasn't fallen for him yet."

"Like everyone falls for Reece? Or gets on her knees for Jaxon?"

"No. Of course, any woman on this campus would marry Jaxon or Reece in a heartbeat. But they *want* Sylvian."

I worry my lower lip with my teeth, trying not to let on that I've already had the pleasure of meeting him. The closer we get to my dorm, however, the more I wonder why I'm not just telling her. What do I have to gain from keeping what Sylvian told me a secret? I don't have to mention the kiss, or the burning sensation under my skin when he touched me. I can tell Harper what he was talking about, though. Maybe that will draw out more secrets from her about what will "destroy me" at Kingston University.

"Where are you going?" I ask as she walks past my dorm.

"We're going to my place."

"To yours?"

"To my apartment." She gives me a radiant smile. Happy Harper has made a comeback. "You're invited to Reece's party, aren't you? I'm quite keen to join in. Forget the cheap freshmen parties this weekend. Reece is a senior now, and the parties at his place over the last few years already surpassed anything you've seen before." She takes my hand in hers as she strides onward with determined steps. I enjoy the way our fingers touch. It feels as if we're actually a team: A team fighting against whatever might come, even if I have no idea what that might be. Harper's by my side. And she has every reason to want to get back at Clarisse and her clique. I'm looking forward to that, too.

I've been looking forward to a college party ever since I was able to spell the word.

I have to take this opportunity now, don't I?

JAXON

A good game needs a good setup. The moment of tension when the chess pieces are positioned. When the cards are dealt. The golf club swung. No matter the game, they're brought to life not just in the actual battle for victory, but also in what comes before and after.

We're in the before now. First, we'll find out which of you are even suitable for the game. We'll sort the wheat from the chaff, find where gold can be struck, what is dust, and what is diamond. Not all of them are like you: fuckable and bold. Some are good for a bit of fun, but only a few are ever actually good to play with.

We've already started sorting out the dregs, but I'm sorry to tell you, Belle, you made the shortlist. Your plush mouth is just begging to be allowed to suck our cocks, and your big eyes are asking to overflow with tears when we show you who we really are.

I have no idea if it's good or immensely bad luck that we like you. I guess it's neither. YOU will not exist anymore once we're done. When we're through with you, you'll have lost your I, your SELF. You'll breathe and exist, and crawl back to where you lived before you came to Kingston. That's all we'll leave of you.

Sorry, not sorry.

Well. Don't make it too easy for us. You don't want us to pick you. Or do you?

6

MABLE

The Crescents' villa is concealed behind an enormous stone wall. The gate to the house stands open and Harper lines up her Cadillac behind the rest of the luxury cars moving along the gravel path toward the lights on the other side of the bushes and trees.

Even from this distance, I know I'll experience more than one new thing tonight.

I've never been in a building anything like the futuristic work of glass art that appears between the fir trees, nor have I ever sat in a car that was worth more than ten thousand dollars. And I've definitely never worn clothes and jewelry worth more than all the money I've made in my life combined.

Harper picked out a fitted shirt and tight jeans for me from her wardrobe. She probably knew that I'd feel most comfortable in that, and she was right. I have narrower hips and larger breasts than she does, a fact the outfit conceals perfectly. I'd never be able to pull off a dress like the one she's wearing. Her neckline touches her belly button, exposing half of her breasts. The lower hem barely covers her bottom above her long, entirely bare legs.

We could hardly be dressed more differently. Her hair flows in loose waves that make her look like a movie star, while I simply tied mine back. I did let her do my makeup, however, and in no time at all, she managed to transform the Mable I know into a stranger who smiled back at me in the mirror as if she owned the world. My eyes and cheeks are highlighted, and I wear subtle lipstick. Harper's lips glow a bright red.

She let me keep my Converse, though she did try to talk me into some inch-high pumps. I'm grateful to my past self for staying firm on that one. The soles of my feet ached just from the few seconds I spent walking up and down her room in them.

Harper resides in one of the six Greek houses on campus. Hers is the largest one, after the one the Kings belong to. The names alone exemplify the contrast on campus:

Rho Chi Alpha is the Kings' fraternity, though no one ever calls it Rho Chi Alpha. Everyone knows it as Alpha Rex.

Rho Gamma Alpha, which is only really called Alpha Regina, is the largest and most influential sorority. The two buildings are idyllically situated on opposite edges of the Kingston Campus. Enclosed by parkland, they offer nothing but luxury. Not only do the houses have outdoor *and* indoor pools, but the rooms are also furnished like suites, each with its own bathroom and space enough for five children to sleep and play in. When I compare it to Harper's room, furnished and decorated by renowned interior designers, my dorm room looks like a dump. I'm determined to turn it into more of a home now. Plenty of things can be bought used online, after all. Having an entire room to myself that I can set up to my liking surely is an opportunity I should take.

The queue in front of us isn't moving, and Harper drums her fingers on the steering wheel impatiently. "You know what you need to do, don't you?"

"I do. I am going to stay away. From everyone. I've heard that works perfectly at a party."

"That's right. You will stay away. From the Kings and from Clarisse and her clique. Alright?"

"Alright. What if Reece speaks to me?"

"What do you think? Ignore him."

"That's not my style."

Harper groans and rolls her eyes. "Sweetie, he's only being nice to you because he wants to fuck you. He talks to you because he wants to fuck you, and he's nice to you because he wants to fuck you. He'll stop the moment he's got you."

"What do you mean, once he's got me? Is he going to trap me and then rape me as soon as I'm naked?"

"God, no! That's Reece you're talking about. He'll fuck you as soon as he can and then immediately erase your name and your very existence from his mind. He absolutely does not need to rape any woman in this world."

"Hm." Sounds like she's speaking from experience. Is that possible? Did she have sex with Reece, and that's why he so nonchalantly told her not to be jealous?

"What? Are you picturing what it would be like with him?"

I can't put on a neutral expression fast enough, and my face is an open book for Harper to read.

"You can't!" she says, stunned.

"Why should only guys take opportunities as they arise? If Reece wants me, I'm certainly not going to tell him no. Why would I?"

"You can't!"

"Harper, have you seen the guy?"

She shakes her head, looking astonished.

"Far be it from me to start a relationship with one of them, or even to bother with small talk. But he's so damn hot. And if—"

"It's a bet, Mable. Every year, they bet on which of them will get the scholarship students into bed first."

My mouth twists into a wry smile.

"Why are you smiling?" she asks me critically.

"That's really useful for me."

"It's what?!"

I lean back into the soft leather of the car seat contentedly and enjoy the tingling sensation under my skin. If the Kings have a bet about who they can bed the quickest, I'm smart enough to take advantage of that.

I'll stay away from Jaxon and ignore Sylvian for the sole purpose of showing solidarity with Harper, of course, but there's nothing at all wrong with Reece.

Nothing at all. I grope in my handbag to confirm that the two condoms are there. If Reece doesn't talk to me, that's fine. It really is. It means nothing to me whether he does or doesn't. To him, I'm just one of many. But to me, he's one of the most attractive men I've ever met.

I've been watching him all week. He took care of introducing the freshmen to a number of processes and opened course registration. While he didn't speak to me a second time, I really did as much as I could to make myself invisible.

I'm going to see what this evening brings. The idea of having sex with Reece tonight is as terrifying as it is exhilarating, though.

"That was just a bad joke, I hope," Harper mutters as we get out of the car. I watch in disbelief as she simply hands the keys to her hundred-thousand-dollar car to a guy younger than us and starts walking to the house without batting an eye.

"No worries. I won't let anything happen to her," the valet says with a grin, which does absolutely nothing to reassure me. In light of the row of expensive cars lined up behind us, however, I can only hope these rich kids know what they're doing.

If I ever end up on the wrong track and find myself in urgent need of money, I know where I can help myself to what I need: any Kingston University party.

I follow Harper up the gravel path to the house, once again glad I'm wearing Converse. A doorman I think I've seen on campus before opens the glass front door for us. Entering, we suddenly find ourselves right in the middle of a bustling party that's nothing at all like anything I've ever seen.

My focus is drawn to the foggy light flashing across the students' faces. The scene is bizarre, if not a little frightening. We've stepped into the eye of a storm and everyone seems to be moving in slow motion.

Though the beat of the music hammers through the walls, something about the lights, the people, and the entire atmosphere makes me nervously reach for Harper's hand, sure that she'll guide me through the surging crowd.

The entire house is made of glass: windows, floors, stairs, and all. It has virtually no concrete, and we even walk past a toilet behind a see-through wall.

Even though Harper is the one who's supposed to draw attention in her pretty, skimpy outfit, many of the glances our way are actually directed at me. I feel as if I'm walking down a catwalk. My hand in Harper's is getting sweaty.

I search the crowd, trying to spot one of the Kings, or at least Clarisse. I want to see her face when she realizes Harper's here with me.

But none of them are anywhere to be seen.

I'm starting to feel like I'm crawling into a rabbit hole. The deeper I go, the larger the trap that snaps shut in the end.

"You'll have some Coke, I bet?" Harper stops to lean over a white marble counter, conjuring up two bottles of Coke and handing me one.

As I reach for the bottle, I notice another curiosity. No one here is drinking. The only bottles to be seen are the ones in our hands. There are no cups anywhere either.

Not a single one.

"What sort of party is this?" I ask with an uneasy feeling in my chest.

Harper's just about to answer when another voice interrupts her.

"I knew you'd come."

My heart beats in my throat as I whirl around to face Reece. He's dressed in a tight white sweater and elegant beige pants, holding out his arms as if to show off the gigantic size of his party.

"Which one of you had to convince the other, huh?"

Harper gives a derisive snort as she turns away. "We're not here to talk to the host," she shouts over the music, trying to pull me along with her.

I stand rooted in place. It may seem crazy to her, but Reece's attention is like a spell cast on me. It's about so much more than simply seizing an opportunity that presents itself. If Harper is right and the Kings want to fuck me, then I don't want to be the victim. I want to be the one in control. And *making that choice* of my own free will is going to make me the victor in the end more than anything.

Reece smirks when he notices my hesitation. "You're here for the host, though, aren't you?" he asks, leaning casually against one of the many glass walls, hands in his pockets.

He looks incredibly good. His blond hair falls over his forehead as if touched by a breeze, his bright blue eyes flash with curiosity, and his physique is better than any model's.

The problem is that, cute as my plan may be, I'm just too stupid to respond with anything sensible at all. I don't have any cool words. Nor do I seem to have any other words either, actually. So I just stand there like a fish on dry land, helplessly opening and closing my mouth. I can't think of anything that might be considered an answer, and I'm making a fool of myself in the process.

Reece's smirk widens into a wry smile, and that smile blows away the fog that descended on my mind the moment I entered the house. I have to say something, a voice inside me demands, I have to respond, I have to be myself and yet so different, I must, must, must, must…

"Do you want to have sex?"

His face reflects the disbelief I feel. Did I really just ask that?

"God, Mable," Harper hisses, tugging on my arm. "Yes, he wants to have sex. Reece always wants sex. He'd eat this entire room for breakfast. Now come on! You don't have to sleep with him to keep him from throwing chicken feathers at you."

I abandon my resistance and let her drag me along. I do notice the way Reece's smile disappears as he stares after me. His expression suddenly so serious I'm afraid I've said something entirely different from what I wanted to.

"God, I need a drink." Determined, I look around, but I can't find any alcohol anywhere. There's nothing here at all!

"There are no *drinks* here," Harper explains. She doesn't let go of me until we reach a dark corner where her scrutinizing gaze moves from my head down to my feet and back up again. "And I think the last thing you need right now is some substance that lowers your virtually non-existent inhibition threshold even further."

"You can't tell me all these people aren't drunk. I mean, they're more hammered than a nail!"

Harper nods meaningfully. "That's right. They're hammered. They're not drunk though."

"Shit. What kind of drugs are they taking?" I look at the students around me with new eyes. At least a third of them are still staring my way like I'm some kind of circus animal. I'm so done with this.

The fact I couldn't get a decent word out in front of Reece is one thing. I'm just not that eloquent of a person. But the constant stares are getting on my nerves so much that I launch an offensive attack and aggressively return stare for stare, holding individual eye contact until my counterpart looks away and moving on to the next.

It takes a while, but eventually I feel unobserved for the first time tonight.

Harper watched silently as I took my time to stare down every one of the party guests. "Alright, girl. You've got some balls. You've got some real balls."

"Well…" I'm about to object. Can't I be a woman and still not take everything they throw at me?

"You asked Reece for sex," she barges on. "Just like that. In front of everyone. You're not afraid to embarrass yourself after that awful week where everyone tried to make you die of shame. You just go and ask Reece for sex *even though* he's friends with Jaxon, the biggest asshole on the planet. And hey, it's not just that, you then proceed to stare down everyone who looks at you. You know what? Forget about Clarisse. I want to officially be your friend, and not because I want to get back at her or anyone else. I don't give a shit about that." Harper puts a hand on her shapely waist and juts her chin out defiantly.

I make her stew for a moment before I laugh. "Yes!" I yell over the music. "Let's officially be friends."

She joins in my laughter. Then she hugs me, and I feel better than I've ever felt before. I don't care that I embarrassed myself in front of Reece. I don't care about chicken feathers and flooded bathrooms. I don't care that Harper's former best friend hates me. For that one second as we embrace at the party, there's absolutely nothing that sets us apart from each other. Not money. Not parentage. Not past. Harper is going to be my friend. I know it, and

I don't need any explanation. It's just how it *is*. It has *happened*. No questions asked.

And maybe one day I'll hate myself for not having thought more about why a woman like her would put up with someone like me.

But this is not that moment.

We move through the house in this small bubble we just created. I've never in my life felt as carefree as I do now. I've never thought less about my mom or worried less about my sister or been less afraid of getting caught in a shootout at a party or getting raped. That's all gone for the moment. I have no worries or fears.

Harper gives me a sense of security that I've never experienced before. It's probably because no one has ever liked me just like that. Or because I never truly liked anyone.

Back in the trailer park, friendships are based strictly on communities of convenience. Loyalty and trust are just as scarce as money is.

As we roam the house, we dance along with the crowd for a few good songs every now and then. They're songs I've never danced to before because I've never felt free enough to just dance. They're songs that feel like a new life, new opportunities, new experiences, all the reasons so many young people go to college: to find themselves, and to grow beyond who they thought they were.

7

JAXON

Rachel's ass glows as red as her hair. Zayn buries himself in her, and even though she's lying limp on the table, utterly spent, I enjoy watching. She did some cocaine shit earlier and screams if we stop fucking her. Maybe she's in pain. She's also soaking wet, though, so he just keeps going. Maybe he'd keep going either way. I'm never quite sure what's going on in that sick head of his.

I've long since finished with her.

It took me less than a day to get the prickly little thing to undress for me. Boring. Just like everyone before her. She knew what'd happen if she came with me, and she followed me because she wanted it to. I only kissed her once—once and never again—and she's been ours ever since.

Devoid of free will, completely submissive, out to get something from us in exchange for her body.

She acts just like every one before her did, and it loses its appeal more each time. I'm looking for a challenge. I need someone who won't surrender the moment I snap my fingers.

"What're you thinking about, huh?" Zayn drops onto the sofa next to me as he fastens his belt. I was so bored I didn't even notice he finished.

Boredom. The curse of the elite.

Rachel is slumped over the pool table, her naked bottom, red from my belt, shining toward us. It's not long before Romeo emerges from the shadows, stalking toward her.

"I'm thinking about how I'm once again the first to get them all," I reply, feeling something along the lines of affectionate distaste as Romeo throws Rachel over his shoulder. He stumbles briefly under her weight, but then he carries her out confidently.

Even though he assures me he only jerks off on the unconscious girls, I watch his departure with unease. Zayn and Reece are sick psychos in their own right, and often go beyond the boundaries of good taste, but Romeo is damaging to our image. The Kings aren't a group of jocks jerking off over a naked woman's unconscious body. We fuck them when they beg for it. We do it with their minds fully involved. They may be disinhibited by drugs, but never incapacitated by alcohol or physical exhaustion.

A woman who can't clearly tell me she wants me is just as unfuckable as a plastic doll would be. I crave the conflict I can see in their eyes, their hearts pulling them in two directions at once. They want me, but they hate me.

That's the attraction.

That's the appeal of the game.

But when the winnings are so freely available, it's like playing poker without any stakes. It's merely exercise.

"Are you sure?" Zayn snaps me out of my thoughts. "Are you going to get *all of them*?" He nods toward the window to the courtyard.

The house where the Crescents celebrate their parties has several individual concrete blocks connected by glass corridors and the inner courtyard where a number of seats are arranged around a blazing fire pit.

I follow Zayn's gaze to see Clarisse sitting in one of the chairs, without Harper by her side. She seems miffed, typing furiously on her phone, as is her way. Whatever has suddenly come between Clarisse and Harper, I don't like that Clarisse's one-time best friend is looking out for our dole any more than she does. Harper spent all of last week trying to get close to Amabelle.

Has Harper switched sides?

Does she really want us to believe that she and Clarisse have fallen out?

"What are you looking at?" Zayn asks me, irritated.

My gaze slides higher, until I see what he actually meant. Reece. Standing with Amabelle, wooing her. My right ring finger twitches.

"What the hell is *she* doing here?" A smooth movement brings me to my feet so I can step up to the window. I watch Amabelle talking to Reece and feel something very much like... anger rising in me. Someone must have invited Amabelle. Harper? Crescent himself?

Zayn comes to stand next to me, cigarette in one hand, glass of whiskey in the other. "You've got to give it to her. She's the only one here who isn't dressed like a hooker."

"Why is she at the party?" I ask calmly, though my tone warns him not to lie to me.

Zayn shrugs. "Reece invited her."

"Why?" I ask with a huff.

"Why not? The opportunity presented itself."

His calm manner makes me lose my patience immediately. My hand snaps up, pressing Zayn's face against the windowpane until he swears at me. Keeping him captive, I lean in toward his ear. "Why is this the first I'm hearing of that? Are you all keeping secrets from me now?"

"You didn't notice because you were busy with Rachel! Are you really going to break my neck *over this*?"

"Damn it! If I find out Reece is fucking her without clearing it with us first…"

"He won't!" Zayn rolls his eyes and adds ironically, "He would never have sex without asking your permission."

I want to spit in Zayn's face for that, but he's right to mock me for it. *Normally I don't give a shit about which of the scholarship students Crescent fucks first, but you… you're special. Shit. And now I've as good as told Zayn that I'm just as stupid as Sylvian, who's a total goner for you and has been for a while.*

What are you doing to us, Dole?!

"Then go and make sure of it!" I hiss. *Make sure Reece isn't the first one to get you… Fuck. I'm pathetic.*

"Okay, man!"

I let go of Zayn and he rubs the back of his neck. I don't like the matter-of-fact way Crescent seems to have invited Amabelle. Who do they think they are? I'm not the fucking *king* of this university because the title strokes my ego. I've worked for it. These little bastards only have one oath to fulfill: loyalty.

"Where's Silvano, anyway?" Zayn asks casually as he slips into the white sneakers he took off during sex for some reason.

"Good question," I growl. "On your way to interrogate Reece, find Sylvian downstairs and take him along."

"Along where? To tell off Reece?"

I twist one corner of my mouth derisively. "Don't play dumb with me. Get out!"

Zayn rolls his eyes again and strolls calmly to the door. He's not afraid of me, which I find annoying in turn. Our friendship is too close already. We know each other's darkest thoughts. We know all of our secrets, no matter how fucked up they are. We share the girls. We watch each other fuck.

Damn, I really should be less surprised he has zero respect for me.

Before he leaves, he turns back once more, his face, worthy of a Michelangelo painting, curling into a knowing grin. "You do realize the bet's off if you send me out to interfere with Reece winning, right? You actually need to give us a chance, too." He glides through the door before I can yell at him for it.

He's right, of course. It's fair play. Everything's different this year, because of you.

It's getting more serious.

But I can't fight it.

Shit. What is it about you?

I pick up the glass Zayn left and give it a swirl to see if he spiked it. It'd be just like him. He's a junkie, after all, though not the sort who'd ever show it.

As I sit down at the table where we just fucked Rachel, I smile in spite of everything, thinking about how Amabelle looked at me when I fucked that girl's mouth. It would be such a waste to chew her up and spit her out again without taking the opportunity to enjoy her first.

If Amabelle is flirting with Reece, she's just as easy to get as all the others. But I really don't need another one who'll take off her clothes the minute I'm even the slightest bit nice to her. Certainly not.

You will want me even though you hate me.

JAXON

Whatever your plan with Crescent is, I know he flew into your web like a suicidal fly. You're different. You're bold. Every warning you were offered shattered against your shield.

I'll teach you to listen to what they say about us.

I'll give you a sample .

A little taste, courtesy of Jaxon Tyrell.

Do you like it?

8

MABLE

Eventually, the bass loses its definition. The thumping slows to half a heartbeat as everyone in the room moves lazily back and forth, like the music doesn't want to let us go. It holds us captive, pulling our puppet strings and letting us fall into a maelstrom, drawing us back in.

I love it.

"Hello, beautiful."

Goosebumps erupt on the back of my neck. The cold suddenly turns searing hot as a finger runs up my bare arm, tender like a soft breeze on a windless night.

"You seem to be enjoying yourself at my party," the voice whispers in my ear, just before I feel lips touching my earlobe and the ice inside me spreads through all of my limbs.

"Fuck off, Reece!" Harper shouts, but I catch her eye to tell her to stop. She needs to trust me. She needs to let me do this. She rolls her eyes but complies with my request. As if by magic, she disappears behind two sweaty bodies. Then she's gone entirely.

Leaving me alone with Reece.

"You sent her away," he mumbles contentedly, like a purring cat, now stroking my bare arm with the fingers of his left hand, spreading tingling heat over my sensitive skin. "And she really did leave. I don't think I've ever seen Harper listen to anyone."

"Are you friends?"

He laughs harshly, sending jolts of electricity through my mid-section. Something about him has changed since earlier. He seems darker. Less filtered. "I'm not friends with any of those spoiled motherfuckers." Reece lowers his lips to the crook of my neck, making me sigh against my will.

Fuck. He's more attractive than is healthy. I don't know if I'm up to this, or to the all-consuming feelings bearing down on me.

"Want to go to my room?"

I nod without thinking about it for even a second.

Emptiness spreads around me like a vacuum as he lets go of me and walks wordlessly through the crowd. I follow, staying behind him to let him push the many dancers aside, and he leads me up a flight of stairs. Once at the top, he seems to disappear.

Shit. For a second, I feel stupid for falling for his trick. Then he's back by my side.

"This way, Mable," he murmurs, taking my hand to lead me across some sort of bridge into a quieter area of the house. He opens the first opaque door I've seen tonight to pull me into the room behind it.

As soon as he closes the door, the thunder of the bass is just a memory.

Reece stops in front of me to give me a lopsided smile. "Hi," he whispers before pushing me back against the door, grabbing my right hand and pinning it above my head. "There are two things you should know before we start…"

"Okay," I whisper against his chin. He towers over me, look-ing down at me, darkness and light at the same time, just like a fallen angel.

"If the sex is good, we can do it again. I'm not the sort of guy who goes in for a taste and then leaves what he could still enjoy."

"Great," I say stupidly, drawing a laugh from him. I'm tense enough to snap. Why can't I just say something sensible? Maybe: Sure, okay. Same for me. Let's find out if we have chemistry and then fuck again if the opportunity arises. Easy as that. Reece, a god, the super-rich model Kingston student, and Mable, the poor trailer-park Cinderella. Sounds romantic, doesn't it? Like something out of a storybook.

"The other thing…" Reece reaches into his pocket and pulls out a black scarf. "You'll be wearing this."

"A blindfold?" Wow, a perfectly normal question, Mable! You're making progress!

Reece nods seriously. "Yes."

I giggle. "You don't want me to look at you?"

He doesn't answer and my nervous giggling becomes a little more intense.

"Alright, why? Are you that ugly naked? Or does your cock not work if someone looks at it?"

Reece frowns, pushing himself away from the door and looking at me disparagingly. "Are you messing with me?"

"No!" I say, faster than I can think.

"You asked for sex. If we fuck, it's on my terms."

My mouth opens slightly. "Ah."

He narrows his eyes. "What do you mean, 'ah'? Damn. You're the weirdest girl who's ever been in this room. Get out."

"Alright." Even though rejection throbs dully in my chest, I turn around. *Get out* sounds a lot like there *isn't* a bet that he can only win if he screws me.

As soon as I open the door, he reaches over my head to push it shut again.

His right hand goes to my neck and he turns me around. He presses me against the door, lifting my chin with a firm grip, bending his head and bringing his mouth electrifyingly close to mine. Reece's breath fans over the sensitive skin of my face, and I start to shake as I slowly but surely lose control of my body.

He takes in my eyes carefully, then my entire expression. Then he kisses me.

Hard.

I moan, a moan that lasts beyond the time his mouth even touches me. For a tiny moment, his tongue shot out and brushed against mine. It was too short to really feel it. It was too dominant for me to participate.

"Get on the bed."

Resistance rises in me like a cat that's disturbed during a nap.

"What else, Mable?" he snaps at me. "Do you want me to fuck you against the door?"

"If you want to sleep with me, can you please be a bit nicer?"

"What?" he snaps. I seem to throw him completely off his game. At least I'm not alone in feeling off balance.

"You're not nice."

"But you are, aren't you?" he asks, eyebrows raised. "Get on the damn bed or I'll come in my jeans and you won't come at all."

My eyes automatically drop to his crotch. His bulging crotch. *And how very bulging it is.* Fuck. An undefined compulsion steers my legs toward the bed. I let myself sink into it. Finally, I lie back and dig my hands into the duvet.

Reece followed me. He's standing at the edge of the bed now, looking down at me with a dark expression before leaning forward and pressing the black silk scarf into my hand. "Think about whether you really want it. I'm not going to touch you without the blindfold."

I'm a little too tense to ask why he wants me to be blindfolded again, but at least he shows me that it has nothing to do with his looks by taking off his sweater and tossing it aside.

Overwhelmed, I take a breath as my eyes glide across his perfect, smooth skin, drinking in every defined muscle, every single blonde hair.

He gives me a wry grin when he notices my gaze. Suddenly, he's braced over me.

I fall back into the pillows as if afraid his flawless body might touch mine. Reece leans in close, lowering his head but not touching me. When his breath brushes my skin, I tremble.

"Are you scared of me?" he asks, pausing, hovering above my belly button. His hooded eyes directed at me from down there make my hormones roar.

"Maybe," I whisper. "Not of you, just…"

"When was the last time you had sex?"

I bite my lip. "Is that important?"

Reece pauses mid-motion and his eyelids lower further. Now he looks like a sleepy god. A god who just uncovered one of my greatest secrets. "You're not a virgin, are you?"

"I'm not," I hiss and pull my shirt down from where it rode up. "Do you do this with every girl? Chew her ear off before you sleep with her?"

Reece doesn't answer my question. He straightens up again, unzips his fly and leans against the chest of drawers in front of the massive bed where it serves as a TV stand. He slips a hand into his shorts and unabashedly touches himself. With heavy eyelids, he casts a dreamy look in my direction before pulling out his cock.

My entire body goes wild. I feel the urge to flee and I'm not sure why. I want to stay but not really be here. I need to look yet close my eyes again and again. I've never had a boyfriend. I've never had the "pleasure" of seeing a male member up close in daylight.

All the sex I've had has just been hook-ups after parties. In the dark. And I've never… really…

"Do you want to touch it?"

I shake my head.

Reece purses his lips. "You really are a virgin."

"And because that's what I seem like to you, you're not going to touch me without a blindfold?"

He leans his head back and greedily moves his fist along his length. Watching makes me dizzy. Perverted thoughts flood my head as I imagine his cock touching me, even if only my stomach, my waist, my… mouth…

I swallow hard.

"Precisely," Reece answers my question in a gruff voice. "We won't touch you without a blindfold."

"We?"

"Do you like what you see?" he asks, his speech suddenly choppy as his breathing grows heavier. "How much do you want to suck me off? Say it!"

I can't get a word out.

"Say it, go on!" he urges. his hand picks up speed. "Mable!"

"A little!" I say, though I have no reason to tell the truth.

Reece laughs, throwing his head back, and then he's coming. His torso trembles, and I want to jump up and touch him. I want to stroke him. I want to feel his muscles twitch under his tight skin. Milky liquid drips from his fist and he wipes it up with the sweater he just took off, his eyes fixed lustfully on me.

"Are you sure you don't want the blindfold?" he asks, his voice so relaxed he could soothe a tiger to sleep. "I'll be right back. Maybe you should leave if you don't want to continue…" The right corner of his mouth twitches as he disappears through the second door leading off his bedroom and into a bathroom.

I take a breath once he's out of the room. His presence makes it hard for me to think, but there's nothing that will get me out of his bed either. I like the passive role that I'm taking on here. I'm curious to find out who he really is and what he's about to do. Even if he's just going to stand there pleasuring himself, I don't want to miss a second of it. After all, it's like an exclusive show he's offering only to me.

What kind of woman would say no to that?

Okay, there are probably a few who would. Not least among them the ones who just don't fancy guys like Reece. But I have a feeling that this will be my last party for a long time, the last time I can let myself go before the term and all of its classes, lectures, and my part-time job start for real. I want to taste it this once. Just briefly. I want to abandon myself and enjoy a freedom I won't have again until my last exam is complete in December.

When the bathroom door opens, I'm still where he left me. Less than five minutes have passed, and yet Reece seems to have changed. The gaze he fixes me with is darker, and he approaches me like a lynx winding its way through the shadows.

Stopping at the foot of the bed, he leans on it with both arms, licking his lips. Then he notices the blindfold in my hand, which I haven't put on yet.

"Oh, fuck it," he growls. He's on top of me in the blink of an eye, lowering his lips to my stomach and pressing his tongue against my navel. A tingling runs through me just from this one caress and my body stretches toward him like a magnet.

Reece's eyes flash as he notices my reaction, and his lips move lower. His fingers undo the button on my jeans and he roughly tugs them off. That's not what I expected. Reece seemed like a gentleman, a man who would undress me tenderly, touch me lovingly, but this is a different Reece. Like some animal inside him has been awakened.

The tip of his nose slides along the edge of my panties and he takes a deep breath in. I watch him curiously. One thing that's useful about this arrangement is I don't have to worry about whether he actually likes me or not.

Reece is aroused, gives off sparks like a bonfire, but I don't know him. I don't even know if I'd like him if I knew him. Maybe he's an asshole. Maybe he torments little children or invests in stocks that cost other people their lives. Who knows? The less I know about him, the better I will be able to enjoy what's happening. His nose moves higher again, nudging my shirt up until he can finally take it off me. Unfulfilled want is wild in Reece's eyes as he pulls Harper's top over my head and tosses it on the floor. His eyes roam over my breasts before he takes them in both hands.

For him, it's a bet that he wants to win. And for me it's…

The pressure of his palms through the cups of my bra is enough to make the scorching heat between my thighs unbearable. I want to have sex with him so bad. I think. I wouldn't be feeling like this if I didn't, right?

Reece smiles at me before stroking my forearm gently and pulling the scarf from my fingers. He spreads it out with angelic patience and places it over my eyes. "Trust me," he says, reaching to tie it behind my head. "You'll never forget this night."

My heartbeat thunders in my throat and I moan uncontrollably as he presses his lips to mine. The kiss is so different from the one at the door. His lips are like those of a stranger, moving gently but firmly.

"You're so hot, Dole," he whispers against my lips.

"Doll? Like plaything?" I ask breathlessly. "Or Dole? Like British slang for charity?"

"Mm-hmm," he mumbles and continues kissing me.

"Not a particularly great nickname," I say against his lips.

He just laughs, and right now, I can't even blame him for calling me that. Desire leaves no space for bad feelings. His tongue dances in my mouth and I return the cautious thrusts of his tongue with my own.

"Just let it happen, yeah?" His voice is lost in my sigh as he slides a hand to my crotch. "This will be different from what you know."

"Okay," I whisper.

"Good girl." I hear the smile in his tone, and his fingers slide lower. He undresses me with his other hand, while kissing my neck at the same time.

Seconds later, I'm lost in his touch and revel in the feeling that he is *everywhere*. I'm naked and the blindfold allows me to let myself go as if I'm alone in my room and simply succumbing to a fantasy.

Reece tenderly takes a nipple in his mouth. His hands are so nimble, massaging my body, caressing me, and making me lose my willpower.

Finally, I feel his lips on my stomach, tongue circling my belly button, brushing over my mound, and then buried deep inside me a moment later.

I hiss and tense up under him. At the same moment, he pushes my legs apart to make more space for himself. As he licks me greedily, I forget I can do anything other than lie there and enjoy it. My body is an instrument, and he's playing it like a master. His fingers circle my nipples one moment, and the next he's pushing them inside me. Then his tongue licks me wildly and without restraint, only to conquer my mouth a moment later. The alternating between sensations is driving me insane. When he turns me onto my stomach, I have only one desire.

"Fuck me," I moan into the pillow. I hear him laugh and feel his hands on my ass. The buckle of his belt hits my sensitive skin when he opens his pants, followed by a hissing slap.

"Fuck!" I gasp. He hit me. He hit me with his goddamned belt!

"You don't get to decide when I fuck you," he growls into my ear.

I should respond to that. I should tell him that this is going too far for me. But strangely enough… it isn't. Some very distant, depraved part of me is enjoying being at his mercy in this way. Being *punished*. At least a little.

His hands knead my butt cheeks, then my breasts, and once again it feels like he has more than two hands. His touch is driving me crazy, making me more pliant by the minute. Then he kisses me.

I've never been kissed like this before, so full of desire and greed, so unstoppable and so tempting. Moaning, I stretch toward him, letting my tongue slide into his mouth and craving more.

He pushes his thumb between my lips. "Suck it," he demands quietly.

I do as he says. There's no other option than immediate compliance.

My entire body lights up when I draw a deep sound of pleasure from him with my mouth.

"Good. That's exactly what you're going to do with my cock," he murmurs in my ear. The next moment, I feel it against my lips.

My first impulse is to refuse. Scenes pop into my head, images of my mom blowing her *lover* right in front of me because she needed money for pills. Everything inside me resists, but Reece holds my head firmly, relentlessly.

"You want it," he murmurs. "Don't you? Let it happen."

I swallow, shaking on the bed, about to let him know I don't, when he rolls me onto my side and moves his mouth between my thighs again. This time he penetrates me with his tongue, and my mouth falls open. Immediately, his cock pushes between my lips, and then deeper.

I've never done or experienced anything like this before, and I can't help but surrender to it. It feels far too forbidden and far too hot.

His cock slides through my mouth, faster and harder, while he licks me without restraint.

I claw at the comforter, trying not to moan too loudly. My body tenses, and finally I let go.

The heat in me overwhelms my senses. My hips lift, arching and stretching toward Reece's talented tongue and through it all I keep sucking his cock.

Even as intoxication grips my every limb and I'm overtaken by lust, I hear him moan.

Then I taste cum on my tongue, and I slump back.

My heart is racing. I'd love to rip the blindfold from my eyes to see what we look like, but I'm afraid that would destroy the moment, and I want to hold onto the sensation that comes from being able to abandon myself and my thoughts.

"You're so fucking hot, Mable," he whispers in my ear. "You did so well."

Why do I feel proud when he says that? Shouldn't I be put off by it? Isn't it exactly what I've always found terrible about men?

But it's quite the opposite. I'm eager for him to continue. Let him demand something from me again. I'm already waiting for him to continue. To demand something from me again. To let me feel more of him. The orgasm only made me want more.

Something moves on the bed. I think he's leaving again. Only seconds pass before he grabs my hair and puts his lips to my neck. "Do you want to continue?"

I nod, imagining he can feel my carotid artery throbbing with the strength of my pulse.

"Say it," he hisses.

"Yes," I breathe.

"Very good." His voice is a low murmur as his lips brush my neck. "I'll fuck you until you can't walk right. You'll smell like me for days. You'll never forget me. *Never.* Are you ready for this?"

I swallow hard once more, and the door crashes open.

Reece immediately moves away, and I pull the blindfold off.

A cold, icy rain washes away all the warmth in my body. Jaxon stands in front of us. Next to Reece, he looks a lot more threatening, a lot bigger, and a lot meaner. There's nothing but disgust in his eyes. Disgust that hits me like a blow, makes me feel small like an insect. Insignificant.

I want to flee from his gaze. It's a look that robs me of all self-confidence, subjugates me. I'm naked and exposed and lying before him like a calf for slaughter.

When he raises his voice, it's like a gun, like he could kill with words alone. "Did I tell you to fuck her?"

Not only has a flood of loud music come in with him, but so has another person. Romeo. I immediately recognize him, even though he looks rather unassuming and I've only ever seen him in that photograph in the gallery. Standing next to Jaxon, he looks exactly the way I feel.

Insignificant. Out of place. Lost.

I pull the sheet over my body to cover myself.

"What's this supposed to be about, Crescent!" It isn't a question. Jaxon's words sound like an order. Anyone who refuses to answer will suffer for it.

Reece shoves his hands into his pockets, unconcerned. Fully dressed again, he's retreated to the bookshelf, taking him farther away from the bed than Jaxon is.

My breath is still quivering. I should leave, flipping Jaxon the bird and laughing on the way out, but something holds me in place. He seems to be pinning me to the mattress with his gaze alone.

"Have either of you touched her?" he asks darkly.

Either of you?

Reece looks perfectly comfortable, leaning against the wall now, and he lifts a shoulder in response.

That makes Jaxon spit, "Disloyal bastard. Fuck off."

"I want to watch."

"Watch what?" Jaxon snaps at him.

I'm glad he does because I'm just as invested in that answer as he is. What's about to happen that Reece would want to stay and watch? Should I run away? Should I run fast?

Reece pulls his right hand out of his pocket to study his fingernails as if he's thinking about filing them then and there. "I'm not going to go. This is still my house. My room. My party."

Jaxon's lips curl into a smile that frightens me more than any horror movie ever has. "Everything that's yours is mine."

Reece looks at Jaxon for the first time, narrowing his eyes.

"Alright, I'll go, Crescent. Nobody can stand being in your parents' opium-soaked house for long anyway. Romeo."

Romeo slides out from behind Jaxon and steps up to his side.

"We're taking her with us."

"What?" I gasp. "No!"

As Romeo approaches me, I scramble back into the pillows, trying to escape across the other side of the bed. He manages to grab me, holding me back.

"Fuck!" I shout as he pulls me around. Reece watches impassively, while Jaxon tracks Romeo with a stoney expression. A rag presses against my nose. Not realizing what that means quickly enough, I inhale, and everything goes black…

JAXON

Y ou wonder if we do this with every girl. Watch her. Get to know her. Stay close to her.

We don't.

Not with all of them.

It depends on who's putting you on the board, Belle.

You're a playing piece.

One of five.

We're the players.

Some of us want to know you better before putting you in play, others love the risk.

Me, personally? I like to know what I'm getting into, and Sylvian's just a stalker. It'll be a long time before you understand what we're actually doing or what the rules of our game are.

By then, it'll be much too late. You'll already have lost.

Does that sound unfair?

It is. It's how it should be. Life's unfair. We're unfair. God is unfair.

Don't waste your fucking life fighting this simple truth.

9

MABLE

White lights glide past my half-open eyelids as I slowly wake up. The surface I'm on is moving. Soft leather. A car. I'm breathing calmly. I feel intoxicated. Far too comfortable for not knowing what happened in the last few minutes—or hours.

For a few seconds, I consider simply letting myself drift back to sleep. It's tempting to surrender to exhaustion, snuggled up in the languid warmth of my thoughts…

"I'll give you a choice."

I startle wide awake immediately. I'm lying on the side bench of a limo, with Jaxon manspreading on the back seat and Romeo at the other end near the driver. I'm not wearing my top. Instead, I'm wrapped in a big sweatshirt, without my arms in the sleeves, Harper's jeans lying across my lap. I dress quickly. I need to be ready for what comes next. *Did Jaxon really kidnap me?*

I feel dizzy. Not just because I don't know where I am or how I got here, but also because of something they gave me. Drugs? Chloroform?

"What choice?" I ask. My voice sounds distant, drowned out by the buzzing in my ears.

"You can keep studying at Kingston as long as you're available·

to me for sex." Jaxon's expression is entirely relaxed. If Reece is as beautiful as a god, Jaxon's as sinfully attractive as the devil. His long legs reach far across the floor. He's wearing black chinos, dark shoes, and, once again, an azure shirt that stretches over his well-defined pectoral muscles. The small lamp by the bar, where chilled champagne waits, casts his features in shadow and turns his dark blond hair black. I want nothing more than to move away from him.

"Where are we going?"

"You're a little whore, aren't you, *Belle*?" The muscles around his lips grow taut. I'm not sure if he's actually smiling or trying to hide his true emotions. "Let me have a taste."

I stare at him. He's an idiot. What's his plan? Blackmail me into sleeping with him? "Do you need to do that?" I ask as neutrally as possible. He doesn't need to know I really want to scream at him. "I mean, aren't there enough women who fall at your feet? Do you need to drug someone like me and kidnap her in a limo?"

Jaxon's jaw hardens. For a fraction of a second his gaze shifts to Romeo before fixing on me again.

"We can have sex if you want," I explain to him. "Not because I'm a 'whore,' though. Guys like you will always outwhore me. It'd be because you look like Mr. Universe. Do you think just because I'm a woman I'm going to tell you no? You may be an absolute jackass, but ask me if I care about that when we're just talking about sex!"

The corners of Jaxon's mouth twist and he laughs. It's a full laugh that makes me smile too. It's like magic. His laugh makes him even more beautiful than he already is. Even more attractive, more beguiling…

I can't imagine that someone like him would even *think* about wanting someone like me. He's surely just talking shit. And for once, I managed—perhaps because of the drugs—to give as good as I got. I remember very well what my friends from the trailer park taught me.

Always act like nothing can touch you.

They defended themselves verbally so they wouldn't be forced to do things they didn't want to do. They were loud and unruly and drew attention. I went through all of those moments where my—much older—friends protected themselves with words.

The guys who are interested in me are usually closer to Quasimodo than to Jaxon. Not even Reece can match Tyrell's looks and—let me repeat myself—Reece already looks like a god turned flesh.

The very idea that Jaxon could desire me—if only for the five minutes it'd take him to come—sends a deep thrill through my body.

I won't sleep with him because I want to keep his family's scholarship. I would *never* do that.

What do I care, though, if he prefers to think I'm prostituting myself?

Without another word, Jaxon spreads his legs wider and starts unbuckling his belt. That's all he does, but his posture is a clear invitation.

"I'm not going to blow you," I inform him flatly.

His eyes flash and he raises his chin. "You won't?"

"I mean, I might reconsider if you go first." Just like him, I spread my legs a little. He's already seen me naked. I can still feel the heat of Reece's touch on me. If this is supposed to be a sick continuation of what happened earlier, the drugs are just lowering my inhibitions even further.

Jaxon laughs again, making me blush, even though I wish I didn't feel embarrassed by it. Of course, he wouldn't go out of his way to make sure I enjoy anything we do. He wants to use me. The idea of blowing him, like Lien in my dorm room, has me resisting, though. A Jaxon who isn't at all like I imagine him to be suddenly appears in my mind's eye. This one is rough and clumsy and careless.

What if the sex is bad despite how he looks?

Do I really want to risk it?

Will he stop if I ask him to?

Can I trust him?

No.

I bite the inside of my cheek, thinking about how I can maneuver myself out of this situation. When we have sex, it'll be on my terms. But will I ever get the upper hand?

"Show me," he demands seductively. His features are suddenly soft and open. "Show me what you're thinking about. Let it happen."

I cast a nervous glance at Romeo.

"Ignore him. Think of him as my shadow. If I don't hurt you, he won't either."

"Sure. Why wouldn't I believe every word you say?"

Jaxon just smiles. "When the new term starts, we usually make a bet. Crescent, Sylvian, and me. We bet on who's going to be the first to have all the fuckable scholarship students in their bed. We weren't sure whether we should even throw you into the pot, though. It's not just that you're a virgin—you also look like someone who has her pussy locked up tight. Since Reece isn't exactly in the lead and virgins are worth extra points, he wanted to seize the opportunity. Just like you did, eh?"

I wonder if there will ever be a time when women are allowed to be as sexist as Jaxon and his friends are. Maybe I already am. I long to feel as free as the Kings. Simply have the sex I want without being considered a slut or a whore. Getting to classify my male counterparts as *fuckable* or *unfuckable* would be pretty depraved, but it'd be amazing at the same time. Will that ever be possible without feeling like I've betrayed all my ideals? "I'm not a virgin," I clarify.

Jaxon's smile remains unperturbed. "Of course you're not."

"What does it matter? How would it make me special if I were?"

"We're assholes, Dole," he calmly explains. *That horrible pet name again.* "You never forget your first time. Our ego enjoys being the one burned into a woman's memory."

I grimace. "You can do the same if sex with you is particularly good, can't you?"

Jaxon turns his signet ring and looks at the reflection the movement creates in the faint light. "Of course. Nobody ever forgets what we do with them. But fucking an untouched woman puts more on the table than just sex. This is the male brain, Dole. Do you really want to have a discussion with me about it? Or do you want to get to what I want from you so you can stay at Kingston?"

"What do you expect?" I ask simply, folding my hands in my lap and trying to cover up the nerves that've taken hold of me.

"You'll take my number. Save me as a favorite. Then you'll get my messages even if your phone is on silent. I'll tell you where I am, and you will come. You'll get on the pill, and wherever or whatever I ask, you'll do it."

My cheeks heat, and I wring my hands, feeling overwhelmed. He can't be serious. Why would he offer me something like that? *It sounds ... almost hot.* "What's the sex going to be like?"

"Good," he replies simply.

"Does that go for me as well?"

"No idea. Can you come within five minutes? The way you react to my words alone, you might. But I'm not going to teach you. That's what your hands are for."

Maybe it's the heady feeling Reece kindled in me, but Jaxon's words make my body vibrate. Quickies with Jaxon, whenever he wants them, satisfy a very, very dark fantasy in me. "What's the catch?"

Jaxon throws his head back with a laugh before exchanging a meaningful look with Romeo.

"You think you can humiliate me by offering me sex?" I ask, a little unsettled. Maybe I'm not prudish enough to understand what he's getting at. "If I offered you sex to stay at Kingston, would you refuse me? Would you feel bad about it? Or would you think: She might be a completely disgusting character, but she's hot, so why not?"

"Is that what you think about my proposal?" Jaxon asks. For the first time, he seems approachable and friendly. "Did you have to learn that in Feminism 101, or do you really feel that way?"

"What is 'that way'? Like a man?"

He smiles. "You don't fool me, Dole. If you were really like a guy, you wouldn't be here. But yes, that's almost exactly what I'm proposing. And I'm impressed by your response. It's always good to have a toy on campus that hasn't been to tea with my grandmother. A toy who likes being a toy and isn't just hoping for an engagement ring. You know my family doesn't give a fuck about you, right? You don't want to get me because you know you don't stand any more of a chance with me than you would at the bottom of the Mariana Trench. You're all about sex. I'm all about sex. Why not take advantage of this wonderful arrangement?"

"What are you talking about?" I hiss at him.

"You don't know what the Mariana Trench is?" He raises a brow. "Did you fake your SATs?"

"I understand all your words separately, but they make no sense all together," I say tersely. I couldn't have strung together this many coherent thoughts in Reece's presence. Jaxon, however, makes me angry enough to stop thinking before I speak.

"I want you to come over here and suck me off, Dole." Jaxon's lips stretch into a smug smile. "If you make me come and swallow my seed like a good girl, and do it every time I send you a message, I'll consider letting you study at the university for a little while longer."

"I'm *absolutely* not going to blow you just because you're a Tyrell."

"You sure?"

"Damn sure!"

"What a shame." He grins at Romeo again. "Sex would be alright for you then, but blowjobs aren't?"

I say nothing.

"Ah, I see. Girls like you, of course, consider blowjobs to be a tool of the patriarchy, but you can still have sex as a feminist."

"I won't do *anything* I don't want to do. Right now, the idea of striking the same pose as Lien doesn't appeal to me at all. What would I get out of it?"

"Lien is the girl who sucked my cock last Monday?"

I raise a brow mockingly.

"You're right. But you don't even realize yet how much it'll turn you on. And I have absolutely no intention of deflowering you in this limo while Romeo watches. I'll give you a taste of what you can expect when our deal is finalized, though." His perfectly chiseled face looks almost friendly. "Just come here."

My entire body has seized up now. This is different from Reece. Not because Jaxon is an asshole—I really couldn't care less about that—but because somewhere at the back of my mind *I want* to please Jaxon. I have the urge—even if I persistently forbid myself from giving in to it—to please him.

Not with a blowjob. Rather, I want him to ... like me?

When I realize what I'm thinking, I want to puke. Jaxon is the last person in the world I *want* to like. What would I gain then, from pleasing *him*? Nothing. Absolutely nothing.

And yet, I have a certain desire to prove to him I can...

I slide along the bench toward him, unzip my jacket to just below my breasts and sit on his lap without further ado. My hands find his shoulders and his my thighs. I planned to do something seductive or expected he would grab me, but all of these thoughts suddenly vanish, and I just stay there.

He looks up at me. His lips open sensually, his eyes are clear and attentive. My jaw is relaxed, and our gazes meet in a way that has my innermost feelings bubbling to the surface.

As if in slow motion, he raises his hand to my hair, and his fingers dip into my ponytail. He pulls off the hair tie, releasing my mane to spill out across my shoulders.

Maybe he feels the same way I do, or maybe he's just that good at seduction. None of what he just hinted at becomes real. On the contrary, he gently massages the nape of my neck, and looks deep into my eyes.

"Touch me," he whispers, and I shudder. "Give in to the desire."

This moment is a thousand times more intimate than anything I've ever experienced. It's different from sex. Or what I did with Reece. There's... a kind of connection as I reach up and trace the beautiful contours of his cheeks.

He closes his eyes and lets me explore his perfection. It's wonderful to have him with me for this moment, as if he's all mine and I have all the time in the world to get to know his appearance.

"How does it feel?" he asks in a whisper.

When I don't answer, he opens his eyes. The intensity of his gaze almost knocks me out.

"Let me look at all of you," he mumbles, pulling down the zipper of my jacket. He's as gentle as a feather falling to the ground as he peels the fabric off my shoulders, exposing me to his eyes once more. This time it feels even better. Genuine. Closer.

I'm no longer wearing a bra and my breasts are uncovered before him.

He tenderly caresses my curves with his right hand, while the other one remains in my hair. There's no way this can be the same man who just tried to blackmail me.

Or the one Harper warned me about.

It's just impossible.

Jaxon is gentle, careful, and his every touch burns my skin as if he was created just for me.

"Flawless," he murmurs, touching my hard nipples. I moan without meaning to, and his eyes flash. "If you go along with the deal, you might be the only one I fuck. I like the way you react to me, your body pining for me like this. All that garbage you throw at me makes no sense at all—but at least it's different from the rubbish I usually hear."

"What do the others say?" I ask in a low voice, still transfixed. I can't move anywhere. I'm perfectly trapped on his lap.

"The other women?"

"Yes," I whisper.

"You're quite curious, Dole."

"I'm just trying to understand why you feel the way you do about women. As if we're worth nothing more than the satisfaction we can offer you."

His mask slips briefly as he stares at me. For one tiny moment, I can see behind it before he schools his expression again. "Am I worth more?"

Now *my* mouth opens in astonishment. "Do you want to tell me—"

"That I don't know a single woman who would fuck me because she really wants me? Yes. The world is filled with whores trying to gain something from the heir to a multibillion-dollar family fortune. It doesn't matter how good the sex is. They never want me for *that*. It's never *because of me*. They crave what I can do for them. Not who I am."

I feel a knot form in my throat and I'm at a loss for words. Can that be all? Is it true?

"You would be the first to be different. But forgive me if I don't believe it." A sad smile crosses his lips and then it's time.

The moment has come.

I bend down to kiss him.

It seems to be the only way.

To kiss him, to taste him, to *be* with him. My entire self longs for it.

Before my lips can approach his, he grabs the back of my neck with both hands, holding me captive in front of him. With that hold on my neck, he pushes me against his lap.

Firm and dominating.

His lust is hard under me.

My breathing quickens and I look at him like a deer in the headlights.

"Don't worry about Romeo," he whispers. "He's just watching."

The moment he says Romeo's name, I can feel his gaze all over me. It doesn't turn me off, though. Quite the contrary, it makes me incredibly hot to know that someone is watching us. *How depraved am I really?*

As Jaxon holds me captive in front of him, he grinds his hips up into me, making me gasp with pleasure as he drags his hardness across my clit.

His movements turn rougher, wilder with every thrust, and we move together, connected almost chastely but in a way that goes deeper than anything I've experienced before.

I lose myself in longing for his perfect body.

Jaxon's rigid poker face cracks, revealing a glimpse of his soul, and I take a sharp breath. A roaring storm of sensations approaches. I can feel his slim hands on my thighs, one of his rings now and then, pressing into the denim.

I can feel his firm lap under me and his strong, muscular shoulders under my fingers. I'm painfully aware of every single inch of contact between us, and I let myself give in as he stimulates me with unrestrained thrusts.

I just allow myself to sink down into it, like a ship on a stormy sea.

Letting myself fall into his arms, letting myself be enveloped by his protective waves is suddenly an overpowering desire. A tug of longing grows in my stomach, and my heart aches as if I've barely gotten him and already lost him. Just the thought that this moment can't last forever creates despair.

I feel an urgent desire to forget my own self, if only I could stay close to him.

The emotions that chase through my chest are mirrored on Jaxon's face. Surprise, desire, hate, hope, longing, and, finally, desperate determination.

His lips are still sensually opened, the contradictions still dancing in his features as he grabs my chin and slowly brings it toward his.

That's the moment when I realize I can't kiss him. I can't do anything he wants me to do. I've never felt anything like it, never hated someone so much and wanted them so bad at the same time.

My heart is a victim. It is inexperienced, uncontrolled, and weak. I have to protect it at all costs. I can't kiss someone or have sex with them if I feel something about it. At least not if he's a self-absorbed asshole like Jaxon.

I pull his hand down, hitting his chin by accident, and slide off his lap. A breath later, I'm back in my seat, my sweatshirt wrapped around me, my pussy burning hot with unfulfilled desire, but my heart cold because my head knows it needs to be this way.

Jaxon's expression hardens instantly as he looks at me with thin lips.

"Never," I whisper. "I'll never fuck an arrogant motherfucker like you." I say it to break what has grown between us. I have to hurt him to protect myself. "I wouldn't even *think* of it. Play your games with anyone, but I will *never* prostitute myself. If you think you need to blackmail women into sleeping with you, then I'm damned sorry for your self-esteem. It does explain why no one *really* wants you, though."

Jaxon's expression has darkened so much it makes me shiver. Still, I have no intention of giving in now.

"You don't get to decide whether or not I study at Kingston," I blurt out, hoping it's the truth. How much influence does he have to withdraw my scholarship? It's all a bluff, isn't it? To intimidate me? The Tyrells can't possibly listen to their son and no one else about who the family foundation supports. Top marks or not. "Stay away from me. I'm not a whore just because I'm using your family's money to fund my studies. If you or your family feel that way, that's pathetic. It's not like the elite in this country have ever cared if they behave any better than the filth they look down on though, have they?"

Jaxon doesn't look like I accidentally bumped his chin. He looks like I slapped him with all my strength. He spends a few moments just sitting there, looking at me intensely, forcing me to wonder whether I judged him a little too harshly. But then he smiles.

It's diabolical and cold like the personification of evil.

"Funny," he murmurs, "for a moment I thought you really wanted it. I thought your body was *begging for me*. Not for what you think I am, not for my name, my money, or my influence over your academic future. I felt as if you wanted *me*. Isn't it interesting that even I can be wrong? No ..." Jaxon fastens his belt and lets his gaze roam around the limo. "You're just like everyone else. A sycophantic slut who thinks life is unfair because her parents couldn't manage to pay the electric bill and had to move into a trailer. Now you expect *me* and *my family* to pay for everything *your* family neglected to. You expect to be lifted up like a baby from the cradle and have the gold others have worked hard for all their lives shoved up your ass. It's *entirely natural* for you to receive a scholarship just because you can memorize answers for the SATs. You never had to do anything. You never *really* had to work hard. Your mom's been on drugs all her life and let her kids go to seed, but *the Tyrells, they're supposed to rescue your pathetic ass, and you have absolutely no issue with giving nothing in return.*"

Tears sting my eyes, which I realize when I open my mouth and a lump in my throat makes it hard to speak. "Of course I don't expect to be rescued!" I whisper to him, even though I'd rather shout. "I'll give back whatever I can, but it's certainly not going to be sex!"

"You're right," Jaxon replies calmly. "Sex was my first approach because there's nothing else I want from you. But if you're stupid enough to come back, I'll think of something. Romeo!"

Romeo reacts immediately and knocks against the glass separating us from the driver.

The limo stops and Jaxon opens the door next to him. "Go."

I look outside and see nothing but darkness.

"Get the *fuck* out of this car," Jaxon hisses menacingly. I'm scared enough to obey. As soon as I pass him, he pulls me back by my hair. I gasp, staring up into his eyes. "You don't want to be a whore?" he whispers, coming dangerously close to my face. "I will make you one. You're going to fuck everyone as you try to climb your way to the top. You'll sell your virginity to the highest bidder. After this semester at the latest, you're going to beg me to forget the disrespect you treated me with. If I want a whore, all

I have to do is snap my fingers, Dole." He raises his hand to do just that. "Soon, you'll be one of the people who comes running when I do."

"In your dreams."

His lips twist into a cold smile. "I hope you enjoyed the party tonight," he says with a laugh, letting go of me abruptly. "It'll be the last bit of fun you have for a long time."

His words make me so angry I tear myself away from him and get out of the limo. I just want to put some distance between us, his stupid words, his arrogant attitude. It's only when I feel the forest floor under my feet that I realize how stupid that was.

"You can't just leave me here!" I shout at him through the open door, but the limo is already pulling away. "I have no idea where I am!"

The door slams shut and the headlights illuminate the dense woods around me before they disappear into the thicket and leave me in the middle of nowhere.

"You're a fucking asshole, Tyrell!" I yell after him. Knowing that about himself probably turns him on, though. "Damn it!" I scream, more to myself than to the receding limo. Angry and disappointed in my own actions, I start to run after it. How could I not have seen this coming? Am I truly that naive? Could I have averted this entirely? Or was this what Jaxon had in mind from the beginning? How long had we been driving through the forest?

And where the hell am I, anyway?

10

SYLVIAN

I open the stall door and push her inside. Her back hits the plastic of the partition hard, but her moans convey desire, rather than pain. One hand finds her neck, the other grips her hip as I pull her close.

Our bodies move rhythmically, arousing each other.

As she pulls up her skirt, I reach underneath and feel that she's not wearing any panties.

A moment later, she's grabbed at my belt and I'm inside her.

The beats of the club mix with our sounds. It's loud, dirty, meaningless, and I already know I won't even remember what she looks like ten minutes from now.

I hate myself while I'm doing this. But it's the only kind of sex I can tolerate at the moment. Non-committal. Quick. The pure satisfaction of lust.

No strings.

No smiles.

No names.

I only realize how bad the bathroom stinks when we've finished.

The girl pulls her skirt down, grinning mischievously. She's high, has taken the drugs I'm selling here, and will probably remember me even less than I'll remember her.

I flush the condom and send her away. It's not long before we're separated in the crowd. I should feel good, refueled, but every time I fuck another high chick, it only makes me feel more disgusted.

Shit.

I'm a loser.

Just one step away from buying sex.

All I have to do is look at one of the little sluts, and they'll follow me wherever I want them to. I only touch them when I know for certain they're high enough. I don't want anyone to remember me, especially not any of them. I'm a shadow. A specter. A faceless, muscle-bound guy with tattoos who sells drugs at Flavor's and can make you come in five minutes.

What does he look like?

I have no idea.

Did you get his number?

Only my dealer's.

I want to drown in the anonymity of my double life. It's not just the cops who'll never know who I really am. It's also everyone else I meet here.

As I return to my usual spot—the corridor between the dance floor, the stairs up to VIP, and the bar—my gaze wanders over the crowd. People are in a good mood. The DJ knows what he's doing. Everyone seems to be having fun.

I should be on the lookout for potential customers, but I'm looking for an entirely different face instead, as if she's still here.

Behind the bar.

The inconspicuous bartender, the girl behind the empty glasses and bottles.

Since she stopped working here, I've felt empty, sinking into quicksand. I drive two and a half hours from Kingston to Philadelphia, only to realize that I'm chasing the past like a physicist who doesn't have the first clue about the space-time continuum. *Shit.*

Mable never noticed my presence. She saw me none of the hundred times I stood here and watched her. She went to the very same bathroom where I just finished fucking some slut. She breathed the same stale air.

And she instinctively kept her distance from me. She scurried past me as if she sensed the danger I represent. Arousing my interest is the most dangerous thing a girl can do.

Mable did.

That's why I'm still traveling to Philadelphia: to stay away from her. It's the best thing for her. It's one way I can protect her.

Protect her from myself.

My cell phone buzzes. There are four people in my life who send me personal messages. Reece. Zayn. Jaxon, and Harper.

Everyone else is business.

Where are you, pissant.

Jaxon.

> *Work,* I reply. *You may have to look that up in the dictionary.*

Fuck you.

He sends a crazy smiley face. Not turning up at the Kings' first party is not an offense he'll overlook. I deliberately broke one of our most important rules—if you can even call them that. They're really more like *laws*: immovable requirements that everyone has to follow. In a world filled with mistrust and mutual betrayal, these rules are all we have. A year ago, I'd never have dreamed of disregarding them.

I can't find you anywhere, he writes.

> *Everyone is taken care of at the Crescent party.*

You aren't here?

> *No. I'm at work.*

I can see he's typing a reply, but he never sends it. He isn't stupid. He knows I'm staying away. The last year changed me, and he's getting nervous because he's lost his control over me. Control is Jaxon's life. It's made up of noble goals, anger, and control. Held up against his visions, I am nothing. Held up against my past, his is a golden track stretching over the horizon. No one else knows Jaxon the way I do. Maybe Reece has an idea of how the man who unites us all under one flag is doing, now and then. But I'm the one who really *knows* Jaxon. He trusts me with his life. There's no particular reason for that—honestly, no one should trust me. It's simply that he wants to. If I ever put a gun to his head, he would smile at me. I don't make the mistake of thinking that'll never change, though. Especially if I keep trying to protect Mable from him. Protect her from *all of* us.

Five minutes later, I receive another message.

Are you trying to win the bet this way?

By running away from her like a bitch?

She asked Reece for sex.

Isn't she still a virgin?

134

Fucking answer, Syl.

I don't know, I type, accepting a
hundred dollars for my last pill.
Anything else you need to know?

When he sends a smiley face, I can almost hear his cold laugh.

Why do you never learn?

It's a simple question that makes my hands tense up. Jaxon knows me just as well as I know him. My soul is open to this son of a fucking bitch like no one else in this world. His question goes deeper. Far too deep. Yes, why don't you learn, Sylvian? Why don't you finally realize that no one is safe from you? I'd had nearly a year to stop Mable from coming to Kingston.

Did I do it?

No.

Because I'm weak.

Because I want her ... there.

Because I've been gambling for a long time, even though I don't want to.

*You won't be able to protect her. Why
don't you give up and just let us have our
fun? If we both want it, all the better. And
Reece doesn't seem to mind either.*

Only Jaxon can manage to get on my nerves like this.

*I won't be playing this year. What can I
say to get that through your thick skull?*

You conceived of this game with me, Syl.

You ARE this game.

And the little Dole will look nice on the board.

You can have her, honestly. It'll be
pure pleasure to watch you.

                No, I reply, trying to discard his words.

He can't force me to play along with his sick game. It's just Jaxon. He has no power over me. I can change. I'm not a monster. Not emotionally stunted. I don't have to spend my life fucking random drugged-up girls in stinking bathrooms because that's all the closeness I can stand.

I'm not the Sylvian everyone thinks I am.

I'm not a son of a bitch.

Not a bastard.

Not a murderer.

Right?

Fine, then I'll take her.

That was a predictable answer if ever there was one. I already expected I'd have to protect Mable from Jaxon. But I can take him on. Jaxon's a weakling compared to what's lurking inside me. Demons tearing at their chains. That make me thirst like a vampire. For blood. For intoxication. For the next kick.

There's nothing I won't destroy on the way to my goal. The destructive rage will stop at nothing, and certainly not at people. Least of all at women. Jaxon rules Kingston University because he's a ruler. I rule alongside him because I'm a *tyrant*.

And who's Mable on this playing field?

Thinking of her, I suddenly see it all spread out before me like a movie.

The way she approached me. The Crown's notepad in hand, pen firmly clutched. Her instincts told her to keep her distance, yet she had to serve me.

"What'll you have?" she asked. Her voice masked her reluctance. She'd already been weakened before I even started to close my claws around her.

When I told her to sit, she couldn't not obey. I could see her compulsion to do as I said. She couldn't have done anything worse than prove to me that, deep down, she's submissive at heart and looking for someone to lead her.

She let herself be caught like a butterfly in my spiderweb.

The way she reacted to what I said ensured her downfall. Couldn't she have ignored me? Couldn't she have been disinterested? But no—she fell for my clear gaze like hundreds before her. My eyes captivated her. The light brown in her irises was all mine. I took her apart, looked at what made her tick. A single moment was enough to learn everything about her.

The nervous red of her cheeks.

Her trembling fingers grabbing at the pen.

Her beating heart.

Somehow she knew everything I said was true, but she didn't run when she should have.

Amabelle, I think, inhaling the smoke from my next cigarette.

An old-fashioned, pretty name.

Just perfect for what I have planned for you.

I flip up my collar and push my way through the sweaty crowd. Faces turn toward me as I walk through the room. The guests are shrouded in fog, and I'm certain that no one will remember me. There's something else that draws their attention to me, though.

It's not my tattoos. Everyone here has those.

It's the money.

I smell like I climbed out of the rich kids' sewer. I just look like one of those guys who shit money, and hell, I kind of do. But it's more than that. Danger is thick on me. I give it off like a perfume that makes people keep their distance by instinct.

I don't usually work in clubs. I've been staying off the roads for years, letting others do my dirty work. But Flavor's in Philly is a dangerous place for smaller dealers, even though it isn't uncommon for big deals to be done in VIP.

Dirty details, a quickly uttered threat, and cash changing hands. Cocaine samples slit open, lips wetted with the stuff for purity testing…

Does Mable have any idea the criminals she served in this club?

Does she know that I'm one of them?

No. No, if she'd known, she never would've exchanged a single word with me. Her record is so clean it hurts. That's another reason why I should be staying away from her.

Far away…

Unattainable…

When my phone vibrates again, I'm already standing in the street, waiting for my Aston Martin. The valet pulls up just as I read the message. It's Harper.

Sylvian? Have you seen Mable?

I read the message and know Jaxon is going to try everything to win this bet as quickly as possible. And that he took revenge on me because I didn't turn up. It'd be easy not to play this game.

Not to follow the feint he laid out for me.

But Jaxon isn't the only player among the Kings.

Who am I actually trying to fool?

SYLVIAN

Hey baby. Something happened. You caught my attention. Woke the wolf in me. That's dangerous. Didn't I warn you hundreds and hundreds of times? But you challenged me again. Alone again. You want me to do the things I do to all the other women to you. You want to taste my poison. To lose yourself.

To risk your life.

You want so much more than you're even aware of.

11

MABLE

I'm going to die of thirst.

It's well into the day when I collapse from exhaustion, too tired to call for help, too lost for hope. I crumble into the moss, rest my head on the roots of a tree and stare up at the sky.

Wherever Jaxon left me, I can't find the road. There's no path except for the one the limo left between the trees. But those tracks lead into the wild, overgrown nothing.

I made it through the night, though every snapping branch made me wince. I've never been in the deep forest at night before. Never experienced the whispering of leaves, the crawling of small animals and the rapid movements of the shadows. Nothing hurt me, but every hour was pure hell. I never want to experience that again. That means I have to find may way out of here by sundown.

But how?

I don't know the first thing about plants, other than that not all berries are edible. Hunger isn't my problem, though. Thirst is.

Whatever they drugged me with yesterday must have dehydrated my body. My mouth is dry as a desert, and even the thought that Jaxon left me for dead no longer produces angry saliva.

I'm parched. A headache splits my forehead.

I don't know where to go, so maybe it's better to preserve my energy until I can think of a better plan. At least I'm not freezing. I've never been so grateful for the August heat.

"Mable!"

An echo in my thoughts, but I listen anyway.

"MAAABLE!"

Someone's calling my name. It's loud enough to reach my ears even through the many branches. Adrenaline rushes through me and I get up.

"HERE!" I shout back, cupping my hands around my mouth. Gratefully, I run toward the voice. "I'M HERE!!"

Newfound courage propels my legs now. I have to run through the thicket, trampling on broken branches, pushing aside bushes, climbing over tree trunks. Then the calling stops, and nothing else follows. Silence descends around me.

Tears sting my eyes as I realize I must be imagining things. I stagger, stumble, fall forward and just lie there. In the foliage, which makes my thirst even worse.

Maybe eating soil would help. Maybe that would make the disgusting feeling in my mouth go away. Children eat mud, and they don't seem to mind. I longingly dig my fingers into the soft forest floor, brushing the leaves aside, scraping off the dry layer and forcing myself not to cry. Every little bit of water needs to stay in my body.

A shadow falls on me.

A shape.

I only have time to blink once before tattooed arms wrap around me and pull me to sitting.

"Mable." Sylvian crouches in front of me, but I don't want to trust his appearance. Of all the people who could help me, he's the last one I'd expect. His hand darts forward, brushing leaves from my hair. I haven't been able to tie it up again since Jaxon undid it.

Jaxon...

One thought of him and I'm filled with murder.

"You're dehydrated," Sylvian says, his voice distant like an echo. "Come on." He reaches under my arms and lifts me to my feet. I'm too weak to walk on my own, too incredulous that another one of the Kings, of all people, is helping me. What's he going to do? Is he trying to give me hope, only to carry me even deeper into the forest? Is he going to leave me lying in the dirt when I want to believe in the good in him for a moment?

I hardly notice where we're going. Only when he lets go of me and I sink to the ground do I realize he's brought me to a stream.

"Spring water," Sylvian explains, bending down on the bank and scooping water with his hands. He immediately returns, prompting me to part my lips by touching my chin, and then dribbling it into my mouth…

The water on my parched tongue revives my spirits. I greedily bring his hand to my lips, sucking and licking the lingering drops off his index finger. It feels good. So good and real and invigorating that I only realize a moment later how he's staring at me.

I let go of his hand and let his finger slip from my mouth.

I can see the same sort of aggression in his eyes that I've already seen in Jaxon's. Aggression coupled with … lust? My eyes are riveted to his and I blink up at him in confusion for the second or two when he doesn't move. Then he seems to force himself to clear his mind and the look disappears from his face.

He gives me water until my thirst has subsided to some extent. Finally, he offers me his hand to pull me up.

His gaze is dark and his figure gloomy and out of place among the brightly colored foliage and chirping birds. His stubble has thickened since he spoke to me at Crown's. His black hair is disheveled, as if he ruffled it a few times, and his clothes smell of stale smoke from a party. It couldn't have been Reece's since no one was smoking there—could it?

"Do you feel strong enough to walk?" Sylvian asks and I nod.

"How did you know where I was? Did Jaxon tell you to come and get me?"

Sylvian raises one eyebrow. "I know how Jaxon's mind works. That made finding you easy, more or less. No, he would've let you die of thirst rather than send anyone."

"Why?" I ask, even though it sends shivers down my spine. Jaxon? A murderer? "What did I do to make him hate me so much?"

"Not listen to me," Sylvian replies indifferently, even though I hear a trace of pain, or perhaps pity, in his voice. "I'll take you home. You sure you can walk on your own?"

"I can."

As he helps me climb over a fallen tree trunk, I notice the black bracelets on his wrist.

"Can I... maybe borrow one of those?"

He frowns but pulls off one of the leather straps and hands it to me.

I immediately tie my hair back in a ponytail. The day's heat is a lot less heavy when my long hair isn't falling wildly into my face and down my neck.

Sylvian seems to know how to get to the closest street, and I follow him silently. We walk through the branches for several minutes without saying a word. I wish I could undo everything. The entire week, my orientation sessions, ever meeting Jaxon, Sylvian, or Reece at all. If I were invisible, would they leave me alone?

What am I going to have to do to get them to ignore me?

"Sylvian." I stop and wait until he turns around to face me. "Explain it to me."

He doesn't look like he's even *considering* saying another word. "Please."

His eyes glaze over, and he stares up into the treetops before fixing his gaze on me again. "Just because I'm not going to let you die out here doesn't mean I'm a good guy. The less you know, the better it is for you. The freedom of the ignorant is a precious treasure, and I'll be the last person to expose you to any more human darkness than you've already seen."

"What's that in plain English? You were talking about Jaxon just letting me die! I might've never found my way out of the forest! What is this, a national park? I could have wandered around for days until I died of thirst! And that's alright with you? You can accept that and think I'll get over it like it's just another stupid joke?"

Sylvian actually laughs then, but it's mirthless and his eyes remain dark. "Do you want me to take you back or not?"

My mouth opens in bewilderment, but he's already turned around and continued walking.

My hands clench into fists on their own. Something is wrong here. That goes for Reece, Jaxon, and Sylvian alike. They're completely insane. All three of them. I should've listened to Harper from the beginning and stayed away from them.

I intend to do just that in future. I stomp after him, hoping that this will be the last time I have to see him. The last time he's anywhere near me. Suddenly I wonder if he was already standing in the shadows on my first day, waiting there, to *watch* me. I bet he was. What can I do to make the Kings lose interest in me? Would it help to act obnoxious? Pathetic? Bitchy? Demanding? Annoying?

Since my life has always been about being well prepared for college, I've acquired all these qualities. Teachers hated me either because I was a know-it-all or too inquisitive. That was a couple years ago, though. Maybe I've forgotten how to make myself unpopular?

I take a deep breath, trying to relax my hands, and it makes me just a bit too slow. Sylvian doesn't manage to grab hold of a branch he pushed aside in time, letting it fly back to strike me even though I try to protect my face. I cry out, in shock more than in pain, and tears well up in my injured eye.

"Mable!"

"Let go of me!" I yell, knocking Sylvian, who approached, sounding worried, away from me. *His friend actually tried to kill me. And Sylvian can't be bothered to explain why.*

"Let me see your eye," he demands.

"It's fine!" I shout, waving my arm at him to keep him away from me and losing my balance. I fall into the leaves and my head spins for a moment.

"Please, let me look at it." He's right above me. So close his scent of cigarettes, vanilla, and a fresh breeze is inescapable.

I slowly lower my hand to show him my injured eye. It stings like anything, but I don't think it's actually damaged because I can still see through the veil of tears. Sylvian gently runs his thumb over the chafed skin. His physical presence right above me is confusing. I should hate the Kings since they obviously hate me, but instead of hate, fascination wells up in me. While Sylvian touches my cheek, I find myself reaching out toward *his* face.

He flinches.

"What?" I ask innocently. "You can touch me, but I can't touch you?"

His eyes scrutinize me as we stare at each other. "You're different from what I expected."

"What did you expect?" I ask in a whisper.

"Not you asking Reece, of all people, for sex."

I laugh mockingly. "Have you looked at the guy? What heterosexual woman wouldn't want to fuck him?"

Sylvian raises both brows.

"Or you, for that matter? You know exactly the effect you have on women. It's not a male privilege to imagine having hot, no-strings-attached sex, you know?"

"Opium takes quite a while to leave your system, doesn't it?"

"Opium?" I ask apprehensively. "You gave me opium?!"

"The party last night." Sylvian is still half on top of me, making no move to leave. "The air was thick with it."

I open my mouth. "That's why there were no drinks ..."

"You've imagined having sex with me?" he says, returning to the actual topic at hand.

A tingling sensation rushes through my body. I haven't before, but when he asks, my mind snaps to it immediately. What would it be like if he were to undress me now? Right here? In the forest? "Not yet ..." I evade his question.

He laughs harshly, a sound that sends butterflies fluttering in my stomach. I should loathe him, though. Why is my body betraying me like this?

Sylvian still makes no effort to move, and the intimate moment between us suddenly loosens my tongue.

"You know those Hollywood movies where the guy has something going on with an obnoxious woman who just wants to rip him off or use him, and all the time you're wondering why he doesn't leave her? Why he even kisses her? And you're pretty sure he's screwing her, even if it's never shown?"

Sylvian's lips are parted, sensual. His eyes attentively fixed on my face. He isn't the type to answer a rhetorical question.

"That's how I feel right now."

It takes a few seconds for the penny to drop. His gloomy face twists into a genuine laugh that brightens up everything about him. The dark circles under his eyes lessen, his scowl gives way to cheerfulness, and his white teeth flash. He laughs right in my face until his mouth suddenly closes and he grabs my ponytail.

Hard enough to make me gasp.

He yanks my head back, straining my neck and exposing my throat. "You know those movies where a killer kidnaps a woman, tortures, rapes, and abuses her for days, and four months later a cop turns up trying to find the body? Except they never manage to do that in real life. Not with people like us."

"My analogy wasn't a joke," I whisper as panic fills my veins. Is that what's in store for me? Did he just tell me what my future holds? Are the Kings deranged criminals who exploit their social status to escape the consequences and always get away with it?

"Neither was mine," Sylvian returns in as low a voice. He releases my hair, running his thumb over my cheek to wipe away a drop of blood. The dark red shimmers on his skin and triggers an annoying fascination. I can't look away even as his eyes flash and he brings his thumb to his lips.

He tastes my blood like a vampire, and my insides freeze.

"You'd better change genres. Kingston isn't a place for comedy."

My breathing quickens as he stands. Trembling, I climb back to my feet.

"*Nothing* is going to happen to you as long as you listen to me." His voice is a whisper on the wind. "If I wanted to hurt you, I would've done it a long time ago. Just come along, will you? Let's not talk about sex anymore. That way I won't forget myself and can just take you home. We'll never see each other again. *Never. Again.* Eventually, this entire trip will be nothing more than a nightmare for you—one that you survived, none the worse for wear. But we do have to leave now. This damn forest, your total naivety, and your constant blabbing about how attractive I am aren't exactly helping me stay in control. Understand?"

"I do," I whisper, nodding. The moment he turns away, I take the opportunity to process what he just said. *Control... Forgetting himself...* What the hell is he talking about? Is he saying that a part of him ... longs to ... rape me? Or to make me bleed even more?

That thought doesn't bring me quite the distress, fear, or panic that I'd like to feel. My skin burns everywhere he touched me. Something inside me demands an explanation, some way to minimize the things that have happened.

Why do I want Sylvian's words to be untrue so badly? What am I getting out of it? His promise that we would never see each other again sounds good. It also sounds a bit too final for the fact that we're studying on the same campus.

"Sylvian?"

He keeps on walking as he turns to me, his gaze so hot that I want to curl up in a ball of flaring lust. God. What's wrong with these guys? And what's wrong with *me*?

"What?" he asks gruffly.

"Which home do you want to take me to? Because if you mean the trailer park, I'm not going back there. Never."

He only spares me a weary look and keeps going. As if I'm not worthy of a sensible answer. Funny enough, he acts like absolutely nothing at all happened. *Everything*'s changed, though. Not least the state of my head.

I pretend to follow him, waiting for him to disappear behind another bush. Then I turn around.

"Mable!" he calls after me, but I'm running.

It's the only thing I can do in this situation. Run away, most of all from myself, before Sylvian's words trigger something in me that doesn't belong here. He's crazy, he's tasted my blood, he's talking like a murderer, and still, I'm... aroused.

First Reece.

Then Jaxon.

Now Sylvian.

Cruelty increases from King to King, and I can't fall for them. Most of all, I can't fall for *all of them*. I have to leave, even if I never find my way back and die of thirst in the woods. That seems to be a better option than giving in to the maelstrom the three Kings are dragging me into.

Branches crack under my feet; leaves fly through the air. My hands are scraped, my clothes torn, yet I keep going. All the way back the way we came, deep into the forest, into rough terrain, up the hill.

"Mable!"

Fuck. He sounds closer than he should be. I turn around to check if I still have a chance to escape. That's the moment he tackles me, forcing me to the ground again. The only difference is that this time, I'm pinned with my back to him.

My face is pressed into the foliage and his hands hold mine behind my back.

He caught me. I want to weep and plead for freedom. I want to give up and fight at the same time. Let the tears out and keep from crying under any circumstance.

His breath rushes into my ear. He's so close. Everything about him is so close, intimate, and terrifying.

He tasted my blood.

He drags me around roughly to look at me.

His eyes are those of a hunter who's brought down his prey.

They're filled with nothing but greed, roaring desire, and endless darkness.

He places a hand around my throat and squeezes slowly. Very, very slowly, while my breath disappears. "If you don't want me to cut through your clothes, take them off now."

My breathing becomes labored. I should be scared, but I trust him. It makes absolutely no sense, and I know that. "What are you going to do?" I ask, trembling.

"Fuck you," he says tightly. A jungle of desire in those green eyes. "To end this bullshit before it starts."

"Why... end...?" I ask tonelessly, flinching when he pulls out a knife. Adrenaline shoots through my body as he skillfully opens the butterfly knife with one hand, and I do something I never thought I would do.

Never.

I reach down and frantically undo the button of my jeans. Sylvian gets off me, standing up to watch. His expression alone makes me brush aside any doubts. If this is still a bet, then I want Sylvian to win. It's sick. Psychotic, incomprehensible, and utterly perverted, but I need it, and maybe I'm glad that it's happening this way.

In a forest.

With a stranger.

Who's tasted my blood and to whom I would give more if it would satisfy him.

I take off my jeans, then open my sweatshirt and lie there, exposed.

He looks down at me as if he wants me and hates me at the same time. "Why are you doing this?"

"You told me to."

His green eyes roam my naked body. A hurricane seems to rage inside him. "Get dressed again."

"What?"

"I'm not strong enough." His voice sounds as if he is speaking to me from a great distance. "Did you fuck Jaxon?"

"No!"

"Crescent?"

"Why are you asking me that?"

"You can't want me. You can't just give in like that."

"You know, I'd rather join than let you slit my throat!"

He laughs bleakly. It never touches his eyes. "Why?" he asks. "Why do you trust me so much? I warned you about us. *In front of the entire university.* And yet you trust me."

I bite my bottom lip and wish I had a clever answer at hand. How does he know that I don't really believe he would rape me? Why can he read me like an open book?

"Nobody can know what's about to happen. Can we do that? You and me?"

When I don't say anything, he starts to take his jacket off, aggressively, like he's mad about it. "I choose to take that as 'Yes, Sylvian. Anything you want, Sylvian,'" he says ironically. Then he grabs his shirt, pulls it over his head and I struggle to catch my breath. The tattoos covering his chest make him look even more sinister. I start to shiver in the warm August day.

Sylvian comes toward me, the butterfly knife spinning in his hand before he closes it and puts it away. He grabs my shoulder, sending a jolt of electricity through my chest.

"The others have taken care of foreplay, haven't they?" he asks, and my eyes widen.

How much does he know?

Without waiting for an answer, he roughly turns me over. His right hand digs into my butt cheek. His belt comes off, and then he's between my legs. His hard cock pushes into me. I'm lying there, pressed into the leaves, motionless as if trapped in a cage. His tip presses relentlessly into me. I'm wet, but also tight. Too tight.

Sylvian pulls my hips up, so I can support myself on all fours, and moves in circular motions to stretch my pussy as he thrusts. He's rough, but he doesn't do anything that makes me scream.

"You should have run faster, baby," he gasps, the words choppy. His shallow thrusts become more urgent, deeper every time. "I'm going to have to hurt you. I can't help it."

"That's okay," I whisper.

"No, it isn't!" he roars, digging his fingers into the flesh of my ass and surging deeper into me.

I cry out. I'm so tight it hurts, but he keeps going.

"Scream louder!"

I obey. Then all it takes is a few firm pushes, and everything inside me dissolves.

He fills me entirely with a deep thrust and a feral growl.

I lie before him as if trained for it, and it's exactly what I want. I want him to fuck me. He seems to have brought out one of my darkest fantasies and is about to fulfill it.

Wild, uninhibited, dirty sex. No foreplay. No kissing. With a guy who radiates danger like a fucking grenade.

His movements grow wilder and wilder.

I abandon myself to him, savoring every thrust and melting with inner pleasure. It's not what I *really* want. It's not what I *imagined*. It's different, rough, forbidden, with someone I hardly know and yet, for some reason, trust.

Sylvian slides his hand around to rub my clit as he continues to fuck me relentlessly. I come without wanting to, far too fast, too hard, and too violently to enjoy it, and I scream out my pleasure.

No sooner has the explosion come over me than Sylvian grabs my ponytail. He yanks my head back, wrapping my hair around his hand like a rope, and forcing me to bend backward toward him. I arch my back and he continues to fuck me, pressing his lips to mine and pushing his tongue deep into my mouth.

"Tell me this is exactly how you want it," he demands. A film of sweat covers his face. Half my body is covered in earth. "Admit you did everything you could to make it happen."

"I want it," I admit, trying not to feel ashamed. Not to be ashamed of the fact that someone like Sylvian has lured out my most secret desires.

"And if the others were here," he growls more loudly, his movements growing rougher. His cock is so hard and huge that I'm sore already. It feels fantastic. It's beyond anything I imagined.

"If the others were here and took you after me, would you want it?" He twists me around as far as he can so he can look me in the eye. "Say it!" he commands, and I let my lids close.

I allow all the fantasies to wash over me for a moment.

Jaxon and Reece. Here. Watching us. Desiring me. Sharing their lust with me. As I kiss them. Pleasure them. Making them mine one by one. Letting them take me at the same time. Holding me captive between them. I want that.

I need that.

And then I scream again.

Sylvian pulls out of me and kisses me roughly until my orgasm fades. The scent of his cum fills the air and it seeps into the leaves. He's so stupid for using such an unsafe method of contraception, but I admit it was hot in the moment.

Great. How many different people has Sylvian had sex with?

He lowers himself into the foliage next to me and suddenly pulls me close. My worry disappears immediately when he puts an arm around me and runs his ringed hand through my hair.

"Girls are usually scared of me when I show them my true colors," he mumbles, stroking my heated cheek.

I feel nothing but connection between us. I say nothing. Maybe we can stay here like this forever. Maybe I can always keep his arms around me as if they're my true home.

"But maybe you're stronger than I thought."

"Maybe," I mutter.

He smiles. An enchanting, somber Sylvian smile. His sweaty hair falls over his forehead, but he continues to stroke me unperturbed. "Did Harper tell you what we usually do with girls like you?"

Goosebumps form on my arms. "She's hinted at it."

"Good for her. That means she listened to us for once."

"Why?" I ask suspiciously, moving away from him.

He pulls me closer. "Because usually we make sure you don't get any help. We want our victims to ourselves."

I'm getting cold, and what's annoying is that it's Sylvian's chest, of all things, keeping me warm.

"I'd usually fuck you and hurt you. Hurt you a very, very great deal. And then you would fall, and I would catch you, and I would fuck you again and hurt you again. I'm a monster, Amabelle. The most harmless thing I do once it takes hold of me is lap up a little blood."

I hold my breath. That can't be right. How is all this supposed to fit together?

"But if you learn to behave yourself, maybe I won't have to be so cruel for once. I don't want to be anymore. Do not challenge me ever again."

"By accidentally hurting myself so you descend on me like a vampire?"

His green eyes flash and I feel the urge to run away from him again. "You have two options. I can take you home. That would be the best thing for you. But if you want to stay at Kingston, no one can know what just happened. And you have to stay away from *every single* guy, not just Jaxon and Crescent. But from Jaxon and Crescent and me more than anyone else. If you even *dare* to approach us, I will forget myself. The control I have to muster to hold myself back, as I'm doing right now, is superhuman. You have absolutely no idea who I am or what I've done or what I'm *prepared to do* if you don't obey me."

I look at him and can't help the tears welling up in my eyes. How can he be so mean when I just let him take me on the forest floor?

"Hey," he says gently, almost sounding upset. He wipes away a tear, rolls me onto my side and studies me closely. His face is suddenly so warm and full of emotion that I feel safer. "Nothing's happened yet, baby."

I sob and laugh at the same time. "You're such an ass."

He smirks, but I know he means it in a friendly way. "Right now, I am the best version of myself that anyone has ever seen. You give me hope. Maybe not everything in me is dark and broken after all. Should we go back?"

I nod and he straightens.

While he fastens his belt and puts his shirt on, I slip into my jeans.

When we're both dressed, he grabs my hand, intertwining our fingers so I can feel his rings, and pulls me toward him. He hugs me for a long time, which gives me strength, and kisses me on the forehead.

"May you never awaken the monster in me, Mable," he whispers.

And I almost wonder if that isn't actually exactly what I want to do.

I wonder if I may be about to fall love with the Kings' monsters.

Instead of whatever good they might have inside them.

JAXON

I knew it, Belle. You turned Sylvian's head, to the point that he's sending you home instead of fighting to let you stay at Kingston. He doesn't want to destroy you. He's trying with all his might not to repeat his past mistakes. What is it about you that makes you the first one who doesn't wake the beast in him?

Never mind that, though. There's four more of us after all.

And we're going to love setting our monsters on you.

12

MABLE

Half an hour's walk later, I'm wondering whether I shouldn't leave Kingston after all. Even though the thought itself feels like dying inside, that's nothing compared to the actual end of my life. It's clear I can't trust myself. I can't resist my attraction to them and I know I'll succumb to it like a gazelle to a lion. Who knows what'll happen when Sylvian stops being "nice"? Or when Jaxon gets it in his head to kidnap me again?

What am I supposed to think of Reece, who watched Romeo drug me and did nothing?

I can take chicken feathers, flooded floors, and bullying. I don't need to be invited to parties. I can even cope with not having any friends at all for a while.

But the Kings are a different caliber.

And they hate me.

I won't learn why, and I'm starting to think that there isn't a reason other than that I didn't want to sleep with Jaxon. He offered me a deal and I declined. He would have let me die in the woods for that.

Even though my thoughts on Sylvian differ, and I believe him when he says he isn't going to hurt me, he's also said that only applies as long as I listen to him. And he warned me about his *monster*. The monster I would love to learn more about right now.

I'm walking into my own trap.

This has to stop.

The night alone in the forest is nothing compared to the feeling that comes over me when I think about leaving Kingston. I had to give *all I had* to be accepted here. I've been looking forward to starting university for nine months. The idea of going to Kingston was planted in my head early on. My teachers told me about the one university where no matter what you studied, you were going to get the best-paid jobs in the entire world—not just because the education is that good, but also because its network is one of the best anywhere. I might've believed that only people whose parents were already part of that network would be accepted... But who doesn't like to believe in fairy tales?

"God, there you are!"

Caught entirely by surprise, I look up from my shoes and see Harper rushing toward us through the trees.

Sylvian takes two steps in front of me, turns around, and his eyes are filled with shadows. "Not a word," he whispers, and I know what he means.

Harper can't learn what happened between us. Is it that he doesn't want to hurt her? Do I have to be honest about it, or can I keep it to myself because it will never happen again anyway?

Before I can answer that question for myself, I'm bowled over.

"Mable, I've been dying of worry!" Harper shrieks as she squeezes me tightly enough to make me gasp for air. "Never again! Never again will I leave you alone with one of those bastards! Never again!"

Sylvian clears his throat behind her, but she ignores him, steps back and takes my face between her hands. "You're bleeding!"

"It's just a scratch ..."

Her face contorts into an angry grimace. "I'm going to kill Jaxon. I'm going to rip his balls off and eat them for breakfast! He wants war?! He messed with the wrong girl!"

"It's okay," I evade, my eyes fixed to the ground in embarrassment. I can't help but notice the intensity with which Sylvian's watching us.

"Nothing's okay!" Harper yells into the forest, the echo reverberating off the hills. "I should've prepared you much better! Those arrogant prettyboys will *never* get near you *again*! You can bet on that." She pats my shoulder and steadies me. "We're not alone. A lot of people hate the Kings. We'll take advantage of that."

"I'm standing right behind you, Harper," Sylvian informs her matter-of-factly.

She just snorts. "You can't hurt us," she snaps. "If you reveal our secrets, I'll reveal yours. It's that easy." Harper hooks her arm through mine and helps me up the last hill. There, on an almost invisible, leveled road, her Cadillac waits. She opens the passenger door for me. "Get comfortable."

"I'll be driving." Sylvian stands on the other side of the car, leaning on the hood with one hand. "Get in the back together."

Harper is about to say something back, as I can see in her stubborn expression, but Sylvian interrupts her.

"I'm driving," he repeats coldly, getting into the driver's seat. "You're still high from last night."

Harper rolls her eyes, closes the passenger door, opens the rear one and slides in. I sit next to her, fasten my seatbelt, and wish I could escape this whole situation. The sudden appearance of my new friend, the realization that Sylvian didn't come alone, and the knowledge that she's in love with *him* of all people mix in my mind to create a cocktail of madness.

Harper grabs my hand and squeezes it. "It's going to be okay," she tells me. I don't believe her at all.

160

Sylvian watches us in the rear-view mirror as we drive in silence.

After a while, Harper smiles at me encouragingly, mumbling something about how I'll feel better after a hot shower. Only when Sylvian turns onto the highway does she shriek again. "Where are you going?"

"I'm taking Mable home," Sylvian states tonelessly. "Isn't that what you wanted?" he asks me. I don't dare object. It's the right thing to do. Right?

"Kingston is the other way!" Harper complains.

"We're going to Philadelphia."

"You want her to give up? You damn liar! Why do I still believe a single word you say? You can't be trusted any more than anyone else in this fucking circle. Pull over and get out."

Sylvian laughs humorlessly and accelerates along the highway.

"I mean it!"

I quickly grab Harper's arm and give her a look that tells her to calm down. "You're putting us in danger," I whisper.

She looks as if I've just told her to stop breathing. Her face turns bright red. "You've already resigned yourself to the fact that he's going to take you back?"

"Jaxon *tried* to *kill* me," I mutter, even though I know Sylvian can hear every word. "What would you do in my place?"

Harper looks at me with pity from under half-lowered lids, making it seem like she thinks I'm missing the obvious. "Jaxon would *never* have abandoned you entirely. He would never do anything beyond a—very nasty—prank."

"That wasn't a prank," I remind her. "I nearly died of thirst."

"He wants you to suffer, not die. You could have lasted the entire weekend in the forest without dying of thirst. If it turned out something happened to you *because of him*, he'd lose more than you can even imagine. People like him don't go to prison that easily ... do you understand?"

161

"I don't," I say flatly. "I don't have the first idea what you're getting at."

"You've got to trust me," she insists, and at that moment I realize how stupid I actually am. Not only did I let Sylvian drive, even though he tasted my blood and threatened me with a knife, but I'm in the back seat of the car with Harper without even wondering why she's here with him.

What's their connection to each other based on?

"Okay," I reply with a hesitant smile. I keep quiet and wait until a sign appears on the side of the highway announcing a service station. "Sylvian, could you pull off, please? I haven't been to a proper toilet for over twelve hours."

He joins the lane on the right and gets off the highway without saying a word. Once there, I put on my most innocent look. "Do you think ... Can I borrow your phone to call my mom?"

"Sure thing," Harper replies, reaching into her bag. "But I have something much better. I've got yours."

"Oh, thanks." I take it from her and unlock it. It feels unreal to hold it in my hands again. *How I wished to have my phone last night... if only to illuminate my surroundings.*

"When I found it at the party, you were gone. I knew right away that something was wrong."

I give her a likely unconvincing smile and get out of the car.

"Want me to come with you?" Harper asks anxiously.

"I think I can just about manage to pee on my own."

She doesn't seem enthusiastic about the idea of letting me go. That's exactly what shakes my trust in her. When she said the word *prison* I could've slapped myself in the face. Why do the two of them want to take me back to the trailer park or the university? Why aren't we going to the police?

Why didn't Harper even bring it up?

What does she think is going to help me to continue my studies

162

at Kingston? Starting some sort of "little war" and retaliating for chicken feathers with water balloons? *How exactly is that supposed to help me against someone knocking me out and leaving me in a forest?* At night?

I head for the bathrooms, unsurprised when the door opens behind me shortly after I enter the service station shop. Sylvian follows me like a shadow.

I give him a cursory glance that's about as innocent as all of my previous behavior and disappear into the ladies' room.

He just follows me, yanking the door open and closing it behind him.

"Could I maybe—"

Before I can finish, Sylvian has snatched my phone out of my hand, tossed it into the sink, and pushed me hard into the wall behind me.

"Mable!" Harper opens the door too, panting like she sprinted here. She notices Sylvian, who has me trapped against the wall, and stops, irritated.

"I'll tell you what happens if you call the cops." His voice is rough and clear. He also smells of forest, of earth, and perhaps even of sex. He doesn't care that Harper is watching us. It must look like we're quite intimate with each other.

She can't think that.

She can't know he was just lying on top of me. That his throbbing body controlled mine. I'm ashamed. I'm so ashamed I wasn't able to resist, even though I wanted sex. Even though that was exactly why I'd gone to Reece's party yesterday.

I'm still ashamed.

Probably because I let three guys get close to me at the same time. How's Harper going to feel about me when she finds out?

I let Sylvian pin me against the wall because I physically can't stop him. Neither my body nor my will is strong enough, though my mind tells me that I should kick him in the balls.

Now.

Quickly.

Painfully.

I can't do it. I can't hate him. And that's the worst thing of all.

"What's going to happen?" I ask, sounding as unimpressed as I possibly can.

"*Nothing*," Sylvian replies. "Exactly *nothing*."

I narrow my eyes mockingly. "That's bullshit."

"Every year there is at least one student from Kingston who reports another student or a professor. There's never any evidence. Most of them are found to be liars in the end. The cops won't take you seriously. You took some drugs, you were wandering in the woods for a bit, and then you made up a story. Even if you could prove it, they'll laugh at you as soon as Tyrell's name comes up. Jaxon's father is well on his way to becoming a senator for a reason. He has supporters. He has fans. Most of all, he has fans among the cops."

"The police need to be fucking reformed!" Furious, I try to shake off Sylvian, but he grips me even tighter.

"No lie detected," he says quietly. "But you've been warned."

"These warnings are ridiculous! Nobody in their right mind would've listened and simply dropped out of the best university in the country on your word alone! This isn't about rape, it's about ... blackmail. Which is actually a lot less bad, but, hey, bad enough to report it anyway!"

Sylvian laughs, stepping back and shaking his head. "Usually, I'd say go ahead and do it. Right now, though, I'm the one who got you out of the forest, and you'll want me around if anything else like this happens in the future. So don't make Jaxon any more annoyed than is good for you. You should know where my loyalty lies in the end."

164

I make a face at him. His words hurt. They hurt far too much. Of course I mean nothing to him. Of course he didn't mean any of what he said. It was just the sort of nonsense one spouts after sex. He won't help me—not if it means going against his friends.

"If you call the cops," Sylvian continues, "Jaxon will wonder why I didn't stop you, and rightly so. Make the call and you won't just be fucking me over. You'll lose someone who *cares* about you. The abyss waiting to swallow you will only grow deeper."

"Why?" I ask urgently. My eyes shift to Harper. She's keeping her distance, wearing an inscrutable expression. "What the hell is this about?! Why does some arrogant, hyper-rich bastard whose father will soon be a senator want me dead? Why? Who am I to him?"

They say nothing and I want to shout at them. Instead, I lower my voice, trying to control my agitated emotions. "You know, don't you? You know the truth."

"There's no sense to it in the way you're thinking..." Harper evades. "It's not about you specifically, Mable. Alright?"

"This whole thing's directed at all the female scholarship students?" I lock my eyes on Sylvian, but his lips remain sealed. "And you really *don't* want me to go to the police? You're complicit!"

They both look at me in a way that makes clear they don't expect the police to ever be a problem for them.

"What do you think you'll be able to do when all this comes out? Buy your freedom?"

"My father is a judge on the Supreme Court. My cousin is the police chief of Washington D.C.," Harper explains quietly. "I know it must be frustrating for you. But American laws were ... well, not necessarily made for people like us, you know?"

Part of me feels like breaking as I stare at her. This conversation seems so surreal, in spite of everything I've lived through. I've witnessed murders. Rapes. Teachers shot at school. Nobody cared. If anything happened at all, the perpetrators were sent to prison for a few months, released, and then just carried on as before. And just when I think I'm safe from all of that, they're telling me things are even worse in the ... elite?

"I'm so sorry, Mable," Harper whispers, coming closer. I stand stiffly as she hugs me. "There's only one thing we can do: Stand up to them. They won't win. They *can't* win. You have to stay at Kingston. I'll have your back. And so will Sylvian."

Sylvian's face darkens. "You don't get to decide whether she continues her studies."

Harper whirls to face him. "You owe me a favor. A big one. I call it in."

He frowns. "You can't call in a favor on behalf of someone else."

"Really? Why not? You know you owe me something. I have everything in the world that I can buy. But as a former friend of Clarisse's, I have to make amends. I can't do that without help. You're going to help me. That'll make us even."

Sylvian laughs, a brittle sound, but he doesn't hesitate. He grabs my phone on the way to the door of the service area, opening it to let us through so we can get back to the car. "That's not how you make amends. But you'll only understand that when it's too late."

"You're not going to play along. You promise me that. You're going to stay out of it and turn everything aimed at Mable away from her. And I'll explain the game to her. She'll know how it works. What she has to do. What it's all about."

Sylvian sighs. But he seems to give in.

Harper seems encouraged. She buys some crackers and leaves the service station. Just before we reach the car, when she can't see us, Sylvian grabs the back of my neck. His fingers on my skin feel like pinpricks. And though it hurts, I enjoy his touch.

Which is wrong.

Oh, Mable. It's so wrong.

Sylvian leans close to my ear. "If you want to stay at Kingston, erase the word C-O-P-S from your vocabulary. As soon as anyone outside finds out what's happening there, you're out. Harper wants to put you in the lion's cage like cheap food. She knows full well the Kings aren't the ones who want to see you bleed. At least not the only ones."

"Talk to the car for all I care, Sylvian," I manage a quick retort for a change as I shake off his hand. "You could be speaking Russian for all your words mean to me."

Harper turns around and giggles, but Sylvian remains serious.

"Я хочу твоё тело," he says. "Другие твою душу."

I don't understand every word, but the meaning is clear enough.

I want your body. The others want your soul.

A cold shiver that'll stay with me for hours runs down my spine.

I approached this too naively.

Kingston isn't your normal sort of university.

The Kings aren't your normal sort of assholes.

Harper isn't your normal sort of friend.

And I'm not normal enough to leave when these sort of things happen to me. Am I just curious to see what's next?

I am, actually.

Is that stupid?

Probably.

Am I risking my life?

Maybe ...?

But what sort of life is it that I'm risking to begin with? What the Kings don't know, what they can't even imagine is this: I have absolutely nothing to lose. The misery I grew up in, that I had to leave my sister behind in, isn't anything worth calling a life. It's nothing that could be taken away from me.

I can't give up.

I have nothing worth giving up for.

SYLVIAN

Your soul is like a little dove.
     The right hands will teach it to fly high.
     The wrong ones will lock you in a cage.
Mine will crush you.
Chirp, chirp, little birdie.
Let's hope I never catch you.

13

MABLE

Sylvian and Harper stay to make sure I'm recovering sufficiently. I try not to think too much about whatever's going on between the two of them. It's not just that I think Harper would be better off giving up on Sylvian, there's also a fair amount of ... jealousy. It's an entirely out-of-place feeling that brings my mind back to when he was on top of me in the forest. When he was inside me. When he made me come. Several times.

The moment I close my eyes, all of those conflicting emotions swamp me. I can see it so clearly, like it's branded on the inside of my eyelids, and I can *feel* it.

They order pizza and I go take a hot shower because I can't get warm. It's not just the lingering cold from the night in the forest. I try not to dwell on what happened. My hormones are going crazy, I tell myself, pushing aside the memory of Sylvian tasting my blood like it's the elixir of life, fucking me like that rough sex was the truth of his nature.

I try not to.

I try to convince myself to stop thinking about him like that.

I can't keep anything from the last twenty-four hours with me beyond the fear and terror.

And yet my hand moves between my legs ... further and further until I reach my clit, and I moan under the stream of water. It's not just Sylvian who appears in my thoughts. Jaxon's there, too. Jaxon holding me on his lap, his breath caressing my skin, his hands moving over my clothes ... His dominance fuels my desire.

And then there's Reece. Reece, running his fist over his cock right in front of my eyes. Again and again, until his face contorts, and he blissfully abandons himself to his lust. Reece, pleasuring me with his tongue and fucking my mouth at the same time...

Fortunately, I don't have to decide which of these thoughts excites me the most. For this moment in the shower, they're all there at the same time. I can't even pass judgment for my insane urges and just keep rubbing myself.

In my imagination ... In my imagination I'm free.

When the door to the washroom opens, I flinch, immediately lowering my hand.

"Reece just gave you his number?"

"Yeah! Cool, right? But I don't think I'll text him. He's not my type."

Rachel and Brittany.

Reece gave Rachel his number. *Great*, I think. *Then she'll probably be the next one to have hot oral sex and get kidnapped.*

No, you're not jealous. Never, oh no.

Should I warn her?

Would I have listened if she'd warned me? I don't even listen to Harper, and I hold her in much higher regard than I do Rachel or Brittany.

I wait until the sound of running water tells me the two of them are taking their showers before I dry myself off.

The cold still isn't gone.

Will it ever be?

***

171

When I come back into my room, Sylvian's waiting there alone. He's leaning against my desk, his serious face full of shadows that make me hold my breath for a moment. His leather jacket looks scuffed; his jeans certainly are. His white sneakers have dirt and leaves clinging to them.

But there's something else about him.

Something much deeper.

His posture, the energy that emanates from him, is like no other person I know. So much mystery surrounds him, so many unanswered questions, so much coldness and night. For a moment, I wonder what it'd be like if I could just walk up to him. Hug him, kiss him, pull him onto my bed.

What it'd be like if he were my boyfriend.

What it'd be like if he kissed me in front of everyone.

If he made me his own.

And then I push the thought as far away as I can.

If you even dare to approach us, I will forget myself.

Sylvian looks up, and his gaze goes right through me for a second before he finally meets my eye.

"Harper's in the kitchen getting cutlery."

"You're eating pizza with forks?" I ask in an attempt to lighten the mood. Wisely, I changed in the communal bathroom and now put my dirty clothes—Harper's jeans and the sweatshirt I had on when I woke up in the limo—in my laundry basket. When I turn around again, Sylvian has moved across the room like a ghost.

He steps closer to me, his breath streaming into the crook of my neck, and I can't stop myself from thinking back to that moment in the shower when I let my imagination run wild.

"I'm not staying for dinner," he murmurs, watching my lips. The fact that he doesn't look me in the eye makes me nervous. "Nobody—least of all Harper—can know what happened in the forest. Do you understand me?"

"We have to tell her," I whisper helplessly.

"No, we don't," he growls.

"Sylvian, she loves you!"

He looks as if he couldn't care less. "You need a friend like her. And if you listen to her, and to me, nothing else will happen to you. In return, she redeemed her favor with me. I can't betray Jaxon. But I will persuade him to do things differently this year."

"Why are you trying to protect me, anyway?"

"Why?" he repeats, irritated.

"Yes? Why you? Why me? Why not one of the other scholarship students?"

He loses control over his face for a moment. For the length of one breath, he appears vulnerable and weak, like a breeze dissipating in a storm.

I look up at him. "I mean—"

"No, you're right," he interrupts, his voice barely audible. "It's a legitimate question. Why you and not Rachel? Or you and not Harper?"

When he mentions Harper's name, I feel terribly guilty. "Are you suggesting that you're doing all this because you … in a way …"

He waits until I can manage to spit it out.

"You have a crush on me?" I squeak, and I'm ashamed to have said it the moment the words leave my lips. How could I *think* that Sylvian would have a crush on me? The sex we had meant nothing to him, right?

"Yes. That's exactly why."

As he says it, everything inside me clenches. I'm not sure how to react, not sure how I feel about it. It's the craziest confession I've ever heard from a man. *A man who fucked the hell out of you, Mable…*

"Let's hope for your sake that I don't give in to my feelings a second time." He lowers his eyelids as if he's agonizing over talking to me. "Harper will give you an idea of what I actually do to people. Pray that I can always control myself. You'd be the first girl I don't destroy."

Before I can say anything—if I could even utter a word—Harper opens the door and Sylvian takes a step back.

"There's pizzzaaa!" she shouts cheerfully as she puts the boxes down on my desk.

Sylvian continues to look at me, which seems to irritate Harper.

"Leave her alone," she mutters, trying to protect me again. *Or to keep us apart, who knows?*

"Yes," Sylvian responds. "That's what I'm about to do." He goes to the door and pulls it open. He pauses one last time before stepping through, and a pained expression appears on his shadowed face. "When Harper tells you what the game is about in a moment, remember that not even she knows the whole truth."

I open my mouth to respond, but he disappears, slamming the door behind him just as forcefully as Jaxon did on my first day.

Lost in thought, I worry my lower lip with my teeth as I go sit on the bed with Harper.

She hands me some cutlery and actually starts cutting pieces off the pizza. Small, tiny pieces that I wouldn't even feel in my mouth.

"Do you mind if I ...?" I ask and simply reach for a piece.

"Oh, sure." She watches me as if she's entirely unfamiliar with the method. "I don't think I've ever eaten pizza with my hands before."

I swallow and say with a grin, "And I think I feel sorry for you for that."

Without further ado, she also grabs a piece and timidly takes a bite. "Really ... unusual," she says, chewing and looking at the pizza in her hand as if it's the most precious caviar. "I think it's good that I have permission to tell you everything. But maybe I should wait until we've digested our dinner."

"Because otherwise it might come right back up?"

She cringes apologetically. "It's not going to be pretty. It'll be worse when you understand that I was watching the whole thing. I don't know if you'll still like me after that."

"Everyone deserves a second chance, don't they?" I ask to cheer her up. We all make so many mistakes, every single day. Some happen by accident, some we'll never be able to change, and some are really bad. But if we stop offering second chances, or third ones, or fourth ones, what makes us any different from the real monsters?

"I love that you said that." Harper puts down her pizza, pulls up her right leg and rests her head on her knee, lost in thought. "All I know about the creation of the game is that it started with Jaxon. And with his father, who set up the foundation. Each year, a portion of everyone's tuition goes to the foundation to fund the scholarships."

A forced donation. Of course the elite hate me. Who likes to give away their money?

"Jaxon built a group around himself that he calls the Kings. This is nothing unusual. Their fraternity is called Alpha Rex after all, and not just because Rho Chi is Greek for RX. Rex is the Latin word for king, and it is *Kingston* University. But they seem to be the first ones to live up to the title."

"By actually splitting people into rulers and subjects?" I ask cynically.

"That's it. From the very beginning, it felt like they'd created a proper 'throne' for themselves. The students on campus just accept it. Presumably because they like to have someone to follow. I was one of them, and it ... well, when you're one of them, it's a bit like magic. There's a reason I fell in love ... with Sylvian. They can be charismatic, attractive, seductive, and absolutely perfect if they want to be."

"But the Kings are only mean to the scholarship students, aren't they?"

"Nope. Anyone who doesn't abide by their rules."

"And what are the rules?"

"Oh, standard totalitarian stuff, like not being allowed to question them, for one thing." Her face twists into a grimace. "There are some good ones, too. If the Kings realize someone's being hurt, physically, whether it's a woman being hurt by a guy or by one of her own, they'll intervene. It doesn't happen often, but it has happened. In this respect, you can be sure of one thing: No one, no one at all, will ever hurt you on this campus. At least not physically."

"Well, that's something."

Harper bows her head and smiles sadly. "The psychological pain is all the worse for it, though."

"Do I really want to know?"

"They're playing a game. It's not just a bet. And it doesn't have anything to do with chicken feathers, at least not directly. It's much crueler and more treacherous."

I wait eagerly for her to tell me more. What's the big secret about the four Kings that nobody is allowed to talk about?

"They're playing ... chess with you."

"Chess?"

"You are chess pieces. Each of the Kings tries to drive the others' pieces... off the board. By any means necessary." Harper takes a long pause, brushes one of her curls behind her ear and then continues in a hushed voice. "They get two pieces to play with: a queen and a pawn. The queen is a female scholarship student and the pawn..."

"Is a male one," I conclude.

"Precisely." Harper looks at me apologetically. "The Kings consider everyone who isn't one of them a 'peasant' but for their game, the male scholarship students are 'pawns.' The Kings use them to ... destroy their opponents' 'queens.'"

"But how do they do that when there's supposedly no violence involved?

"Oh ... Violence is very much involved. Psychological violence. Bullying. Verbal attacks." Harper sighs. "You know ... The Kings really know how to get at their victims. And Jaxon wants as few of you as possible to benefit from his father's foundation."

"What happens when one of the Kings wins?"

"His queen and his pawn are allowed to stay. They can continue their studies."

"And what do the Kings get out of it? I mean, what are they playing for?"

Harper frowns. "That's the thing, Mable. It's fun. It's just fun to them. They gain nothing at all. There's no prize. They play their game because they can. That's all."

I lean back and push the pizza away.

"Normally, the scholarship students know nothing about the game. I told you, the entire campus is like Big Brother. Everyone checks on everyone else to make sure no one reveals anything to the queens. You have the advantage of knowing now. I can help you survive the attacks of the pawns, but it's still going to be tough. It's going to be worse if the game goes on for a long time. Last year, three scholarship students were left by the end and the Kings had to put in some really hard work to get two more to leave before finals in May."

I feel so sick that I wonder why I ever liked the taste of pizza. "Who won?" I ask flatly.

"Last year?"

I nod.

She heaves another sigh. "Sylvian."

I find it difficult to reconcile her comments with what's happened so far. Reece? He's supposed to be one of the Kings? Sylvian? That's what he wanted to warn me about? Jaxon? Was the deal he proposed to me just a pretense? Was he playing with me?

I shiver, wrapping my arms around my chest. "Is the game on yet?"

Harper raises her right shoulder. "Quite possibly. Nobody knows what the Kings *really* discuss behind the scenes. It usually starts with the first party at the Rex fraternity house at the end of September. What's happened so far is just preliminary skirmishing on the part of the peasants. Those who haven't yet received an invitation to Jaxon's party spend the first few days of term trying to qualify for a ticket."

"By playing stupid pranks on us?"

"Yes."

"Harper, all of this is completely insane! How can these idiots have even been accepted to this university?"

She laughs and shakes her head. "They're smarter than they seem. That's what makes them so dangerous. They know. They *understand* ..." Harper clears her throat. "*We* understand that intelligence and hard work alone aren't enough. Being invited to an exclusive party at the Rex house is a basic requirement for a good network. And if the Rexes only invite their inner circle and people who further their game, then that's what people are going to do. Anything to get closer to Jaxon and the others. They're hoping for contacts. They want a place in the exclusive circle around the Kings. That's all there is to it. It's rotten, but not stupid. Just a necessity. At least it is for people seeking power and recognition."

I stick my tongue out and pretend to gag, which makes her laugh again. I can only joke about what she's telling me because part of me refuses to believe it's true.

"If the game starts at this party, will the scholarship students be invited? Why should we even go? Nobody likes us. It would be naive to accept an invitation like that, game or no game."

"You'll get money for it."

"What?"

"Every guest either receives a thousand dollars or pays it. That's how the party is funded. Since you probably don't want to pay a thousand dollars, you'll get it."

"Jaxon pays people to come to his party? I knew he couldn't have any real friends."

"Only those who can't afford what it costs to be there."

"Which only applies to ten people on this campus."

Harper's lips thin. "That's right. Nobody would have the nerve not to pay, even if their family was on the verge of bankruptcy. Except for you. Five male and five female scholarship students. You'll take the money and not care what anyone thinks about you. But yes. The best idea would be not to go."

I'm wondering what to make of that. A thousand dollars? For going to a party and exposing myself to the game? *Is it really worth it?*

"Who's the fifth King?" I ask after a while.

Harper's eyes light up as if she's just as interested in this question as I am. "Nobody knows . The Kings are masked, and that they're playing this game is more like a ... rumor they started themselves. Everyone knows it's happening, but no one's been able to prove it. It'd be pretty stupid of them to leave evidence around, and even though they're top students, they're also pretty immature."

"You don't even have a *clue* who the fifth King could be?"

She leans in conspiratorially. "I think his name is Zayn. But I'm not sure. Sylvian wouldn't tell me."

"But he played? I mean, he really played this game and even *won*?"

179

"Please don't judge me for still being in love with him," she begs, her eyes pleading. "He and Clarisse were why I watched. All I cared about last year was that Sylvian didn't touch any of the queens. That was the only thing that was important to me... I know." She buries her face in her hands. "I'm repenting. Really. But I know I'm no better than they are."

"Hey," I say gently and pull her hand down. "What you describe would make any normal person freeze up. All these atrocities trigger fears in us. And you have to summon the courage to face those fears first. You've done that. I mean, you're sitting in front of me now. You're helping me. You're the *only one* on this *fucking campus* helping any of us. You're a heroine in my book."

"I love hearing that from you, but no." Harper pats her cheeks, presumably to stop herself from crying. "I was born into this world and will always be a part of it. That's the only choice I have if I don't want to disown my family. Yes, I'll try to stand by your side. Maybe it'll be less cruel if Sylvian doesn't play this year."

"He's really the worst of them?"

She purses her lips. "He won, didn't he? In other words, he surpassed even Jaxon in his sadism. What he just said to you at the door, that I don't know the whole truth, he's right. But that doesn't change the fact that the scholarship students who won in the last few years seem dead inside to me. Not to mention those who almost died by suicide..."

"Suicide?" I ask breathlessly. *And I slept with him? Oh God.*

Harper's face goes pale. "That's what they say. Two of them tried to kill themselves last year ..."

"Wow." I lean back and feel the urge to hurt the Kings rise inside me. What have the scholarship students ever done to them that the Kings have to be *so* cruel?

Even though Harper's revelations show me once again that I'm not welcome at Kingston and that it'll be virtually impossible to have a normal college life, I can't give up now.

What she says only fuels my desire to put the Kings in their place.

Surely they have a weakness I can exploit to hurt them in turn.

Can I perhaps even ... compete with them?

JAXON

N o, you can't. No one can compete with us. We're nothing but a bunch of bored, self-important dicks. We're dedicated to pursuing our goals.

My own personal goal is fucking over my father and his idiotic foundation until he has nothing.

Don't blame me for saying so, Belle, but you're nothing but a toy.

An irrelevant little chess piece in a much larger conflict full of intrigue, hate, and betrayal.

And if I don't want you to win, I won't let you win.

It doesn't matter how well Sylvian plays.

14

JAXON

I inhale the smoke from my cigar. My signet ring reflects the sparkling lantern light from the lawn as do the dazzling evening dresses of the students gallivanting around the garden.

Resting my forearms on the balustrade of my balcony, I watch each luxury car intently as it arrives.

"Anything else I can do for you, Jax?" this random bitch who just finished blowing me asks as she clutches my Givenchy shirt with her long fingernails.

"Get lost."

She looks at me incredulously, shocked I would demand only that. *But she couldn't stop me thinking of you, either, which makes her useless.*

With a dramatic howl, she stomps across the bedroom and out the door.

It's not really *my* bedroom. Barely a night has passed with me alone in this room. If it's not Sylvian nodding off on the couch, it's Zayn, too stoned to find his own room once he's done studying. I used to take any girl on campus that I wanted to bed, but that vice is wearing thin.

I know I can have any of them and I'm tired of seeing that truth in their eyes over and over again.

I miss the challenge.

I miss the game.

Even the normal game, the game between man and woman, cat and mouse, victory and defeat. Even if I treated every fucking one of them like shit, they'd still let me knock them up. Hell, I *do* treat them like shit. Every single one. I'm an asshole, a mean fucker who lies as easily as I breathe, and they still let me fuck them. Beg for it, even.

Every single bitch. But you won't, will you?

"Who are you waiting for?" Reece leans on the balustrade next to me, taking in the Rolls-Royce that just pulled up.

I take a sip and sprinkle ash over one of the peasants walking below us. Some of them are too stupid to realize how much I hate them.

"Oh, I can tell you exactly who." Sylvian joins me on my other side, lighting a cigarette.

"About five-seven, big tits, heart-shaped ass, always wearing a ponytail?" asks Zayn. He's standing next to Sylvian, wearing one of our masks and holding the bottle of whiskey I just poured myself a glass of.

Romeo, also masked, appears at Reece's side. "I know exactly which one you mean."

"As always, you know just what I'm thinking." I straighten up, resting my hands on the parapet. My kingdom is spread out beneath me. The entire fucking university at my feet. "I'm not waiting for our Dole in particular, though. I'm waiting for the game to begin."

Our game.

Our sick, perverted, ingenious game.

The game that crowned me.

The game that allows me to control everything.

Me and the men at my side.

When a black sedan pulls up, I know it must be the one that

holds Amabelle. The other girls are already in the building. Every single one of them was picked up personally, even though our fraternity house is less than a mile from campus. Nobody walks here. When else would the students have the opportunity to take out their million-dollar cars?

The car door opens, and we remain silent, expectant.

Every one of my Kings is just as fucked up as I am and can't wait for the moment when shit really goes down. I'm sure Amabelle doesn't mean to, but the moment she steps out of the car, the way her slender feet in her high heels extend to alight on the curb, could be a scene from a movie.

You are beautiful.

That's your problem.

Apart from your strong mind, some really entertaining retorts, and your fuckable mouth, you are, first and foremost, beautiful.

The tip of your nose, your rosy cheeks, and your constant attempts to hide yourself from the scrutiny of others. Compared to you, everyone else is just the idea *of a woman. No one else seems to be as real as you are.*

A rare feeling rises within me. I might call it *enchantment*. Except I'm not one to be enchanted, least of all by pathetic whores who let themselves be fed by my father's foundation. This one is... different, though.

Amabelle straightens up the rest of the way, looking at the house uncertainly, and lets the pale swathe of fabric that makes up the skirt of her dress fall to drape over her hips. Harper did a great job and turned our little Dole into a swan.

Her pretty features are even more striking now.

Her hair cascades over her shoulders, framing her tempting cleavage.

If she was fuckable before, she seems almost too precious to simply screw now.

Of course, Harper couldn't stop Amabelle from coming. None of the scholarship students has ever been deterred from accepting the thousand dollars they receive to attend our party. Harper probably *wanted* Amabelle to accompany her, anyway. I can't remember a single party that Harper didn't attend last year. And if she really has fallen out with Clarisse, she needs someone else to pretend to be her friend, doesn't she?

The daughter of the chief justice emerges from the car behind Amabelle, but I don't pay her any mind.

My eyes remain on the little princess who doesn't yet know what's in store for her.

You've piqued everyone's interest, Belle. You're stubborn, strong-willed, and bold. It started getting dangerous when Sylvian got within a mile of you. Reece also seems to be enthralled by you.

But piquing my interest is deadly, Belle.

Deadly.

Her eyes dart across the lawn. We really should call this place a palace. It would fit better. The main building has two wings and twenty rooms the size of hotel suites. A few groups have formed in front of the pillars holding up the veranda. Not a single one isn't looking at her. They all look at her, just like we do.

Shrinking under their attention, Amabelle walks toward the house.

It's lovely to watch the blood rise to your cheeks. Is that what fascinates Sylvian so much? He is addicted to a beating heart. Addicted to your strong pulse.

And it's rare that I don't enjoy the same things he does.

I take another deep drag and let the smoke escape from my mouth.

"Well," Reece begins. "Has anyone made up their mind yet?"

"I'll take Rachel." Zayn holds the bottle to his lips and lets the whiskey trickle down his throat. "At least she's not going to read her feminist manifesto to me."

Reece raises an eyebrow. He doesn't seem enthusiastic. Not about Zayn choosing Rachel, nor his derogatory remark about Amabelle.

I try not to let my excitement show as I continue to watch her. She follows confident Harper with shy steps. With every second, she seems to want to enter the building less.

That's right. Your instincts guide you well.

But can you really defend yourself?

Her gaze flits over the large fraternity sign, Rho Chi Alpha framed by a lion, and then finds us. She falters. Freezes. Perhaps she's thinking about the wisdom of turning back.

I toast her and smile.

And in that moment, when she can do nothing but return my gaze, torn between the conflicting feelings that pass over her face in turn, I know I want her.

I want her more than I have wanted anyone before her.

I want to hold her neck in my hands.

I want to taste her heavy breathing.

I want her to lie underneath me and beg.

I want to hear you beg, Belle.

I want you in tears, begging for me to stop.

This is entirely different from any other time.

This is worse.

Deeper.

Harder.

After realizing that Amabelle is no longer following, Harper returns and grabs her arm. She glances up at us, too, then grimaces and pulls Amabelle along with her.

I think I know where this storm inside me comes from. Your eyes shine for all of us. You're not satisfied with just one. You want us. You want to taste the concentrated power of the Kings. Feel it.

Suffer it. That's the thing, isn't it? You wouldn't be able to choose.

Not even with a gun pressed to your temple.

At least not yet.

I don't care about any of it. The fucking game or the fucking rules. There's more between us. More attraction than I ever dared to hope for. The idea of chasing all the peasants out of my house so we can devote ourselves to the one true queen inspires me. Immensely so.

"Alright," says Zayn, waving the bottle in his hand. "You'll just have to fight over who gets her."

I roll my eyes. "What?"

"You all like her, Jax," he says with a shrug. "She's a pathetic bitch from the slums, but you stare at her like she's Princess Diana's daughter. Do you want me to prepare lots?"

My left eyelid twitches. *Why does it bother me when he calls you a bitch? Why do I want to be the only one allowed to do that?*

"None of us are using her as a piece this year." Sylvian pushes himself off the balustrade and leans against the old-fashioned glass of the balcony door. Hands in his pockets, keeping his distance again. Can I guess what's coming next? I can, and for some reason, I'm curious.

Even more curious than I was before.

It'd be damn boring to play the same game with you that we play with everyone else.

Imagine us pushing you around the board now that Harper's told you everything and you know exactly what's going on. Where's the fun in that?

Where's the mystery?

"Zayn has a point," Sylvian says.

Reece laughs. "Never expected to hear those words out of your mouth! You agree with Zayn, of all people?"

"Drawing lots won't help us. We know Mable has the most

potential either way. Whoever gets her as a queen will win. We're agreed on that, aren't we?"

Zayn raises an eyebrow, but the rest of us agree with Sylvian.

You're strong, Belle. Stronger than any of the others. If you had just one King behind you, you could destroy the world. All those other bitches in your dorm would fold immediately if four out of five Kings turned on them. You wouldn't.

We're well aware of that.

And so is Sylvian.

"I have a better idea," he says.

"An idea to make our bet even more interesting?" I ask. *I'm getting more and more excited to find out who you'll pick.*

"Yeah." Sylvian lights his next cigarette, mischief dancing in his eyes. I see myself reflected in them, my other half, the monster that can barely be controlled. "Our bet won't work if we play chess with the scholarship students as usual. Even if Romeo gets Mable as his queen, she knows too much."

"What do you suggest then?" Zayn asks critically.

Sylvian takes a deep drag and exhales until he's engulfed in clouds of smoke. "Let's not play chess this year."

"What then?" I ask.

"Let's open an arena."

When he looks me in the eye and the corners of his mouth twist into a devilish smile, I know he's been thinking up rules that surpass even his usual depravity in this game. But are the rules really made for us?

Or are they made for you, Belle?

JAXON

You want to trick us, Belle. You think that you can beat us if you take the money and run.

Well, I look forward to proving you wrong. I'll make you greedy for me, addicted to me. I'll feed your craving until you stand before me naked and hungry and begging me to destroy you.

And then I'll show you that it's better not to try to trick Jaxon Tyrell.

15

MABLE

Harper kidnapped me after my last lecture of the day. I couldn't stop her from dragging me to her apartment. Now I'm sitting on the fluffy armchair next to her vanity and letting her do my hair.

She mutters to herself as she works. Something between "You'll show them" and "Now *you're* the fairest of them all." I can't take her seriously. Next to Harper, I still look like a pigeon next to a swan, and I'm sure any improvement she manages to make will be due to her makeup skills alone. Her hazel eyes dart over my face, scrutinizing me as she applies stroke after stroke with her brush.

After I got my invitation to Jaxon's party, we discussed why I absolutely want to go.

She offered to just give me a thousand dollars.

I told her that the point was it's *Jaxon's* money. I'm not going to take it and buy myself something. I don't need that. I'll donate it and do something good with *his* money.

Harper only half understood why that appealed to me, but eventually she agreed as long as she was at least allowed to dress me up.

I went along with it without knowing what to expect.

Once she's put some high heels on my feet, she finally lets me get up from the chair, and I stagger more than walk toward the mirror.

A four-poster bed the size of my dorm room takes up a considerable part of her stately suite. A desk decorated with family photographs is on the opposite wall, two armchairs are arranged around a fashionable coffee table, and a huge chandelier hangs from the ceiling.

Her—walk-in—closet is larger than the shared bathroom in my building, and her vanity is piled high with makeup products from brands I've never even heard of.

Harper watches me from the side as I step in front of the mirror. I look like them. Like Harper. Like Clarisse. A perfect elite doll. The woman looking at me seems to be making the same movements as I am, but she can't have anything to do with me.

"Well? Do you like it?" Harper asks.

I open my mouth, and so does the woman in the mirror. It's just that my lips are no longer my lips, now plump and painted in a nude shade that harmonizes with my highlighted cheekbones and long lashes. The overall effect is flawless in a way my face has never been.

The cream-colored evening dress Jaxon sent to all the scholarship students with the invitation is less sexy than I expected. It sort of makes me look like the heiress of a royal house at her debutante ball.

As if I didn't resemble a member of the English royal family at her wedding quite enough, Harper slips a tiara into my hair.

"You'll have to wear this tonight. At least you do if you really want the money, which, as I said, you don't—"

"I've always wanted to wear a tiara." I don't mean it quite as ironically as it comes out.

I do look like a princess.

Like the woman I was never allowed to be and never can be.

I think of my mom, who used to tell me that we were rich once, richer even than people like Harper. I stopped taking her fantasies seriously at some point, but there was a time when I believed her.

Back then, it roused all my naive, girlish fantasies and I dreamed of a prince who'd rescue me from the trailer park as his lost love. He'd take me back to the castle where I really belonged.

But it was just a dream, nothing more.

The only princes I know turned out to be dark kings with a penchant for bullying people to death.

A town car picks us up. It's not the stretch type like the one Jaxon used to abduct me, but the kind that politicians, among other people, use. I don't know if I could've climbed into a limo without suffering a flashback. The night in the forest wasn't that long ago and it all started in that damn luxury car ...

The dress, the tiara, the note about the town car, and a list of instructions were all in a box that Jaxon had delivered to my room. If I want the thousand dollars, I have to comply with the items on the list. Well, I've earned money in harder ways before.

It's silly, but I'm also somewhat glad I don't have to walk across campus in these high heels. I'm just as grateful that Harper is coming with me. If I'm quite honest with myself, I wouldn't have dared to brave the party without her. With her, I'm strong. I can laugh at the bullies' pranks and Jaxon's arrogance. I can refuse to take Reece seriously and forget about Sylvian.

But whenever I'm alone… when I'm walking across campus alone, going to lectures alone, buying food alone, then I feel insecure. I feel like a target. Everyone's staring at me, and I hate that feeling more than any other.

It's just a few minutes' drive before we climb out of the car in front of the Kings' stately fraternity house.

Columns support the triangular roof, which is reminiscent of Greek architecture. A huge veranda leads around the main building and stone gargoyles adorn the entrances.

Two wings are attached to the central part of the house, where the entrance hall, decorated for the occasion, is located. All together the structure forms a U-shape and I can imagine the garden behind the three-floor building is enormous.

The lawn in front of the house is lively already, at least until I approach.

I hate being the center of attention like this.

Will this ever end?

I turn my gaze to the Greek letters, the Rex emblem, chiseled into the brickwork above the entrance to avoid having to look at the faces of those staring at me. The trick of staring back obviously only works when I'm in an opium-drenched room and my inhibition threshold is somewhat lower.

Above the emblem, five figures stand on a balcony, and I falter when I recognize three of them.

Jaxon, Sylvian, and Reece. Two other faces are covered by bizarre black-and-gold masks, sending an icy chill down the back of my neck.

They're the same masks as the ones I saw in the chapel.

Five figures.

A bound woman in the chair.

It all snaps into place, and yet the overall picture still isn't fitting together. With everything I know by now, however, I'm certain Jaxon was there that night. Presumably the other Kings, too.

Jaxon's smug smile tells me he thinks I'm here for the money. He believes I can't wait to snatch up his stupid handouts to buy myself food or other necessities.

No. The fact that his father's foundation is supporting me and I have no choice but to accept that money is enough. I won't take a single dollar from the Tyrells beyond that. Not for myself anyway.

"Come on." Harper grabs my arm to pull me toward the huge

building's entrance. "Just ignore them. That's the worst punishment for them."

Is it? I wonder, not sure if that's true. What if the Kings lash out when they don't get someone's attention the way they want?

As soon as the door opens, we're greeted by loud music.

"Baby!" a guy just inside shouts drunkenly, spreading his arms for Harper. She brushes past him as if he doesn't even exist, though. As soon as I cross the threshold, I gasp for air. Let's hope the rooms aren't *full of opium* again.

"This is your first frat party, Mable," Harper whispers in my ear with excitement as she links her arm with mine. "Try to enjoy it, will you? If it weren't for the Kings, we could have the best time. You look great. Look, everyone's watching you."

I don't tell her that I already know what that feels like. A path opens up in front of us and I feel like I'm in a distorted version of *Mean Girls*, where Lindsay Lohan fell into a trash can during a performance. Harper beams by my side, and everyone is watching me. Really, actually, everyone.

The crowd parts in the corridor and we stop in front of a long, old-fashioned counter. Harper grabs two shot glasses off one of the trays being carried around the room and hands one to me.

"Say..." I study the young men holding the trays. "Aren't those students from my dorm?"

Harper follows my gaze. "The waiters? Sure. The Kings use them for their parties all the time when they don't have more important tasks for them."

"More important tasks? You mean when they're not supposed to make another scholarship student's life hell?"

She nods, as if we were having nothing but a casual chat and empties her shot glass. "Trust me, you don't want to stay sober," she says, patting my shoulder. "Let's have a little fun, pocket your money, and get out of here."

"Speaking of money," a man says behind us.

Harper spins around to look at a tall, muscle-bound athlete. Between all the staring faces, his looks warm and friendly. He almost reminds me of home.

She raises her voice and snaps at him as if he attacked her personally. "I'm certainly not paying to accompany Mable to this party, Vance! Jaxon's lucky I came in the first place!"

Vance raises an eyebrow almost imperceptibly. His gaze slides over me. "What's lucky about that?" I recognize his voice from somewhere. "This time last year, you would've been drunk and naked already. Though that seems to be firmly in the past."

"I'll take the thousand dollars for being here," Harper snaps. "Questions?"

Vance smiles wryly. "You're not wearing a tiara."

Harper snorts, unfastens her bracelet and pins it in her hair with two clips, turning it into a sort of golden diadem. "Happy?"

Vance shrugs. "That'll do, yes." That said, he once again disappears into the crowd.

I'm blushing a little. Even though I was never into the jocks at my high school, I find myself following Vance's athletic body with my eyes. If my college life were normal, if I could *think* about who I found attractive, maybe I'd talk Harper into introducing me.

Would have, if, but, maybe.

My college life is not normal.

"I hate that guy."

"Why?" I ask innocently, trying to hide the fact that I want to learn more about Vance.

"Because he could be a real king."

She doesn't explain and I don't dare ask. The last thing I want to do is fall for another king.

Harper takes my hand in hers to lead me into the next room. The furnishings remind me of an old manor house from the movies. Heavy tapestries, old-fashioned picture frames, landscape paintings, parquet flooring, and tufted leather upholstery. The rooms are crowded, and all of this feels a bit more like a student party than the party in the Crescents' glass villa did.

There's even beer pong.

"This is the second and the last party I'm going to this term," Harper explains, finishing another shot she grabbed from a tray as we walked. "Vance is right: I was drunk too often last year and didn't study enough. You'll feel the same way. Once you have your first midterm exams, you won't be able to breathe until after finals in December."

I glance around the room, noting a single person who isn't staring at me.

Clarisse.

She's just a few steps away as a man approaches her. Slender, masculine hands wrap around the back of her head, tenderly grasping her hair and pulling her toward their owner.

He leans down. Kisses her. It's a hard, dominant kiss that breaks something inside me.

Fuck.

I don't have the slightest reason to feel anything of the sort. I hate the Kings, and I hate Jaxon most of all. More than ever since I know what they've done to the scholarship girls the last few years. *What they're planning to do to me, too.* And yet, jealousy sneaks into my heart, as if I really would like to be the one he pulls against himself like that.

I haven't run into any of her clique on campus in the last few weeks. Some attempted to play tricks on us, and everyone treated us like dirt wherever we went, but the Kings and Clarisse, and pretty much all the senior students in general, left us scholarship students alone. I'm sure it must be because studying in Kingston is just so damned demanding. Even if I *wanted to* play tricks on someone, I simply wouldn't have the time.

Since the early days of September, I've either been sitting in the library late into the night or waiting tables. Some days I get up at six in the morning to prepare for lectures when I didn't manage my entire workload the night before. Studying distracts me from waiting to be attacked by one of the male scholarship students, as well as from the question of what I would do if I met Sylvian in an empty corridor.

Or Jaxon.

Or Reece.

Fortunately, that hasn't happened. So far.

"Don't look at him or he'll notice you," Harper warns me, but it's like a magical attraction.

How could I look away?

How could I ever be indifferent to him?

The signet ring on Jaxon's right ring finger sends a reflection across the room as he grips Clarisse's blonde mane of hair tightly and looks over her head with glowing eyes.

At me.

I clench my jaw as if magnets were pulling my teeth together, while an unhealthy feeling dances in my stomach. I feel anger, envy, and shame, but one feeling overshadows everything.

Yearning.

"Harper, let's go," I say.

"Sure, let's put as much space between Clarisse and me as possible."

Is it really yearning that I feel? Maybe it's just hormones because he's hot?

I'm not thinking about sex, though.

I'm thinking about Jaxon's agonizingly smug smile, about sitting there, hands on his shoulders, in his lap, as he just looks at me...

I will turn you into a whore.

"Hi, how are you doing?" Brittany appears in front of us out of nowhere, beaming at us girlishly with her big, pretty eyes. She's wearing the same evening dress I am. "Mable, do you even know how adorable you look?" she asks me tipsily as the music gets louder with every beat. "I mean, I like your style and all, but this dress looks best on you out of all of us!" She giggles. "Stupid, isn't it? That we have to wear something like this? Rachel is totally pissed off, but she says she's never earned a thousand dollars more easily!"

That's what I said.

Brittany brushes her blonde hair back with her fingers. Her makeup and her overall appearance look a lot less glamorous. She's from Texas. In contrast to me, she went to a regular high school, has a regular family, regular siblings, and a regular life. "Are you coming to join us?"

As we follow her, I glance back into the lounge. Jaxon is watching me, and I suddenly wish I could allow myself to drink a few more shots.

But I shouldn't do that.

I can't drink my courage, I can't afford the hangover tomorrow because I still have a paper on my desk that I need to finish for next week. And anyhow, I have to face Jaxon without the intoxicating effects of alcohol.

His eyes are as blue as ice crystals, and that ice seems to be settling on my shoulder blades and melting slowly. The cold is eating its way through the heat in my chest. It sobers me up. Jaxon is a proper motherfucker.

A cocky, disgustingly rich son of a bitch who thinks that money will buy him everything. I'm disgusted that I enjoyed his touch for so much as a second. I hold his gaze without flinching, twist my lip into a snide curl, and raise my middle finger at him.

The laughter on his features is minimal, but it twinkles in his beautiful—no, no, not beautiful!—eyes. My resolve crumbles, my resistance wanes, and I'm wondering if it would help to walk up to him and punch him in the face when Harper grabs my hand and drags me along with her.

"Stop it!" she hisses. "Stop challenging him. Stop trying to annoy him! Just stop looking at him at all!"

I can't, I want to say. But I'm too ashamed that I'm succumbing to Jaxon's pull, and it makes me keep my mouth shut. As we walk to the door across the room, I still feel his eyes on me. The sensation of an icy breath climbing up between my shoulder blades and settling there.

Relieved that we're leaving Jaxon behind, I focus on picking my way through the crowd.

Brittany leads us to the others.

There are fewer people in the next room, which makes it feel more relaxed. Bookshelves and blue velvet armchairs line the walls. The ceiling is high, opening into a corridor on the second floor on one side. Students are chatting in groups up there, too. The wood-paneled room could be cozy without the antlers and taxidermy staring down at us from all sides. The cold feeling on the back of my neck doesn't go away.

Rachel and Kady are surrounded by three athletes. I've been so busy looking out for the Kings, I didn't even think about the fact that there are *other* guys at this university.

"Hey! It's good to see you, Mable!" Kady is waving at me cheerfully. "Have you met Andrew and Jordan yet?"

We shake hands.

It's the first time one of the other students has been friendly to me. Apart from the professors, scholarship students, Reece, and Harper, no one has been *normal* to me.

Harper hangs back.

"You really do look incredible in that dress!" In contrast to Kady, who chats away cheerfully, Rachel remains aloof.

Her disapproving gaze falls on Harper, and I get the vague feeling that a conflict is brewing.

Even though the scholarship students are some of the few people in the room who don't make me feel inadequate, I'm not going to let them exclude Harper. *Should we be just as awful as the rich kids? We have to show them how to be better...*

"Hey, Dole!" Someone taps me on the shoulder, making me whirl around.

It's Clarisse. She stands in front of me in a sexy, extravagant dress that turns her stunning figure into a work of art, staring me down. Harper moves in front of me, but Clarisse treats her to a scathing look. "Stand aside, H, I don't want to talk to you."

"Just get out!" Harper hisses at Clarisse, who proceeds to ignore her. She's accompanied by an escort of equally beautiful blonde women who stare at me and Harper with hostility.

"You think you're special, don't you?" she asks me in a condescending tone. Her beautiful features contort in an arrogant grimace. I'm not surprised this is the type of woman Jaxon likes. "Let me make one thing clear to you: You're not. You are no better or worse than the other charity cases at this university. You're irrelevant and unworthy. All of you! Be grateful our parents fund the places you occupy here despite the fact that you're entirely undeserving. You need to understand that it's up to *us* whether you continue to study here."

"What are you actually trying to tell me?" I ask.

She comes closer, voice dropping a few decibels. "Stay away from Jaxon. Do not come within a mile of him! If I see you *dare* to insult him, in *any* manner, again, I'll cut off your middle finger. Got that? If you think tonight is the perfect time to show the world that you're not worthless, you're wrong. You are *fucking* worthless. Don't you ever question that again." Her mouth twists into an ugly sneer and her long blonde hair hits my face as she twirls around and leaves the room with her escort behind her.

"You were friends with her?" Rachel asks from behind, turning to Harper.

Harper's face is pale, her slim hands clenched into fists. "Excuse me, Mable..." she mutters, before running off in the opposite direction.

I watch her go with mixed feelings. Should I follow her? My friends in Philadelphia are all a lot older than me. If they wanted to be alone, they wanted to be left alone, and they didn't believe in going after people.

How does Harper feel about that, though?

Uncertainly, I remain where I am and chat with the other scholarship students. We quickly forget about Clarisse. Jaxon, Reece, and even Sylvian have treated me to much nastier threats and insults.

First and foremost, I'm at Kingston and have to focus on my studies.

On making new friends.

On having fun. On recharging my batteries to cope with the workload.

Jaxon doesn't matter.

Clarisse doesn't matter.

Nothing matters.

My future is the only thing that matters. My degree. The college itself.

The athletes ask us to dance, and since I can't find Harper, I go with them. The moment we turn toward the center of the room, however, the music turns off. A sudden buzz of conversation fills the space like a bee's nest and then becomes quieter as the lights dim.

Gradually, we're enveloped in total darkness until a spotlight is switched on and pointed in our direction. Then another one joins it. And another one.

Five white circles of light catch us in the end.

"Do you know what this is about?" I ask the others, none of whom respond. My question sounds loud and clear in a room that's become oppressively quiet. I can handle not being able to see anything because the spotlight is shining right in my face for a few seconds, but then I've had it and I step out of the cone of light and into the shadows. Without warning, someone pushes me back roughly.

"Hey!" I gasp, trying to make out the face of the guy who did it. It's covered. All the faces around us are suddenly covered. Ski masks. Scarves. Dark carnival masks. Everyone's covered their face. My eyes dart past the glaring spotlights and through the crowd in panic until I spot him.

Jaxon.

He's leaning on the parapet on the second floor, relaxed, looking down at me. His intense gaze rivets me in place, while his stony face bears no resemblance to the man who laughed at my middle finger not too long ago.

An icy smile appears on his lips as he also pulls out a mask and puts it on. The mask covers his face down to his lips, gilded on the cheekbones and modelled eyebrows and covering his entire forehead.

A voice comes from the speakers all around us. "Sit down!"

All the other women in the circle obey and sit immediately. I remain where I am, standing. What the hell is this?

"Sit down." A guy bursts out of the crowd to push me into the blue velvet armchair at my back.

I brace myself against him, but he brutally presses my arms onto the armrests.

"Play along," he murmurs in my ear, making me shudder. "Trust me and just play along."

Sylvian.

I stop resisting. *The game begins.* The thought rings in my ears. *This is the game, and it starts now. It's just like Harper said. Can I trust Sylvian? Will he protect me from the others just as Harper does?*

Once I feel the velvet of the seat under my half-naked legs, reverent silence returns. I interlace my fingers nervously. The many eyes on me seem to burn into my skin. Every single glance produces tiny stabs, as if they were weapons aimed at me.

"Welcome back to Kingston University." My eyes shoot up. Even though the voice from the speakers is distorted, I'm sure it's Jaxon speaking. But I can no longer see his mask.

Cheers erupt in response to his words and die down as he continues.

"You're all here because you expect great things."

"YEEAH!" The crowd roars and most of the masked people in front of me raise their fists in the air.

"You want to play, play for life and for blood!"

"YEEAH!" The roar gets louder.

"And you want to win!"

The whole room goes wild, and the voice from the speakers falls silent until the crowd has calmed again.

"How about a game of truth or dare?"

One simple question and the building seems to burst into pieces. All the students in the room cheer, stomp, and clap until the voice rings out again.

"Take them to the stage!"

At that command, the spotlights move aimlessly above our heads. Several strong men grab at each of us. I'm not resisting yet. In a way, I'm ready, and if I leave now, I can't stand with the others.

The "stage" they take us to is in the next room, a platform with five chairs arranged on it. This room is huge as well, so the crowd of masked students can easily follow us inside.

The hands that drag us along push each of us into a chair. We all stay where we're put, for which I'm grateful. I hope this nonsense will end more quickly if we submit to it.

"Truth or dare..." Jaxon, disguised as a phantom, appears right in front of us, swinging himself onto the platform and strutting along the narrow parapet, far above the heads of everyone else. Looking at Jaxon wearing that mask, with everything I know about him so far, makes me squeeze the seat of my chair tight. I'm not going to think about what Harper said happened last year. Or about him abandoning me in the forest or how things could get much worse than that. I won't.

"Once again, ten places were awarded to students who have never paid a single cent to this university. That's a bitter *truth*, isn't it?"

Jaxon's words are followed by approving applause from the audience.

"What makes these ten men and women so special that they don't even have to pay to study here?" Jaxon clearly seems to enjoy the entertainer's role. "Our parents and our parents' parents and their parents in turn have worked hard for us to be here today. And then they can't think of anything better to do than give ten places a year to parasites because of so-called political correctness ..."

Female giggling at the back of the audience and male growling further forward.

"These charity cases will take what they can. They're greedy. They think they *deserve* to be here because they were taught in their cheap schools that you can get *something* for *nothing*. They won't thank us for it. They're like poison attacking our ranks and gradually weakening us. They're here to take what is right-fully ours. Once they're successful enough to realize that they, too, won't tolerate being deprived of what they worked hard for over the years, it'll be too late. Only those who aren't thieves themselves, those who take it as a given not to steal from others, understand that taxes and compulsory levies are *robbery*."

The crowd seems to be holding its collective breath so as not to miss a single word from Jaxon's mouth.

"Laziness. Resentment. Envy. The growing clamor for more support, more taxes, more benefits—these are not virtues that belong in Kingston. And yet *they* are here with us." Jaxon points at us as if we're objects on display. As if we belong in a zoo that exhibits poor people who will never belong to the elite. "What will happen twenty years from now? What about fifty? How are they going to feel about giving away their possessions instead of passing them on to their grandchildren? Will they think that's *fair*? Will they then also *agree* to share their wealth with impoverished parasites who have never lifted a finger?"

I clench my jaw. Everything he says infuriates me to no end, even though I fully understand the fundamental issue of taxes and levies. But the point of a fucking scholarship is not to give people like me a chance we don't really deserve. It's about ensuring that students with potential from *all* walks of life can enrich the world with their contributions.

"By the time they're successful enough to understand that they're being robbed just like our families are today, it will be too late. They will have to swallow their own fucking poison. Then it will be *their* children who turn against them because that class knows no honor. It's scum. Scum attending the same lectures as we do."

Tears sting my eyes as the silence breaks and applause and cheers sweep through the room like a storm, strong enough to knock me out. I want to stand up and fight back, say something to refute this rubbish, but I can't. I'm sitting here as if tied to the chair, and I can see that the other four scholarship students feel the same way.

"So... That was the truth," Jaxon concludes, turning around in front of us like a performer, melting into the black phantom mask for a moment and blurring his human shape. "Let's get down to the dares."

My heart thunders in my throat as he turns to us and fixes his eyes on each of us in turn.

"To study at Kingston, your SAT tests are not enough. You need more than your letters of recommendation, the many entrance exams, and the ability to memorize and reproduce knowledge. If you want to be able to hold your own among us, you have to do more than just use your head. You must prove yourselves *worthy*. If we are to admit you to this university—*we*, the ones who *really* decide whether you can study here or you *are stopped* from doing so—then you have to show us *how much you really want it*."

The crowd is muttering. This isn't something Harper told me about. What is Jaxon implying?

"We've prepared a competition for you." His exposed lips twitch, and I don't have to imagine how much he loves letting out the antisocial asshole to pit the five scholarship girls against each other. "You're going to collect points. She who has earned the least on Halloween, after finals in December, before Spring Break, and after finals in May is out. That's only fair, right? You want to prove yourselves. We offer you the chance to do it."

Sarcasm is thick in Jaxon's voice and a few members of the audience laugh spitefully.

Jaxon moves to the side, pointing at the opposite wall. Suddenly, words are projected there.

"Ten points for a term paper," he reads out loud. "You can give

207

something back to those who are here because they can afford to be, not because they have your outstanding intellect. Amabelle gave me this incredibly ingenious idea. You wanted to *give something back*, didn't you?"

I freeze. Not only does everyone in the room stare at me—I'm used to that by now—but I simply have nothing to say. My head is empty. The only thing filling it is anger.

"You will be able to secure a base of points by supporting other students. But don't get caught at it ..."

The crowd laughs while Jaxon paces back and forth in front of us like some kind of ringmaster.

"What's funny about that?" Kady asks next to me, her voice a squeak that triggers another burst of laughter from the crowd.

"Nothing," Jaxon tells her coolly.

"But how are we supposed to do that ..."

Jaxon raises his hand and closes his fingers to indicate that she should remain silent. "You have been accepted to Kingston. On a damn *scholarship*. You have proven that you are currently one of the five smartest women in the United States. A few extra assignments shouldn't be difficult for you, should it?" The phantom turns another circle, flouncing along the wooden balustrade. "You are the reason our exams get harder with every semester. It's no longer enough to be among the best students. Because of your bulimic brains, we have to stuff even more fucking exam content into our heads and vomit it out again."

Murmurs of approval in the back rows.

"Twenty points for a weekly challenge." Another line appears on the opposite wall. "This challenge is for fun more than anything else. Who's prepared to do *anything* to stay at Kingston? Our ancestors were prepared to do anything for it. Are you?"

I dare a glance to my right. Rachel and Brittany look just the way I feel: pale and speechless. They were not ready for the Kings' ruthlessness and are caught off guard by it.

"Thirty points for a *favor*." Jaxon's smile widens into a leering grin. The way he emphasizes the word, that can only mean one thing. "These points are awarded to you by other students. This is about more than just a term paper. It's up to you to decide how many *favors* you can offer and still maintain your studies. Last but not least ..."

A fourth line is projected onto the wall.

Two hundred points for the best grade point average.

"We don't want to disregard the fact that studying at Kingston is about the results you achieve. It wouldn't be right to ignore that." Jaxon solemnly raises his hands and turns to the audience. "There's your *arena*, motherfuckers! Only one can win! Who wants to bet on who it'll be?"

There's a roar of approval. Every single masked student is cheering and clapping. The music comes back on and some of the students actually pull out money and start talking to each other.

Some guy in a mask a lot like Jaxon's, but also covering his mouth, comes on stage. He's dressed in a black shirt, black chinos, and shoes with a gold emblem. The ring on his finger with the Kings' coat of arms must mean he's one of them.

Reece?

Romeo?

Or yet another athletic asshole who thinks he rules the world just because his parents are multimillionaires?

He hands an envelope to each of us. Without opening it, I know what's inside.

A thousand dollars.

I take the money because I want to donate it, but never before has anything felt so humiliating...

JAXON

What did you think of the show, princess? Did you believe my act?

I can be an asshole if I put some effort into it, can't I?

But don't worry about that.

Everything I said was a lie.

I don't think you're particularly clever or even reasonably intelligent. But I do think you're sure to impress us. Aren't you?

16

MABLE

en points for a term paper.
Twenty points for a challenge.
Thirty points for sex.
Two hundred points for the best grade point average.

The words are still shining on the wall across from us, driving home that we're nothing but entertainment for the richest of the rich. No more, no less.

As if, even after all our hard work to get here, we're only good for their entertainment.

As some sort of amusement for each of them.

I tremble as I rise from my chair.

"Mable!" Harper climbs onto the platform to grasp my upper arm. "I'm so incredibly sorry. I'm so sorry!"

"Did you know about this?" I ask her dully. I still don't quite want to believe that that list is anything more than a party gag. It must be another prank.

Harper looks at me like a sad smiley face with a guilty conscience. "No, of course I didn't!" She pulls me down from the platform. "I'll be helping you. With everything!"

"Thank you. That's really nice of you," I say, trying to keep my footing. It's all too much for me. Jaxon is too much for me. Sylvian is, too. Having bedded Reece, even though he's in on this shit, is too much. I feel dizzy and nauseous and want to run. I want to run until I stop hurting. My dream of having a normal time at college is shattered. It's all spelled out for me now. Everyone in the room is just waiting for me to get on board with the points system, to prostitute myself.

What Harper told me sounded bad.

But it sounded like bad bullying, like something I could get through with enough support.

Now, however, all the other scholarship students have become my enemies.

We were pushed onto a playing field and pitted against each other. The Kings themselves are no longer the weapons.

We are.

After all I've already gone through in my life ... After everything that's happened. My mom. Her lovers who were more interested in me than in her. Olive, who I had to leave behind in hope of being able to make a better future for us.

Everything is bearing down on me, making me want to run away. I'm not strong enough for this. I can't stand up to the Kings because they'll always be able to come up with something new no matter what I do. I know that for certain.

"Let's go somewhere quiet so we can talk about this, okay?" Harper leads me through the crowd, but I'm not quite here. I *can't* be here. None of this is real. It's so ridiculous it *has* to be a joke.

"What do you want to talk about? How I'm going to survive in the arena?"

She presses her lips together and I see pity in her eyes. Endless compassion.

I don't want her pity and I don't want *her* as a friend. Not as an ally. Because I can't even see through who she pretends to be to who she really is.

She's in love with Sylvian?

She was friends with Clarisse?

She knows Reece, Jaxon, and all the others?

Can a person change *so much* in just a few days?

Surely not.

But if there's one thing I've learned in the last two weeks at this cursed university, it's that this isn't about what *I* want.

Harper pushes me toward a door, opens it, and maneuvers me through. We end up in a tiny, old-fashioned bathroom.

She pushes me onto the toilet seat and sighs heavily. "I can imagine how you feel."

"You really can't."

"It's so completely awful and stupid. Total childish garbage, isn't it?"

"Except we're in college."

She gives a theatrical nod. "You're so lucky, Mable. This new version of the game is so much better than the sort I know."

I stare at her, trying not to throw up. How can she say something like that?

"Last year..." Harper goes pale in the face and nervously runs her fingers through her beautifully coiffed hair. "Last year, the scholarship students didn't know what was going on at all. They *really* didn't have a clue. The bets still happened, but in the background. People were betting on who would win. The prize was a jet. A ... private jet. Including pilot, fees, refueling for the next five years ... So that's something that even people ..."

"Something that is interesting even for people who will inherit a fortune," I finish her sentence in a flat voice.

She looks devastated. She seems embarrassed by even belonging to that group of people. "Yes." For a moment, all I can hear is the thumping bass of the music.

"And they wear masks so..."

"So nobody can film them when they're going on like that. No one can accumulate any evidence. Or maybe they just love not having to show their ugly faces for once." She tries to make me laugh, but that won't work.

"Why isn't anyone doing anything about this? No one at all?" I whisper. I feel powerless and entirely broken. I know that I will persevere because I have persevered all my life. But just thinking about how these rich idiots are using me for their games is exhausting.

"I don't know!" Harper says, tears welling in her eyes as she drops into a crouch in front of me. She leans against the door, batting her full eyelashes and looking down. "I think there was someone. I don't know who it was. But there's a rumor that one of the scholarship students took the Kings' machinations to the outside world and ... and she was never seen again."

I feel like I'm choking. "She disappeared?" I ask tonelessly.

"She's probably... dead?"

Maybe for the first time, my world really is falling apart. No matter how often I've felt this way before, it was nothing compared to what I'm going through now.

"I don't know for sure of course," Harper whispers, so quietly I can barely hear her. "But what else could've happened to her?"

Darkness envelops me like an inescapable truth, a fact from which I can't possibly escape. "Do they really have it in them to kill someone?" I breathe.

"I don't know, Mable. I don't think so, but ..."

"Damn, if you can't rule it out for sure, why are you in love with one of them, huh?" I snap. I want to take those words back immediately. It's unfair. And maybe I said it out of jealousy more than anything else. Jealousy that's as out of place as I am at this party, in a tiny bathroom with a tiara in my hair.

Harper flinches and looks down. "I never said Sylvian was a

good guy. On the contrary. But as sick as Jaxon and Reece and Romeo are, with Sylvian I always felt..."

Yes. That feeling that two hearts beat in his chest. He tried to protect me. To stop me from staying.

"Compared to last year, this will be better. You know what you're up against. It's going to be so much easier, believe me." Harper smiles at me confidently. "I think Jaxon changed the rules of the game to make it more interesting for the players. Maybe he thinks it'd be boring if you already knew what was happening because I told you. Or maybe he doesn't want what happened last year ..."

"To happen again?" I ask, coldly.

"The thing about Jaxon is, he can be so damn nice that you think he's an ... angel or something. He was around a lot last year, because of Clarisse, you know? And because Sylvian and I ... Sometimes I wondered how someone like him could come up with such horrible games. The same goes for Reece. If I didn't know that every word he said was a lie, I'd ask if he wanted to be best friends forever." Harper gives a teary chuckle. "That's why you have to listen to me and *never* get involved with any of them."

The idea of sleeping with one of the Kings is still arousing. Harper probably considers sex a sacrifice where women surrender part of themselves. In her mind, the woman probably has to have *feelings* about it. Should men really be proud that they can screw any woman they want? Even if she's just selling them her body?

I don't share those thoughts with Harper. She wouldn't understand, and she seems entirely fixated on trying to help me with this points issue. She rummages around in her bag. "The entire campus is monitored by everyone. They'll be watching you, always with phones in hand to film anything that happens around you. It's like *Gossip Girl*, you know?"

"That's what you meant by Big Brother."

"Yes. There's an inner circle, that's who gets invited to these parties, but you can also qualify for it by playing along or uploading videos. You're going to have a lot of stalkers, and that alone will probably be terrible."

"Great," I mumble. *Stalkers. Rich bastards who'll keep a phone camera on me at all times. Always observed. Never left alone.* Yep, that sounds absolutely like what Sylvian was trying to warn me about in his cryptic way.

"There's no way to trick this system, okay? That means you'll have to earn points, for better or worse." Harper fishes out an eyeliner and stands in front of the mirror. I can't help but notice the *Sisley* label emblazoned on the pen. How much does the eyeliner she's poised to use like a marker cost? Thirty dollars? Fifty? "You'll get two hundred points just for being the best." She scribbles a two and two zeros on the reflective glass. "I'll help you. You have an ally, and the others don't. I have contacts, they'll help me find you old quizzes, practice exams with sample solutions from last year, project drafts ..."

I just nod. That sounds like good support, which I can certainly use. But why does the entire thing have to take place in a worst-case scenario of my college days?

"I'm sure you can write a few term papers for one or two of them," Harper considers out loud. "But that hooker thing where Jaxon says 'favors' when he means sex... At least a couple girls are going to turn your dorm into a proper brothel."

"Great," I repeat, feeling my stomach constrict with every thought. Will I ever be able to eat normally again?

"And then there are those weekly challenges. I bet they'll intentionally be embarrassing as fuck. On top of that, everyone can participate, which means you won't be able to gain much ground because you'll all get the same number of points."

"Please stop it," I whisper. "Stop talking about this ridiculous point scheme as if it's something that actually matters."

"Okay." Harper shuts her mouth demonstratively and draws a few tens on the mirror above the sink. Underneath, she draws arrows pointing to the word *victory*.

Tears sting in my eyes. I don't want to win at all, and even less so if it means four other scholarship students lose.

"I bet you're wondering how you'll do this on your own, aren't you?" She turns to me, her eyes shining and her cheeks pink. "But you don't have to. I'll be there. I can really make up for what I did wrong last year. Please let me help you. I'll stay right by your side all term if I have to."

"You need to study too, Harper."

"Oh, I have a trust fund I can live off for the rest of my life if I don't get my degree. But you? Between the two of us, who is it more important to succeed in our degree program for? Besides, you're the smarter one. I'm already having issues, and I really hate everything related to the justice system because it *obviously*," she gestures around us, "doesn't do anyone any good."

I should thank her for all she's trying to do. But I feel too empty and too weak to show her any sort of sincere gratitude.

"Let's get out of here," I beg her. "I want to go to bed."

"Oh." She hesitantly caps her eyeliner. "Of course. I thought you might want to ask a few people if they need any favors that have nothing to do with sex while we're here...?"

"No," I interrupt her harshly, straightening and waiting for her to turn around and open the door. "The only favor I'll do anyone is throwing up in their face if I stay here any longer. I don't think I'd get any points for that, would I now?"

JAXON

Y ou impressed them, Belle. Your fearlessness, your reaction to the unknown. The entire university has stopped looking down on you. They're actually looking at you now. I didn't expect you, of all people, to be such a little fighter. Showing us that part of you was your biggest mistake.

I told you what would happen if we liked you.

I warned you so you could choose not to give us what we're looking for.

But you failed.

As sorry as I am for your soul, little girl, you have aroused our interest.

May God grant you the mercy that it wanders very soon.

17

MABLE

In the course of the next few weeks, the early stages of the game pass me by like deep black rain clouds. Every week there's another one of the many challenges in which Lien, Kady, Rachel, and Brittany compete. Since the party, Lien has kept even more of a distance from us than before. I bet she rightfully wonders why she should even pretend to be friends with us.

A new notice is posted on the bulletin board in our kitchen every Monday. The "challenges," which are nothing more than a deliberate embarrassment, and the points attained to date are posted there. Who keeps track of them is a mystery to me. Harper's probably right, and the campus is being monitored by a Big-Brother-like network of malicious gossip. I wonder if there's a referee somewhere who meticulously counts who has done what homework for whom?

Are the Kings themselves keeping an eye on the big picture even?

In any case, there's a flat zero next to my name.

I'm the only one who pretends the "competition" never even started.

It's not that I *couldn't* do it. Rather, I'm not going to be pushed around by a pack of super-rich assholes with too much time on their hands. I don't know exactly *what* I'm doing, but doing nothing seems like a viable solution. I'm just going to wait and see. What'll happen if I just pretend the game doesn't exist?

Rachel and Lien have already reached 430 points each at the end of the month. Since they went to lectures in bikinis, cleaned the entire campus cinema with toothbrushes, and completed a few other weird challenges, the origin of some of those points is clear. The rest?

Well, students are in and out of our dorm like it's actually a brothel.

I can't imagine that my fellow students would allow themselves to be humiliated so much, but ... but I know what people are like. Maybe they even enjoy it? Most of the guys who walk down our corridor are attractive. If I was here to have sex, maybe I'd even be happy to have that many "visitors"? But doing it just to earn points in the Kings' game goes against every principle I have.

Does it really make a difference who you have sex for?

Yes.

It certainly does.

While I've been going to lectures, studying, waiting tables in the evenings, and ignoring the points system, a kind of bubble has formed around me. The staring has not stopped. In fact, it's only gotten worse. I'm always on alert for when these assholes try to trip me. Bump into me. Laugh when I ask a question in an exercise or call me a whore when I participate in a lab. Out of all of them, I'm probably the one this description applies to the least.

The bullying is getting to me more than I like to admit. It's the little things that converge on me at night. From day to day, I find it harder to focus on the content of my lectures. Harper is the only one still talking to me. The other scholarship students keep their distance. They don't understand why I'm not collecting any points. I'm sure they think I believe myself above them.

They couldn't be any more wrong about that...

I don't have any friends to sit with in my classes. The insults hurt. As does the soft hiss when I enter a room. As do the notes stuck to my backpack in passing.

Get out of here.

Too ugly for the game.

Unfuckable.

What's worse is that I haven't been able to make myself attend Reece's tutorial classes. I'm missing content. I don't know if I can pass the class by filling in the gaps on my own and I have no one to ask. I dread having to sit down in front of Reece and look at him. I've realized he was making fun of me just like everyone else.

At least I'm not bumping into Sylvian and Jaxon on campus.

It's a daily battle, but one that I'm still winning. Ignoring what's happening around me is working. The question is only how long I'll be able to keep it up.

***

On Thursday evening, as I'm on my way to Crown's to cover for another waitress who's got an important midterm tomorrow, I notice the unusually large group gathered in the car park. Already paranoid, I fear for a moment that they've come for me, that there's a new prank planned.

Nothing happens, though, and I enter the bar unmolested.

Inside, every seat is taken.

"What's going on?" I ask Derby, who's already pulling beer at full speed.

"It's like this here every Thursday. Be glad I've given you the other days." He presses a full tray into my hands. "On the weekends, these kids have their own parties. Only outsiders are stuck sitting around here. On Thursdays, though, they run us ragged." He winks. "Now hurry up."

After half an hour, I feel like I've run a race. Working as a waitress is nothing like tending bar. At Flavor's, I would collect empty glasses, but never deliver full ones. And they never let me into the VIP area since I wasn't twenty-one yet. I counted myself lucky. After all, they were always carrying heavy bottles and trays full of cocktails in there.

Carrying the many glasses of beer around the room is more exhausting than my other shifts. Completely worn down, I take a short breather behind the counter and have a glass of tap water. At least the students are distracted enough by their boisterous conversations that hardly anyone looks at me twice. They notice me, yes, but they also ignore me. That's much better than being the center of their attention and subject to their ridicule.

"Right, take these to the billiard room."

"The billiard room?"

Derby nods toward an inconspicuous black wooden door, which I'd previously believed led to a storeroom.

He scrutinizes me as if he's wondering whether I'm fit for the job. It can't be because of the four drinks he put on my tray. Three glasses of whiskey and a Coke. The whiskey isn't on the menu. It's one of those drinks that costs more than thirty dollars and varies in price based on vintage.

"What is it?" I ask. "Don't you trust me to carry that expensive whiskey properly? I've just walked through this mess for almost an hour and haven't spilled a drop."

Derby's mind seems elsewhere. "Well, you better not spill anything. Go, now."

I turn away, secretly rolling my eyes as I walk toward the wooden door.

A black curtain waits behind it, and cigar smoke envelops me even before I push it aside. I'm expecting to find a line of sophisticated professors behind the curtain and am praying silently they're not ones I have classes with when I step through and find four figures playing poker in the cloud of smoke.

Romeo notices me first. The moment he looks up, the others' eyes follow.

It's as if I've traveled a century back in time. The room is almost as large as the taproom, which can seat more than fifty students in a pinch, and looks like an old drawing room. Decorative wooden ornamentation graces the ceiling, shelves of leather-bound books line the walls, the armchairs have armrests that are wider than their seats. Plush carpets sporting oriental patterns, oil paintings of men in tailcoats, and a billiard table that not only looks antique with its golden decorations but has to be as expensive as the rest of the room's furnishings put together complete the setup.

Jaxon takes a drag on his cigar before placing it on the table in front of him. His poker hand follows, his signet rings flashing at me. He wears a classic, albeit very loosely buttoned, shirt. Reece is sitting opposite him. He's smoking a joint rather than a cigar and dressed in a polo shirt and light-colored pants. He looks a bit like a model printed on the cover of some preppy magazine, only much... hotter.

Romeo is concealed in the thick smoke, his face as inscrutable and gray as it was the last time I met him. That leaves Sylvian.

He hasn't even turned to face me. He's wearing his leather jacket again and has a cigarette between his lips. He seems uninterested. It's as if we don't know each other at all.

But we do know each other. We've had sex. It seems like ages ago and yet I remember every single second of it.

I've already felt three of the men sitting in front of me. They've reeled me in, overpowered me, made me come or almost so, and just as many have betrayed me. Reece watched as Jaxon drugged me. And Romeo helped him.

All my instincts are screaming "run," but how would I ever explain that to Derby?

Should I even care about that? I can find another job. Someone in the administration would surely be able to use a hard-working student willing to work for a pittance.

"Are you going to finish bringing our drinks to the table or do you want us to come take the tray from you at the door, *Dole*?" The right corner of Jaxon's mouth twitches.

Running now would mean they win. I realize I'm playing with fire, but I'm relying on Sylvian to keep his word to Harper. Even if it's naive to put my trust in that. "Who'll have the Coke?" I ask and step closer, my eyes fixed on the center of the table. Stacks of hundred-dollar bills lie there in a heap. A fortune. They're playing for it, just like that.

"Give it to me, Mable," Sylvian says quietly, and relief washes over me immediately. He sounds nice. Terribly nice, making me feel a lot safer. He'll protect me, won't he?

"You're on a first-name basis already?" Jaxon asks him with a sneer, reaching for one of the whiskeys from my tray. His arrogant smile sends anger coursing through my veins, and I shiver slightly as I serve the other drinks. "What's with that, Sylvian? Did you not just rescue her from the forest, but also fuck her in the dirt?"

Sylvian's neck muscles tense, but Reece's expression remains blank, as if he has some sort of issue with that. *The Kings don't know?*

"I've got a great hand," Reece says coldly. "Can we finish this round without being distracted by a worthless charity case? I was just about to raise the stakes." He pushes some of his chips into the center without sparing me so much as a look. "Who'll match?"

Romeo also moves his chips into the center, and I turn on my heel, trembling with rage.

"Just a moment, Dole. You need to take my next order..." Jaxon grabs my wrist and I react with lightning speed.

He dares touch me?

He risks coming closer to me, reaching for me?

After all that he's done to me?

I act without thinking. There's not a whole lot that I can do to get back at him, but in a flash, I grab the Coke and throw it in his face. He snorts, releasing me in surprise, and disbelief burns in his eyes as he stares at me.

All the Kings rise at the same time, so abruptly that two of the chairs they were sitting on fall to the floor, and it frightens me enough that I take two steps back.

Romeo, Sylvian, Reece, and Jaxon.

They stand in front of me, all staring at me as if I've committed an unforgiveable crime.

I back up toward the curtain, but Sylvian follows and grabs me before I can escape. "That was a mistake."

"Oh, definitely," I say. "How *dare* Jaxon touch me?"

"Get a rag," Sylvian tells me. "Get a rag, tell Derby, and come back immediately."

"The fuck I will," I hiss, trying to pull away from him.

Sylvian holds me in place with ease. "Do it or you'll lose your job here."

"Bastard," I mutter, freeing myself from his loosening grip and diving out. I'm starting to realize they've stopped bluffing. Can these men really demand anything they want from me because they're the fucking kings of this university? I quickly explain to Derby, stammering a bit, but he doesn't even really listen.

When I return to the billiard room, Sylvian's still standing by the door. Reece's leaning against the table, his arms folded, and

Jaxon's perched on the backrest of an armchair. Romeo's standing by one of the floor-to-ceiling bookshelves, all but disappearing into the smoke clouding the room.

I approach the table with wobbly knees and wipe up the spilled Coke.

"You have to clean me, not the table." Jaxon snaps at me smugly.

I hold the rag out to him. "Here you go."

He raises an eyebrow and I fume, so angry I stop thinking clearly. The only thing I want to do now is get back at him.

"Oh, hasn't little Tyrell learned how to clean himself? What a pity."

His sneer widens and his right eyebrow twitches upward in surprise.

I step close to him and start wiping his shirt with the cloth. "You know, this sort of thing is frequently found among top students. They may be able to solve the most complicated problems, but still be simply too stupid for things like personal hygiene. I bet you have someone ironing your shirts, bundling your socks, and folding your pants every day, don't you?" I keep rubbing at the damn shirt as I speak. "And you probably get off on it when a waitress spills on you. Try to provoke it. You probably even love the feeling of a smelly rag that's already been used to clean countless tables, eh? It must be quite an extraordinary sensation."

Jaxon laughs and grabs my wrist again, but so tightly this time that I don't stand a chance of wrenching my arm out of his grasp. His ice-blue eyes flash brightly. "Why don't you lick the Coke from my face? That would be a lot more hygienic."

A volcano erupts inside me. "Go fuck yourself!" I throw the rag on the table and wheel around to tear myself away from him. Or try to, in any case. Rather than letting me go, Jaxon pulls me back so hard that I crash into him. His other arm comes up immediately, wrapping around me and pulling my back against his rock-hard chest.

Jaxon's hand runs over my upper body up to my neck. He holds me captive, gripping my throat, pushing my head back against him. Emotions rush through me, as if only a few hours passed since we spoke in the limo.

He leans down toward my ear, his breath tickling my sensitive skin before his lips touch my earlobe.

I gasp as heat rushes through my core. My body betrays me, tensing in his grip while Jaxon relentlessly keeps me trapped. I might be able to free myself, but something saps my will away ... I'm left standing here, as if trapped, waiting for what's to come.

"I promised you I'd think of a way for you to show your appreciation to my family and the foundation that pays for your scholarship," he mumbles in my ear. "If it's not going to be sex—and I don't think it would be anywhere *near* good enough to pay off your debt—then you could at least pretend to be a passable waitress, you know? As far as I'm aware, throwing Coke in my face is not generally considered an expression of gratitude."

"It's nothing more than you deserve," I hiss.

"Because I abandoned you in the forest like an animal? I think you deserved that. Just like you *don't* deserve your place here. And now you're not even playing, not even trying to give yourself a chance to win."

Jaxon runs a hand through my hair, massaging my scalp. His touch could be so soothing if he weren't such an ass.

"But maybe you don't *want* to win?" he hisses. "Maybe you're not ready to fight for your dream like the others are. You think you're better than them. But you can't have victory without a game, my dear."

He loosens his grip and I move away. The way he's acting is keeping me from thinking clearly.

"Are you done, Jaxon?" Reece asks in a bored tone, tilting back in his chair and looking at us with half-lowered eyelids. "Why don't you leave Dole alone? She'll be eliminated on Halloween in a few days, so what's the fucking point? We've been waiting for you for ten minutes."

Jaxon treats me to a cynical smile. "I'm going all in."

Reece raises an eyebrow before leaning forward and pulling Jaxon's stack into the center. "Sylvian?"

"I'm out." Sylvian throws his cards down and collects the cash stacked in front of his seat. "Keep playing without me."

"Excuse me?" Jaxon asks.

"I'll take Mable back to the dorm."

"You'll what?" Reece stares at Sylvian like he's lost his mind. "What is it that has all of you going crazy over this beggar girl? Does her pussy emit some drug I can't detect?"

"You want her to lose her job?" Jaxon asks Sylvian, sounding genuinely interested.

"Romeo can cover for her," Sylvian replies.

I try to make out Romeo in the shadows of the room, but all I can see is his silhouette.

"Thanks, but I'll finish my shift," I reply. "And you can order your drinks at the bar."

Sylvian gives me a hard look. "That wasn't an offer."

"What was it then?" I ask, disturbed.

"We are leaving. Now." He turns toward the door.

"Wait, wait!" Reece has gotten up again and is blocking Sylvian's way. "I'm taking Dole home."

Sylvian furrows a brow mockingly. "Are you now?"

Reece checks his watch. "Yes, definitely. You know, Syl, if you want your princess to have a nice evening stroll, I'm just perfect for that. Unlike you, I can be nice and use my mouth to say nice things."

"She's more likely to run away from you, Crescent, than let you take her home," Jaxon scoffs.

"Well, the main thing is that she arrives safely, isn't it?" Reece asks smugly.

I'm trying to find the right words to object when I notice Jaxon's expression. A flutter rises in my stomach as the intensity of his stare touches me.

"She's staying," he decides.

Sylvian and Reece turn to him.

"We're playing to see who gets to 'take her home,'" Jaxon says with a sneer, pulling out his chair. "Sit down, Belle. If you win, you'll get all the money from the pot."

My mouth goes dry, and I know I can't pass up an opportunity like this. *It's so much money. Just, so much money ...*

"What are you waiting for?" Jaxon asks, flashing one of his friendliest smiles.

"No," Sylvian growls and steps in front of me. "You don't stand a chance playing poker against us. We're leaving."

"I don't have anything to lose though, do I?" I ask him, ignoring the cold gleam in his eyes.

A warning. I should always listen to him. To him and to Harper.

But that's a fortune on the table. That's a chance to never have to work again until after I graduate.

"See?" Jaxon asks the group, but he's really talking to Sylvian. "She does want it after all. She wants to play. She's just lacked the proper opponents, am I right?"

I ignore his words, walk past him, and sit in the chair he offers me. "Let's get this over with, I have to get back to work." I don't even try to count all the money. I have a one in three chance of having the best hand and winning. I've never been closer to amassing a fortune.

"Romeo?"

Romeo emerges from the shadows and goes to the door.

"Don't worry, he'll cover for you," Jaxon says with a reassuring smile that makes him seem almost friendly.

"What will Derby think?" I ask nervously.

"That you've forgotten something at home and will be back in an hour," Jaxon replies with a smile. "Romeo will sort out everything for you, and Derby is too stupid to suspect anything."

"An hour?" I ask in a panic. "Let's just play a round!"

"And where would the fun be in that?" Jaxon is still standing next to my chair and he places a handful of chips in front of me. He leans on the back of my seat, bringing his body close enough to mine that I can feel the energy crackling between us like it has since the limo. "You lose if you run out of chips."

He takes Romeo's seat next to me and gathers the money from the center of the table. The huge pile of cash goes to him. He must have just won the round then.

"Who's dealing?" he asks.

Reece gives me a bored look and starts handing out cards.

My first hand is bad and I drop out immediately.

My second one is as well.

The third time I have at least a pair. I match and watch how the Kings react. Sylvian looks about ready to smash the table. He's avoiding my eyes, but his tense muscles tell me he's not happy to have me here. Reece shamelessly returns my gaze. He seems arrogant, very different from the way I've come to know him. It's as if he has two faces.

Jaxon's focus is on his cards alone.

If he weren't an asshole, if he hadn't involved me in a competition that I'm working so hard to ignore, if he'd never thought of abandoning me in a forest, I'd love to watch him at this.

His body's tension reveals nothing about his cards. He treats me like an equal player. Respectful, calm, and with acceptance.

I find it hard to read any of them, and although my hands get better with every deal, I keep losing. Disappointed, I watch as my last token goes to Sylvian. He's won most of mine.

As soon as we've turned over our cards, he rises. "We're leaving," he growls, looking at me for the first time since the game started.

I take a deep breath and admit defeat.

"Wait." Jaxon's smile pins me to the chair. It's not just the money that makes me listen to him. I don't want to leave them, even though that's a thought I shouldn't be having in the first place.

They're assholes, Mable.

Players who bet on your college degree.

To whom you're worth no more than a speck of dust.

Jaxon leans over to Reece's and Sylvian's stacks, collecting the tokens again and putting them back in front of me. His blue eyes flash mischievously. "Another round?"

"The winner takes her home," Sylvian reminds Jaxon with a threatening undertone. "I *won*."

"I would never object to that," Jaxon purrs and fixes his gaze on me. His intensity makes me blush. "But we haven't agreed on the when."

My eyes dart to Sylvian, who gives me a look so dark it almost makes me flinch.

"Let's play another round, Belle," Jaxon suggests seductively. "Win, and we'll give you five hundred points in the arena in addition to the cash. That means you won't get kicked out on Halloween."

Sylvian returns to his seat before I've said anything back. "Bastard," he mutters, reaching for the cards.

Jaxon leans back contentedly, and Reece seems to grow more annoyed by the minute.

Now I'm even more nervous. The tension between the Kings

intensifies until it's so thick it practically pulsates, and I'm right there between them. My playing may have been mediocre before, but it's downright atrocious now. I'm unfocused, letting my mind wander, paying no attention to anyone else's poker face or my own. I'm far too fascinated by the way Sylvian's tattooed hands hold his cards. By how Jaxon's ringed fingers shuffle the deck. By Reece, who's studying me intently, making me feel unwanted, while at the same time drawing my mind back to what we did in his bed. I'm getting hotter by the minute, and I don't even realize that I'm winning.

Only when I reveal my cards do I realize I have two pairs.

"Congratulations," Jaxon tells me with a wry smile. "Interesting to watch Sylvian go all out to make sure you win."

I cast a shy look at Sylvian's face, but his expression remains impenetrable.

"Take the money and let's go." This time he doesn't get up.

I take my time organizing the many dollar notes. One thousand, two, three ... I won four thousand dollars. Just like that.

Fuck.

"Do you want another chance?" asks Jaxon.

A groan from across the room. Reece rocks on his chair before pushing it back across the floor. "I'm going for a smoke, fuckers." That said, he disappears through a side door.

That leaves me alone with Sylvian and Jaxon. Their presence should make me want to get up and leave, but I might as well be pinned to my chair. It's as if the two of them are fighting a battle I don't understand. As if they're rivals and allies who might turn against me at any moment at the same time.

"We're leaving now," Sylvian mutters, fixing his stare on Jaxon across the table.

"I don't think she wants to go, do you?" Jaxon returns smugly.

"She's not stupid. She knows she'll only win if we want her to."

"Oh, just like in real life then, isn't it?" Jaxon's fingers move like he's playing piano on the table. He would certainly make a gifted pianist. "Another five hundred points, Silvano? Come on, that'd definitely put her through to the next round on Halloween."

Sylvian purses his lips. His body language reminds me a little of a snarling predator.

"If you lose, Belle ..." Jaxon tilts his head in my direction. His gaze alone makes me feel unexpectedly hot. "The winner will be allowed to taste you."

My eyes widen. Heat surges inside me, erasing every clear thought I had left. It's as if Jaxon turned up the temperature in the room many times over with just one sentence. I should laugh at him, tell him just what I think of his perverted proposal, but all I can think about is what will happen if I lose.

If Sylvian were to lick me between my thighs.

Or him.

Nothing in the world would make me miss that opportunity. The prospect of winning more money? The prospect of having one of their mouths on me if I lose? That's a win-win. Isn't it?

"Now she's wondering about the catch in that," Jaxon says with a laugh. "Are you in, Silvano?"

"I'm going to take you for your last fucking dollar, Tyrell," Sylvian growls, and I suddenly wonder if they're even friends. How are the Kings connected? Are they even on the same side? Or do they actually hate each other? Is that one of the reasons they play with the scholarship students like they do? Do they have something to prove to each other? Or are they just deceiving me again, and nothing is actually as it seems?

Reece returns, strolling casually to the table and taking his seat opposite me with a radiant smile. He seems entirely changed, as if he just stepped out of the shower. "Still here, Mable? Wasn't Sylvian going to drag you home long ago?"

233

"I just had to give Sylvian an incentive to win, so now maybe he'll stop losing to get Amabelle points." Jaxon deals the cards.

"Ah," says Reece.

We play and I have the feeling the round is dragging on. The three men do things I don't understand. Poker is not my game, but I do know the rules. I like games that are about skill rather than luck. Poker probably is about skill, too, just not skills I have.

The men gamble and I win, then lose again without knowing quite why.

Eventually, I'm left with two tokens and Sylvian's jawline has clenched considerably. Reece has won several times in a row, but Jaxon has also taken the pot here and there.

As I consider playing my last chip—I have three of a kind—I look at Sylvian. I believe he's still trying to help me win. He nods slightly. It's the tiniest hint of a gesture, but I notice.

I match.

The last card is revealed, and I can't help but smile. Another glance at Sylvian and he rolls his eyes. I have four of a kind but no more tokens, so I use real money instead. Sylvian and Reece match. They're both watching me closely and I wonder whether I should go all in just before Reece does.

With a broad grin, he pushes all the tokens and cash in front of him to the center.

I stare at him. How good can his hand be if *I* have four of a kind?

I look at my money with uncertainty. If Reece has the better cards, I'll lose everything.

I can't do it. Another glance at Sylvian. He doesn't move, but I think I understand he wants me to match. But does he *want* to watch me lose all that money? Can I trust him?

I bite my lower lip and fold, and Reece laughs with satisfaction.

"He was fucking bluffing, Mable," Sylvian growls, reaching

for Reece's cards to reveal them. Reece doesn't even have a pair.

"What did she have? Four of a kind?" Reece asks.

I'm ashamed that I fell for Reece's bluff. I was this close to winning the entire pot and all of Reece's money. Bitterness settles on my tongue.

"What a stupid game," I mutter, leaning back in disappointment.

"Your face is an open book, Belle," Jaxon explains kindly, as if he has a genuine interest in me learning the game. "We can all guess your hand before you've even figured it out yourself. You haven't really lost, though, have you?" His voice takes on an insinuating tone.

I quickly count which of the men has the most chips.

Reece.

The right corner of his mouth twitches and he pushes his chair back. "I'll give you some of my winnings for every time you come on my tongue."

My cheeks heat up terribly, and I wish I'd never played this stupid game. No alcohol. No opium. Not even anger that could intoxicate me. No excuse at all. What happened at his party seems like ages ago. We were alone. That time with Jaxon in the limo didn't go very far. And when Sylvian and I were in the forest, it was ... It happened far away from campus and my normal, everyday life. But this is where I work. Derby could come in at any time.

And there are three men in the room with me. Without consciously controlling it, I bite the inside of my cheeks as I stand up.

You'll love it, Mable.

For sure.

It's not a loss. You didn't lose anything. Absolutely nothing.

I walk around the table and stop in front of Reece. My hands are sweaty, and I feel inadequate and small compared to how gorgeous he is.

"Relax, Belle." Jaxon has stepped close to me, a hand on my shoulder, fingers tenderly grazing the back of my neck. "You already know you're going to like it, don't you?"

Unsettled, I turn to Sylvian, who's sitting perfectly still, expression stony, looking about ready to explode.

"Don't worry about him," Jaxon whispers softly. "Sylvian's going to enjoy every second of what's about to happen."

I can't imagine *that*, but I'm not doing it for him. I'm doing it because I'm curious. Because Reece has already shown me how talented he is with his tongue.

He pulls his chair up in front of me and undoes the button on my jeans.

Just his fingers on my skin and Jaxon's hand stroking the back of my neck make me inhale sharply.

He slowly pulls my jeans down. Like a lover, sensitive and gentle. Except that we're not alone. They're watching us. This is a gambling debt that I'm paying off.

I step out of my jeans, and he grabs my panties. My breath hisses out as his fingers dance tenderly over my hips. He pushes the fabric lower and lower, all the way to my knees, and then once I slip out of them, he moves even closer.

I close my eyes as an electric sensation shoots from his tongue through my body. He plunges between my folds and my legs start to tremble.

Jaxon's physical presence and the knowledge that Sylvian is watching us suddenly sends my excitement into overdrive. Reece's tongue delves deeper, pushing against my sensitive clit.

I sigh, letting myself relax into Jaxon's grip as he supports my neck. I my lips fall open, almost like I'm expecting him to kiss me.

Reece sharply inhales the scent of me and presses his tongue even deeper. Then he grabs me, grips my butt firmly, and pushes me up onto the poker table. He pulls up his chair again and spreads my legs.

My eyelids flutter and then I see them. Both of them. Reece between my legs and Jaxon watching me.

There are no words for how much I long for Jaxon to touch more of me. While Reece slides his tongue deep inside me, I want to feel Jaxon just as much. I would do anything to be closer to him.

And at the same time, I'm holding back. I can't let him win, let him feel like I could ever forget what a huge asshole he is. Reece licks me more and more purposefully, and before I can even think about it happening, I feel the wave building inside me.

Jaxon grips my neck tightly, so fast it must be instinctive, as I come. I groan and then wince as Reece moves away, more or less interrupting my orgasm.

I almost kick him because the unsatisfied throbbing in my clit is worse than any rage I've ever felt for the Kings.

Reece's eyes shine and he looks just like the man I saw for the first time at the orientation event. Relaxed. Relaxed and incredibly caring.

"Close your eyes," he murmurs. I stare at him. He can't demand that. I can't give up *any more* control.

"Listen to him, Dole," Jaxon mumbles, and puts his hand over my eyes. The feel of his fingers relaxes me, and I allow it.

For a few agonizing seconds, nothing happens. All I can hear is my own loud breath, but I can feel someone moving. Fear merges with shame. *What am I actually doing here?*

Relief floods through me as I feel Reece between my thighs again. He pulls his chair even closer, spreads my legs wider, and plunges his tongue deep into me as if he'd never been interrupted.

I gasp and claw at the table. Suddenly, Jaxon pulls me back. Following his lead, I lie down on the tabletop as Reece straightens. He holds my thighs in his hands, licking me wildly and stimulating my clit with his tongue while I moan without restraint.

I turn my head to see Sylvian sitting there. His face is dark, and I flinch when his eyes meet mine. He hates me. He hates me because I'm allowing this, because I'm enjoying it, I'm depraved, and I didn't listen to him. I realize I should hate myself too.

I can fall for anyone. Just not them.

"I'm sorry," I whisper, and his eyes go wide.

"Don't you like it?" he asks quietly.

"I do, but ..."

Sylvian shakes his head in warning, and I fall silent.

"What?" Jaxon asks loudly. He's standing next to the table and has been watching me with lust in his eyes. "What did she just apologize to you for, Syl?"

The mood between the men changes and Reece lifts his head slightly.

"What did Amabelle apologize for?" Jaxon asks coolly over me. Sylvian has also straightened and is now staring down at me. Then there's Reece. He heaves a deep sigh before pressing a kiss to my mound and rising to his feet.

"Dole," he says calmly, and I look at him. "Don't get caught up in their game. We're having fun. That's all there is to it. And you can trust each of us, *every single one of us*, never to do anything you wouldn't want us to do." He thinks for a moment. "At least not as long as you're naked and it's about sex."

"Bullshit," Sylvian growls and takes a step toward Reece.

Jaxon stretches out his arm. "Sylvian, is there *anything* you want to tell us?"

Sylvian's nostrils flare and his breaths are short as he fights for control. "I'm taking her home now."

"The hell you are." Jaxon's voice is sharp. "You're going to sit down. And you will watch. Amabelle has a gambling debt to pay off. If you can't enjoy it, which I can't imagine, because you would've killed Crescent by now, just shut up and wait."

I want to slide off the table, but several hands immediately reach out to keep me there.

Reece holds my thighs with a smug smile and Jaxon squeezes my shoulder.

"What really happened in the forest?" Jaxon's voice snaps like a whip.

Sylvian grinds his teeth. "If anything had happened, you'd know about it already, wouldn't you?"

"You're lying. I know your fucking poker face. Why are you choosing her over me, my friend?" Jaxon asks quietly. "Why are you lying to *me*, of all people, to protect *her*?" Confused, I look at Sylvian. Even though they talk about me like I'm worthless, I can feel the tension in the air. Did Sylvian turn on Jaxon because of me? "Why don't you trust me anymore?"

"I do trust you!" Sylvian hisses, and his anger hits me, though it's directed at Jaxon. "I don't trust *me*, you fucking bastard. When will you finally understand that I don't want to follow in my father's damn footsteps even if it seems to work so well for you?"

"Leave my father out of it."

"Hey, guys, Mable's still here," Reece interjects casually. They're still holding me in place, and there's no point to squirming in their grips. Even Jaxon, who's obviously focused on Sylvian, continues to press my shoulders down onto the poker table.

"You're acting just like him, Jax," Sylvian murmurs. "You like her, but you treat her like you hate her. Just like your father would."

Jaxon's eyes fill with a desperate storm of emotions. I almost want to reach out a hand to comfort him until I remember that he's holding me captive on a poker table, half naked.

"I've changed," Sylvian adds. "You should try it. The game will never end if you don't."

The game? Why do these guys always talk in riddles?

I desperately glance back and forth between their faces. Jaxon's expression is the first to clear.

"You're right," he finally says after a few more seconds of silence and lets go of me. "If she wants to go, let her go."

"No," Reece growls. When he wants to get his way, his voice is just as animalistic as those of the other Kings. He grabs me and lowers his mouth to my pussy again. Against my will, I throw my head back, rearing up as he slides two fingers inside me in addition to his tongue, which is busy circling my clit.

Of course I'm wet.

How could I not be?

I'm so wet and willing that I wouldn't be surprised if my body surrendered to all of them.

My hands scramble, trying to find anything to hold onto to physically counter Reece's stimulation. They end up buried in the cash and chips on the table. I'm lying on money and being licked by one of the most beautiful men in the world.

This is the sort of thing that could only happen to me here.

Nowhere but Kingston.

"See, Sylvian? She does like it. You can't really say you want to take that away from her."

I open my eyes and look first at Jaxon's face, then at Sylvian's. Both of them are watching me with naked greed in their expressions. My breath catches as I realize the degree of depravity in everything that's happening here. They make me feel desired because they are looking at me as if I am.

Desirable.

Reece spreads my legs even wider, lavishing the sweetest strokes of his tongue on my pulsating clit, and release surges inside me like a wave of unbridled lust.

"Look at me!"

I obey immediately, looking up into Jaxon's eyes. I let his piercing gaze penetrate me, captivate me until my body succumbs to the tension. My eyelids close of their own accord, I reach aimlessly to my left, grasping a hand—that must be Sylvian's—holding onto it and moaning loudly.

In those few seconds that feel like an eternity, I simply surrender. I give in to all the dark lust I've always felt, which has only increased since my first meeting with the Kings. My most secret dreams, my wildest fantasies all seem to be coming true.

The orgasm washes me away while Reece fucks me vigorously with his tongue, lapping up everything I give him, and then I'm just breathing.

I'm staring at the ceiling.

I'm feeling that hand in mine.

I don't want it to end.

Ever.

A chair moves across the floor, and I slowly come to my senses. Two Kings have moved away, only Sylvian is still sitting next to me because I'm holding his hand. Reece and Jaxon mutter to each other, looking at me as if I'm a stranger to them.

I quickly close my legs, slide off the table, and pick up my pants.

I feel their eyes on me, each of them separately, as I dress.

What do they think of me now? That I'm a slut because I gave in to my lust? Or because I only did it to satisfy a gambling debt?

I'm sure it's something nasty, and I want to get away as quickly as possible.

"Belle."

I shyly turn my head in Jaxon's direction. My ponytail has come undone, and my long hair is falling into my face. Reece looks like I've completely shocked him, and I don't dare look at him directly.

"You don't have to go."

I swallow hard.

"We could play for a while," Jaxon says amiably. "Have some

fun. I can teach you how to play poker."

Sylvian pushes his chair back and stands in my way. "We're leaving. For real this time."

Jaxon laughs, and I'm glad Sylvian is giving me an escape. I pocket the money I won and turn away.

"Remember, Belle. If you want to secure your next five hundred points," Jaxon calls after me, "we're here every Thursday night."

I bite my tongue, allowing Sylvian to grab me and drag me outside.

"What about Derby?"

"Romeo will explain."

"How can Romeo do anything about *my* job?"

Sylvian maneuvers me through the side door, behind which is the car park. I never realized that Crown's is twice the size of the taproom. "Derby's an employee just like you are. Who do you think actually owns the bar?"

I stare at him. Then I look back at the elaborate C in the Crown's logo. Below it, small and inconspicuous, is a Rho Chi Alpha sign. "The bar belongs to the Rex fraternity?"

Sylvian doesn't answer. He only releases me when we reach a black car. The Aston Martin looks almost too plain to belong to a Kingston student.

"Get in."

I obey, wishing I could just walk the few minutes to my dorm. But that wasn't the terms of the bet, right?

Sylvian drives more slowly than he did last time, but he seems a lot more tense. Since his reaction seems to be connected to some sort of agreement among the Kings, which would never fully make sense to me anyway, I don't ask.

Let him be upset.

It doesn't matter to me.

I want to go home. I want to go to bed. I don't want to have to think about how heavenly it was being between them. Or that I permitted too much. Far too much. First and foremost, too many feelings.

"Why him?" Sylvian asks tersely. His neck muscles are flexing, and I would actually feel more comfortable if we stayed silent rather than risk him jerking the steering wheel around in a rage.

"Hm?" I ask absently.

"Reece," he growls. "What is he to you? He treats you like dirt. He fucks a different girl every day. And his fake charm just sucks."

I cross my arms over my chest. Could it be that Sylvian is jealous? "At least he hasn't threatened me, tasted my blood, or abandoned me in a forest. Or screwed me in that forest, then treated me like I didn't exist and made me lie to my friend. And hey, he didn't make an *arena* out of my university life either."

Sylvian angrily slams a fist on the steering wheel. His breathing is an audible rasp, and I'm afraid he'll cause an accident if I say the wrong thing, so I swear to myself to shut up. "I never said that Jaxon and I were any better. The fucking arena was an idea I had so you could win with relative ease. If only you wrote a paper every week ..."

"Then what?" I dare ask. "I still wouldn't have enough points to beat Rachel and Lien, who are screwing half the campus!"

His breathing is so loud he sounds like a hungry wolf. "I told you to *stay away*. And what are you doing? You just let Crescent lick you like he's not Reece fucking Crescent and one of the biggest assholes I know!"

"I'm sorry if sharing me is a problem for you!" I shout back.

He stops the car in the middle of the road and looks at me. There's plenty going on in the jungle of his eyes, but jealousy isn't part of it. "You just don't get it."

I clench my fists. "Stop talking down to me."

Sylvian clasps the steering wheel with one hand and my

backrest with the other to look at me directly. His expression is unfathomable. Beautiful, dark, and unfathomable. "I have no problem *sharing you*. What ever made you think I would? I could've fucked you straight across the pool table, no matter that your pussy was wet from Crescent's lips. And that is *precisely* the problem. No one who has ever been with us is still with us today ... Has ever ..." He falters, agonized. "You don't know what you're doing to yourself. Just fucking play along. Do you know the risk I took to convince Jaxon to change the fucking rules? I risked *everything* to protect you. My own studies are at stake. And in return, you use your body as a poker chip, like some cheap whore?"

"Having fun doesn't make me a whore!"

He faces forward again, starts up the car, and concentrates on the road. "You don't understand." His voice is much calmer now. "I never said you were. I'd believe every word you said if you were. If you were cunning, cold-hearted, cheap, and only interested in your own gain. But you just try to *pretend* you can have sex without ... feelings. It's just not your thing, though. Or maybe I'm wrong. Have you ever once thought about what it would be like if Reece was all yours? Or Jax? Or *me*?"

I chew on my lower lip and look out the window.

"A smart woman wouldn't think that. She would stop as soon as she thought something like that. You have to stop, Mable."

"I don't know how!" I groan, wishing I hadn't revealed my innermost thoughts to him. It's a mistake to show the Kings how much they've already infiltrated my mind, isn't it? A stupid mistake.

Sylvian's knuckles stand out white as he clenches his fists ever more tightly around the steering wheel. When he stops in front of my dorm and gets out with me, I panic.

"I can walk in on my own! What if Harper sees us?" I whisper.

"What do I care what she thinks?" He opens the door for me and walks by my side.

"She's my friend, Sylvian."

"You're not acting the part."

I stop to stare at him. What he says hurts, but he's right. I brought all of this on myself. I let them wager licking my pussy in their poker game because I would've enjoyed it with any of them.

Sylvian keeps walking, unperturbed, and I'm forced to run after him.

I've barely unlocked the door to my room when he shoves me through it. He turns on the light, lowers the shutters and towers in front of me.

"Last warning."

I put my hands on my hips. "Okay, I'll stay away from Reece and Jaxon, alright? Too bad you can't control me and I make my own decisions."

He laughs coldly. "I very much doubt that. If I see one of the Kings between your legs one more time—"

"Yeah? What then?" I challenge.

He looks at me, his eyes dark as night, and lets silence do the talking for him.

Then he takes a step toward me. Without any warning at all, he puts his hands around my neck and pulls me close. His tongue shoves its way between my lips, and he devours my mouth.

Everything about this kiss is wild and rough and typical of him, and for a moment, I forget all that's happened. I forget about all that he's said and allow the storm of emotions to flow through me.

He pushes me against the door. My head hits the wood hard. His hands slide under my shirt, demanding, as he kisses me with urgency and hunger, like an animal.

His belt buckle comes undone. My hands may have found their way under his jacket, yearning for him. I would love to feel him.

I would love to have him. I want to forget everything that could ever stand in our way, and most of all our argument. Or the fact that he ignored me for weeks after we had sex.

But I can't.

"No," I gasp, pushing him away.

He drops his hands and looks at me even more stormily than before. As if he's unable to actually stop, only pause his efforts out of curiosity about what I have to say. As if he'll force me if necessary. There's no more warmth. No feeling.

Only harsh dominance and threatening darkness.

"I can't do this to Harper," I mutter, stepping aside. I open my door with one hand. "Thank you for bringing me home. Good night."

He makes a sound that, with a lot of imagination, could be a laugh. "As soon as she finds out that I've even *seen* you naked, your 'friendship' will be over forever. Good night, Amabelle." He reaches for the door handle and pulls it shut behind him with a clap like thunder.

Amabelle. My name sounds stern and emotionless coming from him. Just like it did from my father. At least that's what I think. A father I hardly remember. Maybe it's better that there's never been a man in my life before, be it friend, partner, or father.

I absolutely don't know how to handle them.

JAXON

Bullshit baby is what we call women who talk enough shit to make them unfuckable. But we're even worse. Not a single day goes by without us spouting constant bullshit to convince those around us that we're not who we appear to be.

We're assholes.

We're really weird motherfuckers.

We've had golden spoons covered in caviar shoved up our asses our whole lives, and we've always been taught that we belong to the elite and need to act the part.

So anyone who's supposed to know our good side, will. We aren't just lying—we are the lie. We are the scam. We wear fine suits and perfect manners like armor, but our souls are as dark as night.

But they're not quite dark enough to overshadow the radiance of our smiles, and that's all it takes to manipulate everyone around us.

You'll love us in the end, Belle.

Everyone always does.

18

MABLE

I manage quite well not to think too much about what happened between Jaxon, Sylvian, Reece, and me. I've spent the last few days studying and working in the library and just about convinced myself it was a slip in judgment.

It's only when I return to the dorm on Halloween and the rest of my dormmates have gathered in the kitchen that I painfully realize that we're the characters in a *Hunger Games* spin-off.

"Hi, Mable." Rachel calls out, and I just *have to be* polite enough to respond.

"Hi, Rachel."

"Have you found out where the points stand? The tally hasn't been updated since last Monday."

I'm standing indecisively in front of the kitchen door, biting my lower lip, and decide to brave the confrontation. I've kept a low profile and avoided the other scholarship students since Jaxon's party. They've played along with the Kings' silly game of their own accord, and yes, maybe I was a tad too arrogant and thought their behavior pathetic. But what do I know? Each of them must have her own reasons. There are plenty of good reasons for them to be afraid of losing their place at the university. Reasons that render them unable to defy the Kings. Those reasons may never be clear to me but still be completely justified. That's not the issue.

The students, pawns, and kings around us are.

"I really have no idea what the score is." I go to the fridge to get a bottle of water. Somehow it feels better to hold something in my hands. "But why do you even care?"

Brittany, Kady, and Rachel are sitting in front of me at the round kitchen table. Five chairs, two empty. Who will be missing tomorrow?

"They're going to throw one of us out." Suddenly I feel brave, and my tongue loosens. "One of us won't be here tomorrow. No matter who it is, the next one will follow in December. Do you understand? You can't win this game together because only one can win if the Kings have their way."

"It's alright, Mable," Rachel says, annoyed. "We just wanted to know if you knew."

I look at her in disbelief. "Why don't we join forces?"

"What do you mean by 'join'?" Rachel asks. "You're never here to join with us. Now that you're going to be thrown out, you suddenly want to pretend we're friends?"

Her aggression toward me catches me off guard. "This isn't about friendship. We can't put up with this."

"Then why don't you go?" Rachel suggests with a shrug. Brittany and Kady don't even have the courage to look up and face me. "If you don't like things as they are, just leave."

"I want to find a way for *all* of us to stay," I say defensively, a quiver in my voice.

"That's not possible," Brittany hisses. She hasn't touched a single noodle on her plate yet. She seems to be wasting away more and more with every day. "The rules are what they are."

"A bunch of morons made those rules as a joke and we're pretending we have to take them seriously! Please—we could just report the whole thing. What's the issue there?"

"Enjoy that dream," Rachel replies cynically. "Go, report the Kings and see what happens."

"Why don't we at least try? We could also write to a larger newspaper. Perhaps the press would report what's happening here. We could talk to activists! What if everyone just *believes* that nothing will help, but no one has ever tried anything?"

"God, how can you be so naive?" Rachel rolls her eyes, flicking her red hair back in annoyance, and rises to her feet. "You're lucky you're getting out of this tonight. Kingston is out of your intellectual league."

I bite my tongue but say nothing more. *Alright, fine.* Let's not stick together then.

In my room, I dwell on the thought of what would happen if I actually did report Jaxon and his friends. The five hundred points I earned from poker won't be enough to keep me here. How do they intend to prevent me from reporting them after they kick me out?

"They'll prevent it quite easily," Harper explains to me later, as we get changed for her Halloween party. When I heard the party was being held in her building and that many people from out of town were coming, I decided I would go. She dragged mountains of bags into my dorm room and dumped them all on the second bed, then spent half an hour trying on one dress—costume—after another and asking me to do the same. "The entire university is funded by families like the Tyrells. If you report one of them, *nothing* happens. Mable, really." She stops in front of me, hands on her hips. She's the only student I know on campus who doesn't come across as an absolute bitch when she does that. "Do you think the members of the university council are *happy to* pay for your scholarships? They're all misers who would prefer not to invest a single cent in you. Scholarships have only been awarded for *four* years, since Jaxon's father set up the foundation and initiative.

And virtually none of the participating parents actually want to be part of it. Mr. Tyrell has prevailed, though, and so they must. Do you understand what I'm trying to say? The hatred toward you doesn't come from the students. It's passed down from their parents. The parents in turn finance the university, and if anyone knows too much or shows they might want to take action against this bullying ... they're simply dismissed. This is Kingston. A system of rule by the family dynasties of America."

"Ah," I say, tugging at a cowgirl costume that covers less of my breasts than my bra. "I'd forgotten about the dynasties somehow."

"I know." Harper heaves a sigh as she sits on the edge of my bed with one leg crossed over the other. "What are we going to do if they really decide you lose today?"

I shrug as if I don't care. Of course I do. There's a limit to how far I'd go to achieve any one goal, though. I wouldn't kill anyone or sell my dignity to some psychotic rich kids to stay at Kingston. If I have to go, I'll go. But something tells me that Jaxon will be true to his word...

"I have a plan."

"You do?"

Harper's cheeks turn pink as she wrings her fingers nervously. "I know it's not perfect. But if they really decide you lose, which unfortunately it looks very much like they will, I'll put you up with me. You can stay in my apartment. I'll bring you the books you need and pay some of the pawns to give you their lecture notes, and I'll get tutors to do private lessons for you. We'll find a way to outsmart the Kings so you can sit your exams at the end of term. And you'll hide with me until then!"

"Are you serious?" I ask her uncertainly.

"Sure!"

"I wouldn't be able to accept something like that ..."

"And why not?! I can't let them win! Not again! We have to do something! It's not just a fight between you and them. It's about all of Kingston!"

New confidence floods me. Maybe I should tell her that Jaxon suggested I play poker for points again? But then she'll judge me, won't she? I know it was wrong without being told. And I certainly can't share about Sylvian...

"So, what dress are you going to wear?" Harper asks, pointing to the large selection lying on the second bed.

I'm flirting with the sweater hanging in my wardrobe. It's not that I don't want to be sexy. I just want to wear something that will make me stand out. Is it vanity if I don't want to look like all the other women showing off their charms? Will any of tonight's female guests be wearing more than scraps of cloth that barely cover their asses and breasts?

"Oh no." Harper shakes her head vehemently. "No, no, no. Not some Billie Eilish rip-off, please? No."

I bite my lower lip, grab the sweater, and hold it in front of my chest. Then I treat her to a puppy-dog look. "Please, Harper. What do I have to lose?"

***

Quite a lot, as it turns out. I had plenty of fun dressing up. My outfit's elaborate, and it was a pleasure to do my makeup with Harper and talk about all sorts of things. Our favorite movies. Favorite actors. Favorite bands.

As soon as we entered the party, though, it's clear how much better it would've been to blend in with the crowd. Once again, eyes follow me from room to room, and once I've been everywhere I realize I've dressed up solely for the Kings.

I wanted to impress them. Stupid, foolish, naive victim of their seduction that I am, I wanted to please them. *Of course*, Harper didn't even invite the Kings to her party. It's all for nothing that I look like an alien amongst all the dolled-up women in super-sexy costumes, and even though many of those present aren't even Kingston students, they still look at me like I'm a leper.

I clearly am the one among them who doesn't belong.

Harper doesn't notice that I'm uncomfortable. She's so busy greeting her friends from the city and making small talk with them that she doesn't notice my weak smile. I try to be a good friend and make the best of the situation. But getting drunk is out of the question for me, and no matter who I approach, I just don't want to start a conversation. I abandon my attempts after the third try. What am I supposed to talk to these people about? The yacht I didn't go on vacation on last summer? The internship at the White House that I'll never be getting?

I wander through the apartment building in frustration until I end up in the stairwell. There may be a lift to each floor, but the staircase is a sight to behold. It's enormous, with curved railings and gilded stone columns. Harper's apartment is located on the top floor, affording her a magnificent view of part of Kingston Park. She and all the other students living in this building each have their own bedrooms, a living room with kitchenette and balcony, a spacious bathroom, and a study.

Yes, a *study*.

Every single fucking apartment has one.

I'm not being disparaging or anything.

I'm just damn *jealous*.

Lost in thought, I walk down the stairs, accompanied by the beats from the respective apartments. The house has turned into a disco and the walls transmit sound like amplifiers.

Once I reach the bottom, I step outside to take a deep breath. I'm still holding the skateboard that I secretly "borrowed" from one of the male scholarship students who live on the top floor of my dorm, and I feel just as out of place as the board.

What was I thinking, not wearing one of Harper's dresses?

On a whim, I put the skateboard on the ground and stand on it. I've never ridden one before, and I'm wobbly as I push off with one foot. Laughter echoes from somewhere in the park as I stumble and almost fall.

Oh boy. Do they never get bored of watching me and laughing at things that aren't funny at all?

I pick up the skateboard again and take it to the street. A few expensive-looking cars are parked next to the pavement. Including a red sports car with an open top.

I prefer not to try any more skateboarding where Jaxon might see me.

"Boo!"

I wince and spin, my heart pounding. A masked, black-clad figure is standing in front of me. That is the same fine mask that I saw at Jaxon's party. A stiff, black face that leaves only the eyes exposed and is gilded at the high points.

The guy takes off his mask and beams at me. "Hello, Dole. I was hoping I'd find you here."

"Here?" I ask Reece critically, glad that no sexual energy is flaring up between us. Maybe it's because he called me Dole. Or maybe my willpower is just surprisingly strong today?

"I've been looking for you at Harper's party all this time. I almost didn't recognize you." He takes a step back and lets his gaze glide over me. "Dude, *is* that even a costume, or do you usually walk around like that?"

I bite my tongue.

Reece circles me, then grabs my hand and runs it over the fake tattoos on my arm. "Shit ... it suits you in a way. But you're the only one who would come up with the idea of dressing up as a tramp."

"*Skater*," I hiss. "I'm a skater, alright? And no, I don't normally walk around in torn tights, boots, and with safety pins in my ears."

Reece raises his eyebrows. "Can you do me a favor and explain to me in what way a 'skater' is different from a 'tramp'?"

"Right. Good night," I say as I try to walk past him.

"Dole!"

Oh God. Not another one.

Reece takes two quick steps, blocking my way and nodding toward the road. "You've been summoned, skater girl."

"My name is *Mable*."

"Come on, we'll take you to a real party!" Jaxon shouts from the street.

Taking a deep breath, I turn to tell Jaxon that I would do *anything* in the whole wide world before going to a party with *him* on *Halloween*. I should've just run away instead of trying to confront him.

I merely need to look at Jaxon for the feelings he and the others aroused in me on Thursday to crash over me with full force. I stand there, struck by the storm that emanates from his smile like it's a weapon.

Jaxon Tyrell is an asshole, and I know it. He's also standing next to his car, though, grinning, leaning casually on the driver's door. He's looking right at me, and all of that fills me with longing.

To feel his insinuating glances once again...

His hands on my neck...

I swallow hard and try to focus on the others standing with him. Two more of them are masked. They wear the same masks as Reece. I don't recognize them, but I suspect one of them is Romeo.

And then there's Sylvian. As usual outside of university hours, he's wearing his leather jacket and a simple gray shirt. His tattoos are real, in contrast to mine. I also remember his kiss as if it just happened. But Sylvian is off limits. Harper is in love with him. Harper is my friend.

She hates the Kings.

I hate the Kings.

I hate them for good reason.

"You know you want to," Jaxon calls out to me. "So get in." He swings into the driver's seat and starts the engine.

I turn to Reece, thinking about pushing past him, and read in his gaze that he's not going to let me get away. "Give me one good reason why you want me to come with you," I whisper. "Harper's my friend and it's her party. She's told me all about you. Why should I suddenly doubt that just because we played a bit of poker?"

Reece grimaces, and the expression makes him seem like a completely different person, not the man whose touch I involuntarily crave. "Harper's mostly talking shit. Why do you think she's friends with you, huh? Certainly not because she's suddenly grown a conscience. She wants to keep you away from us. The other charity cases are no competition for her. You are."

"Competition?"

"Sylvian's looking at you like he wants to fuck you, is what I mean," Reece mutters. He leans forward. He even smells different from usual. Is that part of his costume? "You know, Dole, speaking as a man, you can't have any real fun with most of the sluts on this campus. They're all whores. They want our names, our money, our influence, or at least our looks. No woman who gets her mommy and daddy to pay for her studies at Kingston hasn't been *drilled* to catch the richest, most powerful, most influential guy the university has to offer. They all want to be the next First Lady. Harper wants Sylvian's position. But you, you just want us, don't you?"

My head spins at his words. Is it possible? Can anything these guys say about Harper be *true*? "Harper isn't the one who invented this game," I reply in a flat voice.

Reece laughs, exposing his teeth. Pointed fangs finally give away his costume: a vampire. "We didn't toss eggs at you either, though, did we? Forget about this fucking game, Dole. If we like you, we'll let you win. You won't even have to screw us for it, alright? Just be a good sport and dress a little less like a beggar so you don't get thrown out by the university itself, and we'll let you stay."

His words sound too good to be true.

"So you're coming along then, yeah?" He curls his lips in victory, casually putting an arm around my shoulders and leading me to the sports car. It's strange, but the sparks aren't flying like they usually do when he touches me. There's no tingling, no electricity.

Right. Great, I tell myself. *One less issue with feelings.*

I know it's wrong to go with him. It's wrong, forbidden, naive, and all the crap my mother would warn me about if she wasn't addicted to pills and had any interest in my life.

It's Halloween. I've done all my coursework. I feel confident in my lectures, able to keep up, and I don't have to study right now. I might even allow myself to have a drink. A little something, a glass maybe?

On the way to Jaxon's car, I take out my phone.

"What're you doing now?" Reece asks.

"I'm letting Harper know I'm going with you. In case you end up abandoning me in a forest again."

"Right. We're not going to do that, okay?" Reece looks annoyed and interrupts my text by putting his fingers on my screen. "Didn't I just tell you that she has a gigantic issue with you hanging out with us?"

"One, I don't believe a word you say. Two, I don't have anyone else to tell. Three, I'm not enrolled at this university because I'm stupid. I won't simply be getting in a car with Jaxon and some masked strangers after what happened last time."

Sylvian has silently observed my discussion with Reece. Now he's moving toward us. "Mable, if you don't want to come, then don't." His green eyes gleam in the lantern light. "You know how I feel about you hanging out with us."

"Don't be such a fucking bore, Syl!" Jaxon shouts from behind the wheel. "No one can guarantee she won't be abandoned in a forest again. That's the thrill of the entire thing, isn't it? Would you be here, *Belle*, if we were boring and sensible?"

Sylvian isn't smiling. He doesn't even seem to realize what Jaxon is saying. His gaze is on me, and me alone. I feel vaguely judged by him. Condemned for still being here. For letting myself be seduced, because Jaxon actually has a point. I have become curious. Addicted. These men hold everything in their hands, and more, but they're also ... appealing. Attractive. As hot as gods, each in their own way, and ... they obviously don't mind sharing me.

"Will you protect me from him?" I ask Sylvian. I know he can simply lie. How many times has he kept the truth from me? I don't know him. I can't judge him and I'm a damn bad poker player.

"I will always protect you," he whispers.

Reece laughs by my side, but I feel a little safer.

But what does *safer* even mean? There's not much they could do to me that would be worse than abandoning me in a forest again. If they take me away to embarrass me, I'm ready. If they want to fuck me, then ... I want them to. If they take me just to be nasty, I don't care because I've realized at this point that good character is not a prerequisite for sexual attraction. At least not for me.

And if they are actually inviting me to have a good time ... then I've won, haven't I?

Reece opens the passenger door for me. I get in and he hops into the back seat over the rear door. He settles on the backrest between the two masked men and lights a joint.

The smell of marijuana fills my nose as my mere proximity to Jaxon makes me tense.

His hands loosely grip the steering wheel. He's wearing a black shirt, his signet rings, a simple gold watch, and black chinos. When he notices my stare, he smiles. His canines are also long and pointed like a vampire. "Do you like what you see?"

My neck is growing hot, and I'm glad it's reasonably dark around us.

"What's going on, Silvano? Why aren't you getting in?" Jaxon asks Sylvian. "Afraid to touch a girl?"

"I'm going to Harper's party. I'll catch up with you."

Something about Jaxon changes as Sylvian utters these words. It's as if he's tensing up inside, but I'm not sure of it. His controlled attitude doesn't give me much insight into his inner self.

"A lot of people from the city came ..." Sylvian explains. That sounds like a very strange reason to me.

"Fuck you, Syl," Jaxon mutters. He looks at his friend—they are friends, aren't they?—as if Sylvian just betrayed him deeply.

"I'm going to Harper's party." One of the masked men gets out and jogs toward Sylvian.

Sylvian does not seem enthusiastic.

"I'm going to Harper's party," the masked man repeats. I suspect it's Romeo under the mask, though since it covers his entire face, I can't be certain. Romeo holds out his open hand to Sylvian and Sylvian reluctantly puts something in it. A flat wallet. The object captures my attention as if it's a secret diary.

The guy I think is Romeo walks into Harper's house and Sylvian opens the passenger door. Shadows dance in his eyes, and suddenly, in that split second, I wonder if it's really Jaxon I should be most afraid of.

"Move back, Dole," Jaxon demands, nodding to the back seat.

I turn my head toward him, lean my neck back against the

head rest, and give him a relaxed look. "Who's she?"

Jaxon shows his vampire fangs as he leans in at lightning speed. Without any warning at all, he pulls me close to kiss my cheek, lighting my entire face on fire. His breath merges with mine, his sensuous touch is intense enough to hurt, and my heart skips a few beats.

"Go sit in the back, *Belle*," he mumbles and leans back again.

I swallow hard, do as he says, and soon find myself between Reece and the other masked man. After Romeo—or whoever—got out, Reece took his place. They wedge me in, but ... it's not in any way unpleasant. This really is when I should be telling myself to *stop* liking it quite so much. What did they say? We're going to have fun? Nothing else?

"Nice of you to come along," Reece says, his arm resting loosely on the backrest and his long legs stretched out to either side. His knee touches mine. "I'll make sure none of those weirdos get any closer to you than you want them to be."

"Yeah, that sounds so reassuring, Reece, thanks," I scoff, realizing that I sound tougher than I want to. Part of him has gone back to being as nice as I've come to know him. Since I'm a painfully polite person, I like to return that favor.

Reece smiles and Jaxon starts driving.

"How many girls would like to sit in your place right now, Belle?" Jaxon asks no one in particular. No one answers. Something tells me it's quite a few. The looks we get from those we pass seem to confirm that. Students, those studying with me and strangers I've never seen on campus before. Everyone stares after the sports car with the woman surrounded by four guys.

Maybe they're actually staring at my costume. Sylvian's got the skateboard between his legs.

I fidget in my seat, which makes Reece put a hand on my knee.

"It's alright," he says quietly, his soothing voice enough to send butterflies into my core. I give up. Apparently, I only like him fifty percent of the time, and my body tells me when that fifty percent is happening.

"Well, *Belle*," Jaxon says from the front as he fixes his gaze on me in the rear-view mirror. He's driving slowly, the wind only rustling faintly around our ears. "I'll give you three places to choose from. *I* would take you to our club room. There are rows and rows of old books on the shelves there. An entire room just for us, and no one to get on our nerves with ridiculous costumes and spilled drinks. Disadvantage: We'll have to blindfold you until we get there. You can't know where the room is."

"Until I wake up in a forest," I add cynically.

Jaxon shrugs. "Reece ..."

"I'm in favor of the city." All the warmth that suddenly emanates from Reece again overwhelms me. Something inside me longs to lie in his arms. To let myself be held. Gently. Reassuring. *God, get a grip, Mable.* "We could go to a club where nobody knows us and we're nothing but nameless faces, and just have some fun. We'll slip a few thousand dollars to the DJ, and whenever you want a song, he'll play it, Mable."

That sounds tempting. It sounds tempting because it's not just me who'd be no one.

"Disadvantage: The drive will take more than an hour," he says, but seems to think that it isn't a real disadvantage.

"And you want me to choose?" I ask.

"Forget about that," says Sylvian, turning around to face me and keeping his eyes firmly on mine. His stubble makes him look rougher than the other Kings. Less smooth and flawless. "Reece and Jaxon are suggesting things that will definitely make you lose control. We'll drive to a lake. There's a party there. With people who look just like you do tonight. *We* won't be welcome there, but you will be. You'll hang out with them, and we'll follow you and hope they let us stay. There'll be steel drum fire pits with fresh bread baked over the fire. Have you ever had that?"

I have to laugh and shake my head.

"None of us will be able to get close to you without everyone noticing. No risk. No disadvantage. It's just a few minutes' drive away. You'll feel good. And we'll be fucked because the car alone will give us away as Kingston students."

Jaxon sighs. Perhaps he knows I've already made my choice. Not being the impoverished girl from the trailer park for an evening is just too tempting. A touch of normality, the reminder that there's more to life than wealth and financial security is what made me wear this costume today. I wanted to be a skater. Someone who's free and doesn't pay a single cent to move from A to B. Someone who can be something with *nothing*. I miss that.

I don't miss the poverty.

But I do miss the feeling of a simple life.

Jaxon closes the roof of the convertible and accelerates.

"Really?" Reece asks, sounding shaken. "A bonfire party?"

I nod and return Sylvian's serious look. He suddenly smiles widely enough to expose his vampire fangs.

"Let's swap places for a night," he says, turning back to the front and switching on the radio. "We'll stand out at this party like she would at one of ours."

"I hope she doesn't find out why we're *really* going there," Jaxon says darkly, stepping on the throttle once more. "Because unlike our suggestions, yours is once again part of some stupid plan, isn't it?"

Sylvian doesn't answer, so I'm not sure if Jaxon is just teasing him. But shouldn't I instead be wondering why Sylvian doesn't mind me spending time with the Kings all of a sudden? Where did that change of heart come from? Should I be suspicious?

JAXON

Yes, little Belle. The women at Kingston were brought up to be whores. They spend four years learning how to fuck so they can leave university with the best possible husband and have their children via a Russian surrogate. Some are lucky and get to learn how to fulfill their role in the pathetic feminist agenda out in the world. They don't learn to fuck. They learn that they'll be fucked in their future positions if they don't do exactly what some man higher up in whatever organization they find themselves in says.

It's sad, isn't it? Kingston is an antisocial hell of prostitution, and I still think I should be the first to teach you.

19

MABLE

The party is ten times better than I could've imagined. Fires built in steel drums have been placed a few paces apart on the shore of a lake. Beanbags, blankets, and towels are laid out all around. I can smell fresh bread, woodsmoke, and marijuana.

They send me ahead to ask if we're allowed to join in. One of the women, who's wearing the same outfit as I am, though she's definitely *not* in costume, embraces me in greeting, but has a critical look for my companions. Reece, Jaxon, and Sylvian have come along. The masked man stays with our vehicle. I bet his job is keeping an eye on the sports car. Like Romeo, he seems to be someone who accompanies the Kings, but doesn't really have a proper status among them. He seems to be someone who ... *serves* them.

He didn't say a word on the drive here.

We sit down by one of the fires and Sylvian gets us some dough. He puts flatbreads on a grill over the fire and seems to be just as comfortable in this place as I am. My stomach reacts as I watch him work the dough like he's cooking for us. I can't fall in love with him. I *can't*.

Reece lowers himself into one of the beanbags and Jaxon's

fetched a wooden chair from somewhere. His face clearly says it would be beneath him to touch one of the old blankets with more than his shoes, and he perches in his chair like it's a throne.

"How did you grow up?" Jaxon asks after a while. Reece is passing his joint around. Just the idea of putting my lips on the same paper as these three men ... *Right. Relax. Get a grip on your hormones, Mable!*

"It was fine until my mom started taking pills," I tell him without emotion. "You know all about the rest, don't you?"

Jaxon smiles bitterly as he passes the joint to me. Our fingers touch for a tiny moment, sending an electric jolt through me.

Damn. I quickly draw the marijuana into my lungs, hoping it will calm me down. Usually, this stuff makes me tired. Maybe it'll also take away my nerves?

What am I actually doing here?

With the Kings of all people?

"How was yours?" I ask.

"Ours?" asks Jaxon. "We didn't grow up together."

"You can take turns," I suggest jokingly.

Sylvian's face darkens. He's still standing by the fire, turning the flatbreads, apparently lost in thought.

"I grew up in boarding schools," Reece starts. "Twelve years at boarding school, three at Kingston. In between, I spent two years abroad to learn another language."

"What's it like there?"

"Cold and dark."

"In winter, but in summer..."

"In summer too. That's when it usually rains." He gives me a wink and links his hands behind his neck. "You know, Dole, I can't complain. My life's been really good so far. But I can't imagine the freedom of a child who doesn't have to live up to anyone's expectations. To achieve what I'm supposed to, I don't have any choice but to study. Most of all, I can't choose *where* I study. My entire path in life is predetermined. No deviations, no alternatives. That doesn't make it bad, but it does make everything boring. Predictable. At least I won't also be forced to *marry* who I *have to* marry, like a Tyrell."

I look at Jaxon curiously. "You're being forced into an arranged marriage? Like in the Middle Ages?"

"Middle Ages?" Sylvian sounds doubtful.

Instead of reacting, Jaxon only stares into the flames. His mind seems to be entirely elsewhere.

"Most marriages that come out of Kingston are arranged," Sylvian explains. "Your lack of knowledge about the entire thing makes everyday university life bearable for you. If you knew what it's *really* about ..."

"Stop this drivel, Syl," Reece interrupts him. "He's trying to say the same thing I hinted at before, Dole."

I shift on my blanket. Why does he keep using that word? It's terrible. It's nasty, and it doesn't exactly make me feel good.

"Not a single fucking woman comes to Kingston to *study*."

I narrow my eyes and he waves his hand.

"Yeah, you might have. You and the few who are *paid* to be here, the ones on scholarships. But the others?" He purses his lips, shaking his head. "Nope. Most of them barely pass their courses."

"And why else would they go to Kingston?" I ask critically. "If this is just some prejudice of yours, you might as well take me back to campus—"

"It's not," Jaxon adds. His gaze is clearly on me now. The serious expression on his face makes me shudder. "At some point, the women's movement got big enough, loud enough, that Kingston could no longer afford to accept men only. They started taking on women then. Initially, they were accepted as long as they had a brother who was studying here. Kingston then extended admission, accepting women from other families as well. They didn't choose them based on tests or performance, on some ridiculous certificates, recommendations, or any of that bullshit, as is the case for male applicants. Kingston chooses its female applicants solely based on *money*."

"So most female students are richer than their male counterparts. But because they are as hollow as light bulbs ..."

"Crescent," Sylvian admonishes him, looking in my direction.

"Yeah, so what?" Reece challenges him. "They're stupid, and they do what their families want them to do. Kingston is a fucking *brothel*, Dole. A Crescent like me just has to raise his fucking hand and any one of them will sit on my cock. They send their best hookers after us. That's what's really happening at Kingston."

"Am I supposed to... feel sorry for you now?" I ask the three of them.

"Sorry for *us*?" Reece snaps, and I flinch where I sit. "Hardly. But you women are really fucked if you keep going as you are."

"Right. Go take a piss and calm down," Sylvian growls.

"What?" Reece snarls.

"Crescent," Jaxon also warns.

Reece looks at the two of them in turn, groans and angrily walks toward the car park.

"Was that just ... a pretty weird sort of explanation on why the patriarchy will always survive?" I ask the two of them, not sure if they're the right people to have this conversation with.

"Not necessarily ... weird," Sylvian admits. Our eyes meet. "Crescent isn't wrong. Kingston brings together power and money. The women do have to pass some entrance exams, but it's true that most of them buy their admission. Once on campus, they tend to ..."

"Want to make things easy for themselves," I help him out.

He raises his hands defensively. "I stay away from most of them.

But if Crescent and Jaxon can act like they do and still fuck anyone they want... There must be something to it, don't you think?"

"I'm here too," I mutter. And if there's one thing I'm absolutely not interested in, it's other people's money. Maybe the other
students feel the same way? Is it possible that they simply want
to taste the tempting poison the Kings give off? "Who says they
would actually marry you if they could? Maybe, like you, they
just want some fun and a little casual sex, and all you're doing
is slutshaming?"

Sylvian's expression remains inscrutable, but Jaxon purses his
lips derisively.

"Save your activism for your Twitter followers, will you? We
know a whore when we see one, and we can tell them apart from
women like you who actually just want sex. Would you believe
that? It'd help a lot, because if you classify us in your mind as
the worst kind of trash and think that we despise women on
principle, you're a bit too superficial for what we have in mind
for you."

"What do you have in mind for me?" I ask with a queasy feeling
in my stomach.

"We want you to win the next stage."

"You what now?"

"No one has ever deserved to stay at Kingston more than you
do." Sylvian flips the bread one last time. "We want to suggest
something so you can win."

"The next round?"

"Yes," Sylvian says seriously.

Jaxon catches my eyes, and his blue eyes light up. "Spend a
night with us and collect a thousand points for it."

My heart is pounding.

"In the fraternity house," adds Sylvian.

"Reece, Sylvian, and I will be there. You will be, too. Preferably the week of Thanksgiving, when we'll have the house mostly to ourselves."

My mouth goes dry. "I might've accepted this totally weird and unreasonable invitation if it wasn't about 'the arena' ..."

"We have to justify giving you the points somehow," Jaxon explains with a shrug. "It's merely a formality."

"Why don't you just stop this sick game? It's so stupid!"

"It's not that easy," Jaxon evades. "There are so many reasons for the game, Belle, but we don't know each other well enough yet to even give you an idea of what it's all about."

"The fact is, we think you want it too," Sylvian puts in. "One night. The campus will think we're just using you. But you'll get exactly what you want."

"And what is it that I want?" I ask, trying to hide my nerves.

Sylvian and Jaxon exchange a meaningful look.

"Us?" asks Sylvian.

"You told me to stay away just a few days ago!"

"None of us really want that," he tells me calmly. The jungle in his eyes looks satisfied. "Not you and not us either. Besides, you won't listen anyway, so you might as well accept the consequences. I'll be there and make sure that nothing happens that you don't want to happen."

"Do you expect me to ... sleep with you?" The very idea sends a cold shiver down my spine—and a hot one right through my center.

"We won't force you to do anything," Jaxon replies.

Sylvian puts the flatbreads on a paper plate, leaving them to cool, just as Reece returns.

"Well? Why do you all look like you missed me so much?" he asks cheerfully as he sits down right next to me on the blanket. "How do you like it here, Mable?"

He seems like a different person. What is going on with this guy? He almost seems to have a split personality.

I don't show what I think and let him engage me in a conversation about the party, but barely half an hour later, a woman starts screaming right next to us.

"You!"

Looking for the voice, I find one of the other guests pointing at Sylvian.

"*How dare* you come here!" the woman screams hysterically, her arm bobbing up and down.

Sylvian just looks at her, but as she approaches, he seems to recognize her. "Fuck."

"You murdered my fucking sister! It was you!"

People nearby start to notice. They rise, surrounding us. Some are curious, others dismissive, and a few men prepare for a fight.

Reece grabs my hand as the commotion around us starts to peak.

"Murderer!" the woman keeps on screaming. "You killed her!"

"We're leaving." Reece pulls me up to shunt me through the crowd.

"Who's that?"

"A madwoman."

"Who did Sylvian kill?"

"He killed *no one*," Reece impresses on me. "Some rumors bear strange fruit."

"Don't you want to stay with them? Some of the guys looked like they're raring for a fight."

"I'll take you home."

"Reece, I don't need your protection," I remind him, stopping dead.

He studies me from head to toe. "You certainly do. At the very least, you're a danger to yourself."

I stick my tongue out at him, and he grabs me by the forearm, pulling me away from the lake and back to the car park. The masked man who was waiting in the car comes running toward us. He asks no questions as he jogs past and into the crowd. By now I'm sure that I've seen him somewhere before.

"Put on your seatbelt," Reece demands as he starts the engine.

"Will you explain to me what this is all about? Why would anyone even *think* Sylvian killed someone?"

"No," Reece replies flatly as he turns the car around. "There's nothing to explain. People are sick. If they can't get to us by loving us, they start hating us. That woman hates Sylvian. She wants her hatred to be justified, which it's not. Sylvian would never kill anyone."

It's a bad habit, but my nervousness and insecurity take over to the point where I start biting my nails.

"Oh, fuck, don't do that, Mable." Reece gives me a critical look. He drives the sports car as if it were his own. "How has Syl come off to you so far, huh? He's a caring guy who's always there when you need him, isn't he? Is that what a *murderer* does?"

"You can't ever know…" *He tasted my blood and told me about a monster that would destroy me if I didn't watch out.* I don't tell Reece that one of our neighbors in the trailer park strangled his wife for no apparent reason at all. One day he was the man who loved her, the next he had become her murderer.

Reece leaves me to my thoughts. He stops near my dorm a few miles later. "Do you want me to come inside with you?"

I shake my head, remembering what happened with Sylvian last time and that I absolutely have to get back to Harper's party. The Kings' game of seduction is a lot more confusing than the actual game they're playing. I need some peace and quiet to sort out my thoughts before I allow myself to feel any more emotions.

Eventually, I say, "Sylvian and Jaxon told me that if I spend a night with the three of you, you'll let me win the next stage."

Reece's eyes grow warm and understanding, sending heat through my entire chest. "So? Do you want it, too?"

I look at him, not sure how their offer can be genuine. They're all attractive. Their bodies alone promise fantastic sex. It's exactly what I secretly wished for, and so much more. They're the Kings. They're hot as hell. Just the thought of it makes my clit throb as if Reece has his tongue on it again. "Not if it's a game."

He smiles ironically, leaning his head back. "But that's the way we are, Mable. We play games. We aren't good guys. But what's stopping you from having some fun with us?"

I blush, which makes him laugh. "What will happen after that night? Will you leave me alone?"

"Alone?" His vampire fangs flash in the darkness. "How could we ever leave you alone, Mable? You know it won't end after one night. Least of all if we *all* like it." His right ring finger touches my leg as if by chance. In contrast to Jaxon and Sylvian, he wears only a single ring: the one marking him as a King. "You're special, Mable. I think we all have the same form of no-strings-attached sex in mind, don't we? Why shouldn't we have some fun together?"

I am about to let loose a torrent of words. My head has long been overflowing with lust and shame, and I certainly should share all the thousand reasons I have to not take their offer, but when I turn to him, not a single sound leaves my lips. Damn. I'm sitting there, a fish out of water, staring at the most beautiful man I know. Well, not counting Jaxon, whose character disfigures his appearance most of the time, and Sylvian, who is fiendishly hot rather than picture perfect.

Reece gives me a knowing smile. We're parked just where Clarisse and her gang were on my first day, when they laughed at me. Jaxon spends almost all his lectures sitting with that awful bitch. The Kings can have anyone. What did Sylvian say? Reece fucks a different girl every day?

Trusting them is stupid. It has to only be about sex for me, just as it is for them. "And you're sure you don't just say that to everyone?" I ask in a whisper.

He laughs again. "Pretty sure." It sounds too good to be true. "Ask the girls on campus. Usually, the only thing we say to them is, Get on your knees. And they ask, How deep do you want me to swallow you? That's the only conversation we have with women who aren't our professors."

"Oh. Sure." I feel dizzy and hot. Is it possible? Would every woman on campus truly sink to the ground in front of a King?

"Think about it, Mable. No one's ever won so easily."

I should find the way he talks about the game that stands between my graduation and me, and the fact that it's solely in the Kings' hands whether I win or not, off-putting. But I can't. It makes me feel desired.

It makes me feel so very desired that I have to wonder whether this isn't exactly their plan.

To make me fly high.

And then destroy me.

JAXON

Y ou want us to take you into our arms, don't you? You want each of us to seduce you in his own way. Have you imagined yet what it would be like with all of us, huh? Do you dare to give in to the depravity within you? Or will you continue to stubbornly cling to your imagined superiority?

20

MABLE

Harper can't believe it when she finds out I didn't lose the first round after all. She stands in front of the notice in our kitchen for several minutes and keeps asking me if truly the only thing I had to do to get five hundred points was win at poker.

Yes, I tell her, repeating it over and over again, to avoid admitting that Sylvian played a crucial part—and in a way that had nothing to do with the help Harper believes he's been giving me. I also tell her about the night Jaxon and Reece want to spend with me so I can win the next stage. I leave out the fact that Sylvian is part of that, too. I don't want to hurt her, even though I know it would be better for her to face the truth.

But I already have a plan.

Spending a night with them says nothing about how far we'll go, does it? If I don't sleep with any of them—and certainly not with Sylvian—I won't be betraying Harper again and I'll win the next stage anyway.

Harper didn't even realize I left her party. I found her drunk in her bedroom upon my return, making out with a guy who took off as soon as I walked in. The next day she told me how grateful she was that I'd saved her.

A few more days pass, and the only thing that changes noticeably is that one of the scholarship students has left. Kady.

It comes as a shock. I liked her the best. We never learn where she went or what happened.

Her dorm room was empty on the first of November, and everyone studiously ignores any questions asked about it.

As much as I enjoy attending my courses and learning from the professors and tutors, always knowing in the back of my mind that a bunch of idiots, including the Kings, are going to decide whether I'll be allowed to stay or not is depressing.

Every night, I muse about whether I should report the game after all. Shouldn't I tell *someone* about it?

But what chance do we have if I pit Harper and me against everyone else?

I try to focus on my studies, which are more challenging with every passing week. Homework and exams need to be written, and I have to prepare for finals in the last week before Christmas. My notes are piled inches high, and I'm borrowing new books from the library every day.

Halloween had one good effect, though: I've finally found the courage to go to Reece's tutorial. It only takes listening to him speak and explain one of the new concepts for five minutes to know that all my concerns were unfounded.

Reece is a great teacher.

His explanations are outstanding, patient, and highly accessible. No matter if he's talking to me or to any other participant, he remains professionally distant and doesn't give away anything at all, least of all regarding our conversation in Jaxon's car.

Reece's tutorial becomes a highlight in my week. I allow myself to secretly ogle him as long as I still listen to the actual subject matter. He teaches linear algebra, one of a number of general studies subjects freshmen have to take regardless of their major.

I hardly ever run into Jaxon and Sylvian on campus. I see one or the other passing at a distance sometimes. Sylvian is usually alone, while Jaxon is often accompanied by Clarisse and his other fangirls. I haven't forgotten his proposition to spend a night with them, but I'm glad we're keeping our distance from each other for the moment.

I can't throw myself into anything. I can't lose myself in my feelings.

The weeks that pass without any contact with them help me to focus on my actual goal of getting good grades.

I start getting nervous as November quickly moves toward Thanksgiving. The Kings' game is still going. I can feel it in the stares directed my way. A new challenge is posted in our kitchen every week and the other three scholarship students always jump to do it.

Brittany and Rachel even painted penises on their faces when told to.

None of this changes the fact that I secretly rely on Jaxon's promise. He said that I could stay if I took them up on their offer. But when would that night happen?

On the last Friday before Thanksgiving, I remain in my seat after Reece's class. He's the one I feel most confident talking to.

"Mable, I need to lock the room," he tells me when he sees that I'm still sitting there. It's a good sign that he doesn't call me Dole. This is the version of Reece that I like.

"Can I ask you a question?"

"One that has nothing to do with math, I suspect?"

"Yeah."

Reece runs his fingers through his hair. He looks tired, stressed. Maybe the Kings just forgot about me? Who knows what they have to deal with as seniors.

I shoulder my bag and move toward the blackboard. "It's just..."

"It's what?"

"I really enjoy studying here. So if you ... Jaxon mentioned a 'mere formality' when we ..."

"You mean the night?"

"Not that I'm particularly keen on maintaining my place here that way, but ..."

"But?"

"I'll do it. I probably would've done it anyway, if there was no game. So I feel okay about it."

Reece's expression is inscrutable. I've rarely seen him look so serious. Suddenly I wonder why an attractive man like him, who could have anyone at all, would spend the night with me *and his friends.* And I expect him to tell me exactly that. He should be telling me just how stupid I am to have ever believed that he would plan a night of sex with me. That it was all a joke.

"How about tonight?" he asks. "I won't be around for Thanksgiving."

"Tonight already?" My voice has acquired a much higher pitch.

Reece smiles his wide, dreamy smile. "Do you need more time than that to prepare?"

I shake my head and try to make my voice sound deeper, which doesn't work. "No, it's great," I squeak.

"I'll come pick you up, alright? Seven o'clock?"

"Alright." My cheeks heat up again and I'm completely overwhelmed by the thought that it's actually going to happen. I'm actually doing it. And *the Kings really want me.*

Reece picks up his bag. "I have to be at the other end of campus in ten minutes. See you tonight, then?"

***

Harper drops by in the afternoon to work on my plan with me. I've asked to borrow something from her for the night and she's already told me that she won't let me go without a set of instructions and warnings. The many midterm exams and plenty of homework have meant that we've barely seen each other in the last few days. Now that we have five days without lectures, though, the mood on campus has relaxed noticeably.

I may not want to go home, but I have to. I dread seeing how my sister has been neglected since I left. Everyone else welcomes the free Thanksgiving week as a break from university stress. For me, it's going to be a nightmare.

"I only support this because it's the easiest way for you to win and you can outsmart them," she tells me, pad and pen in her hand, nervously teetering on the edge of my bed. "Because 'one night together' doesn't say anything about what you're going to do, right? You can just make small talk the whole time! Or twiddle your thumbs! Or play on your phone. It's best to pretend they're not even there. You'll win and they'll look stupid."

We giggle. All the same, I'm aware that it will be difficult for me to take her advice.

"Usually, I'd tell you this is a completely idiotic idea," she says. "But *if* the Kings have actually learned anything from last year, they might be trying to make up for it with the stupid points-for-a-night thing. It's pretty harmless compared to everything else. I mean, as long as you listen to me and don't *really* let any of them get to you, you have nothing to lose. No sex, remember? You will *not* sleep with them. Not with Jaxon and not with Reece."

"Can't I sleep with them and ..."

"No!"

"... still not let them 'get to me'?"

"You can't! Impossible! They'll make you feel like you're the only one for them and get you hooked on them forever. Look at me! I am proof of just how toxic they are. Would you want to get involved with two of them at once?"

I shut my mouth and let her think that she's convinced me. We'll never agree on this. Why wouldn't Reece or Jaxon want more after sex? Why does the woman always have to fall for the guy and then spend the rest of her life mourning him? Why doesn't Harper just find another guy, for that matter? She's the most beautiful girl on campus. If Sylvian doesn't want her ... I bite back the words. Not telling her the truth about Sylvian and me is the one thing that leaves me feeling uncomfortable.

"Is Sylvian going to be there too?" she asks, as if she's caught me thinking.

"I don't know." *Lie!*

Harper's eyes take on a faraway look and she shakes her head quickly. "If you want to do something with him ..."

"I won't." *Another lie!*

"I've seen the way he looks at you, Mable," she whispers. "If he wants you, if he *really* wants you, then maybe he's the only one I'd trust if I were in your place."

"Why are you saying that now?" I ask cautiously. "You said he was the worst of them."

"Maybe you can make him happy?" There's so much love for him in her words it ties my guts into a painful knot. "Maybe if he finds the right girl, he can actually be happy. I wasn't the right one for him, but ..."

"No." My throat is dry as dust and I try to swallow. "How can you be so selfless? If he hurt you, he deserves your hate! Not your love!"

Harper spins the pen between her fingers, lost in thought. "That's what they do to you. Once you start loving them you'll never stop." She wipes away a tear without smudging a single dab of makeup and straightens. "You're stronger though!" She beams at me, stepping close and taking hold of both my shoulders. "No matter what happens tonight, Mable," she whispers. "Use condoms. Better yet: Don't use them and just get through the night without sleeping with them! And never, ever, under any circumstances, have *sex with all of them.*"

Just talking about it makes my pussy glow with longing. Fuck. How many before me have the Kings done this with? Will their experience make it better? Or are they going to tie me up somewhere and do things to me whether I want them to or not, destroy me forever?

"If you fuck them all," Harper whispers urgently, her eyes completely clear now and intense, like she's about to tell me something vital. "Then you'll lose *everything.*"

I take a deep breath and nod.

"Promise?" she asks.

"I promise," I lie, two fingers crossed behind my back.

***

As the evening approaches, we stand by the street waiting for Reece. The only thing I've taken from Harper is one of her handbags, which holds my phone—and no condoms. *If I don't take any contraceptives with me in the first place, I can tell myself that I'm not hoping to have sex with them.*

Harper, on the other hand, is carrying an entire suitcase. She's wearing a bright yellow winter jacket, high boots, a dress, and tights. That's it. I'm in a knee-length coat, scarf, hat, and gloves and I'm still freezing.

I watch the black car approaching with mixed feelings.

The limo reminds me of that time Jaxon abandoned me in the forest.

"Well then, my heart." Harper gives me a tight hug. "Don't fall

281

for their games. Don't even think about getting near their dicks, and just enjoy the night! Do you hear me? I'll text you as soon as I touch down in Miami."

Miami. Right. That's where her family spends Thanksgiving every year. The Mitchells have three residences in the States alone: in New York, in Miami, and in Malibu. Why not meet up for Thanksgiving where the weather is best in November?

"Take care." I release her and watch her get into the sedan while the driver takes care of her suitcase.

A few minutes later, a black Tesla pulls up next to me on the road. The window on the passenger side rolls down.

"Get in, princess!" Reece calls out to me.

I walk up to the car and try to open the door.

He laughs while I struggle to get the hang of its mechanism.

"God," I mutter as I slide into the seat. Instead of sporting a regular dashboard, fans, and buttons, the front is dominated by a gigantic tablet computer.

"Fancy, isn't it?" Reece asks with a grin. "Buckle up."

I obey, only to be pressed into my seat with full force a second later. "Fuck," I gasp and look at him in a panic. He just accelerated from zero to a hundred in two seconds.

The engine doesn't make a sound.

"I love this car," he says. "It's too cheap for people on campus, but it's perfect for impressing women a bit, don't you think?"

"Cheap?" I ask, astonished.

"Well, the Model 3 doesn't even cost eighty thousand dollars. That's a scrap car around here." He laughs as he lets the car coast before taking the next bend toward the Rex house. "They just don't understand that things aren't automatically bad just because they don't cost quite as much."

I try to follow his train of thought and find myself failing. Eighty thousand dollars. For a car. Not much. Will I ever be willing to spend that much on a means of transportation?

Reece talks to me in a very relaxed manner during the ride. I quickly realize it's one of the most normal conversations I've ever had with anyone from Kingston, apart from Harper. We talk about all kinds of things, and I love it.

Every normal topic shifts me a little further into my comfort zone.

He's distracting me from the fact that we're getting out of the car in front of the Kings' fraternity house, where he leads me toward the wide staircase, still chatting away. This house is where this nightmare started. Is it going to end here after tonight?

Reece leads me into a cozy little lounge with a fire crackling in the fireplace and pours two glasses of wine. He's funny, entertaining, friendly, and attentive. He waits until I'm done talking, asks questions, laughs when I try to say something ironic, and keeps quiet when I get more serious.

His blond hair falls over his forehead. His smile is engaging and full of warmth. He wears a light blue sweater that flatters his well-defined muscles, and his every movement is dignified, attractive, and elegant.

When he reaches out to take my hand, I pull back in panic. It's not that I *don't* want it, but I'm starting to like it. I'm liking this far too much, and that goes against my plan—and Harper's recommendation—not to let any of the Kings get to me. "Why are you sometimes nice to me and sometimes ... a real asshole?"

"What?" He sounds surprised.

"The part of you that calls me Mable is really ... attractive. But the one who calls me Dole is an ass. How am I supposed to know when you're going to change again?"

His face darkens and he leans back, his posture full of tension. His right hand goes for his glass. He swirls the wine in it before draining it. The ring of the Kings reflects the firelight. It bears a large coat of arms with an ornate K in the middle. "I can't really give you a good answer for that."

"Why don't you try?"

Reece rolls his eyes at me, which makes me feel uncomfortable. Everything up to this moment has been perfect. He has been perfect. The conversation has been perfect. But how could I forget how he treats me half the time? "Why can't we just fuck, Mable?"

I can feel the wine going to my head. Did he just offer me sex? Am I about to say no? Why? Because I suddenly want the guy I'm going to sleep with to be a totally decent man? "I like you," I say, trying to hold his gaze. "If you were *just* an asshole, it might be easier for me. But because you're *also* likable, I just want to understand why you—"

"You like me?" Reece interrupts.

"A little?"

"Do you like me or not?"

"I like half of you!"

"Alright..." Reece looks at me for a very long moment, emotions battling in his expression. When it evens out again, I can't tell which of the many feelings I just saw won out. "I'm not someone you should like."

"Ah," I say stupidly.

"That's why I call you Dole now and then. That's why I'm an ass sometimes. This can't go any deeper than the game. I told you we could have fun. And that's exactly what I meant. Don't get the idea that you like me. And if you don't want to try to kill yourself, it's best to pretend from now on that Jaxon doesn't even exist. That's what I can tell you." He pauses and looks at me. "That raises more questions than it answers, doesn't it?"

I nod cautiously.

"Sylvian was right when he said that you need to be protected. Not because you're particularly ... worthy of protection or particularly poor or vulnerable. You're just naive. You're so naive that it hurts to watch you walk into your own destruction."

I'm also leaning back now. Unable to think of any defense to keep his words from hitting me quite so hard, I cross my arms in front of my chest. It's not much, but it's the only thing I can do.

"You think you can kiss us or let me lick you and *not* fall in love? How does that work? Don't you realize that all I have to do is touch you and my river is going to sweep you away?"

I swallow. "Have you ever heard about hormones that—"

"No," he snaps at me. "Never heard of them. I'm about to graduate summa cum laude from Kingston University. Do you know what I really hate about you? I hate it so much I want to choke you until you let go of that bullshit as if you'd never thought of it in the first place."

"What is that?" I ask tonelessly.

"You think you can take us on." Reece grinds his teeth, finally reaching for the bottle of wine. His hand shakes as he tops up his glass, but not, as mine would, with nerves. He's angry. "You don't know what you're doing when you try to oppose us. If you'd just play this fucking game, if you'd just collect points like everyone else, if you'd just do the challenges, then maybe you'd even win..." He runs his fingers through his hair and puts the bottle down again with a dull thud.

"But if I spend the night here, I won't?" I ask, distraught. I feel like something's breaking inside me. The bubble of safety the Kings created for me, the idea that I'd only have to survive this one night and they would at least leave me alone until finals, bursts, leaving behind a wound somewhere deep inside me. *I'm so stupid. I'm so naive!* "Reece!" My voice cracks. "Is this night part of the game? Are you going to keep me from winning the next stage?"

He takes a deep breath. "It's not a game for me."

Six simple words that sound like a confession of love to my

ears. The bubble of safety closes tightly around me again and I want to revel in it, drop into it, and believe every word he says. "And for whom is it? Jaxon and Sylvian?"

"I don't know." Reece gives me a weary look, suddenly as exhausted and tired as I've seen him since this morning. "But for you, for you it *should* be one. That's the only way you can win. You can't permit yourself any feelings. You... can't fall in love. Don't get me wrong, I wouldn't mind, but I'm saying that as a man, not a friend."

"The more you explain, the less I get it," I mutter, feeling shy. His words sound like magic and somehow also like a dangerous weapon that could go off at any moment.

"I know," he tells me gloomily. "I'm sorry about that."

"Is it so hard to tell the truth?"

"Not necessarily hard, no. But as I said, I'm not sitting before you as a friend. If I were just a friend, I wouldn't be spending this time thinking about what we could be doing with this night other than talking."

I shift nervously on the sofa.

Reece's voice becomes a little rougher. "Mable, have you had sex before?"

"Why are you so interested in that?" I ask with a huff.

"Because all *we* know is that you're a virgin."

Wow. Sylvian really didn't tell them anything. "And so what if I am?" I ask coolly. "Is that what makes me *desirable* to you?"

"You have no fucking *idea*," he grumbles. "I don't give a shit. But if you really are, then let me be the one to ... deflower you. Not because it means anything to me. Rather, precisely because it means *nothing* to me. I'll be careful, and I'll make it good for you. I'll touch you the way you need to relax and make sure that you feel pleasure in it. I won't do anything that you don't want or don't like, and you don't need to worry that *you'll* do something that

I don't want or don't like. Honestly, that would be best for you."

I reach for my glass. Can I trust him? If I could, if I could *trust* him, then I would say yes. I *want* him, I want us to finally go further. But the fear that he's just messing with me has become overwhelming. "Do I have to wear a blindfold?"

Reece rolls his neck before fixing me firmly with his gaze again. "If you really want me to fuck you, yes. Otherwise ... no."

I quickly take another sip of wine. *You can just make small talk the whole time! Or twiddle your thumbs!*

Yeah. Fat chance of that.

"Let's just talk a bit more first, shall we?" I ask nervously. Reece looks like I just suggested that I show him my stamp collection. He looks at me impassively and slowly leans forward.

Kissing him would be the beginning of the end ... What do you really want, Mable? Can you trust them? Can you trust yourself?

"What are you doing here?"

I flinch and turn. Sylvian is suddenly standing in the doorway like some dark omen.

"Helping Amabelle win?" Reece suggests, reaching for a third wine glass. "Go ahead and have a seat."

"Are you trying to get her drunk?" Sylvian asks. His voice has an edge of steel. "You are not going to touch her, Crescent."

"Won't I?" Reece returns, unconcerned.

Sylvian growls as he comes toward me. He grabs my arm and pulls me up. The coat that I've only taken off halfway so far drops off my shoulders, and he stares at my dress. "What the hell are you wearing?" I wish I could escape from the cold he radiates in my direction. "Shit. What do you think is going to happen tonight?"

I give Reece a helpless look, but he does nothing. Just like he didn't do anything when Romeo drugged me. Is that the hierarchy of the Kings? Jaxon, then Sylvian, then Reece? Or are Sylvian and Jaxon leaders with equal rights?

"Nobody is going to touch you tonight," Sylvian growls as he drags me out of the warm room.

"You're touching me right now," I complain, but he only pulls me along with him more vehemently.

"Just come with me." He maneuvers me up a huge, curved staircase. Deserted and without any party guests, the fraternity house feels like an enchanted castle. I'd fall in love with every single corner if I didn't already have some serious issues with not falling in love with the residents.

"You'll sleep in my room tonight, and I'll take you to Philadelphia tomorrow."

"Thank you, that's really very nice, but I *won't* be sleeping in *your* room. Think of Harper!"

"I don't care what you think of it."

"You can't make my decisions for me!"

"I'm making them right now!" A moment later, he stops in front of a pair of huge double doors. He pushes them open and sends me through. "If you can't make the right decisions for yourself, I'm going to make them for you."

His room is furnished in an old-fashioned style, with furniture that clearly isn't his own. A four-poster bed stands on one side of the vaulted room, a seating area with four armchairs on the other. His fireplace is almost as big as I am. There are a few bookcases, a desk with a laptop on it, and a few personal items of the kind that every student accumulates. Notes, keys, headphones, cables, textbooks...

"Why here? Why should I sleep here, with you of all people?"

"Because this is the only place where I can protect you," he explains.

"Protect me from whom?"

He just snorts. "The first thing you're going to do is get changed." Sylvian pulls a sweater out of a chest of drawers. "If I have to look at you in your little fuck-me-now dress for another second, I'll forget myself. Why the hell did you dress like you thought we were having sex tonight?"

My cheeks glow hot, and I bite the inside of my cheek.

Sylvian steps close, sweater in hand, and treats me to a dark look from above. It's beautiful. It's so dark and beautiful that self-doubt takes hold of me with full force. Of course they wouldn't sleep with me. None of them would. I'm an ugly nothing next to them, dressed up in clothes far too expensive that I could never afford on my own, pretending to be something I can never be.

"Why do you think I let you come with us on Halloween?" he asks so quietly that his voice is more of a low hum.

"I don't know."

"I knew that Jaxon would agree immediately. That's why I made the suggestion. You know exactly how the conditions are phrased. Spend a night in the frat house and you get a thousand points."

"Yeah."

"So, spend the fucking night in the frat house! That's all you have to do!"

My mouth has gone completely dry.

Sylvian's jaw tenses, and his rough beard emphasizes how hard the edges of his face are in the dim light. "You weren't really planning on letting us fuck you, were you?"

I don't shake my head quite fast enough.

"Damn it!" he growls and grabs me. He pulls me in front of him and his breath penetrates deeply into my senses. "You can't let us anywhere near your pussy. Not a single one of us. Do I make myself clear? It won't be hard, because we might be the biggest motherfuckers on the planet, but we'd *never* get close to you if you didn't want us to. So put on the damn sweater. Go lie down in my bed and go to sleep. I'm going to go and leave you on your own. Normally, it's forbidden to bring women into the bedrooms. We're the only ones who are allowed to have girls over, and the fraternity house is virtually empty because of the vacations. Still—it's better not to draw attention to yourself."

"Just you Kings?"

"There's got to be some advantage to the title, right?" he asks cynically, closing the double doors to his room with both hands as he walks out backward.

He leaves me on my own, and I have to come to terms with the fact that I'm standing in his room without wanting to be here. *What is Harper going to say?*

I have my phone with me. I can text her. How can I phrase that message in a way that won't hurt her, though? Also, what happens if the Kings are right about everything, and Harper just wants me to stay away from them because she's jealous?

No ... that can't be. The Kings have proven that it's not wise for any woman to get caught up in their game, and Harper rightfully warned me against it.

I can't risk our friendship.

Before I change, I sit in one of the armchairs to think about what I'm going to say to her.

Hey H,

have you arrived safely in Miami yet?

You're probably still on the plane. I just wanted to tell you that Sylvian took me to his room. He says this is the only way he can be sure that nothing more will happen ... Maybe he's even right. :P I don't want you to think I'm betraying you. Wish me luck that I can just sleep and get through the night unscathed.

The answer comes promptly.

*I knew you were going to sleep with
him. Don't bother to apologize.*

What makes you say that? Are you mad at me?

*Mad? Because you're spending the night
in the room of my ex, whom I still love?
Either way, Clarisse betrayed me worse.*

My mouth opens and I let a few minutes pass before I answer so the
hint of anger that would've made me write something nasty can fade.

*I don't want to hurt you. I would
never hurt you on purpose.*

I receive no further reply. Maybe she's thinking that her reaction
was a bit too bitchy. Can I blame her? If she's as madly in love
with Sylvian as she says, she's surely raging with jealousy toward
anyone who even looks at him... Just like Sylvian said.

I make myself more comfortable in the armchair to let my
thoughts stop spinning for a moment. I have to collect myself
so I can actually figure out what I want. Who's telling the truth?
Why does Sylvian think I'm safe in his room of all places?

Safe from whom?

From the Kings?

Or from my own desire?

As I move around on the chair, I can feel that there's something
underneath me. Reaching for it with one hand, I end up holding
a plastic bag. As soon as I realize what it must be, I throw the
bag as if it burned me.

"Fuck!" I mutter, lifting the second cushion as well. Another bag.

My gaze finds the many other armchairs. Would it be wiser to pretend I hadn't seen anything? Should I act as if I never sat down? It would be smarter. But while I may be intelligent enough to pass the courses at Kingston, no one would call me smart. Following an inner urge, I check under the other cushions as well.

I find bags upon bags upon bags.

Each one contains loads of further packets.

Some are filled with pills. Others with white powder.

Drugs.

Before me lies a dealer's stock for a month.

Fuck. What the hell does all of this mean?

21

SYLVIAN

A s I lean against the door to my room, my right heel against the wood, I roll the day's twentieth cigarette.

The nicotine keeps me trapped in a state where I'm lucid enough not to give in to my cravings, yet hazy enough to stop worrying.

It's the end of November.

And I am still a victim of my own nature.

I believed that my former life in the dark alleys, the sleazy clubs, the dirty subway stations was fucked up. But it's nothing when I compare it to what was waiting for me between the gilded taps and tailored uniforms.

Now I'm part of it myself. I'm rich as fuck and influential as a King.

There are a thousand girls I could have. As a King, one learns the art of seduction better than anyone else. Most of the shit Crescent told Mable was true. But it's only half the truth.

Women are not the only ones looking for a suitable partner on campus.

We, too, must choose wisely.

An impoverished scholarship student is the opposite of a wise choice.

It's downright stupid.

It's so stupid that I doubt whether I'm cut out for the master's program at Kingston.

Since last summer, my black soul has been trying to figure out if Mable would break under the things my imagination dreams up, or if she would emerge victorious. It's not about winning as such, but about the idea of finding a girl made for my kind of darkness. Someone who understands me and doesn't run away when she looks behind the curtain of money and power that makes up my life.

I promised myself that I would wait until I could be sure that Mable was suitable. If anything about her seemed too fragile, I'd leave her alone. Another pile of broken pieces is of no use to me. So I'd leave her whole and disappear from her life forever.

That's what I told myself.

Unfortunately, I haven't disappeared from her life.

I fucked her as soon as I had the chance and lost the bet.

And if I'm not careful, she won't just break because of me.

"Sylvian Silvano."

I look up.

Jaxon's shadow creeps up the huge spiral staircase in front of him just before he himself emerges. Flanked by the other Kings, he smiles mirthlessly. "You're not really planning to hide her away, are you?"

I relax and shrug. He won't be able to drag her out of my room, so she's safe.

"She wrote to Harper." Jaxon's smile widens into a wry grin.

My lighter almost drops from my hand. *Are you crazy, Mable?*

"What are you going to do with her, huh?" Jaxon asks quietly, moving closer. I can't give him any answer that would satisfy him.

He's never going to understand that I'm not the same man anymore. *He won't allow it.*

Yes, I fought a war alongside him for three years. A war against victims who never meant anything to me. Against scholarship students like you. But I've gone too far, Mable.

I have become what I've always hated.

Like my father.

Like my family.

I am no murderer.

I. AM. NO. MURDERER.

"You can't fight it, Silvano," Tyrell says. "You want to finish what we started as much as we do."

"Leave her alone," I tell him clearly. *They crave you. They're eager to finally break your tender innocence. Never before has a female scholarship student—or any woman at all—wanted it as much as you do. Wanted all of us.*

It was only through you that we realized what sets actual whores apart from women like you. But they don't know that I took your innocence long ago. And they must not find out. Never.

"You will leave her alone," I repeat.

"Is that so?" Jaxon demands cynically. "Since when does that no longer include yourself?"

"We," I improve grudgingly. "*We* will leave her alone."

"That's why you brought her to *your* room of all places? So that *we* will leave her alone?"

A torrent of anger rushes through me. "Reece would've already fucked her in the parlor downstairs. And I don't trust you in this at all, Jax. I'm the only one who can hold back."

"No one wants to hold back, Sylvian," Reece interjects with a shrug. "We all want her. You do, too. Why are you fighting it?"

"We won't touch her!" My voice shakes uncontrollably. "We will *not* destroy her. We had a deal."

"No, Sylvian," Jaxon corrects me. "We have a *bet*. And I hardly think you'll win it if you keep her locked in your room and have to lie next to her all night. Why don't we just let her fuck Reece? He wins and gets to decide what happens to her."

My mouth goes dry as I feel the greed rising up between us. It surges in me like some hungry predator. "Reece never played. And anyway, he'll only want her until he can get his cock in some other bitch and get off," I say through gritted teeth.

Reece raises both eyebrows. "Me? I wouldn't fuck anyone else if I could have Mable."

"See?" Jaxon says, voice brimming with lust. "Think about it ... If Reece wins, we'll finally be free of this annoying bet. You can have her. I can have her. We can *all* have a *lot of fun*."

My hands automatically clench into fists, and I move toward him.

I don't want them to touch you, Mable. Yes, sometimes I'm just as naive as you are. Sometimes I think I have a chance to protect you.

"Amabelle wants it too," Jaxon states, blocking my way to keep me from going after Reece. "We all know that. *We all know it, don't we, Sylvian?*"

"Crescent will never let her win." *I knew it from the start, Mable. I knew you didn't stand a chance. For the sole reason that nobody will give you one. Jaxon won't let you win. It doesn't matter what Reece or I do.*

"Maybe, maybe not," Reece replies nonchalantly. "Do I have to?"

I take a deep breath.

"Why do you want to save *her* of all people, Sylvian? What's so special about her?"

"Nothing," I answer truthfully. Mable is so normal it should be a turn off. If it wasn't for the blood that immediately rushes to her cheeks when I approach her ... Or the quickening of her heart when I reach out my hand in her direction ... Or the desire and the lust, the longing and the fire, that blazes within her ...

Maybe we have to destroy her first so she can rise again like a phoenix from the ashes?

Otherwise, I can't explain how she, of all people, can stand against us.

"I know what's special about her." Reece has come closer. If Mable thought to put her ear to the door, she'd be able to hear every word. "She's the first woman I've met who doesn't give a shit about money. As long as she has enough to send to her mom, she isn't looking for any more. Mable is right: Compared to her, everyone else is a whore because they're only after money, power, or better grades. But her? She simply enjoys being with us. Just like that."

"She's not the first," Jaxon replies dismissively.

"Is that so?" Reece asks. "Then why are you so greedy for her? If you didn't care about her, you wouldn't have made sure I didn't fuck her."

"On principle," Jaxon mutters.

"Yes, of course. Of course, there's nothing at all between you. No attraction, nothing. You can really see that."

"You're getting on my nerves, Crescent."

"The other girls," Reece leans forward, speaking more quietly, "had a clear favorite among us and only accepted the rest of us because they wanted to keep their options open in case their favorite didn't want them. But she wants us *all*."

"You're making a fool of yourself," Jaxon mocks in an equally low voice.

"*You're* making a fool of yourself because you always want to be right. In the end, she would have let me fuck her countless times by now if you hadn't intervened like vultures. I think I won your stupid bet and I get to decide about her."

"And what would you do in that case?" Jaxon asks with interest.

Reece smirks, then glances at Zayn and Romeo, who have

remained in the background. "Keep her, of course."

"What exactly do you mean by that?" I ask tonelessly.

"Jaxon wants to get rid of her. You want her to be allowed to continue to study at Kingston unmolested. I'd let her stay, and as long as she stays, she'll be our *property*."

I feel both aversion and fascination. *It wouldn't be any good for you, Mable. It would be a disaster. No one has ever survived between us.*

Jaxon looks satisfied. "Face it, Sylvian," he hisses, coming within a few centimeters of me. "You can't save her. Not anymore."

"You know that I can. And I will try until your ego has finally shrunk to the size it should be."

"You're not being very nice to me."

"And you're actually a pathetic son of a bitch who keeps an army of psychos to torment innocent victims."

Jaxon's face goes pale as he puts distance between us with a big step back.

I run my hands over my jacket and stare him down. "Keep it up and soon it won't be the heir to the Kingston lineage calling the shots on this campus or in the *circle*."

"You like her," he states flatly. The other Kings look at me, watching my reactions, but I ignore their stares. "You really like her."

"What if I do?" I stand by that. *You fucked up my brain, Mable. Ever since I first saw you, I haven't been able to stop thinking about you and what Jaxon is going to do to you if you get in his way. But I barely know you. I know next to nothing about you. There's just this fascination ... This annoying, agonizing fascination that makes me wait in the shadows for a day when I can get closer without hurting you.*

But how is that supposed to work?

How the fucking hell am I supposed to hold back my demons?

I can only do that with women who mean nothing to me.

Women who trigger the same emptiness in me as most other people do.

Reece comes closer, his hands in his pockets, and looks at me intently. "How much?" he asks. "How much do you like her?"

I ignore him.

"Reece asked you a question," Jaxon says coldly. "If she means that much to you, Sylvian, then *go* with her. We certainly won't stand in the way of your *happiness*. Just make sure that little bitch never comes back to Kingston."

"Go with God, but go," Zayn interjects from behind, looking at his fingernails as if they were the only interesting sight in the room. "Why are you torturing yourself so much, Silvano? Why are you torturing *her*? You can lead a great life away from Kingston. Buy her an apartment in the city, get her a job so she doesn't miss you when you're here, and take her out to see the world. Sorry man, why are you even making her an object of some sick bet with Jax? What the hell do you get out of her staying at Kingston?"

My breath rattles. I feel backed into a corner. And rightly so. *Why am I so keen to secure your future at Kingston? How far should I go for this?*

"He doesn't know it himself," Jaxon sneers. He has already regained his position. Even when we meet as equals, I have never outdone him.

I just can't do it. The Kings know me too well.

"Fuck you all," I mutter, pulling open the door to my room and disappearing behind it. They won't follow, I know that. As long as I stay away from Mable, they will accept that I protect her.

Even Jaxon doesn't want his toy to break before the round is over.

Mable is sitting in one of the armchairs, still in the smoking hot dress Harper lent her, leafing through a book.

Something has changed about her.

She's done something.

Fuck, where are the fucking drugs, Mable?

I only have to lift one chair cushion to realize that she's not only found my—admittedly weak—hiding places, but also cleared them out.

For a few seconds, I lose the ability to think. For so many shitty days and shitty hours, I gave this girl a wide berth. Kept myself away. Held back. Suddenly, everything has changed. My fingers twitch. I have nine weapons hidden in the room. One's almost within reach, and then there's the knife that I always carry on my body. It's the instincts of a Silvano that make me think for a moment that Mable has tricked me, betrayed me. For a moment, I wonder if she was planted here by the cops or one of my enemies.

But that's not like you, is it? You have no idea who I am, and this is all a big coincidence.

I have to focus and make a decision in a matter of seconds.

"What have you done?" I ask her, trying to control my voice. To sound normal. Relaxed.

I fail.

"What have *you* done, Sylvian?" she asks, closing the book. "Was that the supply of drugs you need to pass exams in your final year of college?"

My right eyelid twitches. *I usually have less patience than this, baby.* "Where are the bags?"

"I've hidden them here in the room." She looks at me calmly. She learns my biggest secret and doesn't even show any fear. "And I called the police. If you tell me who you are, what this is all about, and how I'm *really* going to win this damn game, I'll tell you where to find all the baggies before they start raiding."

My heartrate skyrockets, blood shooting through my veins like fuel. I take three steps toward her and draw my knife. The butter-fly blade swings open. Mable doesn't know what hit her when I hold it to her throat a moment later, her light brown hair firmly in my grip. Her eyes widen in agony, and she looks at me like I'm a dead man about to drag her to hell with me. Not real and yet so close. I can practically taste the blood rushing to her cheeks, and it would be so easy to hurt her in order to get a real taste...

To taste her again...

"Tell me that's not true," I demand calmly. I'm as calm and controlled as I can manage to be when I'm being threatened this way.

Mable's entire body is trembling. Her hands clench the armchair's fabric. She'd expected everything, but not that I'd be like the men she knows. *Worse.*

I should know how you feel. I should know what a university like Kingston means to girls like you. I've been through it myself. To me, a good school was my chance to leave behind the trailer parks, the violence, the fights, pill trips, and gangsters. And that's exactly how you feel, Mable.

You thought you'd escape that shit.

But you were wrong.

Criminals wear tailor-made suits at Kingston University. They're smart, smooth, and cunning. They won't dirty their own hands. They never do. They're many times more dangerous. You could simply run from an insignificant gangster after all.

You could move to a new city, a new neighborhood, build a new life.

But you can't hide from the real gangsters, the Tyrells, the Crescents, or the Silvanos.

Never.

"Tell me, baby," I whisper.

She flinches as the term of endearment leaves my lips. I feel closer to her than ever before. It's a relief that I no longer have to hide my true self from her.

That I no longer have to hide *anything* from her.

Mable's frightened face reminds me of a murky pond in which the moonlight shimmers. The freckles on the pointed end of her nose shine like stars and her full lips are swollen and slick. She was probably chewing on them while she waited for me, uncertain of whether she was doing the right thing; whether it was a smart move to blackmail me.

You've probably already guessed it: It was not smart.

"You know the cops won't come. So why are you lying to me?"

Her cheeks tremble and her mouth seems frozen. "Would you really hurt me?"

I so would. "No," I lie. "I'm not going to hurt you." You believe me, don't you? Just like everyone else always believes my lies. Baby, the shit I've already lied about, you don't want to know. Lesson one: Next time, run. Lesson two: Never trust a King. I fear we've lost the *ability* to tell the truth. "You have to tell me where you hid them. This is about more than that. It's about my life." *It's not about my life. Bullshit. It's about yours, Mable. Right now, I'm electrified. I can't hold back that part of me that Jaxon created in the first place. Or maybe it was always there. Maybe it's simply been given shape.*

I don't know.

The fact is that you are well and truly fucked.

Either way, I'm not even interested in where you hid that shit anymore. I just want to scare you, to make you believe that I would slit your throat, just like that ... Because I'm the sort of man who can do that without ever seeing the inside of a courtroom.

I don't pull the knife back, gently digging the blade into the soft skin of her neck. Smelling her fear as it numbs my senses, the quiet whimpering, the unstoppable panic, but there's more.

This fucking magic between us.

The pulse of unspoken words.

I feel you, though I don't even have you naked under me.

There was more right from the start.

So much more than I know what to do with.

Run away, princess.

Run before I dig my teeth into your flesh and suck you dry like a vampire.

Run now!

She can't run if you're holding her, a voice interrupts my stream of thought. My own voice, my conscience.

I let go of Mable as if her skin burned me, and immediately retreat three steps. My breath is racing, my blood is boiling. I didn't burn myself, I burned *her*. I made a mark with my first touch at Crown's that I can never forget. And then, I reinforced that mark when I pressed her into the forest floor. My cock so deep inside her…

"Why is your life at stake?" Mable asks quietly. Her eyes are shiny with unshed tears, and it'd be nothing but understandable if she breaks down.

She might simply collapse like a tower built of empty hope.

I've scared her. That was my plan from the beginning. But she didn't run away and now the other Kings have gotten her hopes up. That was *Jaxon's* plan.

I warned you about him. Damn you, Mable! I warned you!

Baby, this fucking world harbors too many monsters. Jaxon is one of them.

I am one of them.

And Reece and all the other Kings are just the same.

Why didn't you believe me?

What else can I do but hammer this fact into your head?

I know what I can do.

I have to make a decision. I finally have to decide whether I'm loyal to the Kings or loyal to my conscience. *To you.* I let the knife disappear again, sit down on the back of an armchair, and light a cigarette.

The truth.

The most vicious weapon.

"I lied."

"When?" Mable asks, still frozen. Can she move at all, even if she wanted to?

"Just now."

Mable huffs a brief laugh. It's a sound of surprise paired with anger and despair. Her subtle sense of humor and her ability to see the comedy in all situations are two of the things that set her apart.

"I won't spare you if you stand in my way. That was a lie. If you don't cooperate, I'll have to hurt you."

"What are you? The son of a Mafia boss?"

"Worse."

She visibly swallows. "Is it true what the woman by the lake called you? Are you a ... murderer?"

Worse.

"No. But do you believe me? You shouldn't. You shouldn't believe a single word I say. At least not since Harper told you all about the games over the last few years. Not since you've known that Jaxon is my friend, and that I will always stand by him. You're so naive, Mable," I mutter. "You didn't really call the cops, did you?"

She snorts. Suddenly she's alive again. "I'm naive? Me? Who let a stranger into their room where they're hiding their *ginormous stash of drugs* under the seat cushions like it's porn? You're naive if you thought I wouldn't find that right away! Or does everyone know? Does the entire campus know you're dealing here? That people can get their next hit from you? In that case, I'm sorry, but it did surprise me a little. I hoped I'd escaped the hole I grew up in. But you're exactly *the same.*"

"That's right."

She chews on her lower lip again. *I hate it when you do that.* "I didn't call the police."

304

"Good."

"That would've been stupid. They probably would've made me out to be the one who planted the stuff on you."

"Probably. If they'd come at all."

"So I just flushed it all down the toilet."

"WHAT?!" I jump straight up.

I know, without having to wait for another answer, that she's telling the truth.

Mable's face goes white as chalk.

"You didn't really ..." I mumble more to myself than to her and storm into my bathroom.

All the bags are empty and scattered across the floor.

All of them.

HUNDREDS OF THEM!

"What happened?!" The door to my room flies open and Jaxon appears behind me. He needs two seconds. The first to realize what the empty bags near my toilet mean. The second to determine how I feel about it.

Reece appears next to him. He takes a few moments longer.

We stare at each other.

Did we expect this?

We didn't.

Mable's mixture of detachment, brazenness, boundless naivety, and complete overconfidence makes for a situation that's caught us all off guard. All of these components mixed in a cocktail...

Deadly, Mable. Deadly.

"Okay, she's in for it now," Jaxon murmurs so quietly that Mable can't hear him. "Even you want it." He looks at me challengingly.

"You're an annoying motherfucker, Jax," I hiss at him.

Jaxon grins. "And you're a good, bad boy, Syl."

I'm fighting some internal battles that no one who isn't me

would go through. I'm a fucking psycho and I know it. Even the nicotine can no longer tame me.

So many warnings ignored, Mable.

So many clues overlooked.

You could've left.

You could've run.

Yes, you could've at least been obnoxious, unfuckable, a woman nobody wants!

Instead, you awaken the dogs in us. The beasts.

"You want it," Jaxon whispers.

My head hurts from all the resistance chaining me in place. *I don't want it. Not anymore. I'm not a monster. Not a fucking monster.*

"I'll help you control yourself," Jaxon promises, and at that moment, he releases it. "You won the bet, Silvano. You haven't touched her this entire time and I'll honor that. But now ... it's time."

The ropes loosen, my inner tension evaporates. Jaxon's control is the only thing that will stop me from hurting Mable. *He'll make sure I don't accidentally cut you with my knife after all.* I need Jaxon just as much as I'd like to kill him.

When we return to my bedroom, Mable is standing tall. Like a queen. Unyielding, seductive, she waits for us to dethrone her.

Or to crown her after all?

"You've subjected me to absolute hell," she says with a huff.

You're even stupid enough to explain yourself. Stand up to us. What did they do wrong when they wired your synapses? Why do you never feel fear?

"You made sure that I was made a fool of, that my dorm was flooded, that I constantly had to be careful not to get tripped while waiting tables. I'm constantly approached by nasty students asking if I want to do them 'a favor' for points, and my fellow scholarship students see me as an enemy. You've created a fucking *game* around my chance at a future, pitting me against the others as if I was nothing more than a pawn in your fucked up world of elitist thinking. A character that you sacrifice for nothing but your own entertainment. Jaxon abandoned me in a fucking forest, and I still believed every lie you told me, even started to trust you. I really wanted to convince myself that you had nothing to do with this childish bullshit." Mable's voice gets louder.

We stand there, all of us like hungry animals. With every word, she gives us more reasons to tear her apart.

"Your seduction skills were fantastic. I really fell for it. But then I find these fucking drugs, hundreds of baggies and pills and loads of cocaine, and they're not even *hidden!*"

Her cheeks are aflame and everything in me wants to set her whole body on fire.

"You really are ... children. Children who see this world as a playground, who've never understood suffering or poverty or hunger, who can't *imagine* what it means to work hard to escape that kind of misery! You hand out these shitty drugs and think they're nothing but a *game*, just like everything else! But people are dying because of them! They get sick and addicted and then are forever dependent on antisocial, rich bastards like you! It was the least I could do, the only thing I could hit you with! Because I know that I'll never win this 'game'! You'll see to that! It hurts your pride that I don't even play, so you'd *never* let me win! No matter how much I deserve it!"

Mable has talked herself into a rage, raising her voice and driving the temperature of my blood to a dangerous boiling point.

She's breathing heavy, and she's still gorgeous. Her clear gaze, defiantly resting on us, her graceful neck that slopes to her slender shoulders. Round breasts pressed together in that dress and her bare legs. Smooth, velvety, flawless. Mable is desirable as fuck and the most beautiful woman I've had in my room for a long time. Maybe it's because she really is like a little bird. A hummingbird chirping delicately and singing a cheerful song, not realizing that it's driving the beast mad with its frantic flapping.

Jaxon does nothing more than raise his hand. A simple sign, a quick movement.

Uncertainty flickers across Mable's face. She doesn't expect silence, but an answer.

A reaction.

Oh, you'll get it, don't worry.

At Jaxon's silent command, Reece goes to the door and locks it. Nobody will disturb us. Hours all to ourselves.

Mable looks up at us, watching us as we approach.

Oh, my little, naive, innocent bird.

It's time for you to finally catch fire.

You'll have to burn.

Because only from ashes can a phoenix rise.

JAXON

Bravo.

You are a bad girl.

Anything else would've surprised me. I can smell it on you. I can taste it. I have a very specific instinct. We all do. You can have a lot of fun with bad girls, Belle.

You did exactly the right thing to ensure your downfall.

Once we're finished with you, you'll have nothing left.

No honor, no shame, no pride.

Only the evil in you. That will remain.

22

MABLE

I'm standing before them, aware of everything that I've done wrong. It was like an inner compulsion. All the anger about what happened manifested in pure destruction. Drugs remind me of the darkness of my childhood. The horrific scenes when my mom did things that made her scream just to get that next hit.

I was too young to bear it.

It killed me inside.

Every single night.

Every. Fucking. Time.

The Kings deal that shit like it has no meaning. As if it couldn't hurt anyone. As if what happened to my mom was just a story they told rich kids to keep them from going after their next trip.

I feel so powerless and angry, and at the same time, I'm filled with so much desperate strength and power that it protects me from the realization that I probably just did the stupidest and most naive thing, the dumbest thing, that I could've ever done.

Jaxon.

Sylvian.

Reece.

They're looking at me like they're looking at a mirage. Like nothing that happened was real.

Like it's a game.

A damn game.

Like my life is a game.

Like you could bet it in poker.

"What exactly did you think was going to happen if you did that?" Jaxon's voice is perfectly calm. As calm as the breeze before a storm.

I gulp, not sure if I shouldn't actually be running. No matter where.

"You may be insane, but you're also consistent." He smiles, a hint of recognition flashing in his eyes. I can cope with that even less than if he'd simply shouted at me.

"Why ... why are you even doing all of this?" I ask, my voice quivering. Sylvian is serious, but Reece looks like nothing happened at all. "I mean, what did you really have to do to get all those good grades? Is it just the money?"

"You mean because it's stupid to take drugs or to sell them?" Reece asks with amusement. "You think we're too *stupid* to pass our exams?"

My lips tighten into a line. They can guess my answer to that.

"It's not stupid." Reece shrugs. He moves toward me almost imperceptibly. They all move toward me. "Sylvian is financing his studies. Isn't that damn clever?"

I look at Sylvian, trying to read his shadowed face. "You pay your tuition with ..."

"Dirty, black drug money, yes I do," he replies harshly. His eyes scan me, taking in my every movement. "Not everyone is lucky enough to be selected for a scholarship. I had to find another way."

My mouth opens slightly. *Is it possible?*

"If I didn't sell the drugs at this university, someone else would," Sylvian explains tonelessly. Almost as if he wants to justify his actions. "But then, it would be the Mafia. Assholes from the city who use the drug money to finance even worse crimes. I found this gap waiting, and I filled it. You're not the only one looking for a way to the top. Surprising, isn't it?"

Now everything makes sense. His tattoos. The look that doesn't match the other Kings. His much more mature behavior. The darkness that emanates from him.

"I fought," he explains. "I clawed my way through shit you can't even imagine. And you come here, to my room where I was trying to protect you, and the first thing you think of is flushing a whole lot of my money down the toilet?"

I'm not feeling guilty now, am I? No. They're still drugs. They were drugs. I did the right thing.

"Your fight is hopeless, little Belle," Jaxon hisses, taking another step toward me. "The market won't dry up just because you harmed one of us. The people out there are *greedy*. They're already *addicted* to all the bad things you'd like to banish from the world. You can't save them. None of them. Most of all not with your pathetic *morals*."

I shake my head. "Bullshit."

"No." His blue eyes are practically glowing. "If you want humanity to stop sniffing cocaine like it's air, you have to change it from the *ground* up. And you need to do it in a way that they won't notice. They can't ever realize it's happening."

"What are you talking about..."

"What this is all *actually* about. Our *studies*. *Kingston*. It's about *so much more* than you can imagine. Kingston is not a place where things change. Kingston is the place that produces people who *change things*. We don't just rule the campus. In a few years, we're going to rule the world. Someone has to do it, and if you stick around for a while, you'll understand that it's damn hard to keep the *peasants* out there from running themselves off a cliff. I can only give you one piece of advice here. It's worth a lot, so remember it well."

He takes another step closer so he can reach out and touch me. Jaxon grabs a strand of hair that's come loose from my braid, wrapping it around his finger.

Reece and Sylvian watch him.

Watch us.

"What's your advice?" I ask, trying not to let on how much faster my heart is beating just from being in a room with the three of them.

"Start playing along," Jaxon murmurs. "That's the only way to win."

A breath of icy wind brushes my bare shoulders.

"We have two options now." Jaxon's lips touch my ear, and it's as if thousands of pins penetrate my skin. "We can fuck up your life. Make it a hell you'll never forget, to settle your debt to Sylvian that you'll never be able to repay." He inhales sharply and I do the same. "Or we can fuck you."

Fuck. My pulse is racing. There's so much I should say, could retort, should be doing at this point. But my mind is a blank and not a single word escapes my lips.

Jaxon leans back and smiles.

He smiles at me like he can see inside me. Like he can read the chaos of my thoughts like an open book. "What do you say?"

I open my lips, but it's as if I've forgotten how to speak.

"Oh, fuck it," Sylvian pushes Jaxon aside and grabs my neck. His lips seal over mine, like he's trying not to let too much air escape. He kisses me hard and so full of lust that the chaos in my head morphs into a dense fog and I can no longer think clearly. His tongue seeks out mine and then ... then I just give in.

I give in and thread my fingers into his hair.

Into the thick black hair that I've always wanted to touch, and I sigh like I'm the happiest person in the world.

Maybe I am.

Kissing Sylvian is like finding a part of myself. A piece of my soul that I thought I'd lost.

I unconsciously snuggle up to him, daring to ask for more, and he promptly breaks our contact.

He holds me at a distance and stares at me like I've done something worse than flush his stash down the toilet.

I glance nervously at Reece and wince. His face is so distorted by desire that it frightens me.

Jaxon, on the other hand, smiles calmly. He's turned one of the armchairs toward us and is leaning on the backrest with both hands. "Come on, *Belle*."

It's Sylvian who spins me around, still clutching my neck. He pushes me down onto the chair before he lets go of me. His face is impassive. I have no idea what's going on inside him.

Reece moves around us. The constellation with Sylvian in front of me and Jaxon behind me makes my body tingle. Yes, I truly am naive because I can't even imagine what will happen next.

"I think it's good that she's always tying it back." Reece stops next to Jaxon. I tilt my head back to look at him as he pulls at my hair tie. "I like that virtually no one knows what she looks like with her hair down."

Jaxon smirks vaguely before Reece leans forward.

I didn't think he was going to kiss me in front of the others until his tongue is running over my lips. He grips my chin, encloses my lips with his, upside down, and slides his tongue across my teeth.

His kiss is a lot more demanding than Sylvian's. And there I had thought Sylvian to be unyielding.

I can't help but enjoy Reece's touch. It's familiar. Like I'm kissing a good friend and an old lover at the same time. I can relax with him. The heat it produces in me is controllable. Beautiful, warming, but controllable. And it feels good to retain a little bit of control.

Reece backs off, pushing my head up to make me look forward. A jolt of electricity runs through my body when I see Sylvian kneeling in front of me. His hands slide under my dress just as I catch his eyes.

My darkest fantasy comes true when he pushes my skirt up. Higher. To my waist.

Time passes in miserably long seconds. He takes my panties off. I'm glad he didn't ask permission first. I wouldn't have made a sound. Not a single damn sound. My voice might be gone entirely.

Sylvian grips my thighs and pulls me forward to the edge of the armchair. He forces my legs apart when I would have rather kept them nervously closed before him and kisses his way up my inner thighs.

His lips tingle, and the idea that I'm not alone in a room with him is driving me crazy. The possibility of being kissed again by Reece—or even Jaxon—at any time raises my desire to an all-consuming level.

Sylvian kisses me gently, so gently, and at the same time without even considering that I might object. I *have to* let him go on. Even thinking of Harper doesn't give me the upper hand over my body.

Sylvian approaches my pussy, but that's not what makes me whimper. Reece's hands on my shoulders do that. I melt between them, want to feel them both, as forbidden and irrational as that is. Reece's strong fingers massage me while Sylvian moves higher.

Something like fear rushes through my veins when I think of what it will feel like when Sylvian touches my center just before he does.

He licks me.

He presses his lips into my pussy and traces his tongue around my clit.

I moan against my will, and at that very moment, Reece kisses me again, as if trying to absorb my lustful sound.

My hands clench on the armrests as Sylvian spreads my legs wide and circles my clit with the firm pressure of his tongue.

I automatically lift toward him. My body demands more, and it receives. It receives everything. Sylvian runs his tongue across my folds once and then penetrates me.

Another moan escapes me, and Reece once more catches it with his lips, but he doesn't let up this time. He licks my lips just like Sylvian licks my entrance. A pure rush of sensation fills me. An absolute takeover of my senses. Not just Sylvian between my legs, one of the hottest men in this universe, but also Reece, caressing me.

Just caressing me like he has no problem at all with someone else touching me.

Licking me.

Sylvian's practiced tongue makes me moan without any inhibition, while Reece leaves my lips and kisses my neck with hot desire. It's heavenly, so hot and heavenly that I open my eyes to take in everything happening around me. I meet Jaxon's gaze.

If I was aroused before, now a fire burns in me.

Jaxon's sitting in Sylvian's desk chair, watching us. He's watching us, with that knowing, arrogant, sexy smile on his pursed lips, and it loosens another inhibition. There's too much.

Too much arousal.

Too much heat.

Too many deep feelings, although I've forbidden myself from allowing them since the beginning.

Jaxon, looking at me like I'm the most desirable object in the world.

Sylvian licking me with hot touches, digging his fingers into my flesh and fucking me with his tongue, after sinking between my legs like it's the only thing he's ever wanted to do.

And then there's Reece. His hands pushing the top of my dress down, exposing my breasts. He rolls my nipples between his fingers and sends jolts of electricity all the way down into my glowing center.

I'm breathing far too quickly, in and out as if every breath could be the last one of my life as I know it.

Jaxon's smile widens. Though he doesn't touch me, his gaze is pure gasoline for my inner fire. "You like it, don't you? Don't worry. I won't just sit and watch the whole time."

I let the air escape from my lungs, like his words are the kind of relief I've been longing for, even though I don't want him to know that. My hands find their way into Sylvian's hair of their own accord. I press myself against his face, feel Reece's lips on my neck again, and cry out.

Fuck.

Even before it's over, I know this is the best orgasm of my life.

It lasts for seconds.

It's as intense as an entire lifetime of arousal.

I feel desired.

I've found where I belong between them.

I seem caught in the only real place on earth.

I never want to leave.

Sylvian straightens up while I'm still catching my breath.

He stands in front of me, next to Reece, who's come around the armchair. Jaxon remains seated in the office chair, gently swiveling back and forth.

"Don't you think it's time to return the favor?" Jaxon smiles cynically and I give in to the urge to straighten my dress so I'm not exposed in front of them. "Save yourself the trouble. We'll see every inch of you before the night is over."

"Mable ..." That's Sylvian. He's looking at me like what just happened between us warmed something in him. "If you want to stop ..."

"Fuck that, Silvano!" Reece elbows him in the ribs. "What's wrong with you?" He shakes himself as if to ward off Sylvian's doubts and grabs his belt. "Maybe you should show him what he'd be missing, princess."

I know what they expect, but it takes a lot of effort. There's only been one time I've experienced a blowjob that was erotic. And that was with Reece. Maybe excluding the moment when I stumbled into my dorm room to find Jaxon.

Jaxon, coming in Lien's mouth, looking at me like I was the one responsible for those feelings…

Otherwise, blowjobs have only ever reminded me of the many women for sale in the trailer park on Saturday nights…

Fuck it. That's over.

Erase it from your memory.

This is different.

You want it.

You don't have to do it.

That's why you want it all the more.

I slide off the chair to my knees. As soon as I assume this submissive posture, it's like the sight triggers something in the men above me.

"Now it's getting interesting," Jaxon whispers.

Sylvian seems to be struggling with himself, but finally he steps forward.

He undoes the buckle of his belt and opens the zipper.

I can do nothing but kneel there. Unable to move, spellbound watching his hands.

Sylvian reaches for his shaft and exposes his cock.

My entire body starts to tingle. Suddenly I know for sure that I want it. Crave it even.

I open my mouth and the fire in my body blazes as Sylvian's powerful cock slides over my tongue.

Everything inside me asks for more.

I close my lips around Sylvian's lust and suck tenderly on his tip. It tastes so good. Much better than I ever thought a man could taste. His gliding movements excite me. His hardness caresses my sensitive lips. I open my eyes, look up at him, and he groans.

His eyelids are almost closed, his mouth sensually open as he grips my hair firmly and rams himself into me all at once.

I gasp. And I love it.

More, I think, giving him permission to continue with a pleasurable sound from my throat.

He groans deeper. Rough and seductive. He fucks my mouth just the way he licked me before.

I enjoy every minute to the fullest. I savor it and surrender to my complete pleasure.

Breathing heavily, his eyes glowing, he pulls himself from my mouth to run his thumb over my lips.

"Was that your first blowjob? Because you're not the only one who will remember it forever."

"Let me get in on that," Reece interjects.

"No." Jaxon. He stood up and is coming toward us. "I want you to suck Sylvian's cock until he comes, Belle." The order alone is so dirty it only stokes my lust higher. "You're not done yet."

I look at Sylvian's face with uncertainty. *What does he want?*

"On the bed." Jaxon nods to the edge of the four-poster bed and Sylvian backs away from me to sink onto the mattress, his considerable size still exposed.

"Only if you want to, Mable," Sylvian whispers, affection and earnestness merging in his expression.

"Oh, never mind that," Jaxon hisses. He grips my hair painfully, making me gasp. His sudden brutality frightens me, but not enough to make me want to flee. Jaxon's lips find my ear, and he pushes my face in Sylvian's direction, causing my pulse to shoot up even more. "Sylvian's a little bitch who wants to make you feel like you have a say in this. But I want to be very clear, Belle. If you don't drink his seed like it's your new favorite cocktail, this all ends right then. One orgasm for you, and one for one of us. That seems like a fair enough trade, but that's not where you want to stop, right?"

My breath hitches, but I've long since made up my mind. On all fours, I cross the short distance separating me from Sylvian and take his cock in my mouth again.

"God damn it," Reece moans. "She's so submissive, I could come just from watching her."

"Don't you dare." Jaxon stands next to me, gripping my skull and pressing it down on Sylvian's cock. At first it's humiliating, but that abruptly changes when he starts stroking my head. I know I can't allow myself to feel anything toward him, but just his thumb firmly stroking and massaging the back of my neck brings me deep satisfaction.

I'm addicted to that touch. A junkie who's discovered a simple drug that moves her deeply. Jaxon's massaging hand on my head and Sylvian's cock in my mouth make me crave more. I feel more desirable with every second and get so wet I'm afraid I'm going to drip.

"Keep going," Jaxon murmurs. His hand works lightly, gently, not too forcefully, while my head moves up and down over Sylvian's cock.

Sylvian is looking at me, his gaze transformed. Looking into his eyes while I alternate between sucking him off and licking his tip makes me even wilder.

"Good girl," Jaxon murmurs, only slightly increasing the pressure of his thumb, still stroking, and Sylvian gives a tormented moan.

He leans back to rest his elbows on the bed. His athletic figure is spread out in front of me. His tight shirt flatters his stomach. Without prompting, he tugs at it like he heard my secret wish, taking it off and throwing it aside.

I pause, unable to move for a moment because I'm so captivated by the sight of him. Sylvian's chest and arms are covered in black tattoos. I seem to see them even more clearly now than I did last time. Figures, skulls, letters, weapons, everything blends into a single work of art.

"You like him, don't you?" Jaxon asks.

I can't answer. For one thing, I probably wouldn't be able to manage to form words, and for another, I have Sylvian's cock deep in my mouth.

Jaxon weaves his fingers into my hair and pulls my head back, moving my mouth more quickly over Sylvian's tip. I'm getting so hot I wonder if I can come without touching myself…

But I don't have to.

I tense up violently when I feel Reece between my thighs. It's not his hand that's between them, but his head.

"Oh yeah, lick the soul out of her, Crescent," Jaxon tells him, now directing the rest of my body as well by keeping his free hand on my back. He pushes me down so I sink onto Reece's face. His tongue darts out and I moan loudly with uncontrolled pleasure.

"Fuck his face, Belle," Jaxon demands, his voice pressed and grim.

I move on Reece's mouth while he holds me by my thighs and slides his tongue through my slit. My moans grow louder and louder. Sylvian's cock rapidly glides in and out of my mouth. Jaxon holds me captive, forcing my movements to adjust to the pressure of his hands. Reece pushes his tongue into my pussy and sucks on my pleasure.

I need to feel them all even deeper inside me.

I need to have even more of them.

With a longing tug in my stomach, I look pleadingly at Sylvian, whose breath is starting to grow ragged. His cock twitches between my lips. I desperately want him to come on my tongue. I want to be the one to satisfy him, and then there's Reece...

Reece, who's surrounded my clit with his mouth, and is taking me to heaven with circular movements. He's making me twitch with lust, licking me deeply and deliciously while I suck his friend's cock, and then there is...

Another explosion.

Even better than before.

Even deeper.

I taste Sylvian's seed on my tongue, swallow every drop, suck it out. My core is on fire, Reece is moaning with me, and it barely takes me a second to catch my breath.

Jaxon's hand disappears from my head, and suddenly I know *exactly* what I want.

What I need.

I'm driven by such an inner compulsion that I get to my feet without thinking about it.

Then I stand there.

Before Jaxon.

It's like there's never been anything bad between us. Like every dark word or deed was a lie. There's only light. At that moment, everything is clear and pure. His face seems to be beaming, even though he's not even smiling. He's just standing there, looking down at me and breathing hard.

I can't say whether it's seconds or minutes that pass. I only hear his breathing getting louder. Then he finally crosses the distance between us to tear open my dress.

I do the same. I longingly push up his sweater and undo his belt. He drops his pants, climbs out of them, and wraps his hands around me.

They're everywhere.

On me.

And I touch him wherever I can.

Jaxon feels like a marble god. Warm, velvety skin stretching over well-defined muscles. There is not a blemish to be seen on him, not a birthmark.

Although I can still taste Sylvian's come on my tongue, Jaxon suddenly kisses me and throws me onto the bed.

I sink into the pillows. He's above me. For a moment, it's just the two of us.

Naked, unadorned, violently demanding each other.

He's lying on top of me, my arms resting against my sides. His hips between my legs, his eyes clear and dark, his lips serious and smooth. Jaxon's fingers find their way into my hair, brushing through it. And then he says something I'm sure he honestly means, even if a big part of me will never believe it.

"You really are beautiful."

Maybe I'm not the only one holding my breath in the room. Jaxon grips my shoulder, drives my legs apart, and buries himself inside of me.

I'm frozen and liquefied at the same time. How far and so near in a single moment.

His immense length pierces me, and I finally feel fulfilled in so many ways that I surrender to him completely. I enjoy it without thinking about it.

He takes over my pussy with deep, masculine movements. I love everything about the way he fucks me. His skill entirely lives up to his looks.

My greed for him is insatiable, and I don't know how long we stay like this. Just moving together. Just the two of us. It's a union that goes so much deeper than it should.

In between, he kisses me on the neck, on the cheek, but only briefly. Most of the time we look each other in the eye, letting our souls merge as if they've been desperate for it.

After a while he pauses, his body covered in a film of sweat. He rests his forehead on mine in silence. "Does it feel good?"

"A thousand times nicer than I expected," I whisper.

He makes an astonished sound that could be a laugh and leans back to look at me. Everything about him is so clear, so unfiltered, so real ... I can see the real Jaxon. The man behind all the masks. Behind all the attitudes of the Kings. And behind all the walls he's built around himself. "Nice?" he repeats.

"Yes."

"Is this your first time?" His expression is interested, but I can also see a tiny hint of concern in it.

I don't know how to explain. Should I betray Sylvian? Do I have to? "Maybe."

Jaxon laughs, moving his head so his dark blond hair falls into his face. "Do I want to know what you mean by that?"

"Here, Jax." Reece hands Jaxon a condom.

I forgot about the others, at least for a moment, and even now Reece doesn't really make it back into my consciousness.

Jaxon takes the packet from his hand, puts on the condom, and penetrates me again. I sigh.

"You really have won," he says suddenly. "It's not me fucking you. You're fucking my mind."

"Is that a good thing?" I ask, making him growl.

Jaxon braces himself, pulling me under him and ramming into me. I gasp, breath choppy, clawing at his flawless chest, his muscular upper arms, and melting under him.

He fucks me into the mattress with fast, hard movements and fixes me with his blue eyes. As he rams himself into me ever more roughly, he grips my neck in a firm hold. Then with a final thrust, opening his mouth in silent ecstasy, he comes inside me, pouring himself out in his condom between my walls as his cock throbs.

"Fuck." The curse comes from Reece, not Jaxon. He's staring at us, but it doesn't make me uncomfortable. Instead, I feel so wanted, so desired, and so at home between them that I smile.

Jaxon rolls off me and lies back, breathless.

Courage I didn't know I was capable of takes hold of me. I lean over him and kiss his chest. His hard nipples. He moans with satisfaction as I sink a little lower, kissing his stomach, just above his pubic hair. It's not entirely without ulterior motives. I want to look at his member up close. I reach for his balls and stroke them.

Jaxon relaxes a little more until someone clears his throat.

Reece.

I let go of Jaxon and roll onto my side.

Reece is also standing there naked, with a body just as flawless and attractive as Jaxon's. "I think you forgot a few other people while you were making love to Jax."

"How could I?" I ask cheekily, sliding across the bed toward him. I willingly open my lips and allow him to push his cock into my mouth.

"Dear god," he moans as he fills my throat. "She's perfect!" Even the fact that he's talking *about* me instead of to me turns me on. I suck on his cock, and he thrusts into me hard and fast. "You're so damn hot, Mable. You have no idea how much I'd love to fuck your brains out until every single neural pathway is stamped with the word *King*."

"Don't overdo it," says Sylvian, though he's smiling. He's positioned himself next to Reece and looks down at me with satisfaction. "Turn her on her stomach."

"But it ... is ... just so incredibly hot to fuck her dirty mouth ..."

I tense up, only to relax even more the next moment. Let them talk about me like that. It turns me on. It's okay if it happens while we're doing this. I *am* dirty. This *is* dirty. They're even more depraved than I am. After all, *they're* sharing me, aren't they?

"Crescent," Sylvian says.

Reece moves away with a sigh. He holds my chin up with his thumb and looks me straight in the eye. Everything about him is casual and relaxed. "If you don't like what we do, just tell me 'stop.'"

I nod.

"Say it."

"Stop."

"Very nice. Remember the word. Say it as soon as we do something you don't like."

"I hope I can manage."

Reece laughs at my ironic reply, sending butterflies into my stomach.

Meanwhile, Sylvian has climbed onto the bed. He grips my waist and turns me onto my stomach.

"Wait." Jaxon's moved higher into the pillows, lying there like a lazy god in Olympus. His smug smile has made a comeback. For the first time, it's an incarnation of that smile that I like. He makes an enticing gesture and I crawl closer.

He gently takes my head in both hands. "Look at me," he demands, eyes intense. "I want to see every shred of your lust while they fuck you from behind."

A shiver rushes down my spine. I feel Sylvian's hands on my hips, then the tip of his cock. He spreads my cheeks, slides past them, and pushes slightly against my entrance. I close my eyes for a pleasurable moment and Jaxon registers every change in my expression.

"Is it bad if I don't hold back?" Sylvian asks with a growl.

I'm not sure how to answer that, but Jaxon beats me to it anyway.

"Don't bother. I bet she'll love it when she's sore tomorrow."

Sylvian firmly squeezes the flesh of my ass, then pushes against me again, forcing himself inside me and conquering me with a single thrust.

I cry out in surprise, squirming because Sylvian's thickness astonishes me even after Jaxon's, but Jaxon holds me in place.

"Tell me it's hot when he fucks you."

"It is," I confirm at once, surprised to have my voice back.

"Sylvian, fuck her properly. I want her eyes to roll back with lust."

Sylvian obeys. He pushes his cock, thick and bulging, into my soaking wet pussy, forcing himself into me again and again. I'm tight, I can feel it, tight for his girth, and it feels so different from the forest. Over and over, he thrusts into me, our bodies smacking against each other. Wet and dirty and so wonderfully depraved ...

"Okay, swap."

I tighten up inside. Helplessly, I look up at Jaxon, who's smiling contentedly. Then I feel Sylvian move, entirely different hands take hold of me, and I'm filled again. This time by Reece. Excitement melts inside me, as if all the fire long since turned to lava. Reece pushes himself into me more slowly, more patiently, before he takes me with long, thorough thrusts.

Then they swap again.

My head is spinning. It's all too much for me and yet I yearn for more. More, more, more, more. I can feel Sylvian inside me again.

He rams himself into me with hard, fast, pumping strokes. I crumple forward onto my elbows, exhausted, with only Jaxon to hold me, and all I can do is enjoy it.

Sylvian makes me come. But it's different from the two times before. He hits a different spot. This explosion is short and violent, and I moan so loudly and lustfully that I barely recognize myself.

Then there's Reece, picking up exactly where Sylvian left off and rubbing that spot in me again. This time he's much faster, quicker, and harder. He teases my body to no end, and I ..., and I ...

"Shit, you're not just fucking her, you're catapulting her right into nirvana."

"Don't stop," I plead.

"Wouldn't dream of it, Belle." Jaxon strokes my forehead, then adjusts himself on the mattress so his hips are level with my head. "Maybe I'll get lucky like you and manage to come a second time."

I'm far too distracted and barely notice how he holds my head captive to fuck my open mouth. I just let it happen, just like I let Sylvian and Reece keep taking turns.

At some point, I'm nothing but lust and deep satisfaction. Sylvian seems to know just what I need, and his thrusts are no longer just for me, but for himself. He fucks me until he comes and pours himself inside me. Reece follows, and when I feel his cock inside me, pulsing with release, I reach the end of my strength.

I slump down.

Exhausted and spent, with Jaxon's cock in my mouth. I can still feel him moving, holding his tip between my lips, letting his fist do the rest. With pumping movements, he moves his hand over his length and comes down my throat.

Sated, I close my eyes. Swallow his seed. Lick it off and feel a kiss on my lips at the end.

First from Reece, with his unmistakable smell. Tender, loving, calm.

Then Sylvian. Dominant, possessive, definitive.

And then Reece again. Wild, unrestrained, greedy.

Then I drop away.

Away.

I can still hear their conversation.

Their quiet words.

And I hope that all is well. That everything is fine as it is. Then I nod off.

JAXON

U sually, you'd have to beg, Belle.
I want to hear you beg.
Nobody gets me just like that.
Least of all if they want me.
It really depends.
You went for it, little girl, didn't you?
I hate to admit it, but you won this round…

23

MABLE

I blink. Morning sun, light, and the most exhilarating feeling of my life wake me up. As soon as my eyes have adjusted to my bright surroundings, I recognize the shape lying next to me.

Sylvian is wearing black jogging pants; his upper body is bare. His many beautiful tattoos draw my attention, and I take in the beauty of every single muscle before I notice his piercing gaze on me.

"Hi," I mumble and pull the comforter up to my nose to playfully cover my face, which is flushed with embarrassment.

"Hi," he says sternly. His eyes are darkened by shadows, his black hair disheveled.

"Did we—" I start, but he interrupts me immediately.

"You slept through breakfast. Everyone else already left. I'm flying to Miami in a few hours. I've ordered you an Uber for eleven o'clock to take you to Philadelphia."

The farewell comes a little too abruptly for me. Entirely unexpectedly, I realize the whole thing might've just been a one-night stand. A one-time thing. Okay, I should have expected that. Ultimately, I did bring that on myself, didn't I? "Did I really flush your drugs down the toilet?" I ask to make sure that last night wasn't a dream.

Sylvian lowers a brow. "You did."

I pull the covers over my head. "God, I'm so sorry."

He grabs the blanket roughly and pulls it down again so that he can look me in the face. "You're sorry?"

"I didn't know you were using it to finance your studies and only selling it to rich snobs, probably for double the rate, to take advantage of the whole thing for yourself. If one of them gets addicted, that's different. They can afford rehab and will never have to hit the streets to pay for the next fix, right? So, it was damned reckless of me to just destroy so much value ... Can you still afford your tuition?"

Sylvian's expression is closed. "I'll figure out a way for you to pay me back."

"You will?"

He doesn't respond.

"Are you somehow..." I sit up, careful to cover myself with the sheet, and look at him straight on. "Did I do something wrong?"

"You?" he asks, perfectly astonished, as if he couldn't even think of accusing me of anything. "What could you have done wrong?"

I exhale slowly. "Well, I—"

"Get dressed," he interrupts me again.

His command is clear, and he looks at me in such an intense, demanding way that I obey. Even though I feel uncomfortable dropping the blanket because what happened between us happened in the dark, I get up and turn my back to him. I reach for Harper's dress, put it on and zip it up.

As soon as I'm dressed, I turn shyly in his direction.

Was that really the only and last time?

Sylvian's expression is impenetrable. If I'm not mistaken, there's a flash of pain. For a tiny, almost imperceptible moment.

"Did something happen?" I ask him anxiously. "Are you sure I didn't do something that ... hurt you?"

Slowly, very slowly, he raises a brow. "Me?" he asks, just as taciturn as before, reaching for the pack of cigarettes lying next to him on the bedside table and putting one between his lips. "No."

"So ... is everything okay between us?"

"Of course," he says smoothly, lighting the cigarette and taking a deep drag.

"The Uber ..."

"I'll pay for it."

"You don't have to."

"Who else is going to do it?"

"I booked a train ticket. It cost barely twenty dollars, and I can walk to the station, I don't have that much luggage ..."

Sylvian taps his cigarette on the bedside table and sits up. He opens the top drawer of a dresser without moving a muscle in his face, without even the slightest hint at what's going on inside him. He reaches in and hands me a roll of hundred-dollar bills.

I stare at him.

"Take it. I won't even notice when it's gone. You have more use for it than I do."

"I can't do this ..."

"Don't be so fucking proud," he growls and presses the roll of banknotes into my hand. "It's not much compared to what I *could* give you. Compared to the tuition fees, it's only a few cents. It'll take you years to repay your debt to me. It won't matter if you let it grow by a thousand dollars."

"How do you want me to pay you back...?"

"Not at all, if it was up to me. But I know it will make you feel better, so do it as soon as you've made your first million."

"My first million?" I ask in amazement.

Sylvian looks like he's bored with the conversation. "I know absolutely no one who's been to Kingston and isn't a millionaire today."

"If I'm allowed to stay ..."

He says nothing about this. "Just take it, Mable. It's pure, clean, taxed cash from your beloved fellow students."

I have to smile knowingly. As much as I hate the drug dealers in Philadelphia who destroy the future of so many young people and the health of so many adults, I don't mind Sylvian selling drugs to the "peasants" of Kingston University. "Right, thanks."

His eyes smile for a moment, warm and approachable, before turning dark green again like an impenetrable jungle. My gaze automatically wanders down his attractive body. I'd like to ask him if he works out. Or does some other kind of sport. He's the most muscular one among the Kings, although it's hard to tell much difference between their hot bodies.

"See you ... after Thanksgiving?" I ask, not sure if it's wise to sound hopeful. Of course, it would be fantastic if the one-night stand could turn into something more. A three-night stand perhaps. A ten-night stand?

"Sure," he replies coolly. Not quite the reaction I was looking for.

I reach for my coat, pulling it on and turning the doorknob.

Perhaps I should've guessed at that moment that I shouldn't hope for anything.

That I should hope for absolutely nothing.

***

Thanksgiving rushes by in a blur. On the one hand, that's because I'm relieved to see how well my sister's doing. She can live on the money I send her, together with my mother's tiny social support. The trailer is tidier than usual because there are no longer three people trying to share the limited space, and Olive seems happy.

We've slept on the dining table all our lives. Every night we rebuild our bed there, and with every year that we grew, we had less space to use. Now my sister has half of the mobile home to herself, and she seems to like it.

She's also entered a phase where she prefers to be on her own anyway.

At Thanksgiving itself, I find out why she's smiling constantly: One of her friends from school picks her up, and he greets her with a kiss on the forehead.

I don't mind spending Thanksgiving alone in the trailer with my mom as long as Olive is happy.

I was expecting it to feel like a long fall back to earth, coming back home after being surrounded by the wealth, historical buildings, and manicured parks of Kingston. But it just feels like home.

It may be a poor, run-down home, but it's the place connected to great parts of my past.

Mom's busy with her own stuff the whole week. Without asking questions, she takes Sylvian's money and uses it to pay off a few debts she had with our neighbors. She and Olive use what remains to buy new winter clothes.

Since Harper gave me a box of her old clothes in early November, I'm already all set for the time being. It would probably be wiser to sell the clothes on eBay and work it out with Harper that I keep some of the profits. But I feel more comfortable at Kingston when I don't have to wear jeans from Walmart.

I spend the rest of the week studying, eating cereal, reading, and studying some more. Only at night, just before I fall asleep, do I allow myself to reminisce about sex with the three fraternity brothers…

With every day that passes, it feels less real, less like it actually happened.

There's only one worry that makes me dread going back to Maryland. It's not the Kings, not the fear of running into them and not being able to say a single word, like I'm some lovesick twelve-year-old who can't stop thinking about them *all*. It's Harper.

I betrayed her.

How can I explain?

How am I supposed to tell her about what happened between Sylvian and me?

My conscience grows more guilty with every passing hour. Harper's text message was spot on, and I don't know if she'll ever forgive me. I slept with Sylvian. Not only with him, but with all the Kings.

I have no choice but to tell her the truth.

She's always been there for me so far.

She helped me, supported me, explained what I was facing, and offered me her help. I didn't plan what happened with Sylvian. But I ... just couldn't fight it.

Will she understand?

When I get back to Kingston on Sunday evening, I'm still not sure.

A knot has formed in my stomach, giving me abdominal pain. Deception is one thing. Lies are something entirely different and only make the former worse. I'll *have* to tell her the truth.

I enter the dormitory and immediately hear someone having sex in the kitchen. Loud moans and the rhythmic sound of fucking echo in the hallway. I roll my eyes because I'm used to the building being a brothel, but as I walk past the open kitchen door with my eyes downcast I have to pause.

I stare at the person standing behind Rachel and pushing himself between her spread legs. His steady thrusts push her upper body across the table and the knot in my stomach dissolves into nausea.

Reece looks up and notices me.

I stand there and look straight at him. The sweat on his forehead, the wild lust in his eyes, the blond hair falling into his face.

He curls his lips into a challenging grin. With wild thrusts, he moves between Rachel's thighs and grips her even more dominantly.

I've seen enough.

Worried I might throw up, I scurry into my dorm room and close the door behind me.

A one-night stand.

That's all it was. *Reece isn't accountable to you. Neither is Sylvian. Neither is Jaxon. And you don't owe them the least bit in return either.*

Reece can fuck Rachel whenever and wherever he wants.

Of course he can.

I sit on my bed, trying to drive the thoughts from my head and find myself chewing on my thumbnail. Right. That's an ugly habit that doesn't do me any good at the moment. What did I expect?

Did I think I was going to come back to the Kings still trying to woo me? Did I expect them to ask me out on dates? Was I imagining some sort of polyamorous relationship in the end?

What a joke!

It takes me a few minutes to calm down. I turn on some music to drown out any more noise from the kitchen and set about reorganizing my notes. I have no time *at all* to think about what the Kings do or don't do.

The one person I don't want to lose is Harper.

On Monday, I look for her on campus because she hasn't replied to my messages. Between classes I check all the important hotspots in the hope of finding someone. Both Harper and the Kings are absent, though.

One thing becomes clear to me: I suddenly seem to be invisible.

People still stare at me when I enter a lecture hall or walk through the cafeteria, but nobody shouts mean things at me anymore. I didn't hear the word *whore* even once all day. It's as if I'm under a spell. There seems to be a kind of glass dome that protects me from new attacks.

However, the game continues to run in the background.

Rachel, Lien, and Brittany each had their picture taken naked, covered only with pompoms, and distributed the photos throughout the sports changing rooms to earn points.

On Tuesday, the pictures are passed around while people talk about which of the three is the hottest.

I ignore it, even more so because I'm still busy trying to find Harper. I run into Jaxon instead. It happens quite unexpectedly as I'm on my way to the library.

He's with Clarisse and the others in front of the wide staircase of the architecturally impressive building, and I can tell when he sees me coming.

His gaze is cold, and I'm not surprised to find contempt in it. Did I expect anything else?

I didn't.

Nothing that happened between us was ever made public. On the contrary, the only thing he's done where people could see was either completely ignore me or punish me in some way. The only time there was anything between us was when we were unobserved…

Jaxon puts his arm around Clarisse's shoulders and pulls her close without breaking our eye contact.

As he kisses her, his strong hand with the many rings on it buried in her curly hair, I feel a tiny sting.

It's minuscule.

I managed to keep my heart closed to him right from the start.

I walk past them, pretending that we've never met, and I'm grateful they just let me pass. I briefly feared Clarisse would try to embarrass me in front of everyone again.

Fortunately, that doesn't happen.

After my study hours, I change in my dorm and go to start my shift at Crown's. It's Tuesday, a slow night, and I can withdraw from time to time to continue reviewing my index cards.

Derby comes to me around half past eight and taps on my table. "Over there, billiard room. Keep an eye on them, I'm going for a smoke."

"Alright." My hands instantly turn sweaty. The Kings in the billiard room? Are they going to talk to me or ignore me?

What should I do when they talk to me?

And how should I react if they ignore me?

I take a few deep breaths before pushing the curtain aside.

Romeo, Jaxon, and Sylvian sit around the poker table.

They hand out chips while Jaxon talks about investment strategies.

"The problem is, now anyone can buy into the crypto system. It's like a balloon that's inflated, and no one understands what the air inside it actually is. This is the same shit since data mining ..."

"Would you like something to drink?"

Sylvian and Romeo look up without flinching, but Jaxon narrows his eyes.

"I'm talking right now," he snaps.

"Sorry," I say, trying not to let any memories of that night rise up in me. *Don't let it matter, Mable. You know they're assholes. You had sex with them. You had fun. That's all there is to it.* "Want me to wait?"

"No," Jaxon growls, reaching for the cards. "What do you want to drink? The little Dole is hoping for a tip. But you've already given her enough for the next five blowjobs, haven't you, Silvano?"

Sylvian picks up the cards Jaxon hands him and ignores me.

Romeo is the only one who's eyes stay fixated on me. For the first time, I notice his piercing gaze is so empty that I wonder if he's able to feel anything at all.

"She didn't want to be a whore and yet you insisted on paying her." The corner of Jaxon's mouth twitches.

I groan. *Could he get any shittier?* "Want me to fetch you the menu?" I ask, annoyed. "Maybe that'll make it easier for you to choose from our extensive selection of beverages."

Jaxon rolls his eyes in my direction without moving otherwise. "If you speak to me again," he murmurs dangerously, "as if I were a *nobody*, I'll have you thrown out immediately. Derby will certainly do me the favor of giving you an extra kick in the ass."

My mouth opens in astonishment and tears sting my eyes. I can't believe he's talking to me like that. Wow. That surpasses everything, all the arrogance he's shown so far. He's simply disgusting. Someone I shouldn't waste a single positive feeling on. "Someone doesn't have the courage to admit they enjoyed the sex, do they?" I ask, turning on my heel, and leave the billiard room.

Sylvian's laughter follows me into the bar.

Fuck.

The motherfuckers.

I still don't let my anger get in the way of my work. They want me to treat them like strangers?

Well then, I will.

I fill a tray with glasses, whiskey, Coke, and a couple mixers and return to the room with a professional smile on my lips and a flutter of my eyelashes.

As soon as I reach the curtain behind the door to the billiard room, I hear women laughing. Goosebumps form on the back of my neck as I think I recognize Harper among the voices.

I peer through a tiny gap in the curtain and watch as five other people enter the room.

Reece, Clarisse, a strange guy and ... Rachel. Together with Harper.

I wait with bated breath. I'm not surprised that Clarisse kisses Jaxon like they're a couple. The two are well matched. The stranger sits down between Jaxon and Romeo. He wears a full beard, a baseball hat, and tinted glasses. I've never seen him on campus before.

Reece pulls out a chair for Rachel, who thanks him with a big *fuck-me* grin, and Harper ... walks up to Sylvian and lets him pull her onto his lap.

Fuck.

That explains a lot and yet absolutely nothing at all. What should I do now? Watching Sylvian wrap a hand around Harper's waist, showing her his cards, laughing while she giggles... is painful. The sting is much deeper than when I saw Jaxon and Clarisse. Even Reece doesn't bring about this kind of reaction in me.

Maybe after our night together Sylvian realized he still has feelings for Harper after all? Is that why he flew to Miami? Did they reconcile? I should be happy, shouldn't I? That's what I wanted for Harper. But she could've just told me. She could've written back.

You aren't friends.

I have no friends.

With a deep breath, I push aside the curtain and enter.

The laughter in the room suddenly stops and all heads turn to me.

"I've prepared a few drinks for you," I say kindly and approach the table. "Jaxon couldn't make up his mind and ..."

"Can you stop saying his name like you're even *worthy* of having it in your mouth?" Clarisse asks me, snarling. Rachel laughs. Wow. Sharing a table with the wolves, she is not the least bit better than the pack.

"Excuse me, His Highness of this campus didn't deign to tell me which drink he desired," I reply cynically as I put the tray down on the table. "So in my extraordinary reverence, I put together a selection."

Everyone in the group looks at me like I just suggested playing hopscotch instead of poker.

"Fuck off with your drinks and wait for our actual order," Jaxon says, quiet and threatening. I take another deep breath.

"Yes, Your Highness." I lower my eyelids submissively, trying to ignore Sylvian whispering seductively in Harper's ear, brushing her hair aside and holding her in his lap as if they've been together for years. I pick up the tray again.

I've barely turned around to leave when a leg shoots out from under the table.

I lose my balance, unable to hold onto the tray as I try to catch myself and go sprawling anyway.

Every single glass shatters on the floor and pain bursts in my elbows. I stay put for a moment. *They're not serious. They simply can't be serious. They can't fuck me* so well *and then treat me* like shit. Adrenaline pumps through my veins, and I would've just climbed to my feet and left if Derby hadn't pushed the curtain aside at that very moment.

"Mable," he barks. "What are you doing?"

"Sorry. I was tripped up because some of the guys in this room can't handle how good sex with me was."

Derby stares at me, speechless.

Well, maybe I'm laying it on a little too thick. Fuck. Can I just go back to being the shy Mable who can't get a word out?

"Clean that up immediately," Derby snaps. "I'm not paying you to flirt."

I open my mouth, stare at him, and take a couple of seconds to think about whether I should respond or not. Probably not. No matter what I say, he'll never be on my side.

"Of course." Keeping my head down, I walk past him to pick up some rags. Anger flows through me like electricity, so strong it's like I put my fingers in an electrical socket. Surrendering to the humiliation of squatting on the floor in front of the Kings and their "ladies" and mopping up the spill only adds to the intensity of the current. They're playing poker like I'm not even there. They laugh their artificial, joyless laughter and ignore me. They let me do the dirty work. They're above helping me.

I keep glancing at the table. Sylvian and Harper are so absorbed in each other that they never notice me. And it hurts. Yes, it hurts, but that pain is no more than I deserve.

I betrayed Harper.

Now she's letting me down.

It's alright. Her, I can forgive. She gets to savor her revenge. But everyone else ... Her new friends and Sylvian himself, who was directly involved in the sex ... Why doesn't he do anything? Why did he give me money to support me and ... Was it nothing but mockery? Did he only give it to me so he could say afterward that he paid me for sex?

I can't help but keep looking at them to see if one of them will have the decency to apologize to me. Not a chance.

Romeo stares back at me. So does the strange guy with his hat, beard, and glasses. They look at me and they do *nothing*.

Once I've finished, I return to the taproom and roughly wash out the rags in the sink.

"I'll serve the boys," Derby informs me as he washes a few glasses. "You can carry on in the bathroom."

"Doing what?" I ask him in surprise.

"Well, cleaning."

I clench my teeth. "I'm *not* going to clean the bathroom."

"Then next time don't be a fucking bitch and just serve Tyrell like you should," he grumbles back.

My jaw drops and I don't know what to say for a few seconds. But then I take the rags and go to the bathroom.

Think about it. You can't put up with that. You can't let people treat you like that. I open the window of the tiny bathroom to let some air in. I need oxygen to think.

Think about it.

My gaze falls on the parking lot.

I get tripped while waiting tables?

They call me *Dole?* Like charity? They treat me like … dirt after the hottest sex of my life?

They have a problem with their egos. A very big problem. The idea that comes to mind is as cheap as it is ingenious. I take off my apron, go back behind the counter and look for a felt-tip pen in the drawer where Derby keeps all sorts of bits and bobs.

"Where are you going?" he snaps, just as he returns from the billiard room.

"Oh." I treat him to a surprised look. "I quit." With that, I walk out and head for the parking lot.

A Tesla, a red sports car, an Aston Martin. And so many other vehicles that cost more than the average American's annual salary.

I wait until pitch darkness has descended. Then I go to one of the lanterns that lights up the lot and kick it out. Kingston is a damn old university, and as well-kept and well-preserved as the rooms and parks are, the electrical equipment dates to the last century. A few well-aimed kicks is all it takes for the lantern to go out.

In the shadows, I can devote myself to decorating Reece's car. Sylvian's and Jaxon's follow. And because it's so much fun, I also mark all the ones within a ten-step radius of them.

Nobody notices me.

There are no cameras.

I scurry away in the darkness and lie down to sleep, completely satisfied.

I dream of the Kings' faces when they read what I've always wanted to tell them.

JAXON

Oh, now it's getting interesting, baby girl. You hate me now, huh? You want to fuck me, but you also want to kill me?

Are you prepared to go to war for it?

What a twist.

Unfortunately for you, I'm not a chess piece to be used.

I am the player.

24

MABLE

The next morning, I feel like I'm woken by the smell of explosives, the smoke and stench of bombs and war. It's all in my head, of course, happening on a strictly psychological level.

I don't feel ready when I leave my dorm room. What I did was reckless. Maybe the Kings have a sense of humor and will laugh it off?

They probably won't.

"Hey, trailer-park girl," Rachel calls from the kitchen as I walk past.

I stop, close my eyes, and wonder whether I really want to do this.

Do I want to talk to her?

Do I want to talk to anyone at all?

Rachel isn't alone. Brittany's sitting next to her, stirring her bowl of cereal without eating bite.

"You lost." Rachel nods to the bulletin board that's been keeping us up to date on the *arena* for weeks.

I read the new printout on the board next to the semester schedule with interest.

My points are at 1500. The thousand points are new, but

there's a big *disqualified* stamped above my name. Rachel has 2230 points, Brittany, and Lien each have between 1400 and 1600.

Since I got 1500 points for winning a hand of poker and the night I spent in the frat house, I wonder what the others had to do for their scores. No sooner have I thought about it than I don't care anymore, though.

"So?" I ask Rachel as I turn around. "Are you happy now that my name is marked *disqualified*? I mean, will you truly be happy from the bottom of your heart if I have to leave?"

Rachel raises her shoulders. "Why not? The rest of us *worked* for our points *from the start* and you just whored around with the Kings. Great work."

"And you're any different?" I ask sweetly. "Isn't it like prostitution for you to let any adult man into your room and spread your legs for him? Because of a *game* played for the entertainment of three completely deluded egomaniacs whose aim in life seems to be to maintain a kindergarten-level of maturity into old age?"

"Just fuck off, Mable. You're not any better than any of us just because you think you are!"

"I never said I was! You did! Just now! Instead of us joining forces, you're playing each other. You know that only *one* can win, right? So why does it matter if I'm leaving next? I won't be the last."

Rachel frowns at me. Since she seems about to spit some more verbal vomit in my face, I raise my hand to tell her I don't care what she's going to say and hurry out of the kitchen.

Okay. No supporters. No allies. What do I do now?

As soon as I approach the main buildings of the university, I'm met with hostile glances from all sides.

"You're disqualified."

"Get out of here, Dole, you've lost."

"You can't come in here." A bulky athlete stands in my way as I try to enter the main building for my Linear Algebra lecture. "Admission for students only."

I look at him, annoyed, from under half-closed eyelids and wonder if he can be serious. The wannabe bouncer's wrist is adorned with a chunky Patek, and his joggers are covered in Louis Vuitton logos.

"Right, I'm sorry, I didn't realize."

Some spoiled rich kid going all bouncer? I've never let bouncers stop me before. Who do they think I am? A little mouse who grew up on a desert island? I spent my childhood and youth in a *trailer park*. I've fended for myself for as long as I can remember. We had shootings at my middle school, a different locker broken into and raided every day. Metal detectors and drug-sniffing dogs at the entrances. I got past them the same way I got past the bouncers at the nightclubs. I may have studied a great deal, a great, great deal, back then, but I did also go out. I did have fun.

I was moving through areas these elitist idiots probably wouldn't even dare to go.

Without giving it a second thought, I take the back entrance and shortly afterward I'm sitting in the lecture hall.

Mr. Louis Vuitton Muscleman notices me as I walk in, and his fleshy face contorts into a hyena-like grimace.

I ignore him.

After the lecture—which I spent in the front row so the professor would notice any further attacks, even if I didn't have any hope that he'd protect me—the door to the outside is blocked instead.

Once the professor's left, an entire group of students look at me like I'm scum as they stand outside the door. They let everyone through who wants to leave, except me.

"You can go if you give us your braid as a prize." A black-haired girl smiles wickedly at me and holds out her hand. I quickly grab my hair with both hands. They're not really going to try to get me to cut my hair off, are they?

They are.

"Give us your damn braid or we won't let you through!" she shrieks.

She's probably not used to someone not immediately giving her everything she asks for.

I back away. There's a second exit on the upper level. I just have to get up the stairs…

But they won't let me escape.

Halfway up, someone pulls me back.

Male hands grab me, dragging me along with them. I scream and fight and shout, and the next moment a hand presses over my mouth.

The three of them pull me to the desk, push me to the floor, and grope at my clothes.

"Let's see if she really fucks as badly as the Kings say." The bouncer from earlier grins hatefully at me and yanks on my pants. "Is she worth the thousand points she got? She's certainly stupid enough not to listen."

The black-haired girl laughs, and the sound burns my ears as I try to shake the guys off.

This isn't really happening.

This isn't happening.

They'd never go that far.

Never!

But they are even smaller men than I thought. They rip down my pants. The bouncer's fly is open. I freeze inside, giving up all resistance as panic condenses into inaction in my head. "Please, let go of me," I whimper, hoping that he will.

They laugh again. All of them.

They're standing around me, looking down at me. Ugly faces,

dressed in the most expensive clothes, and a renegade fun in their eyes that I will never be able to comprehend.

I squeeze my eyes shut, praying it will be over quickly and without too much pain. I prepare myself inwardly to be used roughly. I prepare for the pain, to endure the hands on me, to grit my teeth and get it over with. When I feel a soft cock against my thighs, I realize I've lost.

I have lost.

I will have to give up.

This is going too far.

Much too far.

"Enough!"

Relief flows through me when the boys suddenly release me.

They take three steps back, leaving me lying there as if I'm some unappetizing piece of carrion. I reach for my jeans and pull them on, realizing I have no recollection of the last few seconds. As if in shock, like in an accident, I was watching from the outside. Would they really have raped me?

With everyone watching?

"What are the rules at Kingston?" Jaxon has come alone. He strides through the lecture hall, calm and elegant. His dominant, unassailable energy permeates every corner. He's a man that everyone else looks up to. The power surrounding him drenches the entire room like the scent of prestige and wealth. "I think they've just been disregarded."

"She came to the lecture even though she was disqualified!" the bouncer defends himself, pointing a finger at me like I'm an animal.

With a pounding heart, I pick myself up.

Jaxon descends the stairs step by step, his hands in the pockets of his chinos. "I don't think Dole will be the only one to leave us today."

"What?" the bouncer asks in disbelief. The other students are unsettled, speechless.

"We can't allow important rules to be broken on this campus. Not by pathetic scholarship students who think they're special, nor by assholes like you. You're out, Hilbredge."

Hilbredge looks like Jaxon punched him. The color drains from his face, and his eyes glaze over. "But she's a fucking whore and..."

"She'll never leave if you don't scare her *properly*!" the black-haired girl intervenes. "You're far too easy on her!"

The corner of Jaxon's mouth twitches. The contempt he has for this stranger is even more palpable than his contempt for me. That surprises me. Does he really hate the "peasants" that much? "You're right, Nataly." He lets his gaze slide to me.

I shake my head. Whatever he's up to, it looks like it's going to be painful.

"Carry on, Hilbredge."

"What?" I shout in panic and back away.

"Until she apologizes for attending this lecture, even though she's been unenrolled."

I stare at him. I seem to have forgotten how walking works. Jaxon strolls back to the front row and sits down in one of the chairs. One leg extended before him, he puts his hands in the pockets of his chinos and leans back.

He watches Hilbredge approach me, grinning broadly.

He grabs me again. The laughter is even louder. The joy that their King allows this even greater.

"Apologize for not listening to him, Dole!"

"Like hell I will!" I spit, saliva hitting Hilbredge's forehead. That just makes him even rougher, and he pulls me under him again.

Panicked, I lose myself in the search for Jaxon's eyes. He can't allow this.

He would never do that.

The Kings don't hurt women.

Tears cling to my eyelashes as I realize that I have nothing to hope for. I have to bow to him. I have to give up. "I'm sorry," I whisper as Hilbredge pulls my jeans down again. My body's gone limp, exhausted.

"Louder!" shouts Nataly. "We all want to hear it."

"Sorry!" I shout.

Hilbredge grunts and moves back.

"What are you apologizing for, Dole?" Jaxon calls out to me.

"I was stupid." My voice is a rasp and I let my eyes squeeze shut. *So stupid that I fell for you. So naive to trust you.*

"Stupid?" Jaxon asks with a sneer. He comes closer. "You want to apologize for being stupid? I don't think we can accept that."

I open my eyes and stare at him.

"You didn't listen to Hilbredge. You have sullied the halls of this university with your tedious presence when you were no longer allowed to. You thought you could resist. *Our rules. And the finality of the game.*"

I can't produce another apology. I simply can't. Not when he stands in front of me and appraises me like this.

"But I'll let it pass," he says with a shrug.

"It's not anywhere near adequate!" Nataly declares angrily.

"Would you like to join Hilbredge?" Jaxon's voice is calm.

"What? Join him where?"

"He's going to leave us. Rapists have no place at Kingston."

She hisses softly, which seems to mean no.

"What?" Hilbredge grunts. "Why, I have ..."

"You forget that it's still a game. But if you try to rape a woman, you go to jail. The choice is yours, Hilbredge. Pack your things or go to jail. I recorded everything."

Hilbredge collects some saliva in his mouth and spits it at the

King's feet. "Motherfucker." With that, he turns away and stomps to the door.

Jaxon calmly watches him go. Then he approaches me. It's just a few steps before he's grabbed me by the upper arm. Since he has just rescued me, in a manner of speaking, I don't resist when he leads me outside. There he pushes me off him so hard I stumble and fall to the floor.

Great. Savior, my ass.

He bends over me, his eyes dark with disgust. "Last warning. Next time, I'll let them fuck you until your pussy bleeds."

"I didn't lose," I reply angrily. "Nowhere is there a rule that says you must not be provoked! I still have more points than Brittany! Even if this game is stupid, what kind of game would it be if the rules didn't even matter? If you can just decide to disqualify someone because your pathetic egos can't take a little pushback?"

We have listeners. Not only the students who wanted to watch me get raped but also others in the corridor, all turning their heads in our direction.

Jaxon looks down at me.

It's embarrassing enough that I'm sitting on the floor in front of him. But something in the gaze he's leveled on me leaves me motionless. I want to scream at him so loud that he stops being this nasty bastard and becomes the man who's somewhat bearable!

"It's not about the game," Jaxon explains calmly. "You never played the game. The points we gave you were fake, just to keep you here for a while longer. Because we always fuck the scholarship students before they leave. There has to be some advantage to my father shoving thousands of dollars up your ass, right? Admittedly, we took our time with you because we enjoyed watching you fail. But now we're through with you. Deal with it and *finally go home.*"

Tears sting my eyes. It's not the realization that the Kings used me that hurts so much. It's my own stupidity. Does that mean I could've prevented everything if I hadn't willingly accepted his offer of sex?

Are they punishing me in the end for wanting to have *fun* too? It's so ridiculous.

An ideology from the last millennium.

I'd love to tell him what I really think about him. That I don't believe him when he says it was *only about sex*. He was too ... tender for that? Do the other students know that?

Do they know that Jaxon can be as loving as an angel?

They probably don't.

And maybe I was just too turned on to realize that he didn't actually feel anything for me while we were having sex.

I lean back, my hands planted on the stone floor. This ancient stone floor, walked upon by those seeking to learn for centuries. Was this building erected to provide space for a Tyrell to terrorize students in 2020? So he could be propped up as the tyrannical ruler of everything and everyone here?

When I get to my feet in front of him, he looks at me blankly. He hasn't moved. But the fact that he gives me the chance to say something back makes me feel hopeful for a moment.

"I don't believe you."

One of his eyebrows twitches upward in amusement. "What?"

"All the things you said. You didn't make those up."

He laughs out loud, clearly enjoying the fact that everyone's watching us. Then he comes closer again. "Every single kind word I've ever said to you has been a lie. I lied to you so much that you probably haven't ever heard a single true sentence from me. All I wanted was for you to give yourself to us like a whore. You let us fuck you because you thought you could win that way."

"That's not true!" I counter tearfully.

"Isn't it? So you did it because you enjoyed it, then?"

"I did!" I shout and the crowd around me laughs.

"Fine, then you're just a neglected little slut who can't get enough cock. If you'd realized that earlier, you could've earned a lot of points with *favors*."

My pulse is racing, and I can't think straight. They're laughing again. All of them are. But I can't focus on the fact that we have an audience, or I won't be able to get a word out anymore. It's Jaxon alone who draws the seething rage out of me, which lowers my inhibitions to the floor.

"And what does that make you, then?" I ask mockingly, speaking a little louder to make sure everyone can hear me. "You're so fucking pathetic that you have to lie and manipulate women and then share them among you because none of you can sustain a normal relationship! Nobody wants your ugly hearts or your psychotic minds! They only see your money, your power, your status, but they actually hate you! And that's why you always have to look for new victims, because nobody will actually get involved with you, nobody trusts so much as a kind word from you! They all know how disgusting you really are!"

A few seconds pass in which no one says anything. Jaxon fixes me with his blue eyes.

Then he smiles. Unfortunately, I know it's a real smile. None of my words have hit the mark.

"You think so, do you? Pretty big words for a girl from the slums. You know them, do you? The honest, sincere, loving relationships? The fathers and mothers who stay together and face every adversity as a family? The women who don't get beaten by their husbands or dumped in a trailer park where they turn to pills because no one will ever truly love them? If any of you ever need relationship advice, just ask Amabelle Weaver," he addresses our audience, which is growing by the second. "And if you want a good blowjob, ask her for that, too."

Once again, a shower of laughter rains down on me and I do the only thing I can. I punch him right in the face.

Except he nimbly moves out of the way and catches my wrist.

A loud "Ooooh" resounds through the hall.

Jaxon pulls me toward him. His eyes light up as if my anger deeply satisfies him. "It was a bet, Belle. A small, insignificant little bet between Sylvian and me. I told him you'd want me. Even if you knew everything about me. Even if Harper told you all about me. Even if I stood in front of you and revealed all my hatred for the underclass. I bet that you would choose me and that you'd let me fuck you long and deep despite everything. And I won. Which is why I get to decide as I please what happens to you. And since I can no longer use you as a toy and people who deface the world with ugly graffiti get on my nerves, you've been disqualified."

"I didn't choose *you*." There. I said it. I can't let him have that satisfaction.

"You didn't?" he asks casually. "You mean because you had Crescent's cock in your mouth first? Well, if that's how you see it ..."

"It wasn't my first time with one of you." For a moment, I enjoy the irritation that appears on his features. "And if Sylvian and Reece hadn't been there, I never would've trusted you. But keep telling yourself otherwise. Your ego seems to need it. It really is so much bigger than your cock will ever be."

Endless anger flares up in his gaze and I can't help being afraid of him. I quickly tear myself away. Nevertheless, I boldly raise my chin. Maybe I can beat him at his own game. And the fact that so many people are watching us, people who are obviously very interested in it not ending yet, might work to my advantage.

"If it's a game ... then it's for entertainment, right?"

"So?" he asks coldly.

"Let me play, then," I demand. "Until the last day of exams. If I still don't have enough points by then ... I'll leave." I raise my hand and point around me, even though I have to make an effort to hide my trembling. Going toe-to-toe with Jaxon is one of the biggest challenges I've ever faced. "You want something to watch, don't you? I'm sure people would be in favor of it too."

The crowd actually applauds, even if there are many derisive shouts as well.

Jaxon's lips curl up. "It's cute how you try to delay the inevitable."

"Is it working?" I ask with a shaky voice.

Recognition flashes in his eyes. But he says nothing.

"Come on. Disqualifying me because I drew Mount Dick on your windshields? Don't you have any sense of humor at all? Are you really going to exclude *me* of all people? The others are so boring compared to me."

His smile is devilish as he tilts his head and nods. "You really want it to get harder, don't you?" he asks quietly. "Right, until the last day of exams. But between now and then, you're on your own. If anyone pulls you into a corner, I won't be there. Come up with something, Dole. If you don't fall for another two weeks, you'll fall even farther." He winks, walks past, and turns his broad back to me.

All around me there's a buzz of excited, muttered conversations as people pull out their phones. They filmed our conversation, too, but since the university network hasn't cleared access to any social apps, it'll probably be a while before the video goes viral.

Strangely enough, I still have the feeling that everyone knows what happened as I walk across the campus. The trees above me whisper the truth through the park at lightning speed.

Every single student is suddenly looking at me like Jaxon gave them a free pass to rape me, so I make a detour to the student restaurant before fleeing back to my dorm room.

There I lock the door behind me.

I close the blinds.

I switch on the light.

And I make a plan.

JAXON

Yes, we were only interested in fucking you. We've done that. And that's it for you.

You were available just as quickly as everyone else. Admittedly, most of the scholarship students jump on my cock the minute I ask them to, but I'm nice to them.

I was never nice to you.

And yet you chose me.

Me and not Sylvian, who tried to protect you from me.

Me and not Reece, who was always kind to you.

But me.

This much stupidity asks to be punished by no longer being allowed to study at Kingston.

So go, then!

25

MABLE

My plan starts with turning my room upside down. I no longer trust anyone, least of all the Kings. Who's to say they didn't break in and plant something in here? Something worse than a toad?

I look for traces in every single corner. Cameras. Bugs? Whatever.

In the end, I'm reassured to find that nothing is missing, my safe hasn't been broken into, and there's nothing reminiscent of a fascist surveillance network.

I still have eleven days to go until exams. No new material will be covered in the last week of lectures. If I don't go, I'll miss exam preparation, but I might stay alive for longer. Besides, I have to study on my own first and foremost anyway.

I tape a few blank pages from my notepad together to make a poster and write a message on it to everyone who hasn't been quite as successful as me over the semester. I have no idea whether my idea will work, but I don't have many options.

I pull the blinds back up and attach the poster to my window. Then I stow the supply of food I asked for from the canteen in my cupboard, sit down at my desk, switch on my laptop, and start studying. That's why I'm at Kingston after all, and no one can hurt me if I don't leave my room.

It's as simple as that.

And I can focus on collecting points.

A lot of points.

***

Being locked in is an entirely new feeling of freedom. Why'd it take so long to come up with the idea of spending as little time on campus as possible? Of course, I know this is only a temporary solution. Not being able to ask anyone questions, neither tutors nor professors, is taking a toll on my confidence. What if I don't fully understand a subject?

I changed my sleeping pattern immediately. My alarm clock rings at four o'clock. From five to six, I go outside, take a walk, wake myself up, and run through my exam notes. Around seven o'clock, the campus wakes up and I lock my door behind me.

Then the messages start to arrive.

I never would've thought I'd receive so many. But it's almost ridiculously easy to revise or completely write term papers for my fellow students. It's the first term in the undergraduate program. I have several months of intensive study behind me. I can complete most of the tasks required by my wonderful points sponsors who started responding to my poster within a few hours. Some of the messages, however, make me wonder how they even made it to Kingston … I don't have time to think about how stupid it is to write or revise other people's term papers.

The main thing is that I will get points for it.

As the Friday of Dead Week, the week the campus lapses into comatose study mode, passes, I take the poster that reads *Write to me for 10 points* down from my window. The fact that professors may also have seen my advertisement was a risk. If they pretend this game doesn't exist, though, why should they know what that even means?

On Monday morning, I go to our dormitory kitchen after five o'clock for the first time since my plan went into effect. The notice on the bulletin board, which normally indicates the weekly challenge, is missing. That's not a good start to finals week.

I leave the kitchen again as quickly as I can, making my way to my first exam. In the hope that I'll be one of the first and won't be denied entry to the lecture hall by anyone, I set off an hour early.

I nervously go through my notes one last time. The midterm exams were tough already. Am I prepared well enough for the *finals*?

As the lecture hall slowly fills up, nobody pays me any attention. Finally, I walk forward, confirm my identity, and return to my seat.

For the first time, I realize no one in the room is out to shout something stupid at me. It must be the exam situation. They all just want to make it through. They have no time for bullying anymore.

I hand in my test twenty minutes before the end and manage to leave the lecture hall before anyone else. I go straight back to the dormitory. Since all the exams take place at the same time, the campus is empty, and I make it to my room unscathed.

As soon as I close the door behind me, I breathe a sigh of relief.

This is no life, Mable. You can't keep it up. Not for much longer than a few days.

I push aside the nagging thoughts that remind me that I've stepped into the ring with three assholes for a fight that I'll never be adequately equipped for. Even though I *hate* boxing matches, and I still don't *want* to win against any of the other scholarship students.

I don't want to play this stupid game at all.

Do I have a choice, though?

As a reward for my exam, which I'm pretty sure I passed, I take a shower and turn the water to hot. As the heat washes over me, I go through all the calculations from the exam again. *I haven't made any mistakes, have I?*

My skin starts to wrinkle so I turn off the water. I wrap a towel around my body, go back to my room, and realize that I took too long.

My door is open.

The other scholarship students are back from their exams.

I quickly rush through the open door, close it behind me and check my safe. My notes, all my exam preparation, and my laptop are still there.

But there's something wrong with my clothes.

I pull one of my favorite sweaters from my closet. It breaks into pieces.

"No." Tears well up in my eyes. All my clothes are cut up. Every single piece, down to my panties. The same goes for the super expensive, designer dresses, pants, and shirts from Harper.

I sink to the ground, weak and exhausted. Fifteen minutes. I got out of the shower fifteen minutes too late and was already subjected to another prank. Worse than all the others before. I need something to wear. It's just above freezing outside, and it could snow any day.

I can't do it, a voice whispers inside my head. *I'll never manage. I can't defend myself when everyone is against me. Every single one of them. Everyone.*

In tears, I spread my clothes out on my two beds. Nothing can be salvaged. If it was possible at all, I'd need a lot of safety pins, a sewing kit, preferably a sewing machine...

They even stole my winter coat entirely.

I recall the points once again.

Homework. Challenges. Sex.

Nobody has to hand in any more homework this term. The challenges are over. And "favors"—a.k.a. sex—are not an option.

Who knows how many points the other scholarship students collected during Dead Week?

Do I even have a chance of winning?

Or would it be easier to give up?

My towel wrapped tightly around my chest, I have to pursue the mission of finding allies. There's no other option. I can't do it alone.

Never.

I reach for my phone with trembling fingers. I know that I'm grasping at a very short straw here, but it's the only thing I can think of.

Please. Answer me.

What is it? Harper replies after a short time.

She hasn't blocked me yet. That gives me hope. Although I should apologize to her, although I should ask her for help, I can only manage one sentence:

Was it all a lie?

She takes a few minutes to answer.

You tell me. Was it?

I feel the knot in my throat and put down my phone. She won't help me because I betrayed her. Desperately, I scroll through my other chats and the university network. But the only students who wrote to me there were talking about their term papers. Once again, I reach Harper Mitchell's name. She changed her profile picture. Because I'm a bit of a masochist, I want to see if she might have uploaded another picture of her and Clarisse, so I enlarge it. Instead, it's a photo of her from behind, grabbing her hair. A showy diamond ring on her finger.

I sink back and close my eyes so the pain doesn't knock me out. I can guess who she got engaged to.

And that hurts more than anything else.

JAXON

In a way, we have nothing to gain from destroying you. We simply enjoy it. It's a passion, a bit deranged, an opportunity to act like gods. Do what we ask, and you may continue to fight for the chance to study at the country's best university, or don't ... in which case it all ends. Quickly and painfully, though yes, sometimes we might mourn you a little.

Because your heart does mean something to us.

We break it into its individual parts and divide it up between us.

So each of us gets a small souvenir.

Hold on to your heart, angel.

You never know who you'll lose it to next.

26

MABLE

A part from the fact that the slats from my bedframe are missing, my drawers are superglued shut, and detergent is poured into the food in my fridge, which I almost notice too late, finals week is relaxed for me. Though I do have to remove a rat that someone left in front of my safe from my room on Wednesday night, I'm still alive on Thursday. No matter how often I lock the door to my room, they always get it open again. They probably have a master key, and I'm slowly getting used to the idea that I'm only safe in my room if I push a chest of drawers in front of the door before going to bed.

I stole new clothes from the scholarship students who live on the floor above us. The clothes don't fit me, and I look like I'm wearing garbage bags, but at least they let me get away with it. Maybe they don't even know about it because we hardly ever meet on campus.

So far, I haven't failed a single exam.

There are only twenty-four hours left until I find out if I was able to turn the tide of the game in my favor. As I go to open the door to my dorm after my exam on Thursday, I'm suddenly pulled back.

I don't know why the smell became quite so familiar to me so quickly, but I immediately recognize that it's Reece holding me. He just saved me from having the bucket installed above the entrance to the dorm empty its contents onto my head. Red liquid pours out onto the tiled floor and a few thick wads of absorbent cotton float in it.

"God, are those used tampons?"

Reece lets go of me, and I take another step back so the blood-stained water doesn't reach my shoes.

"They actually went around campus collecting tampons just for me?"

"Looks like it."

"They know I'm always the first to return from exams..." I mutter more to myself than to him. "Thanks." I don't look at Reece because I don't feel like talking to him. "Are you on your way to see Rachel?"

"Who?"

Right. Now I am looking at him after all. "Rachel."

He looks like he has no idea who I'm talking about.

"The scholarship student, your new girlfriend?" I help him out.

"Ah," he says, shaking his head. "That one."

"Yeah." Right. How much has he smoked that he can't even remember her name?

"No, I was coming to see you."

"Oh, that's nice. Unfortunately, I won't be inviting you in." I smile sweetly at him and think about how to get to my room without having to walk through blood.

"Then we'll talk right here."

I take a deep breath. "We won't. I have nothing to say to you, and you won't be able to say anything I want to hear. So let's just leave it at that."

"You've become much more talkative than you used to be. More quick-witted. That's ... cool."

I cross my arms in front of my chest. Reece, always the golden boy, is dressed in a black quilted jacket and a white scarf loosely wrapped around his neck. I wear several sweaters on top of each other because I no longer have a jacket. I feel longing rise in me as soon as I see more of him than his face. There's that heat at the thought of how he felt inside me, taking turns with Sylvian ... How he lay under me, how I came on his tongue, his cock in my mouth...

Fuck.

"You keep thinking back to that too, huh?" he asks, stepping ever so slightly closer. "I'm here to ... apologize. In a way."

I take notice. "Are you?" I whisper, flooded with so much hope that only now do I realize how much I long for a happy ending after waking up from this bad dream. I am strong. I am doing my best. I am mastering the situation—somehow. But inside, I am broken. Inside, I don't want Sylvian to be engaged to Harper and both of them to be treating me like shit. Inside, I long for Reece's casual conversation and his tender touches. Inside, I wish Jaxon wasn't just a King, but that I was his Queen.

Inside, I have long been lost.

Absolutely and irrevocably lost.

"I don't know if what I'm going to say will pass muster as an apology. But at least it's an explanation."

"Why are you all ... being like this to me?"

Reece nods. It doesn't happen often, but right now, shadows populate his otherwise radiant face. "I'm telling you this in confidence. Because I like you, Mable. I just like you, without ulterior motive or agenda. But Jaxon is planning your downfall if you don't leave. Just like we said from the very beginning."

"Really, now? I don't remember *you* saying anything like that."

Reece takes a deep breath. "I'm probably not the right person to explain it to you. But this university is not quite what it seems on the outside."

"No shit." I roll my eyes. Story time with Reece? It could be worse for me. "I didn't even notice."

"Save your cynicism."

"Are you going to explain to me why you're participating in shit like this? Why don't you stand up to Jaxon instead of watching me suffer?"

"I can't do that."

"Because you're not allowed to?"

He growls. "Because I *can't* explain it. This university is about more than just college. It's much more than a degree. That's why you scholarship students are not particularly popular. The people here believe that you're going to take something away from them. It's a bit … like the caricature of a Mexican immigrant who supposedly steals American jobs, even though he doesn't even speak English."

"I'm impressed that you're critical of such behavior."

"I don't see it critically. That's just how people react. They're afraid of everything and see everyone as a threat."

"So you're okay with what's happening around me? Because people are afraid and that's just how they are?"

"How am I 'okay with it' if I just don't care?"

"You tolerate it. That's what being okay with it means. If you cared, you wouldn't tolerate it."

Reece looks at me like I'm some stupid zoo animal. "No. I care about *you*."

"Great. Like that's going to change anything for me. You didn't like me enough to help me win. You lied to me!"

"We didn't! You would have won if you had just spent one night in the frat house! But you had to throw away Sylvian's stash and let us …" He sighs and runs his fingers through his hair. "You're just as naive as a caterpillar that thinks its natural predator is a bird and then gets squashed by a shoe."

"What are you trying to tell me, Reece?"

"If you think everyone in this world is responsible for your suffering just because they don't do anything about it, you're *wrong* for Kingston. This is not about *guilt* or *innocence*. To date, no one who doesn't have at least an eight-figure fortune has ever obtained a degree here. Kingston doesn't sort by race or origin or religion. This university connects families who have money. And what happens when a college advertises this to the outside?"

"It attracts even more money?"

"That's right. For years, there has been *no one* born in the States who's richer than Kingston graduates. And now think a little further and you'll see that it's not about studying. Not on its own."

"It's about networking so you can remain the elite of the elite?"

"That's it. Precisely. A degree from Kingston, in particular a master's degree, opens up an entirely new world. You scholarship students might take up places."

"Places?"

"In the circle."

"In the circle?!"

"That's the name of the group to which you are admitted when you earn a Kingston degree summa cum laude. That's why many here have a vested interest in driving you away."

"I don't want to be accepted into any circle at all!"

"Oh, that's not for you to decide. If *they want you*, you will be part of it."

I cross my arms in front of my chest and say nothing. All this sounds like another lie. "And how did *you* get on the leaderboard? Did the three of you prove that you can be particularly big assholes?"

There is a weariness in his gaze that takes possession of me like some creeping illness. "Mable, why don't you just go and leave all of this behind you?"

"What?"

"You don't have to study here. You have a thousand other options. Your life could be easy. You know, maybe we'll meet in three years, after I get my master's, and continue where our very interesting love story started out. We could have a happy marriage. You're rich in one fell swoop, you let me fuck whoever I feel like, we have fun in the marriage bed from time to time, and at some point, when I don't feel like dining out anymore, we have children. And if someone like me isn't around, someone else would be. You could wrap most of the men who study here around your finger easily if you wanted to. You just need to accept that there will be nothing more for you. That you won't be able to study at an elite university, that you might be worse off than the man you marry. But what is all that compared to what's already happened to you here?"

"What has happened?" I ask brashly. "You mean being a pawn in your stupid game? The bullying is not worth giving up my dream."

"Why don't you take this seriously?"

"Because it's silly!"

Reece's eyelids are half closed. I know he won't tell me any more than that. That he's probably already said more than he wanted to. "What's the point of holding on to your pride? Think about it. Giving up is the better option here. And no, I can't promise you anything, but a woman who marries me to keep up appearances and who's even a little more tolerable than Clarisse ..." He laughs when he notices the look on my face, but immediately becomes serious again. "It would be an option. For many of us, it is. At least for those who have enough money, and my family certainly has enough. Women from our circles are exhausting. But you've already figured that one out, haven't you?"

"Is it true that you just wanted to get me?" I ask him directly. "That it was only about sex?"

Reece buries his hands in the pockets of his coat. "In a way, yes."

"It was all just a game? Every single ... gesture? Every word?"

"Not for me, it wasn't." He grimaces like it caused him pain to say so.

I swallow hard. Why do I get the feeling he's telling the truth for the first time?

"Usually..."

"Just say it, Reece," I demand coldly.

He presses his lips together and thinks for a while before continuing in a hushed voice. "No, I can't. I can't reveal the full depth of our darkness to you. That's not why I'm here."

"What then? To explain to me why I, of all people, should be eliminated?"

"Yes." He gazes into the distance for a moment, as if desperate to confess something to me. But he doesn't. He remains silent and I understand that it's all my own fault. That it's just how he says it is. That by having sex with them, I made sure that I'd be thrown out. Drawing mountains of dicks on their cars probably only accelerated the process.

Stupid, stupid, naive Mable.

"How can you live with ... something like that?" I say haltingly. "I mean, who comes up with such ... nasty ideas anyway? You do realize that I just liked it, right? That I hadn't given a second thought to who you are or what this could mean for my career or my future. That I never once thought you were using me. It was just ... It was just ... you. Why do you want to punish me so much for my feelings?"

Reece looks tortured now, like my words alone are painful to him. "Please, just go. It would be best for you."

"I'm *not* going," I mutter angrily. "What have I done to Jaxon that he wants to destroy me specifically? Why not one of the other scholarship students? What's special about me?"

Reece sighs. His eyes dart around as if he wants to make sure no one's listening. Then he leans toward me.

I can barely comprehend that I had all those feelings for him, that he was inside me, naked and heavenly, and now we're pretending nothing ever happened. Did it really mean nothing to him? How does he feel about Rachel? Did he just use her to hurt me?

"So..." Reece lowers his voice, making it sound rough and seductive. I don't let it draw me in anymore. "It's almost unbearable to be someone Jaxon *hates*. But it's much, much worse to be someone he actually *likes*. You were a touch too ... intimate with him. Now he wants to destroy you, if only to kill off the part of him that feels anything other than indifference and disgust."

"Wow. What a realization," I scoff.

"Believe me." A pleading expression appears on Reece's face, and I'm on the verge of listening to him. "If you don't disappear, Jax will be ruthless. If you continue to resist him, he will kill you *himself*. Just... don't be suicidal, will you?"

I feel saliva collecting in my mouth, look at Reece one last time and spit at his feet. "He can kill you next."

With my head held high, I step over the pool of blood and tampons on the floor.

I'm certain he spends a while staring after me.

JAXON

I want to see you suffer, Belle. I want you to break under what you've brought upon yourself. I want you to understand what you've done. I want you to weep. When tears shine in your eyes, I can imagine you sitting in front of me naked, whimpering and pleading. I can imagine that there is no game, that it's just the two of us. And that, in spite of all the fear that fills you, you can hardly wait for me to fuck you again.

But let's be honest.

It never would've worked between us.

I wouldn't do you any good, Amabelle.

I wouldn't just taint you.

I would destroy you.

Though very slowly, I'm starting to doubt that I still actually want this…

But it needs to be done, doesn't it?

You're not going to give up.

And that is becoming a real problem.

27

MABLE

Commuting between the main campus buildings and my dorm has become a habit. After my last exam on Friday, I set foot in the latter for the last time for a month. I make sure no new bucket of menstrual blood has been installed above the door before I walk into the kitchen. Finally, there's a notice on the bulletin board showing the current points.

There's a 1790 next to my name. Rachel has a 2340. Lien has a 2200, and even Brittany has 1800 points.

What has earned her so many points since last week?

It can only be a trick, and I'm annoyed that I even thought about playing the game. I didn't stand a chance. Jaxon wants me to lose, so I lose.

Frustrated, I empty my fridge, sort out what I can't take with me to Philadelphia and make myself a snack on the side. I spin as a shadow appears behind me.

The man fills the doorframe with his stature.

I've seen him somewhere before. He's one of the football players. He tried to collect money from Harper at Jaxon's party, and she warned me about him. What's his name again?

"What are you doing here?" I ask him.

"I have to pick you up," the giant replies in a deep, melodious voice.

"Do I get to decide whether I feel like coming with you, or is this a Kings thing?" I ask as confidently as I can, even though I shrink under his gaze as if he's one of the Kings themselves standing in front of me. No, even worse. This stranger has the kind of charisma that automatically makes me feel small. Not necessarily out of fear, but ... out of respect. He comes in and closes the door behind him. That fills me with unease.

If he's here to rape me ... I don't stand a chance. With sweaty palms, I remain standing next to the kitchen counter and pray he's not one of those guys who'd force himself on a woman against her will.

"It doesn't have much to do with what you want," he grumbles. I suddenly remember his name. Yes, not only did Harper call him that, he is also cheered by his fans in the corridors of the university. *Vance Buchanan.* "Why didn't you ever play along?"

"At the stupid arena?"

He remains serious and looks like he's very interested in my answer. "Yes."

"I didn't want to be pushed around. Not by any of you."

"Don't ever count me among those bastards."

"What are you, then?"

"Do you know who I am?"

I shake my head at first, but then I nod. "You're one of the football players."

"More like a pawn." He comes even closer, and I gulp. "Just like you."

"What do you mean?"

"I was one of the first to have to go through this shit."

"You're a scholarship student?" I whisper.

"I am," he says tonelessly.

Hope wells up inside me.

"Please, help me," I plead, not sure what good it will do. Why should Vance help me? He's obviously worked his way up. He's part of the football team and has made friends in Kingston who celebrate and appreciate him. He'd never give it up for someone like me. Why would he?

The smile he treats me to is more of a snarl. "I have *been helping you* all this time, princess. I respected you for the fact that you didn't want to play along, so I tried everything in my power to get people to leave you alone. It worked reasonably well."

I blink at him. "What do you mean ..."

"Normally, people out there pay us to pull shit on you. I've made sure my boys leave you alone."

"Your boys?"

"The freshmen who started this year. They left you alone because I told them to. At least as far as my influence over them extends. They listen to me. Mostly. If you hadn't let the fucking Kings get to you by the end of the academic year, you probably would've won. But no. You let them climb on you like a mattress. All my fucking effort wasted."

"You ... helped me?" I look up at him in disbelief. "You of all people?"

"What do you mean, me of all people?" he growls. "I am the only one who'd even have a chance to control the pawns. But then you had to go and kick *yourself* out of the game. No one else had to do anything at all."

"I wasn't *playing*, I was having *fun*."

"Fun with what? Letting the Kings fuck you like they'll ever see more in you than trailer-park trash?"

Vance knows a hell of a lot about me. "No," I mutter angrily. "Letting the Kings fuck me was fun. You wouldn't have said no to three women offering you a foursome, would you? Would you have? And you wouldn't have given *a single thought* to whether they might be rich or poor ... You would've just done it!"

Vance looks at me with a dark expression. "You did ... all this for ... fun?"

I look at him doubtfully. "Why else would I do it?"

"You wanted to have sex with four assholes, so you just fucked them? Without even thinking about what that could mean for you?"

"Three of them." I press my lips together.

"No. There are five Kings. Romeo is on the outside, but the other four were there."

"And you? Were you there too? How do you know so much about it?"

"Fortunately, I wasn't. Didn't anyone tell you that getting into bed with all of them automatically puts you on the hit list? Not even your friend Harper?"

"She did," I mumble. *I just didn't believe her.*

"And did she also tell you that they'll disqualify you if you draw Mount Dick on their cars and write that the sex was bad because their penises are small and that's why they're bullying people?"

I have to grin briefly. "That, she didn't tell me."

His eyes also flash with amusement, which makes me feel like there's some bond between us. But then the cold returns. "The game isn't fair. You are simply an object of their entertainment. Part of their *Truman Show*. Your script was written long before you even attended your first lecture."

"You seem to know your way around."

"I won in my first year."

"Congratulations."

"Thank you." His voice jars my memory as he steps closer. "Honestly, I would've liked to have seen you win too."

As he stands in front of me, I remember. "It was you!" I back up. "You stopped me at the chapel and sent me away!"

"I do whatever they ask."

I snort contemptuously. "Great! Another coward who doesn't know how to stand up to them. Who was sitting in the chair? Was it really about rape?"

His deep brown eyes radiate a warmth that does not fit this situation. "Harper. And *no*," he says, stretching, "Jaxon meant Sylvian. When they were together, Harper did everything he wanted."

My mouth opens in astonishment. "What did she have to do with..."

"She was trying to protect you, and the Kings have a problem with anyone protecting their victims." He offers a grim smile. His entire body is muscular and toned. His clothing is simple but it flatters his appearance. He's certainly no less attractive than the Kings. "I'm sorry, princess, but you know how the game is."

"What?" I gasp. "No!" I shout as he takes another step and pulls me toward him.

"I don't really want to do this," he says softly, pressing my body against his chest. "But I *have to.*"

That said, he holds a rag to my face, and I take the poison deep into my lungs. And I know this is the end.

28

JAXON

I have Sylvian pass me a cigarette and light it. Apart from Vance's work, the soft rustling of hands on fabric, the only sound is the snapping of my lighter. I take a deep drag and exhale.

There she sits.

The small, delicate, obstinate queen of naivety.

Entangled in a web of intrigue, lies, and seduction.

Foggy from chloroform, exhausted, and utterly defenseless.

Vance straightens up as soon as he's finished and nods at me.

Amabelle sits with her head bent forward. Still not awake enough to realize what's happening around her.

Have you ever wondered what the male scholarship students have to do to be allowed to stay? Were you not at all surprised that they seem completely unaffected by the game taking place in public?

I'll let you in on a secret, Belle.

They are our soldiers.

Vance is our best man and never hesitates to do what we ask.

A very simple agreement, just as there could have been between us. He's working off his debts to my family, and because he's always been the most unscrupulous of those begging fucks, he's still here.

Did you wonder who was responsible for all the things in your dorm?

The rat in your closet?

The cut-up clothes?

Do you really think any of us would get our hands dirty?

No, that was them.

Vance and his small army of tail-wagging super-losers who, just like you, would do anything to stay at this university.

Well. Almost anything.

Sylvian gives me a look. I can see in his eyes just how much he longs to go down to her. He wants her, more than I ever wanted her, and at the same time, he wants her even less than I could ever imagine not wanting her.

His inner struggle is brutal.

I know that in a way he loves seeing her like this. Tied up. Defenseless. A victim.

He's so sick in the head, little Belle. You'll be lucky if you never find out how sick he really is.

"If you want to fuck her one last time, don't hold back," I tell him.

We're alone. Just the two of us who observed Vance's work. The other Kings are listening in, though. They *always* listen to *everything* we say. Everything we think. Everything we feel.

In this respect, Amabelle, we are a single inseparable unit. We're the light and the shadow and everything in between. I'm not just Jaxon. Not just a king. I am five. Five people in this world with five right hands, with five thinking brains, with five working cocks.

Alright, Romeo's cock might not actually count, but you know what I mean.

"No." Sylvian lights a cigarette as well.

"Ah, that's right. You've got *Harper* now," I tease.

He clenches his teeth. Another ring shines on his left hand. He's gotten engaged. He's gotten engaged because he believes it would be best for him and best for the world to protect it from itself.

He's a lovesick moron, Belle. He wants you and he won't let himself have you. At least the sex is probably good. Harper's practically moved in with us since Thanksgiving, and I hear her ecstatic moans every single night. No, we don't share her. Harper's not stupid enough to put her lust above her morals. She knows she has to choose.

Something you should have learned before you seduced all of us.

"Why her? Is there a reason you're already thinking about getting married?"

Sylvian doesn't answer.

Of course there's a reason. He wants to protect you from himself, so he's fucking your best friend to make you not want him anymore.

Something like that in any case. We're not going to try and understand Sylvian here.

"Why did you lie to me, by the way?" I keep my voice casual.

He tilts his head in my direction.

"You fucked her in the forest. Like I said. You lost the bet and made us think we were still in the game."

He looks ahead again, inhaling the smoke from his cigarette deeply. "That was only half the bet. I still wanted to see your face when you realize you're not getting her."

"I did get her."

"Only because I was there." He grins wryly at me. "You know that."

"Tell yourself whatever you like." *No, you wanted me, Belle. You reeled me in, lured me to you, seduced me. You wanted me, me, me, me. Even Silvano can't deny that.*

"You're so certain that all the girls want you that you can't even admit that she never wanted *you*. She wanted *us*. And maybe Reece. Maybe me. But you weren't her choice, Jax."

Hearing that makes me angry.

"I have Harper," Sylvian replies, hiding his face behind smoke. "What about you? Is there anyone who really likes *you*?"

My jaw almost breaks as I grind my teeth. Fucking son of a bitch. Is that wounded pride? *Does he want revenge on me because I did all of this to you? But if he didn't want it, why didn't he stop me? How much of the sadist who enjoys watching you suffer is still in him?*

"You're trying so hard not to be like your father"—Sylvian looks at Amabelle, who's still motionless in the chair—"that you're already like him. A man you can only hate."

"Thanks for the compliment, bro," I say cynically.

He laughs. "But you have Romeo at least, don't you? He'll always love you."

I'm overcome with the desire to hit him. "Never forget who you have to thank for everything."

He treats me to an ironic look. The green in his eyes can seem so harmless, *don't you think?* "Never."

"Good." I straighten up slowly. "Not long until May now. If I graduate summa cum laude, I might get into the circle as a junior member. Then I can continue to fuck over my father from there."

Sylvian smiles wryly, but his thoughts are elsewhere. He's not interested in my father. He doesn't care about my revenge. The reason for this game matters nothing to him. *Not even my endless secrets do.* All that matters to him is his inner peace.

He won't be finding that for years to come.

When Amabelle stirs in her chair and slowly wakes up, we move back.

"Let the people in," I command, and Vance opens the doors for them. I put on my mask. "Game over, I guess, huh?"

Sylvian's face is only half hidden by the mask, his mouth exposed. No smile. No joy. "Game over."

GAME OVER

We come at her like a pack of dogs—or like wolves, a pack of five whose entire existence is geared toward destruction. Five slender figures. Five concealed faces. Five motherfuckers who are celebrated like stars by the crowd at our backs.

Like heroes.

Like kings.

Reece, Zayn—*Whose connection to each other you still haven't understood, Belle*—Romeo, Sylvian, and me. We hunger for blood, for revenge, for vengeance, and for the pretty little girl looking up at us as if we were her executioners.

Amabelle is trapped.

She has lost and we have won.

The chair she's tied to is bolted to the floor.

She should have fled while she still could. Now she's sitting there. Trapped. Ensnared.

Surrounded by us and helpless, forced to take part in a final little game.

The award ceremony of cruelty.

I break away from the group, stepping forward to roughly grab her hair, pull her head back, and approach her lips. I can smell how her blood starts to simmer under her skin, and for a moment I enjoy all the images that come into my head. Her submissive look, her seductive lips. I feel her under me, feel myself inside her, and watch her being fucked by Sylvian and Reece. *It's such a shame, little Belle. What a shame that you can't stay. Maybe you'll understand the reason at some point. Maybe I'll tell you when I'm powerful enough that no secret in the world can destroy me. But until then, I will remain silent. Until then, you'll think I'm doing all this for fun. Just because I can. That there's nothing behind it.*

That it's really just a game.

I run a finger over her cheek, touching her one last time and savoring the electricity that crackles in the air between us. Regret fills me, a hint of doubt that I'm doing the right thing by letting her go—until I realize again what this is really about.

It's about my position in the circle.

It's about the effort of my work.

Even you can't get in my way, no matter how much a part of me longs for your affection.

"You lost," I hiss. Amabelle looks up at me, her eyes wide like those of a bird that's been caught and can't believe that anyone would clip its wings. *Why do you just refuse to believe in the bad in the world, Belle? Why do you fight that realization and try to see the good even in us?* "Why didn't you just run while you still could? Didn't you know a chess match is almost always over once the queen is out of the game? Seems they haven't told you that. And here I thought this was one of the best universities in the country."

Laughter ripples through the room. By now, every single seat is taken, every single row in the lecture hall filled. We have an audience, a faceless collection of blood-thirsty students who can't wait for our queen to finally topple.

Amabelle treats me to a defiant look, as if she still wants to defend herself against this incontrovertible fact. As if she could take more than this. As if that wasn't enough.

"You still don't seem very scared of us," I whisper, approaching her face. It would be so easy to put my lips on hers. To pull her toward me and just fuck her. In front of everyone, if necessary. This urge to make her *mine* is pervasive, relentless. *What if you were all mine? If there was nothing dark between us? If I was permitted to give in to what I've always had to keep at arm's length?*

Love?

Fucking simple, bitter, normal ... love?

Then I think of everything I would lose if I fell for her charms, and it cures me instantly.

"Oh, I am incredibly scared of you," she replies with feigned fear in her voice, which drives me crazy even now. Every time she meets me with irony and smugness instead of intimidation, I struggle to maintain my composure.

I'm an asshole. I love to break my enemies.

Amabelle doesn't make it easy. She demands ever more cruelty from me. I have to up the ante every time, and all of that fucks with my brain until I can't help but chase her away before it eventually makes me *never let her go.*

"Too bad Kingston wasn't even able to teach you manners," I say slowly. "You really should know better than to lie to me, little Belle."

"Oh, but I studied under the master of deceit, didn't you know?" She just can't stop provoking me.

There she sits, tied to a chair, surrounded by a crowd of students after her blood, confronted by five bastards who want to devour her alive, and she's provoking me.

Me, Jaxon Tyrell.

So maybe she is suicidal after all. Has she still not learned that she shouldn't show me up in front of the peasants like I'm some nobody? My eyes narrow and I have to put her in her place again. This game is never going to end.

Never, unless she's finally chased off this campus to disappear forever.

"You almost won the game, Belle," I say, raising my voice as I step back. "You impressed me. I'm almost sad to have to say goodbye to you. It was so close"—I hold up thumb and index finger, only slightly apart—"and so *very* entertaining. I wouldn't have wanted to miss a moment of these last few months."

As the anger in Amabelle's face reddens her skin, the lights come on at the back of the lecture hall.

Three women enter the upper rows. Zayn and Sylvian break away, go to them, and escort them to us.

Rachel leads the group. The ridiculous "winner" of the stupid *arena* shines like Miss Universe, even though she's nothing. *Nothing compared to you, and that's what I want you to think. You should feel that. I want you to believe that you lost to this whore who's nothing in my eyes.*

Clarisse and Harper stand by Rachel's side. I had to persuade Harper to come, but there she is. Sylvian puts an arm around her waist, Crescent puts one around Rachel's. Clarisse positions herself next to me.

I recognize the pain in Amabelle's eyes. Sylvian and Harper together, that hurts, doesn't it? Something like jealousy boils up inside me.

Yes, he's replaced you, Belle. Simply discarded you with the flick of a finger. Why are you mourning him? Why do you have a thing for him, of all people?

Do you feel anything?

"Oh, are you sad Sylvian picked someone else?" I ask Amabelle ironically. I lean toward her ear but continue to speak in a normal voice so everyone can hear me. "How could you ever believe he'd choose scum like you?"

The audience cheers when I suddenly push her chair back and

she screams. I catch her at the last moment, just before she hits the ground, grabbing the backrest and unbuckling the belt Vance used to tie her to her chair.

"Run," I whisper, and this time she is the only one to hear me. My voice has lost all sense of performance or showmanship. I'm done playing. The only thing I want now is retribution.

You thought you had Sylvian on your side.

But he never was.

He's worse than me.

He will hurt you more than I ever could.

If you only knew that I'm actually doing you a favor.

You have no fucking idea, Belle.

You don't know anything.

"I'll run tonight," she whispers back to me. "But I'll be back in time for the first class of the new semester."

I can hardly believe my ears and my poker face slips. "You wouldn't dare."

"No one, not even you, will keep me from taking advantage of the best opportunity I can expect in my life. You picked the wrong enemy for your game. You'll have to kill me to keep me from coming back."

That idea no longer seems remote. Why do I let this bitch annoy me? This is what guns are for. They're very easy-to-use and *would instantly erase your smile, Belle.*

She slides backward across the floor, toward the door. I let her get away because I can't say for sure what'd happen if I went after her now.

Amabelle gives us one last look. There's no fear in her eyes, no anxiety or other emotion that would indicate that we left an impression on her. She's unbalanced as she pulls herself to her feet, stands upright, and raises her voice.

"See you next semester!" she shouts, earning plenty of boos, before she turns around. She takes flight because it's the only thing she can do.

My anger peaks as I watch her go, feeling like she's the one who just won.

Not me.

Fuck.

I turn to the Kings.

Four pairs of eyes, and they all seem less surprised than I am that Amabelle hasn't given up. *Have I underestimated you? What will it take to bring you down for good?*

There's Reece, who doesn't look like he's going to roll the dice again. Zayn, who's grown tired of playing. And Sylvian, with eyes as empty as an icy storm.

Romeo is the only one who smiles at me.

Romeo knows a thing or two about chess.

And he knows that the last move hasn't been made yet.

"Shit." Harper raises her voice, then suddenly rips the mask off her face. "Everything she said to you the other day is true, Jaxon!"

The lecture hall has fallen silent.

"You are pathetic. All of you!" She turns in front of the audience, then turns to Sylvian. He doesn't react. To Clarisse. Neither does she. Harper's best friend is probably shocked that she's taken off her mask.

"I'm not going to join you." I hear a tremor in Harper's voice. *Cute, she wants to help you? She of all people?* "And if there's only one person who isn't quite as shitty as you are and doesn't join in, then at least it's me!" She tosses her mask on the floor, accompanied by boos and laughter. Then she turns to me. Her eyes are sharp, sharp enough to make a bit of an impression on me. *What a twist.* "You're going to regret every single lie you utter and every single bad deed. Mable will make sure of it. And if she needs help with that, I'll be there."

"Then *go*," I hiss. "We all love watching you fail to carry out your threats."

"Psh." Harper tosses back her hair before storming from the room, taking the same route as Amabelle did. From the corner of my eye, I notice Vance walking after her. Maybe he'll stop her from helping our queen. Maybe he'll join her.

I don't give a damn. Two broken figures against five Kings and everyone else.

The laughter has died down and my anger has flattened. The heavy door of the lecture hall slowly closes behind Harper and Vance, and I turn to face the audience.

I raise my arms so that everyone falls silent. Then I speak and a satisfied smile curls across my lips. *I do love to play.*

"Who's feeling like round two?"

MABLE

I tear through the night, uncertain if anyone is following me. Going back to the dorm is a risk, but I need my laptop during the break. Fortunately, no one's there, and I think they're going to let me escape.

I stuff all my belongings that have any value at all into my bag and scurry out of my room.

I need a plan if I want to return.

I need a plan. I need weapons. And I need allies.

I have none of those.

I have four weeks to prepare before the next semester starts. Four weeks to think about what I'm going to do to strike back at them.

What do we have?

A self-absorbed, arrogant bastard whose father is paying for my scholarship, who would probably object if he knew what his son was up to at Kingston.

A dark, lost drug dealer who thinks he can get away with anything as long as everyone at Kingston protects him, and who's engaged to someone who used to be my friend, even though their engagement is built on a lie.

And a nice, super-rich guy with a split personality who should probably be locked in a psychiatric ward.

No real opponents.

But then there are the masses. The spectators in this game. Those who applaud when I fall, and cheer when Jaxon torments me.

In a way, they're my enemies, aren't they?

They defile my life with slurs and throw stones to hurt me.

It's about time I collected those stones and built myself a castle.

I need a throne that towers above them all.

They won't drive me off the chessboard.

The game has only just begun!

End of book 1

Not ready to go yet?

HI, I'M VANCE

Yes, I'm that asshole from earlier, the one who makes sure everything runs smoothly, because the Kings are only concerned with sex. (Don't worry, you'll find out soon enough why. Later.) I just want to say that if you're angry right now, or feel powerless, or want revenge – the Kings will regret every word.

They will suffer and get a good beating.

From Mable. And if the time comes, from me too.

Mable is not alone.

You are with her.

And so am I.

And a whole bunch of other people who secretly love her.

Or will come to love her.

This series could go on for a long time, if you want. But better not ask exactly how long, because we won't know until the Kings have fully repented for their actions. But if you all say it's a shitty story, one that never should have caused trees to be cut down, that's fine too. Then the series won't be so long. One thing I can assure you: in the end, you will get your revenge.

Mable will get her revenge.

I will get my damn revenge.

And the Kings will cry...

I'll watch and enjoy. I love seeing them pay for all the shit they've done to the world.

Will you come back?
I hope so.
Because without you, we can't do it.

Vance